THE GIRL IN THE WOODS

A Misted Pines Novel
Book 2

KRISTEN ASHLEY

ROCK CHICK
PRESS

GIRL
IN THE
WOODS

A MISTED PINES NOVEL

NEW YORK TIMES BESTSELLING AUTHOR

KRISTEN
ASHLEY

Authors' Note

By Kristen Ashley

There once was a time, at Hoss's Family Steak and Sea, off some exit somewhere in Pennsylvania, when two women were trapped by a raging storm and seduced by a salad bar.

At that time, I shared an idea kicking around in my head about an FBI agent and the no-nonsense owner of a gentleman's club.

I didn't think it'd go anywhere.

And then one of those women said, "You could put this in the Misted Pines series."

That woman, by the way, was not me.

It was gray and blustering outside, but in Hoss's Family Steak and Sea, where the chicken tenders are better than at a carnival, the skies opened up over my head and a light shone down.

I loved Misted Pines. I wanted to spend more time there. It's weird and creepy and seething at the same time it's a beautiful oasis of safety. I wanted to explore.

But Celeste wasn't ready. I wasn't feeling Harry yet. And the twins were too young. I also thought every book had to be in the heroine's voice.

I was wrong.

Thus, Rus and Cin, who would have been just another hero and heroine clamoring around in my head and never see their ink on a page, were allowed to be born.

Another storm took out my internet at home, so when I arrived back in Phoenix, I had no way to catch up on work. My only choice was to write.

So I did.

I mean, even Mother Nature was desperate for this story.

Thank you, Jillian.

#JebidiahLivesInOurHeartsForever

Author's Caution

In this book, the narrative includes frank discussions of sexual assault and violence that might be distressing for some readers.

ONE

The Last One

S tanding in the doorway staring at a dead woman, Zachariah Lazarus knew this case was going to be his last.

He'd lost his wife to this.

He couldn't drop everything, fly five hours, drive for two and a half, stand in the doorway of a room and assume responsibility for another lost soul.

He'd see to her. If he caught a break, he'd find the twisted mess of a human being who was behind it, and he'd put him out of commission. If he didn't, he'd uncover everything he could and leave it for the next guy to use when he stood in a door and stared at a life ended in a grim and tragic way, hoping like hell he'd catch a break.

But Rus was done.

He was heavy with this shit. Struggling to breathe under a boulder he carried, which grew bigger and bigger, threatening to crush him.

He took a single step into the room, fighting against that weight he'd carried for years but only started feeling the day he signed his divorce papers.

The room was cold, incredibly cold. They'd jacked the AC way up to take care of her. It was probably another reason the owner was impatient to get her out of there.

She was lying in a cradle of plastic sheeting, like the other seven had been.

Her back was to the door, just like the others.

She was arranged in a position of sleeping, on her side, one leg hitched and resting on the bunched plastic tucked around her, arms cocked, hands tucked under her cheek.

She'd been anally raped, he could tell by the blood. Rus knew from experience she'd likely also been vaginally raped.

The back of her head had been bludgeoned, her long blonde hair matted and mingled with the color of rust, the stained ivory of jagged pieces of skull and the gore of exposed brain matter showing through the strands.

He'd spoken to his team on the drive there. They'd come and gone and were queuing up evidence to process what they'd found.

At that moment, the local sheriff and two of his deputies were outside, the sheriff not three feet behind him, the deputies trying to calm an irate motel owner who wanted the body removed.

He was going to have to put up with crime scene tape, but cruisers and an active investigation fucked with his ability to rent rooms.

This was too bad, since the man needed the money so he could put some fucking cameras in his reception and parking lot. Perhaps he hadn't already because their presence made his current clientele nervous, but this meant the zero evidence Rus knew his suspect left behind added to the zero video footage would leave Rus and this woman with less than zero to go on.

She'd been there since discovery by the motel's maid yesterday morning. She was still there due to the fact the MO was highly publicized, and the call needed to be made that would put Rus on a plane.

This boded well for the start of the investigation. It said the locals weren't going to mess around. They didn't try to take lead. They didn't start an investigation they weren't going to be able to finish.

They made the call. Rus arranged for agents in the Seattle division to head out and process the scene, gave the locals his ETA and asked that the scene was secured, nothing disturbed, so he could see her as she was left.

Precisely as she was left.

Great emotion put a stamp on a space.

Stand in the doorway after a child's birthday party, you could feel the joy even if you didn't see the mess left behind or smell the residue of frosting.

Stand in the doorway of a crime scene, you could feel the suffering.

He normally let it wash over him like this, taking on the added weight of that despair, smelling the residue of misery.

He stood in that doorway longer, though, and not because she was going to be his last one.

He couldn't put his finger on why, something was just…

Off.

When he couldn't figure it out, he shook it off and moved farther into the room, down the near side of the bed, noting the coating of blood on her buttocks and thighs left from the violations she sustained, the bruising around her ankles, the smears and pooling on the plastic by her head.

She'd been raped here, and murdered here, tied to that bed.

Before that happened, the plastic sheeting had been spread across the mattress, down its sides, along the floor and up the wall. Once the perpetrator was finished, he'd tidied up, positioned her, but otherwise left no trace.

They'd find her blood and sweat and tears and hair on that sheeting.

Nothing from him.

The profilers had ideas about why she was positioned this way, with the worst of it facing the door.

Rus usually put a good deal of stock into what profilers said.

The first three victims, he bought it.

The last four, now five, he knew this whole show was for him.

Rus set about examining the room even though he knew, if his guy finally fucked up, Rus wouldn't pick it up by looking around. It'd be discovered in forensics.

He still did it, just in case he saw something someone else might miss.

He was thorough.

As such, he stood gazing curiously at her clothes tossed in the corner that the team had left for him to see.

Not unusual. The victim's personal effects were meaningless to her perpetrator.

Her purse had been tossed there too.

Again, there was something not right about it.

They were usually in a tidy, discarded bundle. This all seemed flung in one direction to get it out of the way.

It wasn't a massive shift of MO, but Rus was attuned to everything.

He moved away from his perusal of the room because she'd been there too long. She needed to advance to her next violation, a full autopsy, before she was cleaned up and returned to hands and hearts who loved her.

This meant Rus didn't further delay what he had to do next, even if it was the worst part.

He moved to the other side of the bed, the side he'd so far avoided.

Yeah.

This was what always punched him right in the gut.

And this was what made her his last.

From this angle, take away the plastic sheeting, the contusions and scrapes on her knees, ankles, and wrists, she looked like she was sleeping.

No damage to her face, not even a shadow of a bruise. No blood splatter. The duct tape, on which they'd found negligible residue from the fourth victim, giving indication it was what he used to keep them quiet, had been removed with no visible trace.

Always, the face clean and tranquil and waiting for him.

Since the fourth victim, waiting for, specifically, Rus.

As usual, she was a beautiful girl. His guess, early twenties. A long life ahead of her she would not lead. Career. Love. Marriage. Children. Birthdays. Holidays. Vacations. Graduations. Grandchildren. Retirement. Books she'd never read. Meals she'd never eat. Laughter she'd never share.

That was done, it was tragic. It added to the weight he carried, he'd wake up from dreams about it, his mind would wander to thoughts of it when he let his guard down.

But in the end, he could do nothing about it.

It was time to get on with what he might be able to do something about.

Taking a deep breath, he retrieved the nitrile gloves he'd tucked into his pocket, pulled them on and carefully pressed his fingers between the prayer position of her hands.

A chill glided over his skin.

He could feel the edges of the "gift" that the killer always wrapped in his victim's palm, but the other wasn't there.

It was always there.

From the fourth one, *right there*.

He felt around.

Nothing.

Carefully, he lifted her top hand, which shifted the weight of her head since her cheek was resting on them, and he peered in.

The crystal resting in her palm glinted, a pink one this time, but other than that...nothing.

He grabbed his phone, turned on the light, and kept her hand and head raised, leaning deeper, looking closer.

Not there.

With great care, he removed his hand, then slid his fingers between her and the sheeting.

He lifted.

It wasn't there either.

His blood ran cold.

Now he knew what was off about this room, this girl, this murder.

Carefully, he rested her again to the plastic, turned off the light, shoved his phone in his back pocket, and snapping off the gloves, he strode out of the room right to Sheriff Harry Moran.

"I told you not to remove anything from the scene," Rus stated.

Moran's brows drew down. "We didn't."

He couldn't believe what he was hearing. He'd given explicit instructions, and his team wouldn't fuck that up.

"My boys?" he demanded.

"They didn't either."

"Nothing?" Rus pushed.

"Nothing," Moran asserted.

"You're sure of that?" Rus kept at him.

Moran was getting annoyed. "I've been here for twenty-two hours, Agent Lazarus. I was the first on the scene. Your guys came in, but I supervised. And when we sealed it, I personally sat in my cruiser all night and guarded it until your arrival. Nothing has been disturbed, and nothing has been removed."

Rus was reminded that a year ago, this sleepy town in the Pacific Northwest had some high-profile trouble that was exacerbated by an inept sheriff.

One of the reasons Moran had his current position—the old was ousted, Moran was the new.

This meant Moran wasn't dicking around.

"What's going on?" Moran demanded.

"She's good to be moved. Call your coroner. Bag the crystal. The personal effects. Then get her out of here. We'll talk at the station."

And with that, Rus moved to his rented SUV.

TWO

Lore

_____

Rus folded himself in a chair in front of the desk as he watched the sheriff round it.

He was seriously tweaked.

Even so, it penetrated that, from the minute he stepped foot in Fret County Sheriff's Office, he knew he wasn't dealing with some Boondocks Let's Play Cops and Robbers, half-ass operation.

He should have known from the early call.

In Rus's twenty years in law enforcement, seventeen of those with the FBI, he'd noted some, not all, small-town/low-population counties (and some big-city/high-population as well) had piss-all-over-their-patch chiefs and sheriffs who hired men who were the same.

Men who were more concerned about the size of their balls than serving and protecting.

It was a toxic mixture of the need for status and control, and aggression.

It was about getting spitting mad a man took a knee during the national anthem, but feeling fully justified in defacing the American flag by making it black and gray with a blue stripe and putting that shit on everything from their cars to their backs to their coffee mugs.

It was feeling that their badge and their uniform set them apart in some way from the citizens they served, but when it came down to doing actual policework, they didn't know their ass from a hole in the ground.

Rus was relieved the vibe here was not that.

The look of it, the feel of it, was organized, competent and professional.

Including Moran's office.

This was where Moran did the work of serving a community in order to keep them safe, and when bad things happened anyway, as they always did, finding those who perpetrated those acts and doing what they could to aid the path to justice.

What this was not, was Moran's home away from home, where he put his boots up on his desk and shot the shit with his deputies, a bottle of scotch in the drawer he felt it was okay to imbibe from, no matter the occasion or time of day.

He continued to study the guy.

His uniform went to a dry cleaner. He got his hair cut at a barber and not a salon, and he did that on a standing appointment, not only so it didn't get unkempt, but also so he didn't have to waste time making appointments. He kept fit, but it wasn't a religion or part of his identity, it happened in the natural course of his life. He was a good-looking man, and he didn't give two shits that he was.

Right, so maybe there was a bottle of scotch. But that, and the pictures of his wife and what appeared to be his dad and his brother on the credenza behind his desk, was as far as Moran went in putting who he was in his private life in this office.

And that scotch only came out in times of break-glass-when-needed.

This office, and the entire department, was where shit got done.

Moran barely had his ass to the seat of an ergonomic desk chair before he started it.

"You wanna tell me what's going on?"

"Do you have an ID on the victim?"

Moran gave him a good stare as he came to realize who he was dealing with.

During those three seconds, he made the same deduction Rus just did.

Rus was here to get shit done.

Moran sat back and lifted his chin.

"She's local. Brittanie Iverson. Twenty-five. Got deputies who went to school with her, knew her. Not well, but they knew her. Though, the family has kind of a reputation. She was born here. Works at Bon Amie."

"Bon Amie?"

"Burlesque club in the woods."

Rus had been intent on making it to the scene, but it didn't escape him that, to get there, he'd driven through terrain that was dense forest and rugged.

There were towns. There were homes. There were businesses.

But for the most part, this was backwoods.

This area was about logging, hunting, hiking, fishing and keeping to yourself.

So, "burlesque club in the woods" was not something he was expecting to hear.

Moran read Rus's reaction and explained, "We got history. Trapping. Fur trade. Prospecting. Mining. As they had a tendency to do, white men put their stamp on this place a long time ago. And where he went, other things followed. Like the need to get himself some in the wilderness."

"Right," Rus murmured.

"There's a lot of lore around here, what with the lake and all," Moran continued.

The lake and all?

Rus knew Misted Pines was where Ray Andrews decided he was going to test the skills of retired ace FBI profiler Cade Bohannan. He did this by killing girls. A mess that included Bohannan's far more famous girlfriend's contractor getting shot and the exposure of a sex scandal that involved some of the men of the town. And that exposure was perpetrated by those men's wives.

It was big. It was interesting. It was lurid, shocking and had a double celebrity component with Bohannan and his girlfriend—

award-winning, bestselling author Delphine Larue—so he'd followed the case himself. As did all of his colleagues, everyone in law enforcement and most of the globe since it was plastered all over the news.

So again, lore that involved the lake was not what Rus expected to hear.

Rus didn't like hearing unexpected things.

He also didn't get the chance to ask, Moran kept telling him about Bon Amie.

"Think it was Cin's four- or five-times great grandmother who shot her pimp because she was tired of him roughing her and her friends up. The marshal was partial to her, decided it was self-defense. In the clear and to look after women in a place they had nowhere to go and nothing else they could do to put food in their mouths, she took over the bordello. It kept up in that bent until Cin's great-grandmother decided it was time for the Bonner family legacy to move in a new direction. She took them out of the sex trade and into show business. Bon Amie is in the middle of nowhere, about fifteen miles north of town, not easy to find, not easy to get to, but people make the trek because it's a helluva show."

And with that, Rus knew Moran had made that trek to watch the show. Though he wondered if the man did it before or after that gold band hit his left finger.

Rus's mind filled with the image of Brittanie Iverson in plastic.

"You sure they're out of the sex trade?" he asked.

Moran was all about eye contact when he answered, "Absolutely."

Right.

He was sure.

Next.

"Cin?" he queried.

"Lucinda Bonner," Moran told him. "Owner of Bon Amie."

"I'm gonna need to talk to her," Rus told him.

"You want her to have that heads up now?"

First things first.

"Has notification been made to the family?"

Moran shook his head, but said, "Of a sort."

"What does that mean?"

"Brittanie's father is a piece of shit. No idea where the man is, but he's not in Misted Pines or Fret County. And this is a good thing. He drank a lot. Cheated on his wife a lot. Got into a lot of fights with anyone who might piss him off, and that was a lot of people, including his wife. And Brittanie's mom was all about those 'a lots' too. She'd get fed up and skip town a lot, leaving her kids with a dad who didn't give a shit. Once they were divorced, she had a lot of boyfriends, and she had a lot of good times. So yes, she's been notified. But since she was so hungover when I spoke to her, she was mostly still drunk, I'm not sure she processed her daughter was murdered."

Rus understood he was telling Moran something he already knew when he said, "I'm gonna have to talk to her too."

"My advice?"

Rus nodded.

"Go to Cin first. She's not family, but I'll lay money down she knows more about Brittanie than her mother or her brother put together. And I'm not a gambling man."

So there was a brother as well.

And it was interesting Moran referred to this Bonner woman as "Cin."

"But we've got that info for you," Moran went on. "Polly's already put it together."

He didn't know who Polly was yet, but good.

Next.

"Let's talk about this town," Rus said.

He could see Moran was getting impatient, but he didn't give into it.

"You want more lore, or do you want to talk about Ray Andrews?" Moran asked, and Rus knew he was fishing.

"We can get to the lore later, when we figure this out and we're sharing a beer. I want to talk about Ray Andrews."

Moran leaned onto his forearms on the desk and shared, "Probably won't surprise you, that shit hasn't died down. I'm not sure it's going to. Case like that lives forever. We get tourists. And then there's the women."

The women?

He knew about true-crime tourists. People so fascinated with famous cases, they had to go to the place it happened, immerse themselves in it.

Rus thought that was fucked up, but one thing he'd learned in his business, there was no end to the kind of people there were and the jacked-up shit they were into.

And Moran was right, what Ray Andrews did in that town would live forever.

So Rus was interested in "the women."

"What do you mean, 'the women?'"

"Misted Pines has become a mecca for women who are done with being screwed over by men and want to live around those who are like minded. They've shut down their lives and homes wherever they were, took what money they got, and created a space up here. Some call it a neighborhood. Some who don't like it much call it a commune. Some who don't like it at all call it a coven."

Well…

Shit.

"Can't say I blame them," Rus noted carefully, watching Moran closely, wondering which camp Moran was in.

He shrugged, sat back and said, "If they don't cause trouble, it's not my business. They don't cause trouble. But they're an entity in this town, and some aren't real happy about it."

Rus could get that, and he couldn't.

He was with Moran. If you don't cause trouble, he didn't give a shit what you did or why you did it.

But the people of Misted Pines weren't responsible for what Ray Andrews did. They also weren't responsible for what several wives did to punish their husbands for breaking their marriage vows.

Rus knew a thing or two about women whose hearts were broken when their man's mind wandered from their marriage and fixed on something else.

It was just that, in Rus's case, it wasn't another woman.

"Brittanie or her mother have anything to do with this, for lack of a better word to describe it, coven?"

Moran shook his head.

Since this had no bearing on Brittanie Iverson, he had interviews to do, he had an investigation to conduct, so it was time to get down to how they were going to work together in doing those things.

Before he could start, Moran asked a question that had been preying on Rus's mind since he got the call.

"Do you think this is about Bohannan?"

These words came out of his mouth just as a knock came at the door.

Rus twisted that way, but before Moran could call out, the head of a woman poked through.

Rus's guess from the efficient appearance of her helmet of hair and the low-key makeup, this was Polly.

Though, from where that head was located, it was clear the woman was petite.

"Sorry to interrupt," she said to Moran. "But I know you'd want to know, Cade is here."

Speak of the devil.

Rus sat straighter in his chair.

Cade being Cade Bohannan, a man who had his own lore, and deserved it. Rus knew this from more than the stories, he'd gone to a class Bohannan taught.

This could mean a number of things, perhaps good, because Bohannan won his reputation by being one of the best in the business, or bad, because sometimes a retired agent who felt the need to meddle could fuck shit up.

Rus knew he was going to find out which way that would swing when Moran said, "Send him in."

THREE

Blaze of Glory

R us was not surprised at Cade Bohannan's bearded, flannel-shirt-and-jeans mountain man appearance. He'd left the clean-cut FBI look behind when he'd retired, so this was the man who'd taught the class Rus had taken with about a hundred other LEOs.

That said, this man was tense and gave off a vibe as tweaked as Rus was feeling, and he made no attempt to rein it in.

Understandable, considering he was probably thinking what Moran was thinking. That being, whatever was now happening in this town was the same as what happened with Ray Andrews—Bohannan was being called out, his skill at catching killers versus a killer continuing to kill.

Rus was standing when Bohannan moved in, gave a dip of his chin to Moran, who had also taken his feet, and then he was all about Rus.

They shared coloring, both of them dark-haired and olive-skinned. Rus had an inch on Bohannan, but Bohannan had ten pounds on Rus. Both were about genetics, but that ten pounds was all muscle.

He didn't know exact stats, but he did know Bohannan was around ten years older than him and did what Rus had decided to do that very day.

He retired early.

He had his hand out, and when he arrived, Rus took it.

"Cade Bohannan," he said, his fingers closing in a firm hold. "And you're Special Agent Zachariah Lazarus."

"Rus," he corrected. A quick squeeze, no unnecessary statements made, and they broke physical contact. "You made some calls," he noted.

Bohannan didn't beat around the bush. "Yeah, I did. My son, Jace, dated Brittanie."

Fuck.

"Cade." Moran entered the conversation, and his one word had warning dripping off it.

Bohannan didn't miss it.

This was why he lifted both hands to his shoulders, palms out. "I'm here to offer my services. That's it. I've told the boys to stand down. Jace is out, he knows it. But Jesse is ready if you need him."

Rus shot an "explain" look to Moran.

He explained. "Cade's sons, twins, are private investigators."

He looked to Bohannan. "No shit?"

"No shit."

He didn't ask if they were any good. Any father would say yes. Bohannan wouldn't be lying when he said it.

"You said 'dated', past tense," Rus remarked.

"It lasted a few months. I met her. I liked her. Larue wasn't a fan. But she doesn't like any of the boys' girlfriends."

"A few months isn't very long."

"Jace is twenty-eight, and he's not giving indication he's ready to settle down."

No more needed to be said about that.

Though, twenty-eight was young to be a PI.

There was a story there, but now wasn't the time for it.

"He willing to talk to me?" Rus asked.

"Definitely. Though, not gonna tell you your business"—a quick side glance to Moran—"your first stop should be Cin."

And again with Cin.

"That was the sheriff's suggestion," Rus told him.

"We were just about to get to the part where the Crystal Killer just happened to pick a woman in our town," Moran put in, and Rus admired, from the get-go, Moran's capacity to take a step back, on his own turf, and let Rus run the show.

He'd been impatient since the motel, but he kept a lock on it.

Now that patience had ended.

That was a long time to wait. Said good things about him.

What said more was that, when he was done, he didn't make any demands. He finessed it. Diplomacy, it was Rus's experience, was a lost art.

When Bohannan looked back at Rus, he knew that Bohannan was tweaked about his son's ex-girlfriend being murdered.

And he was tweaked about the possibility the criminally deranged lunatic the media had dubbed the Crystal Killer had decided to match wits with Cade Bohannan like Ray Andrews did.

"I figure you aren't surprised I'm curious about this too," Bohannan shared. "Seven women. Now eight. All blondes. All between the ages of twenty-three and twenty-seven. All going missing, tied to a bed in a small, out-of-the-way motel or hotel and continually raped for a period of not more than forty-eight hours, not less than twenty-four, before they're left to be discovered by staff. This short period of time is not enough for a missing persons investigation to get underway. Also doesn't give the perpetrator any time to fuck around. He's going to concentrate on getting what he needs from the experience."

All true.

Bohannan continued. "Victim found naked, positioned, and bludgeoned. The only thing left behind by the killer is a crystal held between their hands. The first one was in Georgia four years ago, the next in Mississippi. These go unrelated until the third, found in Texas, which is when you were called in. Then you had Iowa, Colorado, Illinois and Maryland. You thought he was going west.

He went north, then west again and backtracked. That last victim, very close to where you live. There's roughly three point eight million square miles that make up the United States. Lots of places for him to get his fix. So I gotta tell you, I'm not real happy, since it makes sense he started dropping victims close to you, considering you're investigating him, and I'm all kinds of fuckin' surprised he found his way all the way across the country to here."

"Why are you surprised?" Rus asked.

"You were in one of my classes," Bohannan shot back, and now Rus was surprised, because he sat at a desk in that class, one of several he knew Bohannan gave, but he didn't introduce himself to the man. "Why do you think?"

He wasn't in any mood to play professor and student.

"I'm an investigator, not a profiler," Rus returned.

"Right, then, this guy doesn't want to get caught. He needs this. If he's tracked down, he'll commit suicide by cop before he'll go to prison because he can't live without it. So until Brittanie, I thought the whole Pacific Northwest would be off limits to him after what Andrews did, because he wouldn't want to get anywhere near something that might mean I'd feel obliged to get involved. And right now, I feel obliged to get involved."

"You're right," Rus confirmed. "He doesn't want to get caught. He needs it. He's determined to keep getting it. And if he doesn't, there's a shit storm he's prepared to unleash if I find him. That shit-storm is going to mean he's going to go out in a blaze of glory and take unknown numbers of other victims with him."

Bohannan spoke not a word because from what Rus said, he knew.

He knew what Moran wanted to know.

He knew what Rus told them next.

"Whoever killed Brittanie Iverson isn't the Crystal Killer. It's a copycat. And shit just got real because the Crystal Killer is not gonna like that. If we lift the media blackout I put on this case and he finds out, he's gonna be pissed. And swear to God, if he finds out, I have no idea what he'll do. I just know we're going to like it a fuckuva lot less than what he's already done."

Harry Moran fell forward into both hands on his desk, arms straight, his head dropping.

Bohannan instantly changed his mind about his earlier friendly offer and demanded, "Give me all you got on this fucking guy."

Rus didn't waste time.

He headed to his SUV to oblige.

FOUR

Ivory and Cream

R us had been warned.

He was still unprepared for the road to Bon Amie being so out of the way. Some of it was gravel, some of it was mud, some of it was treacherous, and all of it was through thick, coniferous forest.

He was therefore unprepared for when he saw it.

A large, two-story, stately lodge made of logs, with a wide front overhang under which guests could get out of their vehicles and they wouldn't get pelted by rain.

That happening right then.

It looked like a rustic mansion.

He had no idea how it could serve as a burlesque theater, but as he slowed to a halt under the overhang, he was about to find out.

He'd left the Crystal Killer file with Bohannan and Moran.

Before he'd done that, Rus and Moran decided on a game plan with input from Bohannan. Moran declared he was going to be Rus's local partner, a decision that Rus would make if he was in Moran's boots. So the kickoff was Moran going home and getting some sleep so he didn't fuck anything up by being dead on his feet after being awake for twenty-four hours.

Moran didn't fight this, another indication he had his head straight, not up his ass or thinking with his balls. However, he was going to look through the file before Bohannan took it with him.

After Moran got some shuteye, he and Rus were going to do interviews with the mother and brother.

They'd also agreed his deputies were going to dig deeper, as quietly as possible, talking to the motel owner and staff and knocking on some doors.

The motel was just outside the town, on a lonesome lot set in a mountain, but up and down from it there were businesses and homes.

It was a longshot, but no stone unturned. You never knew when you were going to catch a break, and since this was a new entity he was dealing with, there were no givens.

Anything could happen.

Rus had learned prior to his arrival it had been reported by the desk clerk that Brittanie had checked in herself, and when she did, she did not seem distressed. The clerk had assumed, since she was known in town (and so was her mother), that she was there for a tryst, although to the clerk's recollection this had never happened before.

They did not see anyone meet her in her room.

This, too, was not the MO of the Crystal Killer. He checked in himself, always in disguise at accommodations he ascertained beforehand didn't have any security cameras in the lobby.

So, yeah.

Anything could happen.

While all this was going down, Rus was going to take their advice and go meet Lucinda Bonner.

He looked around as he exited his SUV, seeing there were only a few cars.

Considering it had just gone one, and they probably didn't offer matinees, this didn't seem out of place.

But Polly had set him up with a detailed who, what and where (he was correct: Polly was very short, wore a skirt and sweater set that was reminiscent of the fifties, and had a professional attitude that was liberally mingled with a friendly, I'm-the-second-mom-to-all-who-work-here feel that said she was not only down with that, she nurtured it).

She'd also shared that she'd booked him a room in the Pinetop Lodge that, "Has an amazing view of the lake, real close to Bohannan's compound, which will be convenient for you."

News Bohannan had a compound didn't faze him.

Rus didn't have the money to set roots in a town in the middle of nowhere that had amazing scenery, but if he did, he'd do it on his own compound.

Gates. Lots of fence. All of it electrified.

There was shit that went bump in the night, and Rus didn't want it anywhere near him.

His ex, Jennifer, had remarried, and he still woke up in a sweat that something would happen to her when he wasn't there.

Same with his kids, who were both in college, something he knew they needed to do to get on with their lives. But it messed with his head, because campus life aggravated pretty much every fucked-up scenario that could happen to your kid.

His son, Acre, could handle himself (he hoped).

His daughter, Sabrina, probably could not. She was more girl than any girl he'd ever met.

He loved it.

And it might kill him.

He had plans to meet up with Moran and Bohannan at Pinetop that evening to compare notes: Jace and Jesse coming with Bohannan. Jace, because Rus wanted to talk to him, Jesse, because Rus was intrigued about a set of twenty-eight-year-old twin PIs who were also the spawn of a legendary FBI profiler.

He hadn't rounded his hood when one of the double doors to Bon Amie opened and a woman wearing a masculine-style black suit, black shirt and a black tie, came out. Her hair was severely pulled back from a side part into a bun at the nape of her neck, and not a stroke of makeup was on her fine-featured face.

She was average height, average build, and even though Rus had seven inches on her, kept fit and had been trained to take care of business, he knew it'd be a crapshoot at what might happen if he was stupid enough to mess with her.

Female security.

Now Rus was even more intrigued than he'd already been about Lucinda Bonner.

"Special Agent Lazarus?" she asked.

He reached into the inside pocket of his blazer to get his credentials, but she shook her head.

"Ms. Bonner is expecting you."

Polly had called ahead.

She held the door open for him.

He walked in, not to face a theater, but an enormous open-plan room with vaulted ceilings that looked part chic mountain getaway living room and part chic mountain getaway bar, and the last part was a high-class restaurant. There were lots of huge windows, including the entire back wall.

And the back of the building didn't face forest. It faced a drop-away view of a massive valley, at the bottom of which was a rushing river with white water rapids and rising beyond was dense forest leading up to a snowy mountain peak in the distance.

So the show wasn't the only hot ticket for the house.

It still begged the question as to where the theater was.

The woman who greeted him walked to the side, where there was an open staircase made of rough wood with a banister fortified by polished branches. This was set against a stone wall and rose above an enormous fireplace.

They ascended, and he saw one door at the landing. It would lead to a room situated above the overhang outside. The landing had a view of the entire bar and seating area, through to the vista out the back windows.

Security knocked twice, then opened the door.

"The agent from the FBI is here," she said, then stepped aside on the landing, indicating Rus should walk in.

He did so.

He didn't know what to expect, any of it, including Lucinda

Bonner, but whatever it was, as usual since he hit Misted Pines, he didn't get it.

Pure class, from the threshold to the woman rising from her chair, her attention trained on him.

She was behind a big modern desk of ivory-stained wood with an ivory leather chair behind it, the numerous nail heads that held the leather stretched in place, exposed on its edges. Two armchairs faced the desk, they were boxed in spindled wood, covered in cream upholstery and had tan and brown zebra-print pillows resting against their backs.

The wood floor had a large area rug with an ivory nap and champagne-gold highlights woven into it.

The desk was clear of everything, save an attractive, squat desk lamp at the center, front edge, a short stack of manila folders in the middle, and at one corner, a tall, perfect orchid plant with yellow blooms fading into dark pink centers, sprouting from a gold pot.

The walls were mostly windows.

The only other thing in the room was an oval plinth in a corner, on top of which was a large sculpture of a Native fetish bear crafted from what looked like solidified honey.

The desk faced the door. The armchairs faced the forest.

And the woman in a figure-skimming cream dress with a high neck, no sleeves, and bisque suede, high, stiletto-heeled pumps on her feet, had stepped to the side of the desk, and she faced Rus.

Her makeup and hair looked done by a professional. The knot at her nape the polar opposite of that worn by her security. It was soft and feminine, exposing the long line of her neck, which was a continuation of the long line of her body.

She had ass and hips.

But fuck him, he was a leg man, and her legs went on forever.

His wife had been blonde, and when she cheated on him, she'd picked a man who looked uncannily like Rus.

The man wasn't just her type, it was a way to rub her pain into Rus's skin, causing him to feel the same.

It had worked.

After his divorce, he'd sworn off anything but the most casual of relationships. A woman to go to dinner with. A woman to catch a movie with. A woman to sleep with. And he had two who were happy to share these things with him and nothing more.

One was redhead.

One was brunette.

They were these because, even though they were three years out on their divorce, he'd made a pact with himself that he was never going to hit Jennifer with the bullet she'd sent tearing through his flesh.

Not that she'd ever see him with either of them. Penny lived in Texas. Ruth lived in Philly. He lived in Virginia, as did Jenn.

But he wasn't going to take the chance just in case.

So, after he tore his mind off Lucinda Bonner's legs, then her shoes, he knew this case was going to fuck him in more ways than it already had because she was a brunette.

Fair game.

Shit.

She came forward, hand raised.

"Special Agent Lazarus."

He was not about to tell her to call him Rus, and not only because her voice was low and sultry.

But now that was one of the reasons.

He took her hand. "Ms. Bonner."

"Lucinda," she invited.

So, not everyone called her Cin.

Moran gave him the impression she was a straight arrow, but this woman could lure a man to stray.

Though, Bohannan called her Cin too. That said, it was Rus's understanding he'd only been with Delphine Larue for a short time but had been living in Misted Pines for years. He could see how Bohannan might have earned the honor of using her shortened name too.

She swung the hand he'd let go to the chairs. "Please sit."

He moved to do so.

She walked back behind the desk, offering, "Can I get you something to drink? Water? A soda? Coffee?"

He hadn't had anything since breakfast on the plane. He could use a sandwich. A beverage would just remind him he needed to eat.

"No, thanks," he answered, and then, for both their sakes, he dove in. "It's my understanding Polly spoke to you about what's happened."

Her amber eyes closed slightly, the movement and the thick line of her false eyelashes hiding her response from him.

But the tone of her voice was holding nothing back.

"Brittanie," she said softly.

"It's been explained she worked for you."

She nodded. "She was a dancer. In the chorus."

At this point, she put a hand on the manila folders and slid them across the desk his way.

And again, what happened was unexpected.

"The top is for you to take with you," she said. "It's Britt's schedule for the last two months. Her cell phone number and address. The name and phone number of her emergency contact, Keyleigh, another of my dancers. They were roommates, but Keyleigh moved in with her boyfriend about two months ago. Britt stayed in their old apartment. I've added a list of any boyfriends that she spoke to me about, friends she had outside of the club, and names of all my staff, in order of those who she was closest to who knew her the best. If you like, I'll arrange for you to interview them here in this office when you're ready. The bottom folder is her personnel file. I don't mind if you take photos, but if you'd please read it here and leave it here. I'm not comfortable with you taking it."

The first part saved time, because it was all questions he'd ask and information he'd request.

The second he was shocked about, because often, to cover their own ass, an employer demanded a warrant.

"You're being helpful," he noted with careful nonchalance.

And again, the amber of her eyes became slits as they narrowed, but this time her reaction wasn't hidden.

She was peeved because she was insulted.

"One of my girls was murdered. You're here to find who did that to her. I don't have the skills to do what you do, or I'd be doing that. Instead, I can give you everything I have that might help." She dipped her head to the folders. "So I've done that."

"It's appreciated," he murmured.

Her voice was as narrow as her gaze when she replied, "I don't want you to appreciate it, I want you to find who killed Britt."

Yes.

Insulted.

But more.

She cared about Brittanie.

"Can I ask a few questions about Brittanie?"

She didn't answer verbally. She sat back in her chair, crossing her arms in front of her, not taking her eyes from him, but her expression told him that was perhaps the stupidest question she'd ever heard.

For the first time since he got the call that another victim had been discovered, he felt like smiling.

He didn't do that.

He shifted the top folder aside, tapped the personnel file and said, "Tell me what's not in here."

No hesitation, she launched in.

"Brittanie's mother wanted to work for my mother. She was a terrible dancer and an even worse person. And when I say she was a terrible dancer, she was *dire*. So that explains what kind of person Melanie Iverson is. However, all her life she wanted to work at Bon Amie. Because of this, I think the driving force of Brittanie's life was to do what her mother could not, not so she'd live the dream for her mother, but to put it right in her face that she could do what her mother couldn't."

"You're saying they aren't close."

"I'm saying Britt hated the woman, but then most people who meet her do," she said coolly.

"Is she close with her brother?"

Her lip curled and she didn't bother to hide it.

"Dakota is his father, so no."

He nodded in understanding. "I've been given some insight into the family by Sheriff Moran."

"I bet you have," she murmured.

"Can you explain that remark?"

Her focus sharpened on him and he knew why.

The inference could be made he knew why she knew what Moran knew, and how she came about knowing it.

Pillow talk.

And Rus couldn't say that with his quick retort, he hadn't injected that inference when he asked the question.

It was because he wanted to know if she was sleeping with, or had in the past slept with the sheriff.

This wasn't important for him to know, exactly.

But it put him at a disadvantage not knowing it.

It was a small town and the personalities in it were going to be intertwined. He didn't have ten years to untangle that mess, but messes like that always had some bearing on small-town crime.

He had no idea if he, in Moran's position, colleague to colleague, would admit to having had an intimate relationship with a victim's employer.

Then again, he married at nineteen and never considered stepping out on his wife, so it wasn't something he'd ever have to consider.

He couldn't deny he'd also made this inference simply because he wanted to know.

This was because, complicating matters, at least for him, he wanted to sleep with Lucinda Bonner.

No, he couldn't deny that, even to himself.

"Everyone knows about the Iversons, Agent Lazarus," she said. "And just so you won't put your foot in that stinking pile again, you should know Harry's wife died some time ago. They'd been married a year when it happened. And the reason he still wears her ring tells you all about the devotion he had to the woman who slid it on his finger."

He thought of the pretty, smiling woman in the picture on Moran's credenza.

Fucking hell.

Poor Moran.

Right.

Next.

"What else do I need to know about Brittanie?"

Lucinda let it go without hesitation.

"She didn't want to be like her mother, but in some ways, she was. She called in sick often. It got to the point of a written warning. It was the only way I could put a stop to it."

This, he could learn in her personnel file.

Lucinda kept talking.

"She wasn't very smart about money, and she'd sometimes ask to wait the floor on nights she wasn't performing. She'd get in trouble when it was time to pay rent, but she had a new Louis Vuitton bag. That kind of thing."

This was important.

He could imagine someone who wanted a life that included designer bags finding ways to get them that might lead her to trouble.

Though, if she found that trouble, it's unlikely that person would rape her, sodomize her and cave her skull in. It's hard to pay back a loan or work it off when you're dead.

However, that didn't rule out the possibility by what means she might work off a loan would put her in a position she'd be left in a hotel room by a copycat murderer.

"I have a no fraternization policy," Lucinda carried on. "And she consistently fraternized. She got a verbal about that as well. This was an issue for her. She had a small cadre of friends because she tended to try to steal boyfriends, and sometimes succeeded. All she knew in her life was drama, and she didn't understand how to live without it. So she created it in order to find her safe space, not comprehending it wasn't actually safe."

"It's my understanding she dated Cade Bohannan's son."

She perked up. "Has Cade waded into this?"

"I wish I could share with you, Ms. Bonner, but in terms of how we investigate, I can't."

She let that go immediately too.

"Yes, she dated Jace. I was pleased when they started going out. He's young, but he's also his father's son, so he's a good man, he knows what he wants, and what he doesn't. Sadly, he didn't want drama, and it didn't last."

"You cared about her."

She uncrossed her arms, set her hand on the desk and drummed fingers that were tipped in nails that weren't long, nor were they short. But they were perfectly symmetrical, squared off and painted a soft beige.

Enough to dig into your skin, not enough to tear it.

Unless she lost control.

He took his mind off her nails by looking at her face, which of course made him think about her nails sinking into his skin if he made her lose control.

She was staring at the bare corner of the desk when she said quietly, "She was a talented dancer. And she was a good kid. She wasn't brought up right, but she listened, and sometimes she learned. She was very funny and very full of life. People she cared about, she'd do anything for them if it was within her power." Lucinda lifted her gaze to his. "I liked her. I don't take all my girls under my wing because most of them don't need it. But Brittanie was different."

Lucinda Bonner wasn't as old as he was, he'd put her at thirty-five, tops, so she was nowhere near old enough to be Brittanie Iverson's mother.

But that feeling was there. Her eyes glowed with something deeper.

I don't have the skills to do what you do, or I'd be doing that.

"Did taking Brittanie under your wing pass beyond Bon Amie?" he asked.

She shook her head, the movement melancholy, like she wished she had.

"I didn't let her waitress when she needed money because I didn't need an exhausted girl dragging on the chorus line. Also because she needed to learn how to manage her money. We had conversations. We had moments. And with Britt, there were more of those than any others, past or present. But all within these walls. As much as my girls matter to me, all my staff matters to me, boundaries are essential. If I didn't set them, I'd have a revolving door of broken hearts, girl fights, loan requests and my couch would never be empty."

She took her hand from the desk, put it in her lap, and straightened her shoulders.

"This business has been in my family for six generations. I grew up learning how to compartmentalize while fostering. My family is my family, Agent Lazarus, and my business is my business."

"Understandable," he murmured, holding her eyes.

She didn't need his validation, she didn't say that, not audibly, but he got it.

"Do you think she would do something ill-advised if she had money issues?" he asked.

"I haven't come right out and said it, though I've implied it, but I'll be clear. Brittanie was the master of doing things that were ill-advised. So yes."

"But she didn't tell you of anything that might cause you concern."

She shook her head. "Keyleigh might know something, but I doubt it. Britt was getting old enough to know better. She'd almost lost her job with me, twice. Keyleigh, who's older than Britt and would definitely cast herself as Britt's older sister, could get impatient with her too. I'm sure you can guess why, but she'll also tell you. So if she was up to something she shouldn't be, I'm not sure she'd confide that in anyone. Though, Keyleigh can speak to that better than me."

"I'll need to talk with Keyleigh right away."

"I can arrange for that while you're reading Britt's file."

"I'd appreciate it."

She nodded.

"Was Brittanie seeing someone?"

She shook her head again. "She hadn't been serious about anyone since Jace. And losing Jace was a blow. She suffered for that.

But she was a dancer at Bon Amie. If she wanted attention, she could find it. And she liked attention."

Now they were into something sticky because they were talking patrons.

"Would you have names of those who paid Brittanie attention?"

She leaned forward, put her elbow on her desk and flicked out her hand, palm up.

"Hand me the top file. I'll write them down. At least the ones I know."

Again, unexpected.

He handed her the file.

She took it, put it in front of her, then opened the middle drawer of her desk.

She pulled out an iPhone and a gold pen he knew was Cartier, because he'd bought one like it for his wife for their fifteenth wedding anniversary.

She didn't open the folder and start writing, though.

She remarked, "Polly told me she'd been killed. She didn't get into specifics."

Before she could continue, Rus spoke. He did it low and with feeling because he couldn't talk to her about this, but he didn't want to rebuff her unduly.

"I'm sorry, Lucinda, I can't share much about the case."

"Can you at least tell me she didn't suffer?"

He couldn't so he didn't say anything.

And that was when it happened.

When Lucinda Bonner stopped being the most fuckable woman he'd laid eyes on, including his wife, but only because she hadn't been a woman when he met her, since they met at fifteen.

It was also when Lucinda stopped being a woman he'd consider proposing a friends with benefits arrangement to, because he wouldn't mind long weekends in the Pacific Northwest. Not simply because it was gorgeous out here, mostly because she was gorgeous so he'd be spending that time with her.

Instead, she became the first woman since his ex-wife that he wanted to know everything about. What she looked like when she smiled. What she sounded like when she laughed. Both when she orgasmed. And everything else he could learn about a sixth-generation woman who turned catering to the base needs of a man into a living that involved her wearing eight-hundred-dollar shoes and using Cartier pens.

This happened when tears shimmered in her eyes momentarily, before she sniffed, set her pen aside, picked up her phone, touched the screen and put it to her ear.

She said into it, "Call Keyleigh. Tell her I need her up here immediately."

With that, she put her phone down, picked up the pen, opened the folder, flipped the top page to its back and started writing a list of names.

But even if Rus knew he was in trouble when it came to Lucinda, he also knew that she'd lied.

He was sure she could compartmentalize like a pro.

But Brittanie Iverson meant something to her.

And that didn't stay within these walls.

FIVE

Give a Shit

R us asked Lucinda to remain in the room when he spoke with Keyleigh, and she'd agreed.

She'd also gone somewhere and returned with a box of Kleenex, which had been a good call.

Keyleigh wasn't as beautiful as Brittanie had been, nor was she stunning, like Lucinda, but she was pretty.

She was also a mess.

So much so, he was worried he wasn't going to get anything from her because she couldn't talk through her sobs.

It was interesting, however, to watch Lucinda sit on her side of the desk, removed from the emotional woman sitting next to Rus, and yet exuding warmth and understanding even in silence.

"I-I'm sorry, Ms. Bonner," Keyleigh stammered to her boss. Another something that was interesting, the formal address to a woman who couldn't be much more than seven years older than Keyleigh.

Then to Rus. "Sorry."

"I'm sure Special Agent Lazarus has experience with people who've sustained an unexpected loss, Keyleigh," Lucinda said in a serene, yet affectionate voice. "Take your time."

"I-I can't…this is…it's…*this is crazy!*" she wailed, then buried her face in a cloud of tissue.

Rus glanced at Lucinda to see her gaze on him.

She tipped her head to the side.

He didn't know how he knew what she was communicating with that small gesture.

But he knew.

Push.

He gave it a few moments.

Then he went after it.

"Keyleigh," he began. "It's important to learn as much as we can as quickly as we can after the event happens. This is a shock, I know, but if you could take a few deep breaths for me and answer a few questions, it would help Brittanie."

Keyleigh took her face from the tissues, nodded, dragged in a few stuttering breaths, and her eyes slid to Lucinda.

Lucinda held them and sat unmoving, the rock Keyleigh could lean on.

Keyleigh leaned.

She swiped her face, blew her nose and said, "Okay. I wanna help. I wanna help Brittanie."

Having a window, Rus launched in.

And he learned no, Brittanie wasn't seeing anyone new, or anyone at all in an official way. Though she was seeing a few men casually, but she didn't talk about them much. Keyleigh didn't know their names and got the sense she wasn't that into them and they weren't going to last very long.

Yes, she was terrible with money, but not only didn't Keyleigh know of any other than her usual troubles with overspending, she thought Brittanie was getting better with managing her funds.

Yes, even though it was frowned on, sometimes she hooked up with people she met at the club. These were the men who weren't going to last too long. It never led to anything but some one-night stands, or short-term hookups, and Keyleigh had no knowledge if anything turned weird or sour.

Unfortunately, yes, some of these men were married. Keyleigh tried to advise her not to mess with married guys, but sometimes Brittanie did stupid stuff Keyleigh didn't understand.

No, Keyleigh didn't know anyone who might want to cause her harm, or at least not anyone who would go that far. Brittanie had made some enemies, specifically with female acquaintances whose boyfriends she'd set her sights on. But killing her for that would be extreme.

No, she did not have a close relationship with her mother or brother. Her brother often got into trouble, which Brittanie wanted to avoid, and she avoided her mother outright, and to Keyleigh's knowledge, she hadn't seen either of them in some time.

And through sniffles and barely controlled weeping, Keyleigh couldn't add anything else, but if she remembered something, she'd be happy to contact Rus.

Throughout the questioning, even though her emotion would sometimes get in the way, Rus didn't sense she was holding anything back. It was clear she loved Brittanie, she was suffering at her loss, and she truly wanted to help find who hurt her.

But more, intermingled with all of this, she'd say how funny Brittanie was. How Brittanie would be the one who would feed your cat when you went on vacation or go to the grocery store if you sprained your ankle. How she loved kids and animals.

And life.

She wanted Rus to have the answers to his questions.

And she wanted Rus to know that Brittanie might be flawed, but she was a good person.

When it was over, Lucinda walked her to the door, hugged her, and Rus was impressed how she could be both aloof and tender in the way she held her girl. She then handed her off to the security woman who'd shown Rus in.

Security Sue was solicitous as she led Keyleigh to the stairs.

But filling her place was a woman in a white chef's uniform who handed Lucinda a tray.

She took it, the woman closed the door, and Lucinda made her way to Rus.

She set the tray in front of him, and Rus stared down at a

gigantic sandwich of perfectly rare, exquisitely shaved slices of beef and what looked like melted provolone on a French roll next to a mess of homemade potato chips and a small bowl of au jus. A tall, narrow glass of ice rested beside a bottle of San Pellegrino, and there was another bowl with slices of lemon and lime.

"Angelina makes a superb prime rib dip," Lucinda murmured as she moved back behind her desk.

He watched her sit.

"You seem like a meat and potatoes man," she finished.

"How did you know?" he asked after how she knew he needed food, not about how she knew he was a meat and potatoes man, which he was.

"Are you from the Seattle bureau?" she asked in return.

"No."

She said no more, but he knew she'd put together he'd gotten a call from wherever he lived and from then to now, finding food hadn't been his priority.

He took the ivory cloth napkin that was on the tray, draped it on his thigh, but before he dug in, he said, "Most obliged."

She dipped her chin.

He dipped his sandwich.

She spoke while he took a bite.

"If you wish to come back up here, I can sort interviews for you in my office with staff. If you want, I can make myself available while you speak to them. I think they'll be more comfortable here and it'll be easier for you than traipsing all over Misted Pines. Tell me a time you want to begin, and I'll handle it."

She was right, even though this was a trek, having interviews scheduled would save time. Further, he'd normally ask them to come to the station, which always set people on edge. Last, being in a safe space, without him invading their homes, was definitely a better option.

She was also wheedling her way into his investigation, which he would allow her to do because it served his purpose.

He and Moran would hit the mother and brother in the morning.

Which meant…

"Tomorrow," he said. "Beginning with the top of the list you gave me, starting at one o'clock. I have to warn you, though, this will depend on if we have any other leads we need to follow."

She nodded and picked up her phone.

He ate while she texted.

He spoke when she put the phone down.

"Where's your theater?"

"The basement."

Mystery solved.

"Have you spoken to Melanie yet?" she asked.

He shook his head.

"I want Brittanie," she announced.

He did a slow blink. "Pardon?"

"Melanie won't have the money to pay for anything fitting, and she didn't know her daughter. She couldn't begin to know what Britt would want. So, when she's released, I want Brittanie."

Jesus Christ.

One could say with that, compartmentalization was out the fucking window.

"I'm sure you understand I can't do that," he said carefully. "She'll be released to next of kin."

Lucinda looked out at the darkening damp.

The rain had subsided, but the clouds hadn't gone away. It was September, the day was waning.

What was outside was now the mood in her office.

"Lucinda," he called gently.

Her gaze cut to him. "Please, do what you can?"

He nodded. "I'll talk to Moran. We'll see what we can do."

She drummed her fingers on her desk again.

He watched her openly while he ate.

She was right, the sandwich was superb, though it was a shocker, the potato chips might have been the best thing on the plate.

He was washing it down with sparkling water that he'd put both the lemon and lime in when he broached it.

"I don't know how hard this is," he said. "I've never had

someone I cared about murdered. But I've been where I'm sitting too many times in my twenty years of experience, so I'm sensing you've held something back regarding your relationship with Brittanie."

"You know," was her strange reply.

"I don't," he returned.

"People, on the whole, but women especially have two choices in life. A walk-on part in the war, or a lead role in a cage."

Rus felt his innards tighten.

He knew those words.

They were hopeless words.

Lucinda kept talking.

"Me, and my mother and my grandmother, for generations, have done what we could to offer another choice to the women who walked through our doors. There's freedom in claiming domain of your agency. I've heard countless stories that would shock most, but not you. Brittanie's was neither better nor worse than many others. What she was, was mine."

Now they were getting somewhere.

So he wouldn't spook her, Rus was back to gentle when he prompted, "How was she yours?"

"On occasion, she babysat my daughter."

Well…

Shit.

He'd been right, but damned if he wasn't ticked about it.

Therefore, it was not gentle, but irritated, when he said, "Lucinda, these are things I need to know."

"I wasn't ready to share."

"I can't wait for you to share. You said your relationship with her happened in these walls."

"That relationship wasn't mine. It was Madden's."

Right.

Now he was getting pissed.

"That's bullshit," he clipped. "It's also a distinction you don't get to make, and you know it. I make those decisions."

Her mouth tightened.

She untightened it to hand him more bullshit.

"The walls it happened in were in my home, which is down the valley, and I've always considered it part of the whole of Bon Amie."

"You know this is too important for you to play word games with me, and definitely too important for you to use those games to lie to me."

Her jaw bulged as she clenched her teeth.

She knew.

He swung his arm behind him and stabbed a finger at the door.

"That's your kingdom, Lucinda. You don't get to decide on me. Brittanie was yours, but whether you approve or not, she's now mine."

"You're right," she said tersely.

"I know," he fired back.

She glared at him, and there was sulk in that glare. Seeing it, it was a relief she could be human, and it was a turn-on to know she had some latent cuteness.

But they needed to get shit straight.

"What else didn't you tell me?"

That was when she verbally punched him right in the throat.

"Madden adored her, she adored Madden. So how do I tell my baby girl her big sister is dead?"

"Shit, Lucinda," he whispered.

Knowing he was no longer feeling anything close to pissed, she pressed her advantage.

"I want her, Agent Lazarus."

"I can't—"

"I. Want. Her."

"I'll do what I can."

She leaned his way. "*I want her.*"

"Honey," he said softly, "I can't make promises, but I swear to you right now, I'll do what I can."

She snapped her mouth shut, sat back and cut her eyes again to the window.

"You didn't let her waitress for you when she needed money, but you let her watch Madden to help her out," he deduced.

She refused to admit to that.

She said, "You heard Keyleigh. Britt loved kids."

She let her watch Madden to help her out.

In fact, he'd lay money on the fact Brittanie Iverson was the highest paid babysitter in the county.

"She wanted her own one day," she went on, her gaze coming back to him. "She was going to be nothing like her mom. When someone is starved for love all their lives, they go one of two ways. Either they have no idea what it is, so they can't give nor receive it, or they have so much of it pent up, when they find someone worthy of it, it explodes all over the place."

"It exploded for Madden," he guessed.

She didn't confirm.

She said, "There's nothing more I didn't tell you. You're right. I was testing you. You handled me well, you handled Keyleigh well."

She left it at that, but he got what was unsaid.

So it was half joke, half true when he replied, "I'm pleased to earn your approval."

"I'll have your appointments sorted for tomorrow, starting at one."

Brittanie might now be his, but those were his marching orders.

At that, he couldn't beat back the smile, but he dropped his head to hide it as he stood.

However, one more thing…

He tossed his napkin on the tray and looked to her.

"Is there something between you and Melanie Iverson I need to know?"

She shook her head. "Outside her being shit as a mom so Brittanie felt unworthy and needed to search for that worth in men she could attract or steal, no. This wasn't abuse, precisely. It wasn't neglect, as such. It also wasn't competition, exactly. It was all of those in a unique package that's Melanie. You'll know when you meet her, Agent Lazarus. You'll know more when you meet Dakota. These days, people spend a lot of time talking about how our country has gone to hell. They say we need church. They say kids need discipline and faith. They're wrong. They simply need someone to give a shit."

"I can't argue that."

"I know you can't."

"I'll see you tomorrow at one."

"Come at twelve thirty. I'll have a sandwich waiting for you."

"You don't have to feed me."

"Yes, I do, Agent Lazarus, because in case you haven't noticed, I give a shit."

Christ God, he had a huge fucking problem.

Because he really wanted to kiss her.

This being, of course, before he fucked her.

"I'll be here at twelve thirty," he said low.

"I'll see you then."

With that, because he had things to do, even though he didn't want to, he turned and walked away from Lucinda Bonner.

He was okay with that.

But only because he'd be back the next day at twelve thirty.

SIX

Filled His Soul

O n the way back to town, Rus made four important calls.
The first was to Wade Dickerson, Moran's deputy in charge when he was out of commission. Rus recited the list of patrons who'd shown Brittanie attention. He also gave him the list of boyfriends Lucinda had written down. He then told Dickerson they were persons of interest, and why, and he left the man with the mission of having chats and gathering alibis if they were to be had.

The second was to Ben McGill, his local FBI lead, who assured Rus he'd be delivering the things Rus had asked for to Pinetop Lodge within the hour.

The third was to his son, Acre, who was a junior at the College of William and Mary studying Criminal Law and Psychology.

And yes, that meant Acre wanted to follow in his father's footsteps, though he wanted to skip the being-in-the-army-for-four-years part, along with the being a cop for five (instead, after graduation, he was going to enlist in the Marines, this flip-flopping what Rus did —Army first, then he went to school for five years while working).

After serving, Acre wanted to apply right to the Bureau.

He got Acre's voicemail.

"It's your dad," he said after the beep. "I'm on a case in Washington state, but as usual, I'd like regular indication you're alive, eating, hydrating, studying and using condoms. Text me."

The last was his daughter, Sabrina, who was a freshman at the University of Florida. And even though she'd only been there mere weeks, evidence was suggesting her major was researching all the ways you could make an entire year at college into a spring break.

She answered.

"Daddy!"

Everything about those two syllables filled his soul with what had been leaching from it since the moment he got the call about a new dead girl.

"Hey, baby," he replied.

"Oh my God, how did you know I needed you to call?"

"Because you go over your new bikini allowance weekly, so you need me to check in and approve additional expenditures? Just a guess."

She giggled.

And that sound filled him enough to get through the next forty-eight hours.

"No," she said. "But if you're offering."

"I'm not," he replied.

Another giggle, and then, "Okay, I have a friend who's thinking he wants to be in the FBI. Will you talk to him?"

"Are you dating him?"

"Yes."

"Then no, I already hate him."

A long trill of giggles through which she cried, "Dad!"

As usual with Sabrina, he gave in.

"Yes, I'll talk to him. But I'm on a case. It'll have to be later."

Her tone changed when she asked, "You're on a case?"

It wasn't the PTSD left behind from an absent dad. After his marriage had imploded, he'd had long talks with his kids about that.

They'd assured him what he was doing now, which was what he'd always done—carved out time to let them know they were on his mind always—had given them what they needed. That and the rituals they had before he left and after he returned from travel.

No, it had been Jennifer who'd needed more.

And she deserved it.

He just didn't give it.

What he was hearing from his girl now was a daughter worried about her father doing a necessary job that she knew burdened him in ways she wanted to alleviate, but she didn't understand her continued health and growth and vibrancy did the work for her.

"I am, Sabby. In Washington state. But I'm always available if you need me, though I can't talk to your guy right now."

"Okay."

"Everything else good?"

"Yes."

"You going to class?"

"Of course!"

Lie.

"Your mother and I are paying for you to actually learn something down there," he pointed out.

"Every new day of life is learning."

Fucking hell.

"We mean the kind you get in a classroom," he clarified.

"Dad, it's just so sunny down here," she replied. "Like *all the time*."

"It'll be gloomy and snowy and cold when you flunk out and have to go home to your mom."

"I'm going to class," she stated quickly.

This didn't mean she *had* been going to class. It meant his threat penetrated and she *would* be going to class.

"That makes me happy."

"I'm glad."

"Okay, I gotta go. I'll call in a few days, but I want texts from you."

"Okay. Be safe and love you."

"Love you too."

They disconnected.

Acre would text because Rus asked him to, and knowing Rus

was on a case, he'd continue to do it once every two or three days so Rus would know he was good.

This delay between comms wasn't because he didn't want to keep in contact with his old man, or because he wanted to give him space to do his job. It was because Acre was serious about his studies. He was serious about partying. And he was serious about getting laid.

Keeping in contact with his father put a crimp in his overtaxed schedule.

Knowing he was on a case, instead of his two to ten texts a day from his daughter, now Sabrina would add to that and text when she saw a flower she'd never seen before, when she heard birds singing, when she saw the fronds of a palm tree sway, when she enjoyed the refreshing tang of a lemonade, when the sun was shining, or the moon had a lovely glow.

Yes, he would hate any man who won her heart because the abundance of love in it she had for the man in her life had always only been his, and he wasn't feeling like he'd ever be prepared to share.

On that thought, the GPS programmed to lead him to Pinetop Lodge told him a left turn was coming.

It didn't take him through town.

Instead, he turned on the outskirts and climbed what would probably be considered a hill here but was a mountain in Virginia. The road led him straight to a large, attractive hotel that had successfully fused the feel of the Swiss Alps and Washington rusticity with a broad hint of Native appropriation.

He pulled in the front and a valet raced to his door.

He was sensing this was going to usurp more than his approved daily expenditure on room and board, but he nevertheless angled out of the SUV and gave the valet his keys.

A bellman was already at the back gate of the vehicle.

"Checking in?" he asked.

Rus was in the opened back passenger door getting his laptop and briefcase when he answered, "Yeah."

He grabbed his bags, the bellmen led, and check-in was practiced and fluid.

He was glad for the moist atmosphere considering there was a goodly amount of stone, but the lodge was mostly made of wood, so a fire would suck, but might not be annihilating, as he was led to the top floor and into his room.

Definitely taxing his per diem.

He handed off some bills to the bellman who'd hung his garment bag and rolled his suitcase into the closet in the bedroom before he discreetly closed the door to the suite behind him.

And Rus was left in a suite that had a living room, a bar with sink, microwave, refrigerator and two stools on the outside, a romantic fireplace and a balcony with two lounge chairs that had a view of another mountain/hill across the way, and at the bottom of the hill the hotel was on, a large lake shrouded in a heavy coat of mist.

In other words, the view was outstanding.

The bedroom also had a fireplace, an armchair and ottoman, and a king bed with white sheets, a fluffy duvet, a red plaid blanket spread along the bottom, and two blue toss pillows with red moose on the front propped up against an abundance of pillows that would cater to the head support needs of any living human being.

Sabrina would scream with glee at the bathroom.

He was just happy to see a clean shower.

He pulled off his clothes, got a change that was more comfortable, but didn't unpack seeing as he'd be relocating somewhere else after tonight, since the cheapest room here was probably out of budget.

He took a quick shower, dressed and decided to live it up, hitting the mini bar for a beer.

By this time, McGill was texting to ask his room number.

He gave it, and while McGill was on his way up, Moran texted that he was on his way, and Bohannan was en route too.

Before the locals arrived, Rus had time to debrief with his agent, getting a detailed verbal report of the investigation of the scene, the motel and its surroundings, spreading pictures across the round table by a window, the easier to enjoy room service with a view.

It was too soon to get into anything meaty. Tests would take time to run, prints would take time to process.

They had something bigger to discuss when Moran and Bohannan joined them.

And that was not only sharing ideas about why someone used a serial killer's MO to murder a local woman, but also how to strategize the FBI's continued involvement, namely Rus's.

Because Moran could request FBI assistance, but that assistance would be from the Seattle division, as it would be in what was not a federal crime, it was a local one.

SEVEN

Your Wins

M cGill had a beer, a boot to the edge of the coffee table that was covered in a mess of pictures and reports, and had turned on the fire, because, like Rus, he knew this was the only chance he'd get, so he was going to live it up, and it wasn't even his room.

"The copycat thing, the AD is going to be cool with you being here," McGill said.

"I need you," Moran said. "And I don't mind making a call to share that."

"The Bureau Chief isn't going to want anyone here but you," Bohannan said. "It's not going to be an issue. What's going to be an issue is containment. The local media is already sniffing around. They know we have a body. And Misted Pines is on radar, so they're hungry. You were right. Your guy can't know anyone is using his MO."

"What's this?" McGill asked.

Rus looked to McGill.

"He's made threats, credible ones, that he can remotely detonate something, somewhere, he hasn't said where for obvious reasons," Rus told him. "But wherever it is, it's going to cause damage, in property and human lives, if we get too close or do anything he doesn't like."

McGill wasn't enjoying a taste of the good life anymore, he was staring at Rus.

"He's communicating with you?"

"He leaves me notes with the bodies."

"Jesus, fuck," McGill bit off, taking his boot from the coffee table and sitting up.

"This is why I knew it was a copycat," Rus explained. "Details have gotten out. Too many. That's the one we've kept to ourselves. Everything in Misted Pines was done by the book. But they didn't know that, so they couldn't include it."

"How do you know the threats are credible?" Moran asked.

"I tested it after body seven, saying something coded that only he'd get during a press conference," Rus shared "He got it. I wasn't done with the presser when a small bomb went off in a park in Alabama. It was a risk I didn't like taking, orders from on high told me to go for it. They were convinced he was bluffing."

Everyone in the room wore understanding expressions.

Sometimes, they didn't get it right, and with the stakes they played, getting it wrong had terrible consequences.

"Fortunately, only a dog was injured. The little guy didn't make it. His owner was hit with some shrapnel but was fine. When all was said and done, the locals blamed it on a faulty gas line. But we knew it was him because, at the time of the explosion, the FBI switchboard got a call from a landline in a house in Maine. The man who called asked, 'See?' and hung up. When local agents stormed the house, there was no sign of him. We found out later the owners were in Europe on vacation. And as usual, he left no trace."

"Okay, first, allow me a moment to shiver that there might be random bombs anywhere in the US this guy can detonate on a whim," McGill remarked.

Rus was right there with him on that, he lived that shit every day.

"So okay, now how do you know he'll be pissed someone is using his MO?" McGill asked.

At that, Bohannan entered the conversation.

"Because, among other things, he's a malignant narcissist. The world revolves around him. He's never wrong. He's the best at everything. He feels he has carte blanche to live his life as he sees fit without question. He's extremely proud of his crimes, and because he is, someone copying them will infuriate him. Not only does he get off on the fear, control and pain his victims feel, and the physical acts of violation, this is his art. Someone usurping that is going to threaten his dominion. He probably spent years on sexual assaults his victims were too terrified to report before he ratcheted that shit up and began bludgeoning. He can't have just anyone making it look easy."

McGill nodded to express he took that in while Rus marveled at the fact Bohannan had such a close bead on the guy after only an afternoon with the file.

Bohannan kept going.

"Rus is his victim too. He knows Rus is frustrated. He knows Rus wants to stop him. And by threatening to cause even more harm, he knows he's controlling Rus and forcing him to experience fear. This guy turns Rus's eye with a crime the Crystal Killer didn't commit, he'll take it as a violation. He feels like he owns Rus. No one takes what's his until he's done playing with it."

Bohannan looked to Rus, and when he did, he didn't appear happy.

"They should have pulled you off the case on the first note. This guy should never have had anyone to manipulate."

Rus was surprised Bohannan had this reaction. He knew that wasn't the way they rolled.

"So an agent has to start from scratch with each new victim?" Rus asked, watching Bohannan carefully. "It stymies an investigation and gives him what he wants because, if every new agent has to take time to get up to speed, he has more time to get away."

Rus then told him what he had to already know.

"Plus, as uncomfortable as it is, it's good he thinks he has a relationship with me. He's communicating, and in doing it, could give something away."

"It's too much pressure on you," Bohannan returned.

There was something else there. Something Bohannan was getting from the file that he wasn't sharing.

However, Rus sensed it wasn't the time, or maybe they weren't in the company, to press it.

"You know the job, if you can't take the pressure, you get out of the game," Rus replied.

"Yeah, I know the job, which is why I got the fuck out of the game," Bohannan retorted.

"And this is why, once we find who killed Brittanie, I am too," Rus shared. "The problem with that is, I know the Crystal Killer isn't going to let me go easy. And I have a daughter."

The room went dead silent.

"So, yeah," Rus said into the void.

"Right," Moran started then moved them past something no one in that room had any power to do anything about that evening. "Let's deal with what we can deal with. The press."

"Stick with limited information released," Bohannan declared.

"I got that, Cade, but how do I keep the maid, and the desk clerk, and Brittanie's own mother quiet if someone offers them their thirty-second interview of fame?" Moran asked.

Rus reached to a piece of paper and shook it, reciting the details of the report written on it. "The maid, Gentry Anderson, found the body, exited the room, and called 911. Your deputies were there within ten minutes and entered next. The owner arrived after some time and wasn't allowed to enter the room. There's no indication in this report anyone entered except the maid."

He looked direct to Moran before he concluded.

"And you yourself made the excellent decision to order the exterior cordoned and shielded so no one could see in while the scene was investigated. Is that not true?"

Moran nodded his head. "It's true. The maid went to the desk clerk after she called it in. He wasn't there and she was flipping out, couldn't find him. Even though she knew he had a habit of being at the vending machines getting cookies because, apparently, he's prone to taking random breaks that included eating cookies, which could be a result of the fact he also took random breaks to smoke weed."

"So we only have to keep the maid quiet," Rus said.

"And Melanie and Dakota Iverson," Bohannan added.

"They don't need to know the specifics," Rus stated.

"No, they don't," Moran agreed.

"So it's the maid," McGill finished it.

Moran pulled out his phone in order to get someone on making sure the maid kept to herself.

"Cin give you anything useful?" Bohannan asked.

"The use of her office and scheduling service. She's setting up interviews tomorrow afternoon with her staff."

Bohannan's lips in his beard curved. "Unsurprised."

"Brittanie babysat for her," Rus told him.

The lip curve faded. "Fuck."

Moran stopped texting, so Rus looked to him. "She wants us to convince Melanie Iverson to release the body to her."

"I don't know the woman well, but on first impression, I suspect the minute Iverson knows Cin wants her, Iverson is going to dig in, when before, she probably couldn't give two shits how her daughter was laid to rest," Moran told him. "She'd do this for no other reason than to be a pain in somebody's ass."

"We're gonna have to finesse that."

Moran's brows went up. "You told her we'd get Melanie to release Brittanie to Cin?"

"I told her we'd do what we could. But somehow, we're going to get her to relinquish claim to Brittanie so Lucinda can take care of her."

Moran and Bohannan exchanged a look.

Rus would be worried about this if they didn't know Lucinda. Therefore, they knew she was the kind of woman who found ways to wrap everyone around her finger.

Considering what he was doing for her was innocuous, and he knew they all knew it would be for Brittanie, he didn't mind they thought she'd gotten the twist on him.

"I think it's important for her to know how much a funeral costs," Bohannan suggested.

Yes.

It was best for Brittanie.

"And she needs to understand the state will handle it if the body isn't claimed," McGill put in.

"Right, so we got a plan on that," Moran said, then shared he was done with it by getting into the most important topic of the night. "Now, anyone have any fucking clue why someone would copycat kill a woman in my town? Is this just some sick fuck? Or is it something else."

"My call, something else, and still definitely both. You want her dead, and you want to get away with it, it's a good plan to kill her in a way suspicion is going to turn in another direction that is nowhere near you," Bohannan suggested.

"So she steals a few boyfriends," Moran replied. "Who hates her so much they do that to her? It takes planning. It takes effort. It takes follow through. It's grisly and it's personal. We won't know what we got until the coroner makes her report, so all we got right now is that it's gotta be a guy."

"It's cute you've never heard of a dildo," McGill ribbed.

Moran wasn't in the mood to make light of the situation, even to take the edge off.

He proved this not only by not shoveling it back, but by what he said next.

"You saw her. It's overpowering her. It's tying her up. That wasn't sexual assault. It was sexual brutalization. And she checked in herself, and so far, we've had no indication she has lesbian or bi tendencies. So she checks in, odds are she's meeting a guy and that guy is our perp. She hits a motel out of town that doesn't have security cameras, it's probably a married guy."

"I wouldn't know, but I suspect some married men don't feel guilt at taking in a burlesque show," Rus remarked.

"Cin's list," Moran said.

Apparently, Dickerson had briefed his boss.

"It's all we got right now," Rus replied. "Along with the ex-boyfriends."

"List?" Bohannan asked.

Rus filled him in.

After he was done, Bohannan nodded and muttered an approving, "Good."

"So we got that, interviews with family, staff who might know something, and fuck all else," Moran bitched.

"It's more than I have on the Crystal Killer," Rus pointed out. "And I've been working that for years."

"You've looked into the plastic sheeting?" Bohannan asked.

Moran jerked up his chin. "Any store that sells it in that amount anywhere in the county, which is one store, has not sold that amount to anyone," Moran told him. "We're pushing out to other counties. But I'd guess it was bought online."

Rus jumped in.

"Any joy on the crystal?"

Moran shook his head. "On the other hand, there's a lot of New Age shops in the county. We've shown the picture around. No one remembers selling that particular one. We're going to cast a wider net on that too."

"How are you on warrants?" Bohannan asked McGill.

"We're working on the bank, we'll have it tomorrow. Another couple of days for her bank to get us data. Credit cards and cell will take longer. She's in the queue to get a tech guy to work on her laptop. I hope to have access to email soon."

Rus already knew this because it was part of his morning briefing before he even got to the scene.

But while McGill was sharing, on mentioning the ex-boyfriends, it hit Rus unusually belatedly that a couple of guests to their party hadn't showed.

"Your boys coming?" he asked Bohannan.

"About that," Bohannan replied.

He said no more.

Fuck.

"Let me guess, Jace doesn't know he's out, like you suggested, and Jesse is with his brother," Rus said.

Unfortunately, Bohannan's response to that was valid.

"I think we can all agree that our first instinct upon learning a woman who shared our bed got dead, especially what they did to Brittanie, we'd do something about it. I'm giving them a day to realize this is a stupid play. Then I'm reining them in."

"I want to see him sometime *soon*," Rus demanded.

Bohannan nodded. "I'll make that happen."

This didn't break up their party, but since there was nothing more they could do that night, Bohannan led a team-building exercise, which was essentially shooting the shit so they could all get to know each other better.

McGill had a long drive home, since he lived in Seattle, so he left first.

Bohannan had a beautiful woman who was at home, so he left second.

Rus was travel-weary, and he needed a fresh start in the morning, so he didn't give indication he wanted to bond further with his new partner.

No slight was taken, Moran knew it before Rus had to say it.

He was on his way out when Rus broached their last topic for the night.

"The Bureau isn't going to pay for this room, Harry."

"I know. Tonight is on my department. The remainder of your stay is sponsored by Cin."

Shit.

That felt good when it shouldn't feel anything.

"She contacted you?"

"She contacted Polly, who contacted me. She wanted you moved here from wherever you were staying, not knowing Polly put you here to begin with. Though, once Polly got a call from Cin, she changed your reservation to a suite."

Of course she did.

He'd barely met Polly and he knew he liked her.

"I'm not sure that's going to fly," he noted.

Moran looked him dead in the eye and advised, "Man, take your wins where you can."

And on that sterling piece of advice, that was the end of the discussion and the evening, because, after Moran clapped him on the shoulder, he walked out.

EIGHT

Unicorn Heads

The next morning, Rus sat shotgun next to Moran in his cruiser as they drove to Melanie Iverson's house.

"Got official approval this morning to stick with the case," Rus told the sheriff.

"Good news," Moran replied, relief underlying his tone.

"And I know my guys have been over it, but I'll want to get into Brittanie's apartment sometime today."

"We'll do that next," Moran replied. "It's on the way to where Dakota works."

"Great," Rus muttered.

Moran drove.

Rus took in the landscape wondering if he'd ever get bored of fir and spruce.

He then decided he wouldn't.

"And here's where Brittanie grew up, feast your eyes," Moran said as he turned them into a drive.

Outside of the natural beauty that surrounded it, it was far from a feast.

The yard was scrub. He'd say the house needed a paint job, but it didn't. It didn't even need two weeks of handyman services.

It needed to be condemned.

Moran parked. They got out.

As they walked up to the house, Rus had to curb his desire to phone animal welfare to report the emaciated pit bull chained to a pole cemented in the ground. The dog had an overturned water bowl and no shelter in sight. Rus then had to concentrate on not falling through the spongy boards of a deck that had once been a pretty sweet front porch.

Moran knocked while Rus was careful of their combined weight distribution on the slats.

Moran knocked again.

He was about to knock a third time when the door was pulled open, and there she was behind a dilapidated screen door.

Melanie Iverson.

Jesus Christ.

She might have three days of makeup on her face. It appeared she just painted over the last, even if some of it had made it to places it wasn't supposed to be. Her hair was a rat's nest, dyed a brash version of Brittanie's natural color, with half inch white-gray roots. Her cheeks were sunken. Her skin was sallow. She was overly thin. The lines around her lips betrayed she was a lifetime smoker, even before the smell of it hit him.

And she was visibly in a very bad mood.

"You tell her fuckwit of a father someone offed her?" was her greeting.

Two seconds in her presence, he knew exactly what Lucinda was talking about.

"We've been unable to locate Mr. Iverson," Moran replied.

She opened her mouth and both he and Moran leaned back at the smell that emanated from it as she—no other way to describe it —cackled.

Once she was done doing that, she said, "I'll bet."

"I'd like to introduce you to Special Agent Zachariah Lazarus," Moran said.

She squinted his way like she was looking through smoke, which was either habit, or she was too vain, or poor, to get glasses.

"Special Agent? Like, FBI?" she asked.

"Yes, ma'am," Rus said.

"Ma'am, huh," she grunted and returned her attention to Moran. "So she finally made it to the big time. FBI is on her case. Or can't you deal with some little slut getting murdered in a motel room?"

Annnnnnnnnd...

Rus was done, mostly because he knew this was a waste of time.

Moran, however, was feeling stubborn.

"Can we talk to you for a few minutes?"

"No," she denied. "And you can tell them reporters to fuck off too."

At least some good news, she wasn't interested in talking to the media.

Moran had released a name that morning and the fact she was found dead in a motel room. Dead, not murdered, and they were waiting for a coroner's report to know more.

Still, the media got the jump on them.

"It'd really help if we could have a few minutes of your time," Moran pushed.

"Listen, she had to be making some bank up there at,"—she leaned back and swayed—"*high and mighty* Lucinda Bonner's joint. Her mom asks for some cash to help her out of a squeeze, what's she say? Don't bother trying to figure it out, I'll tell you. 'Go fuck yourself.' That's what she said. So you don't have to think hard on what that means. We weren't close. At first, I was shocked. My kid, murdered? Goddamn. Then I remembered she was a bitch, a whore and a tightwad. So I got over it."

Yup.

Totally got what Lucinda said about this woman.

Even so, they were there, so Rus gave it a go. "Are you saying you haven't had any contact with Brittanie in a while?"

"Whoa, you're a sharp one," she jibed. "No wonder you're in the big leagues."

"We're trying to establish—"

She cut him off. "No, I haven't talked to her, it's been probably four, five months. No, I don't know who might wanna off her. I didn't like her much and I'm her mom so, real sorry I couldn't narrow down that field," she said sarcastically. "Now, are we done?"

They weren't.

"Your daughter has passed. Once the autopsy is conducted, we'll need to know what funeral home you want her taken to," Rus told her.

"Say what?"

"She needs to be laid to rest," he pointed out. "It's a sorry business, I know. And expensive, but—"

"I gotta pay for that shit?"

She was incredulous.

He began to feel nauseous.

"If someone goes unclaimed, the state handles it," Moran put in. "Or sometimes good Samaritan citizens will—"

Melanie cut him off.

"I don't got no money to pay for no funeral. Someone wants to pitch in, that'd be cool. Never understood why people went overboard with that shit. The person it's for can't enjoy it."

That was all they needed.

Now, for their last matter of business.

"Do you feed your dog?" he asked her.

"What?"

"Do you feed your dog?" he repeated.

She leaned forward, but he didn't know why, because she didn't do it far enough to see the side yard where the dog was chained. Still, she looked that direction.

She came back to him.

"Not my dog. My boy dumped it on me."

"Do you feed it?"

"He gave me a bag of food, I put some out for him."

"When was the last time you did that?"

"Yesterday."

No, now he was done.

"That's a lie," he stated coldly.

She squinted at him again.

Moran jumped in. "At this juncture, you should know, abusing an animal is a criminal offense."

That shook her. "It's not my animal."

"It's on your property," Moran noted.

She was more horrified about this than her daughter's murder or the possibility of having to pay for her funeral.

"You're saying I can get in trouble for my son's stupid dog?"

"Are you saying your son has abandoned that dog and you need to surrender it to the proper authorities so it can be cared for?" Moran asked.

She stared at him a beat and then said, "Take it. Dakota can get another one if he wants a fucking dog. You want its food?"

Fifteen minutes later, they'd realized the dog didn't have the energy, or temperament, to give them trouble. Rus had filled its water bowl from a spigot on the side of the house so they could at least hydrate the poor pup. They got him unchained, and Rus led the dog to the cruiser and helped it into the back while Moran went to the porch to nab the bag of food that had spilled all over the slats because she'd tossed it out.

They then drove not to Brittanie's apartment, but to Moran's vet.

"SHE WAS NEAT," he murmured, moving through her apartment.

"Yeah," Moran agreed, doing the same.

It wasn't unexpected with what he'd learned about her.

On the one hand, she lived life, had friends, hooked up with guys, some married, stole boyfriends, wasn't great with money, which would indicate some levels of either busyness, immaturity or irresponsibility that might lead to not taking care of her home.

On the other hand, Lucinda would never let her babysit if she was a total mess, she was loyal, she'd dicked around and nearly lost her job but then toed the line to keep it, Keyleigh had been undone by her loss and Lucinda was hiding that she, too, was deeply affected by it, which would indicate Brittanie had her shit together…or was trying to.

This was why it was important to look at where a victim lived, to learn more about her.

Her apartment showed which way that swung.

He could see the money she spent here. She cared about décor. She cared about quality. He couldn't say anything was top of the line, but nothing was cheap.

But she took care of what she had.

No dishes left in the sink. Toss pillows on the couch carefully fluffed and arranged. Fresh vacuum marks on the rug.

She also liked Keyleigh, and what looked to be Keyleigh's boyfriend, Declan. They had good times together if the framed pictures told the tale. And she had fun backstage at what had to be the burlesque. She also had friends there. Lots of bright smiles. Lots of horsing around. She cared about her friends, she surrounded herself with them even when they weren't around.

And Madden, Lucinda's daughter, was adorable. There was no mistaking the parentage of the dark-haired, maybe six, seven-year-old girl with a missing front tooth who was hugging Brittanie and giving a peace sign to whoever took the photo.

Big sister, little sister.

Undeniable.

Rus moved from the photos to the bedroom.

There was a little mess there. She didn't bother putting away clothes she took off, but she didn't let them sit forever and pile others on.

The last thing she wore before she dressed to go to the motel was on the floor in front of the closet.

Jeans, a sweater, a pink bra, socks with little unicorn heads on them, and high heel booties.

He'd seen the pictures of her home, McGill had brought them to his suite last night.

But being there…

Smelling hints of her perfume mingled with whatever was wafting off those wood reeds women set in scented oil, he got insight into the Brittanie Iverson who left the hovel she grew up in and got in money trouble to give herself better than what she'd had.

Not only that, it meant something to her.

She'd earned it.

It mattered.

That boulder he was carrying got heavier.

They both took their time in her space. They could find no letters, journals, notes, or anything that could give them deeper insight into Brittanie's life or relationships, just as the first team had come up empty on these things.

They were ready to leave at the same time.

Moran started the cruiser, but he didn't put it in gear.

"Fuck," he said.

"Yeah," Rus agreed.

"She had unicorns on her socks."

Rus turned to Moran. "Suck it up, man. We got work to do."

Moran did what he was told, audibly through his nose.

"Let's hit the brother," Rus said.

Moran put the cruiser in gear.

"I DON'T KNOW where he is. I don't care where he is," the manager of the local big-box home improvement store told him. "I'm just glad he's no longer here."

"Was he let go?" Rus asked.

"Well, yeah. After half the time he doesn't show for his shifts, and then he gets caught loading three chainsaws he didn't buy in the trunk of his car in broad daylight, like working here is a free ride to a storewide salad bar, he was let go," the manager replied.

"When was this?"

"We've had three weeks and two days Dakota-free, and you'd be right about how bad it was that I'm still counting that shit."

"Why didn't you call me on the chainsaws, Rob?" Moran asked on a sigh.

"Because this kid is bad news, Harry," Rob answered. "I don't need him pissed at me even if I don't want him stealing from me. I don't want to put up with him showing sometimes, not showing others. Having to ride his ass when he does show. Having to keep an eye on him, or have my assistant manager keep an eye on him, so we don't have to deal with a sexual harassment complaint. I mean, the chicks that work here, they can take care of themselves. But we all got our limits, you know what I'm sayin'? And corporate *way* frowns on that shit. And since I know these women, I frown on it a whole lot more."

"Yeah, Rob. I know what you're saying," Moran affirmed.

"His customer service was a nightmare," Rob carried on. "So I put him on stock. He's on break out front, hanging on the patio furniture eating a taco, and a female customer walking in, he calls her fat. While wearing a goddamn store smock. I have to tell you, I was thrilled he tried to steal those chainsaws. It gave me clearcut reason even he couldn't mess with to let him go. I tried with the fat thing, but he raised a ruckus that, shit you not, had me checking all the cameras I got on my house."

"He threatened you?" Moran asked.

"He's bad news, Harry," Rob repeated. "You know the Iversons. Only good one of the lot was the girl, and now…" He shook his head, looking sad.

"Did you know Brittanie?" Rus asked.

Rob shook his head again. "No. Seen her around. I'm married but I'm still a man. Girl that pretty, you notice. Not that way for me, though. I'm not a skeeve. She near-on could be my daughter. She came in, usually with her friend, buying the girl shit we got. Pots and plants and shelves and stuff."

"You hear anything about her? From Dakota? Or gossip?" Rus asked.

More head shaking. "I wish. I wish I could lead you right to whoever hurt her. I know Dakota real well, but not in that way. He didn't share about his family. He came to work, gave me a migraine, and left. That was Dakota."

"Do you know if he had a girlfriend? Who he hung around with?" Rus kept at him.

"Nope," Rob answered. "Though, I would be floored any woman would have anything to do with that pervy asshole. And he wasn't about making friends with his workmates, so if he had any outside of work, that'd surprise the shit out of me too."

Nothing.

All morning, except unicorn heads that drained all of the shoring up his girl Sabrina gave him, they got nothing.

Moran ended it. "We'll stop taking your time. But thank you for talking to us."

"I hear anything, Harry, you know I'll call."

"Appreciated."

"Good luck to you," he said, his gaze taking in both of them. "I mean it."

Rob loped off, and Rus and Moran moved to the cruiser.

Once they were in, he asked Moran, "You got an address on Dakota?"

"Yeah, his mother's house."

Dead end.

Though, he suspected that pit bull had not been regularly fed for three weeks.

So Dakota loses his job, dumps his dog on his mother and skips town?

Moran started the cruiser up. "What about the dad?"

"We're working it. Nothing so far."

"Do you want me to punt that to McGill?"

"Wouldn't hurt."

Rus pulled out his phone.

"It's slow going pinpointing those men and finding time to chat, but Dickerson says he's going to have a short list of possibles by this afternoon," Moran pointed out.

"Right. So how are we feeling about what we just heard?"

"We're feeling like the brother was a piece of shit, and he could have wanted money and thought his sister was his cash cow, like the mother did, and got pissed she didn't pony up," Moran started. "But it doesn't sound like he's smart enough to try to put us off the scent by copycatting a serial killer's MO to that degree. And I'll need to buy a year's worth of mints to deal with the epic puke I'll need to unleash if he could do that to his sister."

"Yeah, that's where we are," Rus muttered. "You want in on the staff interviews?"

"Absolutely."

With that answer, once he texted McGill, he pulled up Lucinda's name on his texts.

He'd gotten her number before he left.

Now, he had to touch base to ask her chef to make another sandwich.

NINE

Ever Created

"How was your reuben?"

"It was a damned fine reuben. But I'd drive all the way up here for just five of those chips."

Lucinda smiled.

It was after the staff interviews, which she'd scheduled thirty minutes apart, but they'd only needed fifteen, and in some instances ten.

The intel they got ran the spectrum of what they'd already learned, depending on if Brittanie flirted with your man.

She was either loved or put up with.

Not hated. Unless someone was a really good actor.

They'd done the top six on Lucinda's list, and one who Lucinda threw in to shake things up because she wasn't Brittanie's biggest fan: three dancers, a bouncer, the doorman to the theater, a waitress, and one of the sous chefs (Bon Amie had a full menu they served on the upper floor, and a tapas menu they served in the theater).

The six who were close to her were devastated she was gone. The one who wasn't hip on her was shaken up, and being human, openly upset about what happened to a woman she knew.

Lucinda had invited Rus and Moran to come back and speak to other staff during breaks or lulls whenever they wished.

He didn't yet know Moran's plans, but Rus was returning that night.

Now, Moran was on the landing taking a report from Dickerson about possible leads.

And Rus was alone with Lucinda.

"I'm sensing things aren't going well," she prodded gently.

"I started my day with Melanie Iverson talking to me through a screen, then Moran and I rescued her son's dog that she was slowly starving."

Angry pink dots hit her cheeks, her eyes widened for a second, but she clamped down on her reaction before she asked, "How's the dog?"

"He'll be at the vet a few days."

She nodded.

"Though, she has no interest in laying her daughter to rest, so you're clear to go on that."

Her face got soft.

Amazing.

Her voice was soft too when she said, "Thank you."

Also amazing.

His turn to prod.

"I saw a picture of Madden at Brittanie's. She had a missing tooth."

Her lips curved. "That would be two years ago."

"She's cute."

"She's the most beautiful being ever created."

For the first time in a very long time, Rus let loose a full smile.

Her eyes widened again when she saw it, though this time she didn't get a quick lock on it, or the different kind of pink that hit her cheeks.

Terrific.

He wasn't reading it wrong.

She was into him too.

It was him who should lock it down.

Of course, he didn't.

Instead, he teased, "Shame she's got a mother who's not proud of her."

"She has a tough life."

He didn't believe that for a second.

"I have to push back, seeing as my daughter is the most beautiful being ever created," he told her.

"Isn't it a miracle?" she asked quietly. "How so many of them are roaming this earth."

It was.

They were both very lucky.

"How old is yours?" he asked.

"Nine. Yours?"

"Eighteen. My boy is twenty."

"You're not wearing a ring," she noted.

Definitely into him.

"Divorced. You aren't either."

And he wasn't hiding he was into her too.

"Madden's father had definite ideas about which gender in a relationship should make the most money. Seeing as what he thought should be the way wasn't the way between us, he's down in Oregon with his new partner. He sees Madden two weekends a month, six weeks in the summer and alternating holidays."

"Rough," he muttered.

"Not for me, and not for Madden either," she stated firmly. "She doesn't need to be around a man who will inhibit in any way, either openly or subconsciously, who she might wish to become. She loves her visits with her dad. Since he doesn't have a lot of time with her, he goes out of his way to make them special. She comes back feeling important and adored. Which is what she should feel. Not limited and burdened by expectations."

"My ex made more than me when we were married, and she still does," he shared.

The cat's-got-her-cream look that hit her face, he felt in his cock.

Fabulous.

What he asked next took them both out of that zone. He did it for that, and he did it because he was worried.

Therefore, he went gently.

"How'd she take the news?"

Her lips turned down, she took in a quiet breath, and she answered, "Not great."

He sensed that was an understatement.

It was her turn to change the subject.

He knew it was coming when she leaned into both of her forearms on her desk and said, "You're good at this."

"Pardon?"

"Your job. It's frustrating you that you aren't further with this case."

"It's early."

"You're still frustrated."

"Yes."

"So you're good."

"I've worked with the Criminal Investigative Unit for fifteen years, and in that time, I've had some wins."

"I talked to Bohannan about you this morning. He knows people. He asked. You've had more than 'some wins.'"

She was right.

Rus shrugged.

"Why's the FBI involved in a small-town murder?"

Shit. Fuck.

Ambush.

"Lucinda," he warned.

"It would have been nice if Brittanie had someone who thought she was the most beautiful thing ever created."

"You don't need to guilt me into working hard for her," he bit out. "I've got that covered."

A small sliver of regret, followed by another of alarm, flashed though her eyes before she said, "You're right. That was uncalled for. Forget I said it. Instead, tell me what I can do to help."

"Secretarial services, meeting rooms and a flashy suite work great."

"Agent Lazarus."

Fuck him.

"Rus," he corrected.

One side of her mouth depressed in surprise.

That happened around his name often, though sometimes it was his full name, which he was never surprised people found it interesting and sometimes even thought it was fake.

Most of the time, though, it was about people thinking they should call him Zach.

"Rus," she said.

Yeah.

As he expected.

His name sounded really fucking good in her mouth.

And yeah.

He should lock this down.

"It's the least I can do," she said.

"I'm going to be in that room to sleep and pore over reports and pictures that hopefully will tell me something. I don't need a suite with a view, a bar and a living room."

"You need quiet when you need it. You need rest when you can have it. When that time of day comes, you need somewhere you look forward to being so you can relax. And I need to feel like I'm doing something for Brittanie."

It was the last part that had him giving in.

"You play dirty," he muttered.

She rested back, murmuring in return, "You've no idea."

The door opened and Moran walked in, talking.

"Right, most of the men have solid alibis, but they won't be voting for me in the next election because two are married, one is separated but wants a reconciliation, and none of them were fans of my deputies showing at their places of work to ask about their connection with a dead woman who was a burlesque dancer."

"Comes with the territory, buddy," Rus replied sympathetically as Moran sat down.

Then, right in front of Lucinda, who gave them the list but didn't need to know the results of them working it, he continued sharing those results. "Three possibilities. One married. Two single. One of the singles was an ex-boyfriend we can't locate, not Jace. The other two were Bon Amie."

"The married one doesn't have an alibi?" Lucinda asked his question.

"She's out of town. Gets back tomorrow."

Lucinda lifted her fingers in front of her and clicked the tips of her nails on one hand against the tops of the nails on the other, a small smile flirting with her full lips. She looked like the magnificently beautiful Disney villainess, the one you silently rooted for, who just sent the cloying, innocent heroine spiraling down the white-water rapids at the bottom of her palace.

"The coven is going to eat this up with a spoon."

Her glee was unhidden.

But fuck.

Rus forgot about the coven.

"First, I'll make it clear that talking about an investigation in front of a civilian is not my favorite thing," Rus began.

Moran showed zero guilt at this.

"Second," he turned to Lucinda. "Do I need to point out this could be rough on your business?"

"Agent, please," she drawled. "I could tell every wife and girl-friend her man comes to watch our show, flirts with the girls, and takes that further if given the opportunity, and men will still come to our show. They can't help themselves. You must know that a great many of your number think with a certain part of their anatomy."

He did know this.

He was one of that number when he was around Lucinda.

He decided to pay attention to what he should be paying attention to.

"We can't worry about the coven now. If we have any hope of him opening up to us, we need to get to the married guy before his wife gets home. When she's home, he's lost to us, and we have nothing. Between the glut of fingerprints they'll be sifting through from that motel room, and the excess of DNA, no witnesses, no motive, we need a man who will talk. And he'll know nothing about anything that has a thing to do with Brittanie the minute his wife comes home."

Moran stood. "Then we better go."

Rus stood too and looked down at Lucinda. "I'll be back tonight."

She held his gaze two beats too long, and damn, but he was willing to stand there if she held it a thousand beats more.

Then she purred, "I can't wait."

Christ, now she was openly flirting.

Before they left, Moran said some words of thanks that included ones that were more heartfelt around the reuben.

They were in the cruiser on their way back to town when Moran said, "You two are cute."

Jesus.

Suddenly, he was annoyed he'd been saddled with a good cop, meaning an observant one.

"Fuck off," he grunted.

Moran chuckled.

Rus sighed.

TEN

Twice-Baked Potato

_____

W hen he returned to Bon Amie that night, he was vaguely surprised at how full the car park was.

And he was definitely surprised when the female security employee saw his car, came out to stand under the overhang and waved him that way.

He drove in.

A valet, also female, jogged from behind her stand to Rus's door.

He did the getting out, handing over the keys business, then walked to the double doors.

Security Sue was there with legs planted and arms crossed on her chest.

Oh yeah, and she was also wearing a smirk.

"She wants you," she announced.

Rus made no attempt to hide his beleaguered sigh.

This only made her smirk get bigger, but she dropped her arms, turned and walked him into the club.

Things were hopping upstairs, and it wasn't just men, or even predominantly so. Women were there too, on dates or nights out with their partner, or in groups for a girls' night.

This reminded Rus it was Friday.

Security Sue didn't lead him to the stairs.

She led him to a table in an intimate corner, the one that had to have the best view.

It was four-top size, two chairs set catty-corner, the top set for one, and that place setting was not in front of Lucinda, who was seated in a chair. In front of her was some clear liquid in a martini glass with a perfect twirl of a lemon rind swimming in it.

Security Sue slinked away after she accomplished her mission and Rus asked, "Are you feeding me again?"

"Yes," Lucinda replied.

Earlier, he'd tried to block out today's dress, mostly because the skirt was as tight as yesterday's, even though the upper part wasn't. But he'd seen the back, and there was a triangle cut out that exposed her from between her shoulder blades to her waist, and also shared she wasn't wearing a bra. It was in what he was realizing was her signature color scheme, a cream that had the barest hint of pink.

It played havoc on his ability to concentrate then.

It did the same now.

She reached to pull out the empty chair and patted the seat.

He could see why her ex found her emasculating.

Rus, on the other hand, was mentally cataloguing all the shit she was pulling in the event he could get his back when he had her naked.

He sat.

A female server was at his side instantly.

"Can I get you something to drink?" she asked.

"Beer," he told her.

"We have—"

He interrupted her. "It's gotta be cold and wet, that's it. You pick."

Her panicked gaze flew to Lucinda, her need to provide the best service she could to her boss's guest right in front of her boss at odds with his request.

"Let Morley decide," Lucinda ordered.

The server took off.

"Morley?" he asked.

"Our bartender. She's the best mixologist in Washington."

"I do beer and I do scotch. A bourbon if it's smooth. Vodka if there's tonic. That'd be lost on me."

She picked up her martini glass and murmured, "That's too bad."

He was reminded he needed to put a lock on it.

Earlier when he was there, it was fun, his day had only been half-frustrating by that point, with the promise of her and a good sandwich in the middle of it, and she'd delivered on both.

Now he was tired, grouchy, at loose ends in finding the killer of a beautiful, dead woman who many people liked a whole lot, and she had unicorns on her socks, so he picked his strategy and went for it.

"I think I already shared I'm not into playing games, Lucinda."

"I'm not either, Rus."

"I'm able to feed myself. I'm not here to eat. I'm not here to flirt. I'm here to observe and talk to your staff."

"I know why you're here."

"So maybe I should do that and not drink a beer with you, with my back to the room."

"I know my customers. I've spent time in this building since I was able to walk."

"And?"

"And I'd like to know how your evening went and who you talked to."

"I've told you I can't discuss the case with you."

"And I just told you I know my customers. You met with them. I don't know which ones they were. But I could guess. I can also tell you if they're full of shit, or if you got the truth out of them."

Damn.

Now he wanted her take.

"Ezra Corbin and Lance Shultz," she guessed.

Got both in one.

Fuck.

"Why were those your picks?" he asked.

"Because Ezra Corbin fucked Audrey Pulaski, though somehow

he flew under the radar of the OGs, probably because his wife never found out. I warned Britt there was nothing there for her. He's a serial philanderer. And he's able to do this because his wife travels for business. And Lance Shultz because he was the only single man on that list."

"Audrey Pulaski?"

"The mother of Alice, the eight-year-old Ray Andrews killed when he started his reign of terror."

"Jesus," he muttered as his beer was served.

This also meant that the OGs she referred to were the wives club that outed their cheating husbands in the most explicit way imaginable.

All of them had had an affair with Audrey Pulaski.

But Ezra dodged that bullet, a fact Rus found surprising, because the guy was full of himself, had all the answers at the ready, but Rus still got the impression he wasn't all that bright.

Now he knew why, if Ezra stepped out on his wife frequently and he was still married to her.

When it came to lying, practice makes perfect.

"Are you going to refuse food?" Lucinda asked, cutting into his thoughts.

"You got a steak?"

"Filet, rib-eye or strip?"

He turned to the server. "Rib-eye. Medium rare. And some of those potato chips."

"Angelina's twice-baked potatoes have won awards," Lucinda noted.

"Change it to that," he said to the server.

The server nodded and took off again.

Rus took a draw from his beer.

Yeah, Morley knew what she was doing.

"Let me guess, Ezra was smooth as room temperature butter and Lance was freaked out," Lucinda deduced.

And again, got it in one.

She could be helpful, he knew, because she was being helpful.

And she wanted desperately to help.

He had a bad guy to catch, so why was he fighting it?

"According to Ezra, he'd spoken to Brittanie once between dances when he was here entertaining business associates."

Because he was sharing, the relief and gratitude in her eyes that she let him see made her so beautiful, it nearly bought her a kiss.

He managed to control himself.

She spoke. "He lied."

"I know. He was very sorry to hear of her death. But although he understood we were just doing our jobs, he was frustrated to have two visits in a day from the sheriff, since he absolutely knew not one thing about her, outside the fact she worked here."

"Do you like him for it?"

He felt his lips twitch at her terminology.

So she watched cop shows.

"I think he's good at lying. I'm not sure that extends to being good at getting away with murder. His veneer is thin. He strikes me as kind of a moron."

Her lips curved.

Yes, Ezra was a moron.

"And you were also correct about Lance," Rus continued. "He was freaked, admitted to sleeping with her, and knew, since he did and people knew about it, he'd be a suspect before the first set of cops came to ask him questions."

Rus took another sip from his beer before he went on.

"The weird thing about that guy was, even though he has no alibi, and he was adamant that he had nothing to do with her death, I got the vibe off him he was getting some thrill out of being a suspect. Or at least being questioned."

"Lance is gay and fucking my doorman. But if his father found out, he'd lose his mind and cut Lance out of an inheritance that's probably around ten million, but it'll be more by the time that particular bigot leaves this earth. Lance is not in Seattle with his family. Instead, he's here, so he can secretly be who he is with less chance of getting caught. But he openly flirts with burlesque dancers, and sleeps with them to seal the deal, just in case anyone asks. You questioning him because he had sex with the victim might get back to his dad, which would prove he's heterosexual, when he is not. However, if things got concerning for him, he'd pull a rabbit out of a hat, because he's active. Barrett isn't the only one he's sleeping with, and no doubt he has an alibi. Just not one he's willing to produce until his choice is outing himself, or prison."

Barrett was her theater doorman.

"So, if it's either of them, you lean toward Ezra?"

She looked to a view that was now purple and midnight blue, the rapids a moving shadow and stars twinkling in the sky.

She took a sip of her drink.

She put it down.

"How did she die?" she asked the window.

"Lucinda."

She turned to him. "He's into kink."

Right then.

Here we go.

"What kind?"

"Pain. His."

"So, receiving."

"Yes."

"How do you know?"

"I have a friend who has a certain clientele and a well outfitted room in her basement. He's a regular."

"Will she talk to me?"

"Doubtful."

Fuck.

"If you asked pretty please?" he pressed.

Her lips quirked. "I'll try."

That was his girl.

"Did he ask this of Brittanie?"

"He brought equipment and requested she use it on him. She tried her best, but it wasn't her thing. This was when she broke things off with him."

"Do you know how many times she was with him?"

"No, but it was more than once. Enough he got comfortable and tried to groom her into something she wasn't interested in. However, unless I'm mistaken, it didn't last long."

"Do you know if she threatened him with what she knew? Maybe to tell his wife?"

She shook her head. "I would have told you that already if she did. But he wasn't that important to her. He wasn't like Jace. He was a man who gave her attention. Made her feel pretty. Made her feel wanted. Regardless, she'd never do that. She lives in this town. The coven's OGs were thorough with their revenge. Against my advice, Britt was sleeping with a married man. More than one. But she'd never, ever expose herself like that. Not in Misted Pines."

He was surprised. "So the coven goes after women?"

"The coven is ever changing and growing. The originals were not fans of Audrey, and for a reason. But to my recollection, they never went after her. However, what it is now isn't under their control. Though, Wendy, one of the OGs, moved into that neighborhood with them. If they have a leader, it's her. The top dog OG, Lana, is loved up and living with her lover. She's out."

That was less surprising.

"You have to be single to be in the coven?"

"You have to use men like they use women to be in the coven. You can play. You can share. But you can't keep."

"If these women discovered Brittanie was sleeping with married men, would they retaliate?"

She shook her head again, but said, "I've no idea. But I'd lean toward no. They come here. To the club. They drink. They eat. They watch the show. On occasion, they pick up toys and take them home. They're big tippers and respectful, of me and my staff. I don't equate big tips and respect to a female business owner with budding murderers."

"So what is this? A loose bunch of women who live close to each other and share a set of rules?"

"Good question. No one knows. You have to be a part of their crew to know. That said, it isn't a bunch of women who live close to each other. They own a *neighborhood*, Rus. It's small, upper middle-income homes, maybe twenty-five of them. It was built around five years ago. The first women who came to town bought houses for sale in that development. I think it was a fluke. They got to talking. Maybe did some mild recruiting. Somehow, probably the internet, they became known. The rest either bought other houses that went up for sale or offered the owners a price they couldn't refuse. I don't know how many of them there are, exactly. Maybe fifteen. Seventeen. But they all live in that neighborhood. I haven't been there, but it's my understanding most of the other houses are for sale."

"Why?"

She lifted a single shoulder.

"Intimidation?" he suggested.

"Oh, most assuredly," she told him. "Any collective of women is intimidating to people for some reason. Even if they don't do anything but hang out, become friends and go on the prowl together."

She was scoffing.

He was being serious.

"You seem to want to downplay this. But we're talking more than a dozen women coming from somewhere else, having the means to take over a neighborhood, and living by a certain set of rules. That sounds like something to take seriously."

"Is this why the FBI is involved?" she pushed. "Because fifteen women have been identified as a hate group?"

"It isn't why I'm here, but would you describe them as a hate group?"

"I'd know them to point them out, Rus. But I don't *know* them. They seem friendly to me. They're not standing by the side of the road throwing rocks at cars with male drivers. And as far as I know, men aren't dropping like flies or having bizarre accidents because their hexes are working."

That was funny, so he smiled at her.

Then he noted, "You think I'm going down the wrong path."

"I don't know what to say because I don't know how Britt was killed. Was it poison?"

This again.

Christ, she was stubborn.

"Lucinda."

"Gunshot?"

He sighed.

She leaned his way with impatience. "Why won't you tell me?"

"Why do you want to know?"

"Because poison says woman. And maybe a gunshot too. And my girl was sleeping with married men, meaning they have wives. And she was killed at a fucking *motel*, for God's sake."

He leaned her way as well, getting face to face.

"Sweetheart, how about you leave the detective work to me? You're invaluable as an informant, and I appreciate all the help you've given. I also get you very badly want justice for Brittanie, so you want to find who hurt your girl. But I'll take it from here."

Her irritated face also had signs of latent cute.

He didn't allow himself to get stuck on that.

"Tell me about the motel, did she go there often?" he demanded.

She shook her head but didn't sit back.

He knew why, and it wasn't because she worried they'd be overheard. It hadn't escaped him none of the tables around them had patrons, this she'd arranged so they could speak freely about the case.

No, she stayed where she was because he was there.

"We were close, but I wasn't her confidant. So I don't know for certain, but I don't think so."

"The desk clerk knew her but had never seen her there before."

"That feels true to me when it comes to Britt. She liked nice things. That motel isn't nice. She wanted attention, but she wasn't about to accept less than she deserved. They either came to her place, she went to theirs, or they treated her to a night at the Pinetop or in Seattle, *not* at a motel."

"I bet you taught her that."

"Of course I did."

He grinned at her.

She watched his mouth as he did it.

His steak arrived with great timing.

Lucinda kept him company while he ate, and they put the case aside.

He learned Madden won last year's spelling bee and wanted a microscope for Christmas.

She learned Acre's and Sabrina's majors, and he received his first genuine broad smile when he told her about Sabrina's bikini budget.

And she did not lie.

The twice-baked potato was *insane*.

ELEVEN

Done Fighting It

The lodge had a half-mile running trail through the woods above the building.

The next morning Rus ran it three times, and in that altitude with the steep inclines, and the fact he didn't get back to his room until three in the morning and he'd started running at six thirty, it kicked his ass.

Nevertheless, he hit his room and did his sit ups and pushups before he jumped in the shower.

He had a towel around his waist, wet hair and was about to shave when a knock came at the door.

He looked through the peephole.

Room service.

He opened the door. "Sorry, there's been some mistake. I didn't order breakfast."

"Compliments of Ms. Bonner," was the reply.

He nearly burst out laughing.

He didn't, but he was smiling when he stepped aside, and the guy wheeled the cart in and set the food up on the table by the window.

When he left, taking the cart with him, he didn't hand Rus the wallet to sign off on the bill.

Guess she was taking care of the tip too.

He quickly shaved and put on some shorts, olive green khakis, a belt, and a pressed white button down. He then went to the safe, pulled out the file from under his two guns and sat down to breakfast with Brittanie's murder as company.

But his mind wandered to last night.

After Lucinda left him to it, he'd spoken with Morley, Emma, her assistant bartender, Emeril, Security Sue's partner (he wore the same black suit uniform as Sue) and half a dozen other staff members before he wandered down to the theater.

It had been like going back in time.

Obviously, the upper floor had been updated, and that had happened recently. It was stylish, expensive, subtle and comfortable.

It was Lucinda.

The downstairs was her great-grandmother.

The first thing he noticed were the pictures on the walls around the staircase down to the lower level.

A hundred years ago, they would likely be considered pornographic.

Now, they seemed like art.

After he was waved through by Barrett in his doorman booth (cover charge was twenty-five dollars for bar and general admission seating, fifty bucks for a booth, this was hefty and still, there was a two-drink minimum), he entered Washington State's version of Moulin Rouge. Except the lush reds, blues and black were replaced with black, purples and pinks.

It was a large space, but still seemed close and intimate.

The bar to the side was long, manned by three people and packed two deep.

The cocktail waitresses wore old-fashioned, little black dresses with pink or purple frilly petticoats under skirts that were so short, they exposed white panties with ruffles at the seat.

The small, semi-circle booths staggered back along the space in front of the stage had black velvet seats and pink or purple velvet backs. The round tables had black tablecloths and small candles in pink glass on top.

In the back of the theater, there was less posh seating and space to stand and watch.

He lived close enough, and his daughter was interested, so they hit New York for weekends that included musicals and the ballet.

So when the numbers came on the stage, Rus saw talent, but there was a reason they weren't in a big city trying to get their big break. They were good, it worked, but mostly because the women were attractive and each number was so sexual, it was almost a choreographed group striptease.

The stars of the show were the costumes and the sets. Each dance lasted a good while, but there was at least a ten-minute lull in between so they could wow the crowd with something entirely new and patrons had plenty of time to order fresh drinks.

The place was packed, so it wouldn't be cool to take the time of staff to ask questions.

But word got around he was there, and several of the dancers came and spoke to him between sets.

They were Brittanie's friends, so they had reason. They wanted to help.

But he learned nothing new.

He waited it out, had a few more chats after closing, and was pleased to see Sue, Emeril or one of the bouncers escorted all female personnel to their cars even if this was the middle of nowhere and the parking lot was brightly illuminated. Not to mention there were numerous visible cameras trained on the lot and the building.

Since she left him to it after he'd finished eating, he'd not seen Lucinda. She was either busy, or, with the way she spoke about her daughter, she went home to her girl.

That morning, he was dragging.

It was a risk to have such a late night when he had no time to sleep in. That was something he wouldn't blink at doing when he was twenty-five. Now forty-five, it no longer caught up with him, it dogged him.

But when you had nothing, you had to take every shot to find something. Anyone could have seen or heard something that would give him a lead.

The risk didn't pan out.

But even as he drank coffee, texted Moran about a meet up, sent in a progress report suggesting they look at other sexually-motivated open cases to ascertain if there had been another copycat they hadn't caught, re-read the reports written for him, examined photos he'd already examined, wrote notes on a yellow legal pad about any little thing that struck him, and ate eggs, bacon and toast, he didn't regret it.

What he felt he had now was a full picture of Brittanie.

She had her flaws, but she was a good person.

Whoever did this to her was the one with the damage. Unless they turned something up in her bank accounts, texts or emails, the motive would be as twisted as the murder, and none of it would land on Brittanie.

He got a responding text from Moran, and it was time to roll out.

He wanted back in the motel room. He wanted to return to her apartment. And he wanted to hit the local lab where they were processing what they'd found in the room.

He'd been to these places and examined the pictures. He saw the pile of her clothes in the corner.

But he wanted to inspect things more closely.

Items spoke.

And when you had nothing, you had to find something else that might talk.

He wanted the brother, the father and the ex-boyfriend they couldn't find, but he wouldn't be doing the leg work on that. McGill and Moran's deputies were on it.

He also wanted to go back to Ezra Corbin.

It was pure gut, but he felt Lance was out.

There was no reasoning or evidence for a revisit to Ezra, outside the fact he had no alibi.

He just didn't like the guy.

Now was about going over old ground just to make sure they didn't miss anything.

He called down to the valet to have his car brought around, secured the files in the safe with his guns, left his dishes where they were, tied the laces on his tan shoes, pulled on a dark-blue blazer, and exited his room.

The first thing he noticed in the lobby was Madden, Lucinda's daughter, wearing a corduroy skirt, tights, ankle boots, and a chunky turtleneck sweater. She was sitting in a chair, her dark head bent to an iPad, her adorable face screwed up in concentration.

He swung his head left and saw, standing and talking to someone of authority in the hotel, Lucinda, wearing tan, wide-legged trousers, a slim-fit matching tan turtleneck, and an equally matching cardigan that fell to her ankles. On her feet were chocolate suede, stiletto-heeled boots.

Until that moment, Rus had tried not to think about the fact he'd left Bon Amie without any reason to go back, the slim chance she could get her dominatrix friend to speak to him being his only thread to spending time with her again.

And he wasn't thinking about it because he wanted more time with her and wanting time with Lucinda shouldn't be what was on his mind.

Regardless, he was both exasperated, amused and pleased she was there now, with her daughter in tow, for whatever her reason could be.

He was about to move her way when someone stepped in front of him.

Close in front of him.

In his space and face.

"Are you the agent from the FBI?"

He stopped dead and looked down his nose at the woman who had waylaid him.

She appeared young, but her long hair parted down the middle and hanging in sheets down the sides of her face was gray. She was wearing a denim shirt, jeans and one of those colorful blanket jackets. Also a lot of silver and turquoise jewelry. Her makeup was subtle, but there.

She was attractive, but not his type. He was about women who were all woman, and although she was all woman, the masculine bent to her dress and her aggressive demeanor were not his thing.

He took a step away.

"I'm sorry?" he asked.

She didn't repeat her question.

She asserted the answer. "You're the agent from the FBI. The one investigating that woman's murder."

She didn't give off the air of a reporter.

He still went cautiously.

"Can I help you?"

"Can you confirm you're investigating the murder?"

"You are?"

She thrust out a square hand, no polish, short nails, lots of heavy rings and bracelets. "Ellen Macklemore."

He took her hand and made light work of squeezing and releasing. "Are you a reporter, Ms. Macklemore?"

"I'm a concerned citizen."

Shit.

It was a guess, but he suspected it would be a correct one.

She was in the coven.

"What can I—?" he began.

Her eyes were going up and down him as he said those three words, and she interrupted him.

"Day off?"

Oh, hell no.

FBI wasn't about being the men in black anymore.

But he didn't owe her that explanation.

"Ms. Macklemore—"

This time, as he spoke, she twisted her neck to look Lucinda's way.

He did the same, and saw she was still speaking to the member of staff, but her eyes were on them, and they were narrowed.

Great.

He hadn't experienced it fully, but another guess he would suspect was correct: Lucinda pissed was not a good thing.

Ellen returned to him.

"Enjoying the local scenery?" Before he could speak, she went on, "A woman is dead and last night, you were on a date."

He was being watched and talked about.

Small town, that was going to happen.

But fuck this bitch.

He held his shit and informed her in as light a voice as he could muster, "Please know, how I spend my time is not your business."

"It certainly is when my taxes pay your salary."

The favorite refrain of the entitled.

And one guaranteed to piss any cop right the fuck off.

Rus was not immune.

"You're wrong, but just to alleviate your fears, last night, I had dinner with the victim's employer while discussing aspects of the victim's life and this case, on which Ms. Bonner was extremely help-ful, as she's been since we started the investigation. I then spent the night interviewing people who worked with and knew the victim, and immersing myself in her place of business, so I would under-stand more about her, the life she led and who she shared time with. I got back to my room at three in the morning. It's now nine, I spent the last hour going over what we have on her case, and I'm heading out to meet the sheriff to continue our work in finding who did this. I take my job seriously. I take this case seriously. And I can guar-antee you, since I've been up to my neck in the life cut short of a vibrant young woman, I know her better than you, and I care a great deal more that the person who ended her life is brought to justice. Now, do you have anything else to say?"

She looked chastened, but was opening her mouth, when Lucinda slid in by his side.

"Well, hello. This is a surprise. Do you have out-of-town visitors you're coming to see?" she asked Ellen Macklemore smoothly.

"I…no," Ellen replied.

"Visiting the spa?" Lucinda suggested.

"No, I—"

"Certainly you're not here to cause trouble for a man who's devoted his life to civil service," Lucinda drawled.

Ellen opened her mouth.

She got nothing out because Madden was now there, asking, "Mom, is this the FBI guy?"

He looked down at her.

She stared up at him with a frank gaze that was not her mother's amber but instead hazel, with more green than brown.

"Would you please excuse us?" Lucinda's pure frost crackled toward Ellen. "Special Agent Lazarus has things to do today, and he doesn't need unnecessary delays."

"Then why are you here?" Ellen snapped.

"Because he needs me to introduce him to someone, and we have a brief window, so if you don't mind, we must be getting on with it."

Ellen glared at her, schooled her features, looked to Rus and said, "Good luck." Then she painted a smile on for Madden before she walked away.

"She doesn't seem like much fun," Madden remarked before Ellen was out of earshot.

And she heard it, if her shoulders tightening told the tale.

Rus swallowed his chuckle.

"Baby, what have I said about saying out loud everything that pops into your head?" Lucinda asked her girl.

Madden tipped her head toward her mom. "You said be honest in all things."

"We were talking about something else at that time," Lucinda corrected.

To that came the cheeky, "We were?"

Lucinda assumed a look of a woman searching for strength that God gave her an astute child and what that meant in times like these and for the rest of her life.

He moved to save her.

"Madden, I'm Rus." He offered her his hand.

Her eyes got big with excitement when she stared at his hand.

She then took it, shook it hard about five times, while saying,

"Hi! Will you come talk to my class? Say yes, because I already told them you would."

He let her go and didn't swallow that chuckle as Lucinda clipped, "Madden Emery Bonner Rhett. Really?"

"What?" she asked her mom. "You told me to make my own opportunities."

Lucinda looked to the ceiling and prayed, "Oh my God."

Rus busted out laughing.

He couldn't help it.

The latent cute had surfaced fully, it was all wrapped up in her precocious daughter, and he was loving every second of it.

She turned to him. "Do you think this is funny?"

"Did you miss the laughter?"

The peaches and cream of her skin turned more peach than cream.

He cut her a break and again looked down at Madden.

"I'd be honored to talk to your class, but I'm doing something important right now, so it might be later when I can do it."

How the fuck he forgot what he was doing was investigating the death of her unofficial big sister, he had no clue.

But those hazel eyes filled with tears right before they disappeared in her mother's long cardigan after she crossed to her and pressed close, hiding her face.

Lucinda rested one hand on her head, the other she wrapped around the back of her neck, and she looked to Rus.

"Sorry," he mouthed.

She shook her head in an *it's not your fault*.

She then crouched in front of her girl, cocooning her with arms and thighs, and they had a whispered conference.

And it was witnessing that, Rus was done fighting it.

He wasn't going to embark on an affair with his vic's employer.

But he was going to get to know her along the way, and when the time was right, he was going to embark on an affair with his vic's employer.

And maybe, if it kept going the way it was, for the first time since Jenn, he was going to allow himself to have something meaningful with a woman he was interested in.

Madden nodded, pulled away, Lucinda straightened, and Madden looked up at him, swiping at her face.

"Sorry, Mr. Lazarus."

"Nothing to apologize for, sweetheart," he said gently.

She nodded and took her iPad back to the chair she'd been sitting in when he first saw her.

He turned to Lucinda.

"I made a call," she told him. "I said pretty please. Do you have time this morning to meet with Thea? She has a break between her nine o'clock and her eleven thirty."

"Just so I have this straight, we're taking your daughter when I interview a dominatrix?"

"No. We're dropping her off at my mom's along the way."

Full immersion in the Bonner family.

He shouldn't be.

But since he was done fighting it, he was.

That being totally there for it.

TWELVE

Official Capacity

I ndira Bonner had let her hair go gray.

It was a thick mass of waves and curls with streaks of white that were natural and beautiful.

He was surprised, however, because she was young, at least too young to retire and leave the business to her daughter. Unless he was reading it wrong, she had Lucinda late in life, and over the years she'd simply taken care of herself.

Or maybe she was still involved, just not day to day, and she'd handed the helm to Lucinda and kept in the background.

She indicated she was well aware of her granddaughter's recent loss, but this wasn't the only reason she enveloped Madden in a grandmotherly hug that was so warm and openly nurturing, it seemed at odds with the fact she was home on a Saturday, about to babysit, and she was wearing an outfit much like her daughter's. Except she didn't have the cardigan, the white sweater wasn't a turtleneck, and her smart slacks were charcoal gray.

Things got more interesting after their quick introduction led to another one when a tall, good-looking, dark-headed man, around Lucinda's age, showed up behind Indira.

"You're here," Lucinda said to him.

"In the flesh," he replied, his attention on Rus.

Lucinda delayed no further. "This is my brother, Porter. Porter, Special Agent Lazarus."

Yeah.

Total immersion.

"Rus," he invited the man to use his nickname, offering a hand.

Porter took it. "Hey."

They broke contact, the man glanced at Lucinda, his mother, then claimed his niece by throwing her over his wide shoulder to her delighted squeal.

"Sundaes," he declared, walking away.

"Yay!" Madden cried.

"It's nine thirty in the morning," Lucinda called to his back.

He waved a hand and didn't bother even looking over his shoulder as he kept walking.

Madden lifted her head, grinning huge, and said, "Bye, Momma. Bye, Mr. Lazarus."

"Later," Rus called.

Lucinda said nothing.

They disappeared.

Indira shifted into their line of vision.

"We have this, go," she said to Lucinda.

"I don't want her eating a sundae at nine thirty in the morning, Mom," Lucinda decreed.

"There are times for nine thirty sundaes, my darling, and this is one of them," Indira refuted with the god's honest truth. Before her daughter could say more, if she was going to, Indira looked up at Rus. "It's nice to meet you. I'd offer you coffee, but I think time is tight for you."

"It seems it is. Another time. And it's nice to meet you too," he replied.

Indira made a shooing gesture, and since only Madden had made it over the threshold, the door was closed in their faces.

He looked down at Lucinda.

"You have a brother."

"One. Older. Annoying. He needs to settle down and have kids of his own so he'll stop spoiling mine," she groused.

"Hmm," he hummed his disagreement to this statement, since he not only spoiled his daughter, he spoiled both his brothers' daughters.

And their sons (and, in his way, his).

She gave him a side eye then turned to walk down the steps toward his SUV.

Her mother lived in a gated condo complex. Rus had been surprised at its existence in this area, mostly because the gate was manned, and it was clear HOA fees were hefty. The condos were semi-detached townhomes, and they looked huge. On the way to her unit, they'd passed a clubhouse, an outdoor swimming pool and tennis courts.

It seemed more suited to Scottsdale than rural Washington state.

He stood at her door while she climbed in the vehicle, he closed it for her and only got into it when he was in, and they were moving.

"There's money in Misted Pines."

"There's money everywhere. But this is a weekend playground for people in Seattle, and though it's more of a drive, Spokane. It's a tourist spot for those out of state too. Pinetop Lodge has one of the best spas I've been to, and I know spas. We get weekend warriors. We get write-off corporate getaways in the guise of conferences. There's fishing, hiking, trail running and riding. And there's skiing close. The locals keep the local places secret. There are a lot of 'keep out' and 'private property' signs, and everyone encourages outsiders to take those seriously. We have no industry but the tourist industry, some logging and a quarry. So if people stopped coming, the town would die."

Shit, fuck, and everything damning.

How hadn't he thought of this before?

"What?" she asked, clearly sensing his change in mood, or maybe he hadn't kept the fact he was suddenly pissed at himself off his face.

"Your mom retired early," he noted, and had to admit the words sounded strangled.

"We all do. You can't keep things fresh if you've been doing it for forty years. But that wasn't what you were thinking. So what were you thinking?"

The Bonners ran their ship tight, but she was correct, that wasn't what he was thinking.

"Your brother isn't involved in the business?" he asked, instead of telling her what that was.

"My brother manages the stage, particularly building sets. He likes working with his hands. That also wasn't what you were thinking. So, again, what were you thinking?"

All those elaborate sets were her brother.

And this was news.

"Did he know Brittanie?"

"He probably saw her around, but as much as it makes me feel the need to gargle with acid because these words are coming out of my mouth, even I, as his sister, know he's exceptionally handsome. The girls flirt with him all the time. It not only annoys him, it wastes his time. He's not a time waster. And he's into fresh-faced, let's-have-a-picnic-after-a-three-hour-hike mountain women. He's also highly intelligent and understands you don't shit where you live. So if he said more than five words to her in the four years she worked for me, I'd be surprised."

Rus had barely met the guy, and he liked him.

"Rus," she warned.

"Brittanie checked into the motel herself."

"All right," she prompted when he said no more.

"We're looking local, but what if it was someone from outside Misted Pines? I take it these tourists and business conference people hit up your club?"

"Absolutely," she replied. Then he knew she got him and just how difficult it would be to track down someone who wasn't local when she said a soft, "Damn."

"Keyleigh didn't mention anybody. You didn't either."

"No. And again, if she set up a tryst with someone, she would not go to that motel. Even if they were from out of town and for some reason she wasn't comfortable with taking them to her house.

97

She'd expect them to pay, and she'd expect something like Pinetop. That's the most exclusive place in town, but there are others, not as nice, but definitely nicer than the motel."

"Still, it's a possibility."

"I'd say outside possibility, Rus."

"I don't dismiss any possibility until it dismisses itself."

"Of course."

"Gotta make a call."

"Of course," she repeated.

He pulled out his phone and called Moran. He got voicemail, shared his thoughts, then reiterated what he'd texted earlier: once he was done with Thea the Dominatrix, they'd meet up and get on with the day.

But now that included having a discussion about a possible out-of-towner drifting through and killing Brittanie.

Thea lived on the opposite side of town from Lucinda's mother. It wasn't that far of a drive. They were going to be early and couldn't show until she was done with her nine o'clock.

Because of this, Lucinda directed them to stop at a place with a shockingly (in this part of the country) progressively liberal, in-your-face mural on the side of the building, and a sign on the front that was clearly made from reclaimed materials.

It declared that inside was Aromacobana.

Their local coffee spot.

So an explanation of the liberal mural.

They went in and immediately stirred a lot of interest.

This interest wasn't about Lucinda's version of a casual outfit that would go better lunching in New York City than picking up a coffee in a grunge-loving-progressive-lefty coffeehouse in rural Washington.

It was what was obviously making its way through town about who he was and the time he was spending with her.

As annoying as it was that Ellen Macklemore felt entitled to drive to Pinetop Lodge and confront him about how he was spending his time investigating this case, Rus had never been one to give any fucks to what people thought of him. This was one of the reasons why he cut his military career short.

It wasn't that he didn't like authority.

It was that he was more of a freethinker than the military allowed you to be. Until then, he'd lived an entire life where thinking freely was frowned on, and more of that turned out not to be his gig.

This was also why he didn't continue as a cop.

And it was what led him to the FBI.

Structure. Support. Rules and regs.

But leeway to be your own person and encouragement to explore and share your thoughts.

Though, he couldn't say he didn't have some pride standing at the side of a beautiful, elegant woman and strongarming her at the cashier so she'd finally let him pay for something.

One thing he had added proof of after taking a sip, the libs knew how to make a damn good coffee, and that was the case from sea to shining sea.

They were back in the SUV and had resumed their journey when he noted, "Ellen Macklemore, the woman in the denim and turquoise, is in the coven, isn't she?"

"She is." Lucinda confirmed. "Though, I was surprised at the open offensive."

"Not as surprised as me."

"Now, what are you thinking?"

"I think thou does indeed protest too much on occasion."

She sounded surprised. "You're back to the coven?"

"She thought I was having dinner with you. It's none of her business if I break for dinner or who I do it with. By last night, I hadn't even been here two full days, and someone's in my face about how I'm spending my time?"

"Welcome to Misted Pines."

This stunned him.

"Really?" he asked.

"Did you not see that mural? Much of our citizenry has opinions, and they aren't afraid to state them openly. Since the Ray

Andrews debacle, the town council meetings are a free-for-all. I go for entertainment value alone."

This made him feel better.

"Don't run into Kimmy, whatever you do," she advised. "She'll tell you exactly who killed Brittanie, and she'll be very wrong but think she's very right."

"Kimmy?"

"The woman who runs our holiday shop. And no, we're far too small, no matter the tourists and out-of-towners, to have our own dedicated-to-holidays shop. But Kimmy makes a go of it against the odds. She's also our local conspiracy theorist. She knows who killed JFK, and she's pissed as shit Cade Bohannan hasn't taken her directly to meet with Director Wray so he can reopen that case."

"Oh yeah, help me keep a wide berth from her, baby," he muttered.

Her voice was warm and amused when she replied, "I'll do my best."

They made what was left of the ride in companionable silence, and she guided him to a house that was alone, if not remote, quite like Melanie Iverson's, but it was in much better condition.

There was a lone Subaru sitting outside, indication the client was gone.

They walked up together, and Thea already had the front door open, standing behind a screen, wearing a big, warm-looking, plush robe.

"Well, shit," she said as greeting, staring up at him. "Did Hollywood cast you, or are you for real?"

"I told you he was fun to look at," Lucinda murmured as Thea pushed open the screen door and they walked in.

"Special Agent Lazarus," he introduced himself when the screen shut behind him and he'd offered his hand.

Thea took it, smiling and declaring, "I'd clear a whole weekend for you."

"Honored, but no thanks," he replied, friendly at the same time formal.

"The fun I could have," she said to Lucinda.

Lucinda appeared stricken, then annoyed.

"No offense, but I'm here to talk about a murdered woman," Rus stated.

The fun she was right then having at his expense, he didn't mind, exactly.

But that didn't negate the fact he wasn't there to have fun.

Not to mention, he could see, he'd been around mirrors, and he knew he was handsome. It was nice when women thought the same, and even nicer when they shared it.

What wasn't nice was having that conversation in front of him, when, if he and a male friend did the same to a woman, especially if she was acting in an official capacity as he was right then, it would be considered at least harassment, and definitely what he felt it was in that moment.

Inappropriate.

Thea appeared instantly contrite and muttered, "Sorry."

"I appreciate the compliment, and I appreciate you being willing to talk about a client. I can imagine it took a lot for you to make that decision. It could come to nothing. It could also mean a great deal to this investigation, which frankly, you should know, puts you out there. But I hope you take no offense when I point out we both have things to do."

She nodded, and apparently okay with the "puts you out there" part of his speech, she said nothing and gestured them farther into her home.

This was the living room, no tools of the trade here, and he was relieved. He didn't judge, and a good two (or seven) toys were nice to have in your arsenal, but intimacy was intimacy.

And living life was living life.

Thea took a seat. Lucinda took a seat. And Rus looked down at Lucinda.

"Any chance you'd give us some space?" he requested.

"None at all," she denied.

He blew out a breath and took his own seat.

"You're here about Ezra," Thea started it.

"Yes," Rus confirmed. "How long has he been a client of yours?"

"Three, four years. We have a standing, every other Saturday afternoon appointment. Today is not his Saturday, by the way."

Rus dipped his chin to note he got that, mentally documenting the lengths of Ezra's trail of lies that as yet had gone undiscovered by his wife.

She continued. "His wife thinks he's golfing. In the winter, no clue what he tells her he's doing. No clue what he tells her about paying my fee. He also comes in when she's out of town."

"It's my understanding he's into pain?"

"Yes. Mild. Nothing deep, intense, physically scarring. No fire play or blood play." Both shoulders went up then down. "It's pretty pedestrian."

"Have you explored deeper?"

She nodded. "In the beginning, he requested that. He didn't like it. Used his safe word. We don't go there now."

"Have you been uncomfortable with any of his responses or requests?"

She shook her head and surprised him by giving him the skinny.

All of it.

"He takes a paddle. He takes a crop. Light whip work that won't cause lasting marks. He's ringed or caged. Likes the pain in his groin of a confined erection or not being allowed to orgasm. I honestly think that's mostly what he enjoys, since he takes a crop there too, but he definitely likes to be dominated. Told what to do. Light disobedience so he'll be made to do it, with pain, but not much of it."

"Humiliation?"

"No. None. Not into that at all." She moved to the edge of her seat. "Listen, Agent Lazarus, I've been doing this a long time. It's natural, these tendencies, finding ways to live out your fantasies. It's more normal than you know."

"I know how normal it is," he replied.

She took a second to assess him, saw what she needed to see, no judge and here in an official capacity. He then saw her finally relax after their rocky start.

She kept speaking.

"But I do get clients who I move out of my practice with firm guidance of where they should move on from me. I can tell it's not about getting what they like. It's about something else. Damage to their psyche that they shouldn't be working out with me, or anyone like me. They need another kind of professional. Ezra has a wife who makes a lot of money. I don't know if he loved her in the beginning, or he loved her because of the life she could give him. I do know she's made it clear she thinks his needs are sick, and she wants nothing to do with them. He doesn't love her now, he's said that straight to me. But he stays with her because of what he'll lose if he doesn't. She doesn't give him what he needs, that's why he sees me. Why he sleeps with anyone else who will take him, that's about him just being an asshole."

"I'm assuming with all of that, you two talk and this isn't just business?"

"We talk. He complains about his wife. He complains about his golf game. I listen. This is a safe space for him."

"Did he ever mention Brittanie?"

She shook her head.

"I can imagine this is a safe space for all your clients," Rus remarked. "So out of curiosity, why did you agree to speak with me about Ezra?"

She had a ready, honest reply.

"Because I don't like him. I'll take his money because he's a good sub, and it's fun to work him. But he's a dick. This is my business. I work part-time at The Joy of Joy to augment income, but this is what pays my bills." She tossed a hand out to indicate Misted Pines. "And where I live, I don't get to pick and choose my clients."

"So he comes to you just to get his kink, which is his natural proclivity. And there's nothing deeper there that might snap and make him do something extreme?"

"I didn't say that."

Fucking hell.

With the way she'd been talking, he didn't expect that response.

He glanced at Lucinda as a pulse went down his spine.

She was looking at him.

"In the beginning, when we were exploring?" Thea asked.

Rus returned to her and nodded.

"He seemed disappointed. We had discussions during aftercare. I could sense he was upset he couldn't take more, so we explored options. We ran the gamut, or at least the gamut of what I'd offer. The only thing we added that took was ass play. But I never shook that feeling that he was searching for something else. After Cin called me, it struck me that if we didn't try it, no self-respecting Domme like me would do it. And although I'm not into seriously extreme play, I know people who are. They don't live close. He'd have to go to Seattle. But I suggested them to him. I don't know if he ever tried them. I just know he never stopped coming to me. Now, if I can't get him off as well as someone else can, he's not going to pay me what I charge to get something that isn't as good as he can get elsewhere. And men can't fake orgasms, and since we have no emotional connection to speak of, he'd have no reason to do so anyway, so…"

She let that trail off.

But Rus was stuck on what she meant.

"No self-respecting Domme would do it?" he queried. "What does that mean?"

"People think anything goes in my world because it isn't their world. And yeah, if you aren't in the life, it'd all probably seem extreme. But there are very strict rules. There are always boundaries. And hard passes. Standard. Across the board."

"Like?"

"If it's illegal. Assault. Non-consent. Stranger danger that's not set up beforehand so the person who's being attacked didn't consent to that attack prior. Say she, or he, just won't know when it's going to happen, or who'll be doing it, but they arranged for it to be done. That kind of thing."

Rus's chest was beginning to feel tight.

"Do you think he'd enjoy assaulting someone?"

"No, but I think he might enjoy watching it or being made to do it."

Fucking *fuck*.

He could feel Lucinda's eyes on him.

But this...

This was a damn solid fucking lead.

The man he'd met last night was calm and collected, and an inveterate liar.

Rus had seen that before and it hid a monster underneath.

This man had been lying to his wife for years about multiple affairs, and a standing appointment with a Dominatrix.

If he could fool the woman he was living with for years, he could put two law enforcement officers off the scent for thirty minutes.

"I need to be clear I do not know that's what he's about," Thea asserted. "I just know he wanted something more. And a good prostate-induced orgasm wasn't all he wanted."

"Is there anything else you think I should know?" Rus asked.

"Just that I'm firing him as a client. Our next session will be his last. I've taken on a few new subs, ones I like. I'm finally in the good place of getting overloaded. I've been squeezing them in"—another double-shoulder lift—"because money is money. Truth is, I need to lose someone. Which was another thing I started to think about after Cin's call. I don't know if he did it. I hope he didn't, because that would mean I'd have to hire industrial cleaners to deep clean my dungeon, and I'd personally have to shower for a week. But he really is an asshole, and I'm glad to have an excuse to see the back of him that's not going to hurt my ability to pay my cable bill."

His phone was vibrating in his pocket, but he ignored it, stood and said, "I appreciate you talking to me."

She stood too and came to him. "I really do hope it isn't him. But just in case..."

She looked vaguely nauseous.

"I hope it isn't him either."

For your sake.

They said their goodbyes, got in the SUV, and he was digging out his phone when Lucinda said, "I apologize for how Thea started that. It wasn't appropriate, and I inadvertently fed into it. Though, I have to admit, sharing about your good looks was part of my pitch to get her to talk to you."

"It's okay," he muttered, distracted, but still processing the pleasure he felt that she said out loud she thought he was good-looking, at the same time seeing he had a missed call from Moran.

"Was she assaulted?"

The feeble tone of her voice made his attention race to her.

"She was, wasn't she?" she whispered, her skin pale, her eyes speeding over his face.

It wasn't professional, but then again, neither were the endearments he'd been using, and they had both moved out of the strictly professional space last night at dinner.

Touch was another matter.

However, with the look on her face, he couldn't stop himself from cupping her jaw and leaning toward her.

"Lucinda—"

"Just tell me."

"She was raped."

She swallowed, closed her eyes, and turned toward the windshield.

He slid his hand to her neck, gave it a squeeze, and he didn't like it at all, but he then had no choice but to let it slide away.

She opened her eyes.

"How'd she die, Rus?" she asked the windshield.

"The autopsy hasn't been done yet, but preliminarily, we believe it was significant trauma to the head."

"Violently," she whispered despondently. "She died violently."

Yes, she did.

His phone vibrated in his hand.

He looked down at it.

He wasn't going to take it, but it was Moran again.

"I have to take this, honey," he said gently.

"Do it," she replied shortly.

He took the call. "Lazarus."

"I know you're interviewing someone, but you need to cut it short and come to the station right away."

"What's up?"

"Jace and Jess found Dakota."

Holy shit.

Moran wasn't finished.

"And Brittanie's dad."

Well.

Damn.

THIRTEEN

Not A Subject

H e had another reason to like Fret County's woman-behind-the-sheriff when he came into the station with Lucinda at his side, Polly intercepted her while Rus kept moving.

He looked back, and he felt his gut lurch, because she didn't appear ticked or stymied to be left behind.

As she had been the whole ride there, she was lost in the knowledge of how Brittanie had spent the last hours of her life.

"I'll call you," he said.

"Okay," she replied woodenly, her eyes on him, but he knew she didn't see him.

And his gut lurched again.

He wanted to be with her.

But he had work to do for Brittanie.

The story of his life when it came to women.

He made his way to Moran's office.

The door was open, he stood in it and knocked, seeing Moran behind his desk and on the phone.

The man looked up, motioned for him to come in, then motioned for him to close the door.

"Right, right," he said into his phone as Rus did as motioned and sat in a chair in front of Moran. "Lazarus is here. Yeah. Okay. We're on it. Let me know if there's more. Later."

He touched his screen and looked at Rus.

"Fuck, man, everything is exploding."

"I want to know, but Lucinda is out there, and she needs a ride to her mother's."

"On it," he mumbled and picked up his desk phone.

"I had to tell her how Brittanie died. She's not in a good place."

Moran's gaze came to him, he nodded, then said into the phone, "Get Polly to take Cin Bonner to her mom. I want Polly to do it. And find a way to let her know that Cin just found out how Brittanie Iverson died. She needs to handle this with care." Pause then, "Great."

And he put the phone in the cradle.

"Where are Jace and Jesse, Dakota and Gary Iverson?" Rus asked.

"Cade showed. He's talking to his boys somewhere. Dakota and Gary are in separate interview rooms, waiting for us to speak with them. They're pissed as shit."

"Please tell me the Bohannan twins did not do something to fuck all this by abducting the brother and father of the victim in order to bring them in," Rus begged.

"No, I mean they're pissed as shit Brittanie was killed. They were holed up in some hunting cabin, it's owned by a friend of Gary Iverson. No cell service. No internet. Apparently, they've been mostly getting drunk and shooting bottles and doing shit I don't know, because I have a job and a life. They came in of their own accord. Which is good Jace and Jess talked them into it, because, as I noted, they both got guns and they both got a reason to hunt anyone down who might have looked at Brittanie wrong and shoot him in the face. And right now, since they just found out she's been murdered, they're all hepped up to do that."

Rus blew out a breath and sat back in his chair.

"I'm deputizing them," Moran went on.

Rus felt his eyebrows shoot up. "What? Who?"

"Jace and Jess. They're good with an interview, hate to say it, but better than any of my people. They're also good with communication. If anyone can calm these guys down, Jace and Jess can. And these guys are far from calm. I'm prepared to hear someone shouting and tearing my station apart at any minute. But we don't have time to deal with that. We need to get to the lab."

His neck suddenly itched.

"Why?"

"Because they've had some time with the stuff they took from the scene. And another break from the Crystal Killer's MO, the plastic sheeting was wiped down. I don't know what happened in that motel room. I do know that the coroner is close to finalizing her report, but about five minutes ago, she called and told me, down Brittanie's right side, the one she was resting on, there are carpet burns. Even if we moved her before you got there, we probably wouldn't have noticed them. They were reddish marks but came up stronger post-mortem. I think she was taken off the plastic, it was wiped down, then put back on it and struck in the head there. The blood was there, and that was undisturbed. But I think she struggled on the carpet. And I know our perp wiped down the plastic because he worried he left something behind. And he should be worried, since he did. They found a pubic hair that was not Brittanie's on the very edge of the sheeting. They didn't get everything, Rus. And it's viable. The whole shaft, with skin. He left something behind. If we find him, we can put him there on that goddamned plastic."

It was gut, but he'd learned to go with his gut.

From the minute Thea said, *I didn't say that*, he felt the niggle.

But now it was more than a niggle.

A lot more.

Therefore, urgently, Rus ordered, "Right now, you need to send deputies to pick up Ezra Corbin."

A light lit in Moran's eyes. "The dominatrix give you something?"

"It's a little thin, but I think still solid. And if we can break him in interrogation, yeah. It could get way more solid. So we need a warrant to get his DNA. Get on that, and I'll tell you on the way to the lab."

And again, Moran reached for his phone.

RUS DID NOT TEND to get squeamish.

The FBI normally didn't investigate homicides unless there were extenuating circumstances. Like the perpetrator abducted their victim and crossed state lines, or it was a serial killer, or the local authorities asked for their assistance.

Still, seventeen years on the job, five more as a cop, four as a soldier, and he'd been deployed, so he'd seen death.

And he'd been in autopsy suites.

Even with all that experience, he'd never learned to divorce himself from the fact that the person on the table had their most precious possession stripped from them against their will. And there were people who cared about them who were grieving.

For Rus, it was always personal.

Standing, listening to the coroner, with Brittanie naked on a table in front of him, the Y-cut on her chest stitched shut, it was the worst in his career.

It wasn't that he'd investigated her life deeper, felt he knew her better. He worked at being thorough in all his cases.

It was Lucinda.

And Madden burying her face in her mother's cardigan.

"Bludgeoning," the coroner was saying. "A mess was made, but there were depressions left consistent with a hammer."

"Is there something you need to show us on her body, or can we cover her?" Rus asked abruptly.

She startled and looked to him.

"I get she's a subject to you and you have to be removed from it," he continued. "But she's been through enough, don't you think?"

"Of course," she muttered, moving to grab a surgical drape.

He felt Moran's attention on him, but he looked to his shoes while the coroner covered Brittanie.

He lifted his head when she started speaking again.

"Like I reported earlier, there was no skin or blood under her nails. We did find fibers from her fingers, both carpet and hemp. She possibly tried picking at the rope she was tied with. Those fibers are in the abrasions around her wrists and ankles too. Carpet fibers in her toenails, and as I said, fingernails."

"She was raped on the floor," Rus said dully.

"It would seem consistent to being on all fours on carpet," the coroner replied. "I compared the fibers I found with some retrieved from the hotel room, and they're the same. That said, she only had carpet burns on her side, not on her knees or the palms of her hands. With the way she was assaulted, if it was on carpet, she'd have burns."

"Any residue around her mouth?" he asked.

She nodded. "Glue, yes. From tape."

"Messy?" he asked.

"Sorry?" she asked in return.

"Did you find a lot of it?"

"There was an attempt at cleanup, but not much. So I suppose."

More evidence this was definitely copycat and not CK getting sloppy.

He might one day get sloppy.

But not this sloppy.

"The bleeding, bruising and internal injuries indicate she was raped while she was alive."

"Is there evidence of more than one person assaulting her?" Rus asked.

"Yes, and no. Yes, in the sense I believe she was physically assaulted by a penis, both vaginally and anally. And yes, in the sense that she clearly sustained a prolonged assault. But a possible no, because she was penetrated by something else a single assailant could use to keep assaulting her even if he wasn't able to sustain an erection. I found latex proteins internally that are consistent with a prophylactic. Silicone doesn't leave a residue, but whatever was used was much larger than even a very well-endowed penis."

"So somebody else could have been there," Rus stated. "And it could be any gender."

She shook her head. "I can't rule that out. I found no hairs or other organic matter on her body that weren't hers. But even though they didn't clean her up down there, that isn't entirely out of the ordinary. Especially if condoms and gloves were used and she was moved around. Hairs could have fallen away. And I found latex powder around her wrists, ankles and neck, also in her hair. Someone touched her in these places wearing gloves. Gloves don't carry that much powder, so either a single assailant wore multiple pairs, or there were multiple assailants wearing gloves."

The hairs fell away, or at least one of them did.

They'd gone to the coroner's office from the lab. He'd seen the dark pubic hair himself. They were now far more closely examining the hairs and anything else combed from the carpet.

Ezra Corbin had dark hair.

And there was someone else there.

Rus would stake his career on it.

"Tox screen indicates she was given a mild sedative."

Rus's attention sharpened on her.

Her eyes wandered to Brittanie. "I wish I could say it was enough she didn't feel or know what was happening to her, but it wasn't. Though, it was enough to render her incapable of real struggle, and definitely she couldn't have fought back."

Christ.

Not even a fighting chance.

"Anything else you got for us?" Moran asked.

She watched Moran ask the question, but on her answer, again, her gaze drifted to Brittanie. "In this case, I'm afraid it's what you see is what you get."

"I appreciate you working on a Saturday, Dr. Pfeiffer," Moran said.

"I've been working Saturdays for seven months, Sheriff," she replied. "Too many stupid people doing too many stupid things. I'm sorry it took me so long to get to her. The three ODs, the road rage idiot, the two Darwin Award nominees who tried to make a trail bike into a motorcycle then climbed on for the test drive, and the guy who had no idea how to clean his brand-new gun came in first."

"You sure they're not all Darwin Award nominees?" Moran asked.

"No," she replied shortly.

Moran's lips quirked and he said, "We gotta get back to the station. Thanks again."

Rus lifted his chin to her, and Moran and he started to walk away.

"Special Agent?" she called.

He turned back.

"She's not a subject. I did everything I could for her. But she's safe here and she has been from the minute I got her."

"I didn't mean to imply differently."

"I know, I just want you to know, I did all I could for her."

He studied her.

Yeah.

Brittanie ate at her too.

"Obliged."

She nodded.

They left.

FOURTEEN

The U S of Fucking A

In the genetic pool sweepstakes, for her short life, Brittanie
Iverson was a clear winner.

Rus knew this, standing at the viewing glass, watching a twenty-
eight-year-old calm, composed version of Cade Bohannan sit and
study Dakota Iverson as he prowled the room, punching air, kicking
walls and making empty threats.

Dakota was thin, weaselly, short, already losing his blond hair,
and Rus would guess they didn't have running water up in that
hunting cabin, because he looked like he hadn't taken a shower or
put on clean clothes in weeks.

Listening to the going's-on, Rus didn't know if the guy loved his
sister, or he was pissed at the world and using this as his excuse to do
something about it.

"Whaddare'ya doin', sittin' there?" he demanded of Jesse
Bohannan, and he did this slamming a chair into the table opposite
where Jesse was sitting.

Jesse, lounged back, one forearm on the table, which was fortunately bolted to the floor, one hand resting on his thigh, long legs
stretched out and crossed at the ankles, didn't move a muscle.

"What the *fuck!*" Dakota stabbed a finger at the wall. "My sister's killer is walking free, *asshole*."

"What I'm not doing is kicking a wall. A wall didn't kill Brittanie," Jesse replied, cool as Brad Pitt playing poker in *Ocean's Eleven*.

Rus wasn't sure that was the way to go.

They were contemporaries, though. Jesse was a built, good-looking guy who clearly had his shit tight.

Dakota was probably the way he was, not only because his mother was who she was, but because he'd been bullied at school.

The cool guy gives you attention, you don't act like a dick.

You act like the cool guy.

"Now, I came in here because you'd calmed down and said you were ready to help," Jesse continued. "Are you not calm? I mean, we're trying to find who did this to your sister, and you can be a part of that. What doesn't help, is you being a dick and punching air and getting pissed at me. I need you to talk to me, Dakota."

That did it.

He wanted to be the cool guy.

Dakota pulled out the chair and sat down.

Jesus.

He'd never seen it go down that easy when someone was that riled up.

"Fucking hell," Rus muttered.

"I know. It's uncanny. They're goddamned savants with this shit," Moran muttered at his side.

"It's just, she's my sister, dude." Dakota tried to sound like he was explaining his behavior, but there was a whine to it.

Jesse nodded understandingly, two cool guys bonding.

"I get it, bud. Seriously, the worst. I feel you."

"Yeah," Dakota huffed out.

"When'd you last see your sister?" Jesse asked.

"I dunno." That was sullen. "Fuck, she told me she was gonna help me find a job. *Fuck!*" he exploded.

"Dakota," Jesse said warningly.

"You know, she had it so together. Sweet crib. Sweet job. Cool shit." Dakota's small eyes narrowed on Jesse. "Why'd your brother dump her, hunh? She was happy with Jace. Real fuckin' happy."

"We're not talking about Jace. We're talking about Brittanie. When did you last see her?"

"Went by her crib when that asshole canned me. Three weeks ago. Said I didn't wanna go back to living with Mom. She got me. Man, did she. She said I could crash on her couch, and she'd ask around to see if she could get me something to tide me over until I could, you know, get my career back on track."

Rus and Moran exchanged a glance on the words *career back on track*.

"I said I needed a vacation. I was gonna hook up with Dad and chill out. She told me not to go. She said she'd buy a bed for that extra room where Keyleigh used to stay. Said we could be room-mates for a while. Did I take her up on that shit? *No.* I coulda saved her."

Jesse further proved his mettle by keeping a straight face at that.

"Did she talk about anyone she was seeing? Anyone who maybe she was having an issue with? Someone who was causing her problems?"

"You think I'd go off with Dad if she did?" he demanded.

Yes, Jesse did. So did Rus and Moran.

Jesse didn't give that away either.

"She could have tried to blow it off," Jesse noted.

"She didn't say dick to me," Dakota returned. Then he stabbed the table with his pointed forefinger. "I'll tell you this shit, you listening?" He didn't wait for an answer. He kept tough guy stabbing and talking. "You said she was killed at that motel. My sister wouldn't go to that motel. She was class, man. Jace knows it. You know it. Everyone knows it. She was a dancer at Bon Amie. She wasn't a skank. She wasn't my mom. She wouldn't go to that motel. Someone had to drag her there. She probably died going through the door to a room, it was so beneath her."

And again with the motel.

But she checked in.

Not in distress.

"I want to talk to the desk clerk," Rus said just as Moran said, "We gotta go back to the desk clerk."

They looked at each other.

Then Moran flipped the switch that muted the audio and they turned around to the viewing glass to the other interrogation room.

Jace, an exact replica of Jess, was leaning against the wall, ankles crossed, arms crossed, chin in his throat, eyes on the man slumped at the table, weeping.

Momentarily, the thought of Sabrina meeting one of these two guys skimmed through Rus's head.

He'd still hate sharing all the love she had to give.

But at least he wouldn't wake up in a sweat worried someone might hurt her. A threat came to their door, Rus could convince himself just looking at these two, they could vaporize it with a hard stare.

Moran flipped on the audio, and they heard the weeping.

"Mr. Iverson," Jace said low. "I need you to pull it together and talk to me. When did you last see Britt?"

"You shouldn't have left her," the man sobbed into the table. "You shoulda kept her safe."

Rus got tight, and he hadn't even met Jace yet.

He felt Moran do the same.

Worst of that, he watched Jace do it.

These two fucking wastes of space?

Laying that shit on a guy who went out there, turning stones, trying to do something for a woman he was no longer seeing?

Fuck.

And…

No.

He pivoted on his shoe and stalked out.

"Lazarus!" Moran clipped.

But he was out the door.

He took the three strides to room one, yanked the door open, and he walked right in.

Jace straightened with a start from the wall.

Rus had his hand out. "Jason. Special Agent Lazarus."

"Sir," Jason greeted, giving him a shake, his eyes sharp and taking in everything about him.

Christ, he'd never felt so seen in his life.

Could he talk Sabrina away from the sunshine to the pine trees? At this rate, with her lack of interest in her studies, and these fucking guys, he'd take a community college.

Rus let him go and turned to the table.

The man at the desk had lifted his head.

Rus saw it then.

Take years and experience from Melanie and this man and maybe, there was a hint of Brittanie there.

Just a hint.

Maybe.

Lucinda was right.

Although he was taller, more built, he was Dakota in twenty years.

Including the fact he had very little hair.

"Mr. Iverson. I'm Special Agent Zachariah Lazarus of the FBI. I'm helping local law enforcement investigate what happened to Brittanie."

The man wiped his nose on his sleeve. "FBI?"

"Yes, as you can see, we're all taking this very seriously."

"FBI," the man breathed.

Rus fought a sneer because Iverson was impressed his daughter's death brought in the Feds. Just like Melanie, though her way was less complimentary.

He took a seat across from the man.

"Now, what I'm going to say, I'll preface by sharing I mean no offense. I know this is tough on you. I feel for you. But you didn't kill your girl. And we need to find that person. So, taking this time getting you and your boy to talk is time we can't spend looking for who did what was done to Brittanie. To do that, we need to know everything we can from everyone we can talk to, especially those closest to her, about every little detail we can dig up that might lead us to the killer. So, can you please tell us when you last had contact with your girl?"

"I don't...I wasn't..." His face crumbled, he did a snot take all over the table, and wailed, "*I wasn't close to my precious girl!*"

Christ.

"Mr. Iverson, please pull it together."

"You!" he shouted suddenly, pushing to his feet.

Rus rose too.

"You! You shoulda been with her!" he yelled at Jace.

Rus moved into his field of vision. "They broke up. It happens. It isn't his responsibility. Look at me."

Iverson didn't look at him.

"*Look at me!*" he roared.

Iverson did a full body shake in surprise at Rus losing it, and he stared at Rus.

"For three days, he's been busting his ass to find anything that would help, including finding you. What have you been doing for the three days Brittanie's been lying in the morgue? Don't you fucking cry again," Rus gritted when the man's face started collapsing. "Man up, goddamn it, and tell me when you last saw Brittanie."

"I haven't seen her in months," he admitted.

"Right. Do you know if she was seeing anyone? Do you know if she got caught up with someone that made you uncomfortable?"

Iverson puffed his chest out. "My daughter wouldn't get caught up in *shit*. She was a dancer at Bon Amie!"

Rus nodded. "I've been learning everything about her, and she was a good person. People loved her. It isn't good people who do bad things. But that doesn't mean bad people don't get to them."

He shook his head. "We weren't that close. She'd…she'd…"— he looked to the table—"she'd slip me money, you know, when things were tight. But she didn't tell me things."

She had a nice apartment. She might have a designer bag or two.

But mostly, it seemed it was the weight of her deadbeat family hanging on her that led her to needing money, and she probably didn't tell her friends or Lucinda because she thought it was embarrassing.

He hoped to Christ it wasn't money that took her to that motel.

If it was, Brittanie dead, these motherfuckers alive, he wasn't sure he'd be responsible for what he'd do.

"Even so, think hard. Is there anything you can give us that might help? Anything at all?" Rus pushed.

"I'll think about it. I just…" He dissolved into his chair. "I just didn't know her real great, you know? She was young and had her life ahead of her, and I'm an old piece of shit. She's not gonna hang with me. My boy, he hangs with me. We're men. But to her, I'm just an old piece of shit. You know?"

Oh, he knew.

"You keep thinking and you tell us, Mr. Iverson, if you think of anything."

He nodded and looked beyond Rus.

"It wasn't you, son. I'm just a piece of shit," he said to Jace.

"It's okay," Jace murmured.

Rus turned to Jason and jerked his head to the door.

They both walked out.

"You don't take that on," he ordered the minute the door closed them from Iverson.

Jason's jaw bulged.

He felt someone approaching, but repeated, "You don't take that on."

"Take what on?" Bohannan asked from behind Rus.

"Look at me," Rus said to Jason because his attention had gone to his dad. "Did you hear me?"

"Yessir," Jace replied.

"She's not yours, she's mine. Did you hear that?" Rus pushed.

"Yessir."

"Say it."

Jace's Adam's apple bobbed.

"Say it, Jace," he pressed.

"She's not mine, she's yours."

"You do this work. You know what I mean."

"Yeah," he whispered.

Yeah.

He knew.

"I get it. I do. I'd feel the same as you. But don't let that meat suit in there get under your skin."

"It's tough," Jace admitted.

"I know. He feels guilt, and no matter what kind of person he is, his daughter is dead. He's striking out. Don't let it get under your skin."

Jason nodded.

"I need you to stand down, bud," Rus told him.

His gaze went over Rus's shoulder, again to his dad.

He got it back when he said, "I don't need anything fucking with this investigation. You're good at what you do. That's obvious. Moran deputized you, like this is the Wild fucking West. But it isn't. It's the U S of fucking A, and when we get this guy, you and I both want him going down and staying down. No one fucking it. Yeah?"

Jace's nod to that was stronger.

"Yeah," he agreed.

"Good work," Rus grunted, turned, jutted his chin to a deeply concerned-looking Bohannan, and he started to walk away.

He needed a breath of fresh air, because being in that room with Iverson answered the question that no, that hunting cabin didn't have a shower.

He stopped when he heard, "Yo."

He turned and Moran was coming out of the viewing room, holding his phone.

Rus didn't know him well enough yet to decipher the look on his face.

He walked back to stand with Bohannan, Jace and Moran.

"What?" he asked.

"You're not gonna believe this shit," Moran said.

"*What?*" he bit out.

"Ezra Corbin has skipped town."

They talked to him last night.

Last.

Fucking.

Night.

God.

Fucking.

Dammit.

FIFTEEN

Because I'm Here

"This is impossible to believe."

Sherri Corbin was standing in her living room, staring at them in horror.

"I need your promise, Sherri, that if Ezra gets in touch with you, you'll call us. You find out where he is. You ask him to come home. We need to talk to him," Moran said to her.

"About that girl *who died*?" she demanded.

"Yes, he's a person of interest," Moran answered.

"This is unbelievable," she hissed.

"I'm sorry, Sherri," Moran said.

She looked up to Rus, to Moran, back to Rus then she stormed to a window and stared out of it.

"You sure he's left?" Moran asked.

"I've only sent fifteen texts and called seven times, no answer. Not one," she said to the window. She whirled to face them. "His entire suitcase set is gone, half his clothes are gone, and he took *twenty thousand dollars* from our joint account. *Twenty thousand!*" she screeched.

"Sherri, please calm down," Moran said soothingly.

"You calm down, Harry. For God's sake, my husband is gone, he

123

stole from me, because I made that gol darned money, Harry." She slapped her chest. "*Me*. He's always got some business deal he's cooking up, but nothing ever comes of it. He's always wining and dining investors, out golfing and schmoozing. And he's wanted in connection with a murder! Of some young girl!"

Rus had to admit, that was worth screeching.

Little did she know he wasn't out golfing, at least not every time.

He was out getting his ass fucked and his cock swatted, among other things.

"We're going to be monitoring his credit cards. His phone." Moran dipped his head to Rus. "We've already got the FBI on that. We'll find him, but it'll be better for him if he comes in on his own."

"Did he kill her?" she asked.

"We just want to talk to him," Moran answered.

"You think he killed her."

"We just want to talk to him, Sherri."

She leaned toward Moran and snarled, "This is *insane*."

She was right about that too.

"I'm so sorry," Moran said, and it was genuine.

Moran wasn't getting to it, but someone had to.

He was the outsider, so it was going to be him.

"Do you have a family computer?" he asked.

Her chin went in her neck. "Who has a family computer anymore? We both have laptops."

"Did he take his?"

He could tell she didn't know with the expression on her face.

"It would also be helpful," he kept at it, and her attention focused again on him, "if we could get a DNA sample for Ezra."

Moran made a noise, but he didn't intervene.

Her eyes closed.

Slowly.

Yeah.

She was understanding what was happening.

Rus felt for her.

She was pretty. Curvy, and held it great. Fantastic hair and skin. Wore a close-fitting dress that hugged her curves like she was as proud of them as she should be. It was Saturday, late afternoon, and she looked stylish and put together.

Rus had things he liked in bed that maybe some women might not get off on. If you were honest with yourself, most everyone did. It wouldn't be fun if your wife told you she thought it was sick.

However, Ezra could have said that to Thea, and never breathed a word of what he needed to his wife for fear of losing her, her money and their lifestyle.

They'd run him, and he had no real job to speak of. His LinkedIn profile said he was self-employed with a business that offered "wilderness conference planning."

They had a really nice house. Definitely top of the line everything.

Ezra had been the expansive man of the house last night. King of his domain.

But it wasn't his domain.

It was hers.

If she scraped him off because she didn't want to explore his kink, considering it didn't sound like he was a real winner, his domain would shrink to nothing.

Yeah.

Rus could see that lie.

They should warn her it was going to get worse. They should warn her the cheating would come out, and the kink, if he did it.

Now was not the time to warn her.

Now was the time to get her on their side.

Moran was good at his job, and he knew this.

That was why he said gently, "Just call us, Sherri. I hate this is happening, but we need your help."

"Harry, you will be the first call I make if that jackhole gets in touch," she shot back. "And that's a promise." Her attention returned to Rus. "Now, I'm gonna go look for his laptop. What do you need for this DNA?"

It had been an up and down day.

And fortunately, that was another up.

"NO, man, she didn't seem distressed. She seemed happy. Excited. And no, I didn't see anyone meet her in that room. I didn't even see a car pull in the parking lot. Like I told all the other guys, she was totally cool."

The desk clerk from the motel, who was again working that night, was talking to Rus and Moran.

He wasn't done.

"I'm serious. At first, I thought she was meeting someone she really liked. Then, when no one showed, I thought, well maybe she just needs a break. You know, like one of those staycations. She's in there giving herself a facial or something."

"How many people from Misted Pines take a staycation at the Better Times Motel, Brad?" Moran asked.

The day getting to him, his sarcasm was biting.

"You know, it's quiet here," Brad snapped. "Our business is matinees, man. That's when it gets noisy, all those cheaters fucking during their lunch hour so they can go home to their husbands and wives after work. At night, it's smooth. The stars come out really bright. Our pool doesn't suck. It's kinda nice. Maybe a family that doesn't have a ton of cash to drop on the Pinetop or the Hideaway stays. But they're not noisy. Their TV might be loud if they bring a Roku, 'cause our cable here is always on the blink and the walls are like paper. But I'm serious. She was hot. I wouldn't lie. I want you guys to find out who snuffed her like everyone else in town does."

He put his hand on the desk, and the look that came over Brad's face made his stomach turn sour.

Like all the rest Brad had just said, he didn't hesitate to unleash what was on his mind.

"I mean I'm sittin' here, my thumb up my ass, while some hot chick is being killed seven doors down. You think I've slept, man? No. Not since that night. Not a fucking wink."

That had to be true.

His eyes were red-rimmed and shadowed.

Rus felt for him. That would haunt him too.

Brad kept talking.

"You think I haven't thought over and over, what did I miss? Why didn't I look out, see if she got in the room okay? See if she had someone in her car. Did I forget someone pulling in? Did I nod off? No. I didn't. I'm a night owl, man. *Fuck*."

"Okay, Brad, we believe you," Rus said consolingly.

"Just find this fuck, okay?" he bit off. "I might sleep again, you find this fuck."

"We're doing our best," Moran assured him.

"Right," he muttered. "I don't wanna be a dick, but shit, man. I need this job, and I wanna quit. I park at the back and walk all the way around on the outside so I don't have to go by that crime scene tape. It's fucked up."

"We just need to be thorough," Rus told him.

"Yeah, I'm gettin' that. Shit."

"Thank you for your time, Brad," Moran said.

"Okay. Yeah. Whatever."

Rus and Moran looked at each other and turned to leave.

Something made Rus turn back.

"All the other guys?" he asked.

"What?" Brad asked back.

"You said, 'all the other guys' you talked to. What guys?"

"Your guys," Brad said.

"Specifically, who?" Rus pressed.

"The deputy guys that day she was found. Then the FBI guy, same day. Then the deputy guys came back again the next day to tell me to keep quiet about it. Then the Bohannan twins showed. Then that guy yesterday."

Rus went solid and his neck started itching again.

To his knowledge, no one had been sent to re-interview Brad.

"What guy yesterday?" he queried.

"I don't know. He was dressed like the FBI guy." He tipped his head to Rus. "Nice pants. Blazer."

"A reporter?"

"No."

"You sure?"

Brad suddenly looked unsure. "I don't know. I didn't ask."

"Did he show you credentials? A badge?"

Brad started getting pale. "No."

"Are you certain it wasn't a reporter?" Moran questioned.

"I…do they have to tell you they're reporters?"

"They don't, but they should," Moran told him.

"He didn't say that, and he didn't show me a badge. I just assumed, you know, with the questions he was asking. It was about, like, you know…*he knew*. I've been following and the press doesn't know dick, seems to me."

The itch got stronger.

"He knew? He knew what?" Rus asked.

"He knew…you know…"

Now Brad was uncomfortable.

"We don't know," Rus pushed.

"He knew, you know, what Gentry knew."

Gentry, the maid.

"What does Gentry know?" Rus asked with forced evenness.

"You know, the plastic, like, it was ritual and stuff."

No one knew that.

Except the cops.

And Gentry.

And apparently, she told Brad.

"Gentry isn't supposed to be talking," Moran pointed out.

"I know, man," he bit. "But, see, she and me are going through it. We can't talk to anyone. So who do we talk to? Ourselves. Okay? You gonna arrest me for trying to get some fucking sleep? Or Gentry, because that shit was fucked up, man."

"No, we're not going to arrest you," Moran assured.

"Goddamn," Brad muttered.

"Please, if you speak to anyone else, ask to see a badge if they say they're law enforcement, or ask them to identify if they're press, and what outlet they work for," Moran requested. "But mostly, don't talk to anyone unless it's someone you know for certain you should be talking to."

Moran lifted his hand to Rus, Rus knew what he was asking, pulled out his wallet, got a card and gave it to Moran.

He took out his own and walked them to Brad.

"You have questions, you either call Special Agent Lazarus or me, directly," Moran instructed. "We don't pick up, you call the sheriff's office and talk to Polly or Wade Dickerson. Okay?"

"Yeah," Brad mumbled.

"What did this guy look like?" Rus asked.

"Older than you. Close cropped hair. Took care of himself. Not as tall as you. A little pudge. Not much. He was fit, for an old guy. But not as fit as you. I mean, he didn't look like an action film star. He wasn't a fucking Henry Cavill look-alike, you know, like you. But he was clean-cut. I thought he was a cop. No, I thought he was FBI."

"White?" Rus kept at him.

"Yeah."

"Dark hair?"

"Brown. Like, not light or dark. Just brown, going gray."

"Facial hair?"

"Yeah, a mustache."

"Eye color?"

"I don't know. I thought it was weird, he was inside the lobby, it was around this time, so it was dark, and he never took off his sunglasses."

Jesus, *shit*.

That itch came stronger, but with it there was a mild bolt of a thrill.

"Rus," Moran murmured questioningly.

"Can you do me a favor and write down everything you remember about the guy? Call me, I'll swing by and get it. Give it to me and me alone. Okay? Everything you remember."

"You're freaking me out, man," Brad warned.

"I'm just being careful. You want to be careful too, for Brittanie, don't you?"

"Yeah. 'Course."

"It doesn't mean anything," Rus lied. "Just being careful."

"I can be careful. I work tomorrow night. Come by and get it. Cool?"

"Yes. Thanks, Brad."

"No problem," he mumbled.

They moved out to the cruiser.

They were in, Moran had started up and they were moving out when Moran asked, "What was that?"

"What would you do if someone stole your art?"

A silence so total, it felt like it was an entity filled the car.

Moran broke it. "You think the Crystal Killer talked to Brad?"

"I don't know." Yes, he absolutely did. "I think it's a possibility."

"Brad's right. We're getting calls. We've had reporters come in. They've been antsy for information. But days have passed, and that's died down. We haven't given them anything more. We've been putting them off. The details have not been published. Which means Gentry and Brad might be talking to each other, but so far, it hasn't leaked. So how does he know?"

Rus turned his head to look at the sheriff.

"He knows, Harry, because I'm here."

Moran didn't take his eyes from the road as he said, "Fuck."

SIXTEEN

I'm Not Scared

I t was good that Lucinda was so damned smart.

He thought this as he walked into his quiet, well-decorated, relaxing room, flicked off his shoes, shrugged off his blazer, clicked on the fireplace and went to the bar.

He saw the red wax of the hotel-bar-sized Maker's Mark, and he tore into that fucker.

He'd be sure to pay for it himself when he checked out.

He poured four fingers into a glass, walked to the couch and collapsed to his ass.

He took a sip.

He stared at the fire.

He took another sip.

He stared at the fire some more.

He wondered if he'd have enough energy when he was done drinking to make it to the bed.

He then realized he hadn't had a thing to eat since the food Lucinda arranged for him.

Which meant he was smirking when he pulled out his phone and checked it.

Text from Acre, *I'm alive. I'm stocked. But if you're feeling generous, don't hesitate to send condoms.*

As ever, reading that, Rus was wondering at the wisdom of making himself a safe place for sex talk with his son. He didn't want him to do anything stupid, like get a girl pregnant or get or give an STD.

But…

Jesus.

Text from Sabrina, *Going to bed! Love you, Dad!*

And there was his girl, all grown, and she still texted she was going to sleep.

Better than Maker's Mark.

He still took another sip.

Then he texted them both, sending his love.

Next up, text from McGill, *Alerts in place. Credit cards. Airports. Etc. His cell is off. But we're on him.*

He hoped Corbin either came in or screwed up, and he hoped he did one of them soon. He wanted the man's ass in jail. He wanted to know who his partner was, because Rus knew he went to that motel with a partner, someone who called the shots.

He wanted this done.

And if CK was there, he wanted him to have reason to get out of Misted Pines.

Whoever caught that case when Rus did whatever Rus was going to do next could find him somewhere else.

Text from Bohannan #1, *Appreciate you. What you did with Jace. Won't forget it.*

That came in before the text from McGill.

Text from Bohannan #2 came in after it, *Harry called. I'm going over the file again tonight. I want to tweak my profile with this new possible. Larue wants you over for dinner tomorrow. Doable?*

He texted back, *Doable. Give me a time and see you then.*

Then he went back to the text that came after Acre, but before Sabrina.

Text from Lucinda, *I'm sorry I zoned out like that with you. I already*

knew it was something bad, or you would have told me. If you want, call me
when your day is done.

He was tired as fuck.

But he didn't hesitate.

He went to her name, hit info, hit her number and put the
phone to his ear.

He drank more bourbon and stared at the fire.

"Hey, Rus," she answered.

Not all better, but her low, husky voice in his ear sure helped.

"How you doing?" he asked.

"Better. Um...I don't know how to tell you this, you might
already know, but I sense I'm kind of your local touchstone, and I
feel it's important for you to know, so I'm just going to tell you.
Rumor is flying you guys are searching for Ezra Corbin."

"We are, though I didn't know rumor was flying."

"His wife, apparently, is beside herself."

That was true.

Rus took another drink.

Then he said, "It's been a day. I had three hours of sleep. And
you know what?"

"What?"

"It sure felt good coming back to this room."

Soft laughter.

Damn, he'd like to see that. He'd had a few smiles, no laughs.

But it sounded good.

"I grew up in a cult," he announced.

"I...pardon?"

She sounded stunned.

As she would.

"My name," he began. "I grew up in a cult. It was a Christian cult.
When I was two, my dad was in a car accident. He died, or his heart
stopped, for about a minute. They brought him back, and when he
recovered, he was different. At least that's what my grandparents said,
my aunts and uncles as well. He went on about all that white light
business. Said he saw Jesus. Got hooked up with this guy who was off,

but he had a following. A pretty big one. It wasn't anything weird. It wasn't Koresh or Jim Jones. But it wasn't mainstream either, and it was insular. Very insular. Take away the polygamy, adding books to the Bible and women dressing in outfits from the eighteen hundreds, and it was kinda fundamental Mormon. In other words, intense."

"Well, wow," she said carefully.

Her response didn't sound promising, but he kept sharing.

"Women were definitely quiet, subjugated. But everyone did what the elders told you to do. Dad was an elder. The head preacher man, Richard, was the top authority and essentially told the elders what to do. He said Jesus brought Dad back from the dead. He used Dad a lot in his sermonizing. It was him who changed Dad's last name to Lazarus. Dad did it legal for him, Mom, all of us. The name I was born with was Sawyer Wells, but I was too young to ever remember being that kid. They changed my first name, and my brothers' names too. Because Pastor Rich told them to."

"That's quite a story," she said quietly, not in a *Christ, you're fucked up* way, but a *go on* way.

That was a relief.

He went on.

"When I was eighteen, the only means I had to get away and feed myself, I enlisted in the Army. My ex, we went to high school together. For three years in school, we were together, dated, but my parents never met her because I wasn't allowed to be with her. They'd picked a girl for me from our church. Arranged marriages, now, that was a thing."

"My God."

That was a *Christ, that's fucked up*, but still a *go on*.

He again went on.

"Yeah. Jenn saved me from that. She was normal. Her parents were great with me. They got it. They helped cover for me. Helped cover for me to do normal high school kid things. Helped cover for my brothers too. One was older, one was younger. Obadiah was older. He was getting close to being married off. He was flipping out. He didn't want to get married at twenty to a girl he didn't like. He knew her, had grown up with her. And I agree. She wasn't a good person. That didn't matter. What Pastor Rich said, went."

"This is…"

She didn't finish that.

"A lot, I know." Rus finished for her.

But if they were going where he wanted them to go, she had to have this in order to make the decision if she wanted to go there with him.

So he kept giving it to her.

"Jenn's parents let my brother live in their basement, got him a job. When he fully cut ties with the church, he changed his first name back to what he was born with. He changed it to Lucas."

"Okay," she said, talking softly, like she was snuggled in, listening.

This time, *go on* meant *I'm interested in learning about you.*

This was a relief too, and it felt good.

"I went into the Army. Our church was pacifist. Mom and Dad cut out Lucas. When I went to basic, they cut me out too. Jedediah, he kept his name, but not like I did. He changed it legally to Jeb, which is what we all called him when we weren't around the church members. He got out too, with Lucas's, Jenn's parents' and my help."

"So, none of you talk to your parents anymore?"

"Not for a while. Jenn and I married at nineteen. Lucas got married to his first wife at twenty-two. Jeb was engaged. Mom was hearing stories. She was pissed she was missing out. I'm not sure she bought into the whole thing anyway. But she loved Dad and she was glad he wasn't dead, not only because she loved him, but when he had his accident, she had two little kids, and one on the way. At first, I figure, she was happy to do anything as long as it made him happy. But she used to do things like sneak us sweets or a pop when we weren't allowed processed foods. Or we'd fake feeling sick to get out of going to church, and we went to church Wednesday night, Saturday morning, Sunday morning and Sunday evening, and that's a lot, and she'd back our play. She'd take us to places where we could watch TV, since we weren't allowed to have one at home. Shit like that."

"She broke free?"

"She told Dad it was her and her boys, or the church. There was some push and pull, but he picked her. And us."

"That's good."

It was.

Very good.

"It took a while. Lucas, particularly, had an issue and he wouldn't let go of it. He didn't have a Jenn to go to so he had some normal. He was pissed Mom and Dad knew he didn't like the girl they were marrying him off to, and Dad was adamant he go through with it. He wanted to play football. They didn't believe in organized sports."

Rus took in a breath and then kept giving her some of the shit of his life.

"Mostly, they didn't believe in members spending time outside the flock. For kids, if you wanted physical activity, you worked for one of the church members' businesses. For free. Even if it wasn't about physical activity, if you weren't in service to the church, starting at thirteen, fourteen, you worked for someone for free. Lucas is a financial advisor now. He has money, about twenty rental properties. Even when he was a kid, he'd fight with Dad, wondering why he was busting his ass to make someone else money. And asking Dad questions, like how someone made money off Lucas's back, then they gave it to the church. Asked him why Pastor Rich had a ten thousand square foot house, we were living in a two-bedroom, and Pastor Rich drove a Mercedes, and Mom and Dad shared a Chevy minivan. And yet, Dad managed three branches of a local bank and made six figures."

"These are good questions."

She was right.

They were.

"Pissed Dad off because he didn't have good answers. Once the reconciliation happened, it was a rough go, but it got better with time."

"So everyone is together now?"

"Yeah. Mom and Dad live in a house bigger than the one we grew up in. Mom's happy. I think Dad's a little lost, mostly how he gave twenty plus years of his family's life to that, and now he's seventy and that time is just gone. He eventually saw it. We had a family meeting. We decided it was too much of a pain in the ass to change our names back to Wells. All the wives would have to change. Lucas had a daughter by then. Jenn was pregnant. So I'm Zachariah Lazarus, but secretly, I hate it. It sounds made up because it is. That's why I like Rus. I gave that to myself. Simple, and somehow, it's just mine."

"I get that. And I like the name Rus. It's very you, and not because it's simple. Just open and honest and modest. Definitely you."

Nice.

"That was a lot," he noted.

"I don't know. My many-greats grandmother was essentially human trafficked, ended up in a whorehouse slash saloon at fifteen, in a fur trading town in the middle of nowhere. At seventeen, she shot her pimp because he was an asshole and then took over his girls. And we've stayed in that business, for the most part, for over a hundred and thirty years."

"Somehow, your back story seems more normal than mine."

And he got the soft laughter again.

"I abandoned my wife for my job."

There, he did it again.

"Oh, Rus," she whispered.

"I did. You get caught up in it. I was away from home a lot. She had a job too. Made good money and to make good money, there's stress. And she had the kids. And the house."

"Did you get what your dad got? The ultimatum. Your job or her?"

"I came home to her fucking some guy who looked like me in our bed. I knew the minute I saw them I'd never be able to get over it. Thing is, she didn't ask me to."

Lucinda said nothing.

Still, he agreed, "Yeah."

"That wasn't nice," she snapped.

"She warned me."

"She warned you she was going step *in*, that being in your bed with another man?"

"Not in those words, but I knew she was unhappy. But I was working a big case. I would have let a lot of people down if I walked away from it, as she'd asked me to do. And I was a soldier, then a cop, then an agent. What am I going to do? Become a PI? Consult for one of those firms that do hideous shit but pay a lot of money, so I have a boat, but I can't sleep at night? Give up the field for a job teaching, which might kill me?"

These were good questions.

Because now that he knew he was getting out, what was he going to do?

He had two kids in college, for fuck's sake.

They'd saved, but he had condoms and bikinis to buy.

"No, you do what you love. You do what you're good at. And your wife finds a way."

"There's gotta be compromise, baby."

"Says who?" she retorted. "Sure, if you lose your whole family because you placed them in a cult and made five people live in a two-bedroom house, you think on things. You marry a soldier, who becomes a cop, who goes into the FBI, you know what's happening."

"You're only defending me because you like me," he teased.

"I do like you, Rus. But I'm defending you because, even if you grow apart from your husband, even if the way your life became is not something that makes you happy, you walk away. You don't fuck another man in your marital bed for the sole purpose of causing pain to someone you at least used to love."

Rus stared at the fire.

"I can't believe she cheated on you. *You.* My God," Lucinda said in his ear. "What a bitchy thing to do."

"She was hurting."

"So she hurt you?" she asked. "Jaeger and I were drifting apart.

I have a problem. I'm a strong woman who likes men. Quote-unquote *real* men. Like it or not, it's not progressive or current or hip anymore, but for me, it's the way it is."

Jesus.

That was good to hear.

"What can I say?" she asked rhetorically. "I grew up in a fucking wilderness around men in trucks who chop logs as recreation and bathe in freezing cold creeks like they're Jacuzzis. It's what I know."

Now Rus was staring at the fire, sipping bourbon and smiling.

"Or maybe it's just what I like," she continued. "Sadly, this type of man, for the most part, is at odds with the woman I am. This, too, is a generational flaw. Mom and Dad divorced because Dad couldn't deal with being home with me and Porter while Mom was managing the business. Gramps was hilarious, and he loved Gram a lot, she loved him too, but after they had Mom, they didn't live together. They got together often. But they didn't live together. So I fell in love with Jaeger. We committed to each other. I realized we weren't going to work, and we sat down and worked out how not to be together. We don't hate each other. We talk. We even call each other and catch up. I don't talk to him all the time, but I know what's going on in his life, and he knows what's going on in mine, and a lot of that doesn't have to do with Madden."

She paused.

And then she said, "What I didn't do was get pissed when he said he got a job offer in Oregon where he'd be getting paid a lot more, and he wanted all three of us to go. And I refused, because, you know, seven generations of Bon Amie, I'm not walking away from that. I've been waiting to get my hands on it since I could form coherent thought. When he dug in, I didn't get angry and find some guy and arrange for him to discover us fucking. One, because Jaeger would have torn his head off, and I'm not a big fan of blood on my sheets. And two, because that's just nasty."

"Gotta say, you're pretty funny when you're off on one," he ribbed.

"The point is, Rus," she huffed out in exasperation. "She made you feel guilty for being you, then she did something really awful, and for some reason, you think you deserve it. When you don't. Ezra deserves someone being really awful to him. As far as I know, you don't. Though, maybe your ex does."

There was a warmth in his stomach that had something to do with the bourbon.

But mostly it was her.

"Did I mention I like you?" he asked.

"Yes."

"So, in case you didn't put this together, me landing all of this on you is to lay it out because I like you."

"Yes, Rus, I put that together."

"Not scared?"

"Honey, I'm Cher with less makeup and no plastic surgery and a lot better head for business. And you're asking me if I'm scared?"

"What?"

"Have you seen *Burlesque*?"

"Your show? Yeah, I caught it last night."

"No, the movie. With Cher and Christina Aguilera."

"No, I haven't seen that."

"Of course. On second thought, it doesn't strike me as something you'd rush out to see," she murmured.

"Is it good?"

"Have you heard Christina Aguilera sing?"

"I think so."

"It's good. Even Jaeger liked it, and I thought his eyeballs would melt if he watched it."

Rus started chuckling. "Let me guess, he chopped wood for recreation and took baths in creeks."

"I still have wood he chopped, and he's been gone for two years, and I have three fireplaces in my house."

At that, Rus burst out laughing.

"Can you chop wood?" she asked.

"There's an art to it. I found that out when we were in Colorado for a vacation and we rented a house. But I got the hang of it. It's not neurosurgery."

"Or catching a killer."

That felt warm in his gut too.

"That either, baby," he said quietly.

"Let me be clear, I'm not scared."

That felt the warmest of all of it.

His voice was rough when he said, "Good."

"You can make your move at any time, but apparently, I'm coming to Cade and Delphine's for dinner tomorrow. My guess, either Cade or Harry said something, and Delphine is match making. So, you know, I probably wouldn't say no to after-dinner drinks in your room."

He was smiling, but uncertain, when he replied, "I'll bear that in mind."

"Or wait until you're ready," she said gently.

"I got a killer to catch, honey."

"I know."

"How's Madden?"

"Sleeping now. We got word Brittanie is finally at the funeral home. We're thinking Tuesday or Wednesday for her services. Probably Wednesday. Maybe, after that, Madden will have some closure and a sense of peace for Brittanie, and she'll have fewer dark times. We lost Gram about a month after Jaeger moved away. This isn't her first loss. But you never get used to them."

"No, you don't."

After that, they talked a little while longer, they didn't get into anything heavy, and by the end of it, she sounded sleepy. He knew he was, so they signed off.

He finished his drink, turned off the fire, went to the safe and got one of his guns, ambled into the bedroom and set it on the nightstand.

He had just enough energy to strip to his shorts and brush his teeth.

Then he got under the fluffy duvet, arranged the pillows so they were perfect for his head, and fell into a dead sleep.

SEVENTEEN

Hawkins

R us slept until he woke naturally.

Which meant he was out of bed at nine seventeen, feeling refreshed.

He put on clean running clothes and managed the trail five times before he headed in.

He was stopped by an employee who asked, "Would you like breakfast sent up now, Agent Lazarus? Maybe pancakes today?"

This being how they knew yesterday when to send up breakfast. Lucinda had them on the lookout for him.

He suppressed a smile, popped his earbuds out and requested, "Could you give it half an hour? And you pick, but something healthy."

Lucinda had been correct. He was a meat and potatoes man, and if he could eat that with the addition of peanut M&Ms and a variety of pies and cookies, that'd be awesome.

But his body needed additional nutrition.

He went to his room, did his sit ups, added some exercises for his obliques, then planks, mountain climbers, a few burpees and ended on his pushups.

After that he took his shower.

He was shaved and in jeans and another long-sleeved tee when room service showed.

That day, coffee, granola, fruit, yogurt, toast and cold-pressed juice, something, at a taste, he knew had apple, ginger and kale.

He did not pull out Brittanie's file.

He didn't open his laptop and check email.

It wasn't that Sundays were rest days. He'd had one lifetime of that, and now he didn't let anyone tell him what to do with his days.

It was that he learned, sometimes you needed to step away from a case in order to see that case.

If you immersed yourself too fully in it, you missed things.

This had worked for him when he'd found the father who'd abducted his daughter, then killed her, because, for some fucked-up reason, that was preferrable to letting her live with her mother.

And it had worked for him when he'd found another guy, who'd grabbed his girlfriend and her little sister, because he'd gone off his meds, and he'd holed up somewhere with them and no one could find them. Until Rus found them.

And it had worked for him on a serial rapist case, and another serial murderer, both who he'd help stop before they'd notched too many victims on their lists.

The only time it hadn't worked for him in an intricate or intense investigation was CK.

His mind had been taken up by the music he listened to while exercising.

But now, eating, with nothing but the view of mist on the lake and clinging to the pines to take his attention, he let everything crash in.

Was he right with what his gut was telling him about Ezra?

What were they missing? What drew Brittanie to that motel?

Who was Ezra's partner, and was he wrong to think there was one? Is this guy a guy who could have acted alone?

To-do list material:

Circling back to Thea for names of her colleagues who did the "more extreme" stuff. Running through them to see if Ezra made contact, and possibly finding his partner. Ascertaining for certain

Thea knew what was coming and advising she plan for it if she was outed for what she did for a living when all of this went down. Intensifying the search for the one missing boyfriend they hadn't found, and ruling him out...or in. Following up with his team on Brittanie's bank statements, cell and laptop.

He gave time to wondering about how Jace was holding up.

And more to what he'd do next since he'd made the decision to leave the FBI, and rethinking that decision since he had responsibilities.

He had five years before he could officially retire.

It was lunacy to quit now.

But if he requested it, could he be reassigned to the Seattle office?

Which of course brought to mind the sound of Lucinda's laughter, and her defense of him.

Which further brought to mind something he'd never thought about because he'd convinced himself, or maybe Jennifer had convinced him that he owed her something.

She'd saved him from the cult. He'd told her that more than once. He'd been grateful for her love and support, also her parents', and he'd shared that often.

But that didn't mean she owned him or his time, like Pastor Richard thought he did.

He now worried he'd gone from thinking that was what he had to give to one entity in his life, then, maybe out of habit, he gave it to another.

But it was fucked up what she did. She knew he was coming home. She knew when.

And she was fucking some guy who looked like him precisely so he'd walk in on them.

He thought that was on him because she told him it was.

But it wasn't.

What Lucinda said made sense.

It was on Jenn.

Now, they were over. She'd moved on. But they shared kids, and he did not call her to shoot the shit and ask what was going on with her life because, for the most part, she acted like she was entitled to be a bitch to him because he'd betrayed her.

When it was the other way around.

Rus had emotion around this. He was pissed about it, and the significance of that anger, he had an urge to tell Jenn he was feeling it.

However, at this time, he wasn't sure it would serve any purpose.

What needed to work for their kids worked, and he should let it go.

Further, he wasn't certain even if he shared she would rethink what she did. That was how deep she was in feeling she was warranted in her actions, which was part of why she'd done such a bang-up job of convincing him this was true.

But the fact remained, if she was done with trying to make him the husband she needed, she should have walked away.

Instead, she did something else, and it was Rus who'd been holding the weight of that, not Jennifer, and it had started digging under his skin.

And last, what was on his mind was the fact he was relatively certain CK was in Washington, and what that meant about how closely he monitored Rus's movements.

By the time he'd decimated his breakfast and sucked back the dregs of his juice, he'd sifted through all of this in his head, which meant he was able to set it aside.

He then made a plan for what was next for his day.

He called down to have the valet bring his vehicle around.

He grabbed his phone, his wallet, his credentials, pulled on a sweater and attached his gun to his belt.

He was not a gun person, even though he had to be.

And since he had to be, he made a point of knowing how to use it.

He was at the range a lot. He worked toward marksmanship awards, and had won a few. He scheduled time in the simulations. He took care of his weapons. And he did all of this solely because it was part of his job, and should he need to use his firearm, he wanted to use it right, and if he or his colleagues were in danger, he didn't want to miss.

He did not own a personal firearm. He had only the two issued to him by the Bureau.

Though, when he was fully out of the game, he'd purchase one. He'd put enough people behind bars not to own one. But much more importantly, he knew how deadly a gun was, he respected that, and he'd own one responsibly.

During investigations where it was unnecessary for him to carry, he didn't. The higher-ups weren't thrilled with his choice, and leaned on him, but not too hard, because he produced results.

But it was Rus's experience it intimidated witnesses.

He did not need to sit in Lucinda's office with a gun at his hip while he talked to her staff. He needed them to open up and share. He needed people like Sherri to give him DNA. He needed people like Thea to trust him with information that was a threat to her livelihood. And along his journey in law enforcement, he'd learned carrying a gun did not help any of that, and in some instances hindered it.

Many cops thought a gun gave them authority or was an indication they held it.

Rus was of a mind, either you naturally had authority, meaning you knew what you were doing, and you could communicate that to people along with the fact they could trust you, or you didn't.

And if you didn't, then you shouldn't be in the job.

If you needed a gun as a prop, rather than what it was—the very last tool you had no choice but to reach for in an urgent situation—it was a prime indication you had no business being a cop.

But the possibility of CK being close, he was going to carry.

He walked out to his SUV, drove into town and parked close to Aromacabana.

He got a coffee and sat outside on a chair that looked purchased at a yard sale, cleaned up, painted and set outside on the wide sidewalk next to a small table and another chair, neither matching, both also probably bought at a yard sale.

Rus then did what he'd been meaning to do since he got there, but he didn't have the time.

He took in the town.

He'd driven through it a half a dozen times, and first impressions were, it was Mayberry.

There was no McDonald's. There was no Starbucks. There was an old movie theater that had one screen. There was a diner that looked stuck in the fifties, and it was called the Double D, so it probably was. There was a five and dime, and Rus hadn't seen one of those since he was a little kid.

A flower shop that had buckets of colorful blooms on the sidewalk under its front window.

A greengrocer, which also displayed its goods out front.

It was idyllic.

It was Americana.

It seemed safe and quaint and perfect for a weekend away from the big city, even though a girl was murdered five miles away in a motel where people daily broke their marital vows.

Even though it was a place where men still cheated on their wives regardless that, a year ago, four of them from this town had been nationally humiliated. This leading from an eight-year-old being brutally murdered in a way even Rus couldn't finish the report, and as mentioned, he wasn't squeamish.

Not to mention, the town's foundations had been built on usurping Native land, killing animals for their coats, and otherwise raping its natural resources, all while fifteen-year-olds were pimped at bordellos.

And Rus felt all of it.

The seedy underpinnings that, no matter the coats of paint you slapped over it and coffeehouses you opened in it, never faded away.

It wasn't the nostalgia of Mayberry.

It was the nostalgia of Hawkins in *Stranger Things*. Where, beneath it, every horror you could imagine was seething, working constantly at finding an opportunity to make it to the surface, and if that didn't succeed, as was the case for Brittanie, pulling you under.

Rus took a sip of his excellent coffee, thinking, fuck him, that was what made him perfectly comfortable sitting right there.

He'd never want Mayberry.

He needed Hawkins.

He was Hopper, knowing no matter what he did, life was going to suck, but doing what he could to fix it anyway.

He could see himself buying flowers from one of those buckets and taking Lucinda's shit when he gave them to her, all while monitoring that coven, because he knew they were up to something, and it might start innocent and supportive and about the sisterhood, but in the end, it would be no good.

He took another sip wondering if Moran needed a full-time detective.

Rus didn't want to wear another uniform, but he did want to do the work.

And fuck it, so he was only five years away from full retirement.

The Crystal Killer could be done playing with him, walk up to him sitting right there, and shoot him in the face.

Life was too fucking short.

His father was miserable because, not only the best years of his life, but the best years of his wife's, he'd squandered. They had money because they both still worked. Their retirement bought one-hundred-percent wool carpet for Paster Rich's living room, put gas in his Mercedes and paid for his timeshare.

Rus liked it here, a whole lot better than the choked-with-people hassle of the East Coast.

He'd be far away from his kids, but they didn't have to rely on telegrams to communicate.

Misted Pines seemed a magnet for some seriously bad shit.

So they'd need a good detective.

On this thought, he went for his gun and nearly spilled his coffee down his sweater.

Because, getting the drop on him in a way he'd never share that shit with anyone for the rest of his goddamned life, was a round woman wearing a headband made of those stick-on bows you put on presents, a sweater that had rows of the same down the front, with snowman earrings dangling at her ears.

She threw herself in the chair across the small table from him.

She stuck her hand his way.

And said, "Heya, I'm Kimmy."

Shit.

EIGHTEEN

Justice for Brittanie

"**D**on't look scared, I'm not going to talk about Kennedy," she said as encouragement for him to shake her hand.

It wasn't much, but he shook her hand, and he found it interesting she knew but didn't care, someone had warned him about her.

"You're the Fed," she declared when he let her go.

"And you own the holiday store."

"Cin told you about me, eh?"

She seemed proud.

So he felt safe to nod.

"So, you know, the town's buzzing," she informed him.

"I've heard a few things," he replied.

Apparently, that was her indication to launch in, because that was what she did.

"I didn't know her, my granddaughter did, and she said she could be a bitch."

She stopped speaking and put her hands up in a *Don't Shoot!* gesture, maybe due to his expression, since he knew she was talking about Brittanie.

"Her words. Not mine," she continued. "I asked my girl why. She said, 'She's a maneater, Gran.' I asked, 'What in the dickens does that mean?' She said, 'She steals people's boyfriends. That's not right.' So I said, 'You mean, she's providing a public service.' And she was all flustered. 'What do you mean, Gran!' And I was all, 'Well, if your man's head is turned by a pretty face, then you best be knowing that while he's your boyfriend, and not later. So it seems to me she's helping the female population by showing these boys for who they are before a girl gets her heart broken.' She saw the wisdom of that, I think."

"That's an interesting take," he said.

And it was.

"I got a lot of those," she told him something he already knew. "You a Christmas person?"

"Not in September."

She waved a hand in front of her face. "Oh, don't worry. I've moved the Labor Day stock out, and the fall and Halloween stock in. It's not all Christmas all the time."

Her green and red and bow-festooned outfit said different.

"Good to know."

"I don't know Ezra either. I just know Sherri. She's a holiday person."

That tracked.

"Always thought she could do better, though," Kimmy continued. "No clue why. Now I know."

He gave no indication what she said interested him, and asked casually, "You know what?"

"That girl? Murdered at the motel?" She gave an impressive fake shiver.

"He's only a person of interest," Rus lied.

"He did it," she declared.

He agreed with her assessment.

Nevertheless.

"It wouldn't be good for anyone in this town to sidestep due process."

"Yeah, you gotta worry about that, but I can have whatever opinion I want," Kimmy retorted. "I don't know him, but it's a small town. I've seen him. He's a bum wearing nice clothes because his wife can afford them. He checks women out when Sherri's not paying attention. But he doesn't bother to hide it when she's not around. I mean, when are men gonna learn? Bobby offed himself in his garage, for heaven's sake."

"Bobby?"

"Lana's dead husband. Not gonna say rest in peace for that guy. I've seen more of that man than is healthy." She dug into her pocket, presumably from what she said next, for her phone. "You seen the videos?"

He knew exactly what she was talking about now, and as such, his voice sounded clogged when he answered, "Yes."

She read his tone. "Mm-hm, you bet. Anyway." She stood. "I need a coffee. I need a brownie. And I need to open my shop. I open late on Sundays."

"Smart to give yourself a day to sleep in."

"Agreed. Good luck to you, Agent."

"Thanks, Kimmy."

She wandered into the coffeehouse.

Rus took a sip of his drink, not knowing whether he felt ambushed or privileged.

He looked up this time before she got too close.

"Agent," she said.

She was tall. She was attractive. She knew it.

She reminded him of Lucinda, but her edge was cool and cutting, where beyond the veil of Lucinda's, there was nothing but warmth. The obstacles you faced to get to the heart of this woman were barbed. The ones to Lucinda's were clever. You had to take time and put effort into figuring out how to maneuver them, but they didn't cause pain along the way.

"Hello," he greeted.

"May I sit?"

"Sure."

Although it wasn't exactly welcoming, she took his invitation and sat, carefully aiming her very nice ass to the seat while holding her takeaway coffee.

"I'm Lana," she introduced.

He'd just heard her name.

She explained how he knew her even though he already knew.

"I'm Malorie's stepmother. Malorie Graham."

Dead girl number two for Ray Andrews.

And Lana was the ringleader of the posse of wives who'd obliterated their husbands.

He sat up straighter, saying, "Nice to meet you, Lana."

"I don't want to take up a lot of your time, but I feel you should know, there are rumblings. Some people are demanding a town council meeting where they want to force Harry to explain what's going on with what happened to that woman at the motel."

Shit.

"Thanks for telling me."

"I understand you all have to do what you have to do how you have to do it. I mean, I know much more than others how there's a certain way to go about these things. But the town has some post-traumatic stress. That isn't on Harry. It's on Dern. Our last sheriff."

"Right."

"Still, that kind of thing doesn't fade away. It was only about a year ago that…"

She didn't finish.

"I know," he said low.

She took a breath into her nose, and it came off as a supercilious sniff, but he knew it wasn't.

She was reliving something hideous, talking to him.

Still, she was taking the time to do it and it said a lot about her.

"If they call a meeting, I'll come and explain that it isn't exactly in that woman's best interest for the police to share every little thing they're doing. I don't know if it will help. We have a lot of characters in this town. But most people are normal. Rational. They'll listen to logic and back down."

"That's good to know."

"Also, what Ellen did is not okay."

Right then.

She was taking the time to address all of it.

And he wondered if Lucinda was wrong for once, because Lana knowing what Ellen did just yesterday morning wouldn't suggest she was out of that group.

"They were very angry when they found out about the murder," she carried on. "Ellen is more…" She searched for a word. "*Militant* than the others. They heard about what happened to Brittanie Iverson, and obviously, as anyone would be, they were shaken."

It seemed he now had the opportunity to learn more about this coven, and Rus didn't squander opportunities.

"I've been hearing a lot about your friends," he noted leadingly.

She was not a woman to be led.

"Wendy is my friend," she corrected. "And I like some of the others quite a bit."

In other words, not all of them.

More words than that, she and Wendy talk, but she's not one of them.

"There's a reason, or many of them, why they're all where they are," she shared. "You'll never understand because you are who you are."

"A man," Rus deduced.

She tipped her head to the side in a, *clearly*.

To return her favor, but more, to win her trust because she was a woman you wanted on your side, he said, "I'm here right now to get a bead on this town, the town where Brittanie lived, and maybe where her killer lives. And I'm here to take a break. I've made some decisions based on information and gut. I've been immersing myself in Brittanie's life. I need to shake it off. I need to hit it tomorrow with clear eyes and a fresh perspective."

"You don't have to explain to me."

"Yes, Lana, I do, and since you're one of the few people in this town who deserves that explanation, you know why I do," he said quietly.

She looked away.

And the name hung between them.

Malorie.

"The town is going to do what towns do," he told her. "Wendy and her friends are going to do what they do. This makes no difference to me. I know what I need to do, and I'm going to do that no matter what anyone else thinks I should be doing."

She returned her attention to him. "They're harmless. Wendy and her friends. They've been hurt. Badly. Misery loves company, for some."

He nodded even though he wasn't sure he believed her.

Then again, Lucinda said something about how groups of women were intimidating, even if they were just hanging out together.

In the past, groups of women wore white and burned bras for rights, and hashtagged their solidarity by announcing their membership in a club they'd been given no choice but to belong to.

Men who gathered had put on hoods and burned crosses, and cut a swath of terror through entire states. And that shit still hadn't gone away, with more male collectives pulling up gaiters and putting on khakis and taking to the streets to claim rights they already had in abundance.

Maybe it was Rus, who lived the ideals of a father who wanted to belong to something that gave more meaning to life, who was hanging his damage on people who didn't deserve it.

Then again, the word "militant" never gave him warm feelings.

"I won't judge the whole by the one I encountered," he promised her.

She nodded, lifted her coffee to him in salute, and said, "I hope you find justice for Brittanie soon."

With that, she got up and strutted away.

But he agreed with her.

He hoped so too.

He finished his coffee leisurely, because so far, it'd been useful sitting out on the sidewalk in Misted Pines.

He had some people walk by who paid attention to him, dipped chins or even said hello.

But Kimmy and Lana were his only new acquaintances.

So when he was done with his coffee, he went in and bought a few things to have in his room should he get peckish and to take to the Bohannan's.

He then strolled down the street to buy some flowers for his hostess that night, Delphine.

NINETEEN

Born This Way

E arly that evening, Bohannan sat Rus down in his office with a beer and the door closed.

Delphine had been thrilled with the cookies and the flowers, and he'd been reminded that she wasn't just a world-renowned author.

In a former life, she'd also been the star of a sitcom Rus had not been allowed to watch when he was younger.

That was a wild life trajectory, but he knew of wilder ones.

In other words, she was beautiful and outgoing and friendly, and right off-the-bat, very funny.

He met Bohannan's daughter, Celeste, as well.

She was pretty, sweet, shy and would be the perfect foil for Rus's ballsy, knows-what-he-wants-and-goes-after-it son.

He stopped coupling off his kids with locals, which would bring them closer if Rus followed through with moving out here, when Bohannan got him a beer and led him to the office.

He'd asked Rus to come early because he wanted work out of the way so they could enjoy dinner without CK hanging over their heads.

Rus was at one with this idea.

That said, first things first.

"Christ, man, what devil did you make a deal with to score this house?"

Bohannan smiled.

He was right on the lake. His view was even better than the one from Rus's hotel room, which was only about a seven-minute drive away, down the mountain and around what he had a feeling was Bohannan's property.

And it was a compound. There was a tall, sturdy fence that disappeared into the woods and a gate with a call box you had to use for them to buzz you in, unless you had the code, which Bohannan did not give to him.

Rus wasn't slighted. If he had this setup, he'd have to be a lot tighter to those he gave access to as well.

"My ancestors founded the town," Bohannan informed him. "We got this land, probably by taking it."

Well, that explained that, though Rus was struck by the coincidence that he was dealing closely with two people who had deep roots in an area of the country that was almost as far away from Plymouth Rock as you could get.

Guess if you found what you liked, you didn't move away.

Bohannan was studying him.

"You getting ideas?" he asked.

"I like it out here," was all Rus was ready to say, not that he didn't feel like sharing with Bohannan, just that he wasn't ready to say it out loud.

"It'd be nice to have a brother here, in that way," Bohannan replied.

Rus had to admit, that felt good.

He knew from friends who were agents who had been reassigned, if you went somewhere new, especially at his age, it wasn't easy to develop a social circle. Those had all been established years before, and although you could be invited in, you still always felt like the odd man out.

Including in your new bureau.

And this could be even tougher on spouses.

Unless retired FBI agents made a habit of ending up here,

Bohannan and Rus would be the only ones who shared that bond.

"And it'd be good Cin had a man whose balls didn't get in the way of his brains," Bohannan finished.

He couldn't be any clearer about his opinion on that.

"But that's out of turn," he muttered, still watching Rus closely.

Rus liked the guy, so he gave it to him.

"Not really. You, or Harry, called it as it is. We're talking. I know Lucinda's coming tonight. But she knows I need to focus on the case. When it's done, though, I've made it clear I want to keep getting to know her. And she's receptive to that."

"Glad to hear it, she's a good woman."

"I know. So it's a compliment you feel we might fit."

Bohannan jerked up his chin, and Rus felt relief they were off that subject when he watched Bohannan put his hand flat on the fat case file that shared the trail of torment of the Crystal Killer.

"I can't say I disagree with what the profilers said about this guy," Bohannan started it. "Malignant narcissist gone off the rails. The staging, at first, was an act of intimacy for him. He feels emotion for them. Not in any way we understand, but they mean something to him. It continued in that bent, but he started to clean their faces when you came on board. He did this as a gift to you. To show you what good taste he has. To show you when you walked in what his power was, but when you saw them from the front, that was what he worked with. The beauty he owned, until he was done with her. And he wanted them to look beautiful for you too."

Rus nodded.

He'd heard all of this before.

At least all of it before the last part, which was something that turned his stomach.

"I also agree with the profilers that the notes he left, too short for them to establish a language pattern, not too short not to have meaning, were definitely for you. He knows you're investigating him. Though I don't agree they're important."

This was new.

"They dismissed the crystals, and I think that's a mistake,"

Bohannan asserted. "Those are how he's really communicating with you."

Rus felt a tightness hit his shoulders because he'd always thought the same.

He'd researched crystals until he got a low-key stress response if he saw a New Age shop.

But he couldn't put his finger on why he felt they were important, other than he knew his suspect didn't do anything throwaway.

It was all important.

Rus wasn't the perp, or a profiler, so he didn't know how it was important.

Bohannan continued.

"Case in point, victim number four. He put a malachite in her hands. Malachite is known in those circles as a protection stone. Also healing. Balance. They blew it off because they didn't feel it pertained to him, where the other stones seemed to have some connection to the perpetrator. They thought, when the message changed, they were headed down the wrong path, reading too much into it. It was just a calling card, the stones selected at random. He's proud of what he does, and he wants his victims linked. Or it was a way to throw you all off, send you down the wrong path, away from him. I think…"

Bohannan stopped talking, and the sense Rus had as to why made him move his head side to side on his neck, because all of a sudden, his shoulders got so tight, they caused pain.

"I think that stone, and all the ones after, were for you."

He didn't get it.

"He wants to protect me?"

"Bear with me on this, Rus," Bohannan urged. "I was feeling this when I first worked the file, but the fact he might be in town makes me believe it. And the other profilers who worked this case did not have that to work with. You and him, traditionally, are adversaries. Adversaries can admire each other, but they're still adversaries. I don't think it would enter any profiler's head what I'm about to say when you have a suspect like the Crystal Killer."

Rus braced.

Bohannan gave it to him.

"The way I read it, he thinks you appreciate what he does. He sees you as a connoisseur of his work. He doesn't consider you a fan. Or a protegee he's grooming. He considers you a collector. He thinks of you as a kind of soulmate."

Bohannan shook his head while saliva filled Rus's mouth.

"That's not the right word," Bohannan said. "He thinks you're the only one who appreciates the work he puts into what he does, and since that's important to him, he's inflated what your relationship really means. Once you came on board, he stopped being frustrated that people didn't get the beauty he created. He convinced himself somebody understood. And for that, you are very, very important to him."

"You gotta know, that skeeves me way the fuck out, Cade," Rus growled.

"It would me too," Bohannan agreed. "But breaking it down, it makes twisted sense. No one, not even him, is more intimate with what happened in those hotel rooms. No one, but you. You've spent days, months, years on his work, and he's not a well man. It's easy for him to feel, or more, convince himself you're enjoying, even relishing what he does. He doesn't even spend that much time on his victims. By that I mean what he does when he kills them. He definitely spends time choosing and finding where he's going to kill them. Covering his tracks along the way. I'm sure he takes pictures and relives what he's done. Even so, I'd lay money on the fact you've spent more time on what he's done than he has, and he knows it."

Yeah, it was twisted.

But it made sense.

Bohannan kept going.

"Running it down, victim one had a Carnelian. This denotes energy and ambition. It's thought of as a source of creativity. Protection from adversity. His beginning."

Rus nodded.

He knew this too, more than he wanted to know it.

"Crystal two, Chrysocolla. More energy. More creativity. But also wisdom. Self-expression. Crystal three, Tourmaline. Again, creativity. Grounding in the present moment. Protection against negativity. These are all for him. Victim three is when you enter the picture. And then there's victim four, with the Malachite. Victim five held an Obsidian, which is also for you. Protection, but also it guards against attack."

Rus was well acquainted with all of this as well.

Though he never considered it was for him.

"This was a shift in meaning," Bohannan noted. "It could be about him worried he's going to get caught. But that's off-profile. He's confident. Not a man to worry. So that's why the profilers began to doubt the crystals meant anything."

That was exactly why.

"Victim six, rose quartz," Bohannan stated. "This is often equated with love and relationships, and that threw the profilers way off. That, as you know, is when they completely gave up on the crystals. Because, for the most part, this is meant between lovers. But it's also about caring and compassion and connecting on a more profound level. It has connotations of finding your inner truth. By this victim, he feels that's what he's establishing with you."

"Jesus Christ," Rus bit out, feeling a cold creep into his blood, because this made sense.

Too much sense.

Bohannan dipped his head understandingly, but he kept talking.

"The last victim, he's reaching out to you. Pink Halite. Unconditional love. It provides a shield against people who would hurt you. Now, I don't think this love is physical love. He's not homosexual or striking out against the world because he is and doesn't want to be. He doesn't have issues with his parents. He wasn't bullied. He doesn't have psychological wounds that have abraded away the tools every human needs to live harmoniously with others. He's genuinely mentally ill. He was born this way."

And again, Rus had heard all of this.

Bohannan carried on.

"He lives his life. He might be married. He's good in bed, loving, giving, demonstrative. He feels he takes care of his victims. He feels they're privileged to be of service to him. So he's going to take care of his wife, his partner. And if he's in a relationship, he truly loves his partner, or he does in how he understands that emotion. He might be so deep into this, and we know he's smart, so he could also be manipulative and convincing, both traits of a malignant narcissist. So she could know what he's doing and approve of it, allowing him to go out and make his art. But bottom line, you mean something to him, Rus. And I don't think he's here in Misted Pines to protect his work. He's here to protect you."

The fuck?

"What's he protecting me from?" Rus demanded.

Bohannan shook his head. "I don't know. Someone wasting your time and valuable skills on something undeserving of both. Maybe he fears for your safety because this is a wildcard. The good news is, my take, and I could be wrong, he would never hurt someone you care about. He would not cause you pain. He'd never hurt you, not directly. You mean too much to him. Honestly?"

Rus nodded again.

"I think you could retire, and he'd back that play. He might even go so far as finding something new to do so he'd have a new agent to impress and connect with, because that is now deeply involved in what he needs to get out of his scenes. His new crimes would be so different, no one would ever know. The cases would never be connected. He'd start all over again. And the Crystal Killer would just fade away."

This did not sit well with Rus.

Not at all.

Which was why he demanded, "Are you shitting me?"

Bohannan shook his head.

"This is very convenient, Cade," Rus remarked.

"Think of the life trajectory of a narcissist," Bohannan suggested. "At the end of his life, he's either used up everyone who loved him, and he's totally alone. Or he's left with only those he's groomed, usually since birth, his children, but also there are partners he's either conned, and they fell into his web, or they came to him with such low self-confidence, they put themselves in his hands. But one way or the other, he's had plenty of time to demand their unconditional love, no matter his behavior, and that's all they know, so they give it. Or he selects the chosen few to cover in his love, smothering them with it, so they become addicted to it and mirror his behaviors by giving that back to him."

This was definitely the case of a narcissist, so once again, Rus nodded.

And Bohannan kept going.

"But it's rare he has any true friends. He's usually driven away his family, at least those not directly connected to him. Now think of a narcissist's pattern with relationships. He discards people who have no more meaning to him, usually those who have figured him out and call him on his shit. He picks up new ones who don't know just how disturbed he is and convinces them of how amazing he is. He then becomes obsessed with them. They're everything. They're perfect. They fulfill his every need. Until his flaws show, and they point them out. Then these new people are cast aside, and he always casts them aside, even when they break things off with him. He convinces himself he's the one in control of it being over. The other scenario, they fall so deep under his spell, they're his forever."

Again, all shit Rus knew.

Bohannan had more.

"Now think of a narcissist who feels he's finally found his equal. He has no flaws, and his equal doesn't either. It's impossible. No one is as smart as he is. No one is as anything as he is. This is a miracle, to finally find a true connection. To finally find that one person alive in billions who appreciates you just as you expect to be appreciated, and he returns that."

The cold hadn't stopped creeping in, so now Rus was fighting the need to shiver.

"But it makes sense," Bohannan continued. "You aren't competition. You aren't going to turn the eye of his wife. You aren't going to earn the love of his children. You aren't going to go out and rape and murder women. You aren't going to call him on his day-to-day bullshit. You aren't going to take anything he has. And he wants nothing you have. And you can bet he looked into everything he could as to your accomplishments. He knows how good of an agent you are. He knows they sent the best to find him. And he's not going to destroy someone as good at what they do as he is. He admires you. It would be a sacrilege. It would be like destroying himself."

Bohannan's gaze became hyper-focused on his.

"There may be one person he'd put it all on the line for, Rus, and that's you. And yes, what I mean by that is, if he's here, there might be one window of opportunity for you to catch him, and that's now. When he's making himself vulnerable to protect you."

Rus sat back in his chair, whispering, "Fucking hell."

"Another guess?"

Rus needed it, but he didn't want it.

Still, he jutted his chin at Bohannan for him to give it.

"He's a tall man with close-cropped brown hair and a mustache. He didn't appear to Brad like he usually does, in a disguise. He went to Brad as just who he is, not only to ascertain what on the face of it seemed too close for comfort. A young, beautiful, blonde woman murdered in an out-of-the-way motel that didn't have security cameras, something that drew you to the scene. But he was definitely there because your presence indicated that something was fishy, and it pertained to him. He knew you'd go back to Brad. He knew you'd go back to that motel."

Bohannan's chest expanded with the massive breath he took in.

And when he let it out, he lowered the boom.

"For the first time, no disguise, he was there as the man he is to say hello to you."

TWENTY

Pumpkin

"This is humiliating," Jess muttered.

"That's two hundred dollars, Jesse!" Madden crowed.

Jesse handed her the one hundred and fifty dollars of Monopoly money he had left. Then he flicked the top hat piece off the board, plopped back into the sofa in defeat and declared, "I'm out."

Madden giggled.

"You're vicious, and I think that dice is weighted," Jesse accused on a tease.

Madden giggled again and cried. "It's your board!"

Jesse cracked a smile. "Oh. Right. Well, whatever. When you own all of Misted Pines and I'm late on rent, remember what a good loser I was."

Madden burst into gales of laughter.

Rus grinned at Lucinda at the same time wondering if this might be a good read of the future for Madden, successful Misted Pines tycoon.

Lucinda smiled back, knowing it was.

They'd been playing Monopoly for an hour and a half.

Rus had purposefully lost half an hour ago, not a difficult feat since the Bonner women were relentless.

However, he did this because he wasn't into board games seeing as, when he was growing up, not allowed TV or a ton of other activities kids should be allowed to do, they played a lot of board games.

Now, he hated them.

Since Jesse was out, the only ones left were Lucinda and her daughter, both with huge piles of money in front of them.

Obviously, Lucinda had brought Madden for dinner, and Rus was pleased she did.

He was because Madden had lost Brittanie, and more than usual, she needed her mom. Also because Rus loved watching them together, seeing as they were so damned cute. Last, he knew it was Lucinda's indication she was putting no pressure on him to take what was happening between them further when he had other things he should be thinking about.

And her understanding his need to focus meant a lot to him.

Oh yeah.

And, since she brought her daughter, he'd learned the important fact she was insanely competitive, so was her girl, which was important to know.

"Call it a draw?" Lucinda asked Madden.

Madden brought her hands up in front of her and twiddled her fingers together, a move akin to what Rus had seen her mother do a couple of days ago.

"No, we're in it until the bitter end," Madden announced.

Watching this, Rus thought Disney had missed the boat.

They shouldn't have been focusing on the singing, dancing fairy princesses.

They should show young girls how awesome it was to be the cunning queen.

On this thought, he felt something strange and looked to Delphine, who had her eyes aimed at the kitchen.

The expression on her face told him what he'd see even before he peered over his shoulder to follow her gaze.

Jace had opted out of the game but had hung with them until he'd wandered to the kitchen with his dad, after Bohannan had done what Rus had done, and successfully lost early.

Jace was now walking out of the kitchen toward the doors to the back deck, Bohannan with a face full of worry watching him go.

That night, Rus had found it surprising they'd all known Delphine for what amounted to a short time, considering she was so close to Celeste, it seemed she was her mother. And she doted in a loving, shovel-a-lot-of-shit way on Jesse and Jason, which also appeared like she was the proud mom of two grown men.

Part of Rus's job was to get a bead on people and places. But if he'd walked in this house with no information, he would have told you Bohannan and Delphine had been married for thirty years and had three great kids.

Delphine being perfectly in tune to what Bohannan was right then perfectly in tune to said it all.

Rus shot Lucinda a look, glanced through a concerned Celeste and Jesse, who had his eyes to the back door and a muscle jumping in his cheek, both of them clearly having decided to give Jace space, and made a decision.

He rose from his chair.

"Excuse me," he murmured.

He took his beer and headed outside.

The air was chill in that wet way that made a little cold seem biting.

Jace was on the end of the back deck, staring into a heavy fog, which clung to the lake so thick it almost cloaked it, and it encroached toward the house, so all Jace had to do was step off the deck and he'd disappear in it.

Rus came to stand next to him.

"That's a lot of fog," he noted.

"Hot springs," Jace replied. "In the summer, smooth as glass and you can see from here to the other end of the lake, which is a hike. Minute it gets cold, though, the warm off the water hits the air…" He took a drag from his beer, swallowed, and explained, "Misted Pines."

Absolutely Misted Pines.

"That's got to be a lot of hot springs," Rus remarked.

"That's what everyone says," Jace replied. "The good, we could swim right now, and it'd feel like summer. The bad, mist hides shit, so if they drained this lake, the bottom is probably covered end to end in bones."

Another indication of the lore this town carried.

"Harry told me there were stories," Rus shared.

"Yeah. He tell you of the buried treasure?"

Of course there was buried treasure.

"Nope, he failed to mention that."

Jace jerked up his chin.

"One of our ancestors buried it somewhere close to here. Jesse says we should take a break, go hunting for it. I'm not in the mood, but it'd be good if we found it. Honest to God, people these days are so fucked up, it's a wonder we're not always chasing assholes off our land who are obsessed with finding it."

Treasure hunting was a big deal, so that *was* a wonder.

Though the gate and fence, and the three very serious-looking men who lived on the property—because he learned that night Jace and Jess had homes on it, in other words, the Bohannan compound was a true compound—might have something to do with keeping people away.

"DB Cooper is a big thing up here," Jace declared, seemingly out of the blue. "They have festivals and conventions. This guy was carrying a bomb, he hijacked a plane, probably scared the shit out of the flight staff, demanded money, then disappeared into the night. After that, they made him a folk hero. Said he stuck it to the man. Like that money he demanded, and got, wasn't taxpayer money. I mean, the people were the ones this dick stole from, and somehow, he's twisted into a hero so big, decades have passed, and people are still obsessed with him. They admire him, wear T-shirts with the artist's rendering and have podcasts talking about him. When, bottom line, he's an asshole and a criminal who put people in danger solely for his own ends."

Rus couldn't argue that.

He didn't know why Jace was talking about it, but he couldn't argue it.

"I hope, when he jumped, he slammed right into a mountain,"

Jace said. "Died right there. Not only because that'd serve him right, but because it'd serve all those morons right to be obsessed with a dead man who didn't get away with shit."

And Rus couldn't argue that either.

He was worried Jace had brought up Cooper because many also twisted killers into heroes, Ray Andrews being one. Not a hero, as such, but the guy looked like a male model, so he had a cult following.

Jace had been close to that case too.

And maybe Jace was upset that would be what would happen with who killed Brittanie.

Jace pointed the bottom of his beer bottle into the mist.

"We found Malorie out there, tied to our dock."

Yeah.

Ray Andrews was on his mind.

Since Jace felt like talking, Rus settled in, crossing his arms on his chest, his beer on the outside.

And he said nothing.

But he knew what Jace was talking about now.

Ray Andrews had come to Misted Pines to play with Cade Bohannan and Malorie was a pawn in that game.

So Rus knew where they found her.

"She wanted to move in together," Jace said.

All right then.

That wasn't Malorie.

That was Brittanie.

And here we go, Rus thought.

"We'd only been seeing each other a few months. It was too soon. She was talking that and hinting marriage. I liked her. But we were nowhere near something like that."

"Okay," he said low to encourage Jace to keep talking.

"We got in a big fight when I put her off. I don't mind fighting, but she was quick to get pissed, so it happened too much. And you can't force a man into making a move like that."

"No, you can't," Rus agreed.

Jace slugged back more beer.

Then he said, "Honestly, I didn't wanna break up with her. She was funny and sweet. I liked her a lot. But I wasn't ready for that, and she wouldn't let it go." Long pause, then, "It got too much. So it was me letting her go."

Just like most men would do.

Rus got to the meat of it.

"I can say it a thousand times, and you won't get it until you get it, still, I'm going to say it. You couldn't have stopped what happened from happening."

"I know," he whispered.

He did, and he didn't.

But Rus felt one day he would.

"I don't get why she went to that motel," Jace muttered. "It's not her. Like, her biggest dream was to take a vacation in LA and stay at the Beverly Hills Hotel. She was all about spas and room service. She said she wanted to have a vacation where, for a while, she got to live like Marilyn Monroe. Just stay in bed for days and days and read and watch TV."

"Sounds like a good vacation."

"Yeah," he grunted, and took another drag from his beer.

"I gotta warn you, we might never know why she went to that motel."

"Yeah," Jace repeated, and finally, he looked to Rus. "It's killing me, man, not being out there, finding this guy."

"I know."

"I know how she died."

Shit.

But of course he did.

Rus uncrossed his arms so he could clamp Jace's neck where it met his shoulder and squeeze, but he said nothing.

"You don't have to worry about me," Jason assured. "I have my shit tight now. I know, if I find him, I'll fuck this."

"Right."

"I just don't know how to live with knowing how she died."

"You'll learn how to live with it when you understand you'll never be able to live with it. That's the difference between men like you and monsters like the man who did that to her." Rus gave him another squeeze and removed his hand. "I'm sorry, Jace, you will never come to terms with what happened to Brittanie. But you will come to terms with knowing the fact you can't is a good thing. And that will get you by."

Jace's demeanor changed to one that was a great deal less concerning.

"Thanks for being honest about it. Delly's all about healing, and if she keeps making me cupcakes, I'm gonna get a gut. Celeste thinks she can love away everything. But…" he blew out a breath, shaking his head, "it's kind of a relief to know it'll never go away. Not that I want to hold it. Just that I don't feel like a freak, knowing I'll never get over it."

"You're not a freak," Rus asserted.

Jace nodded, turned to the mist and took another draw from his beer.

Then he said, entirely to himself, "This year, she's gonna get my whole pumpkin."

Rus had no idea what that was about.

What he knew was it wasn't his to have.

So he didn't ask.

He just stood at Jace's side in the mist and drank beer.

TWENTY-ONE

Pearl Buckle

R us was back in his room, his shoes off, the fire on, his gun on the coffee table, and the last of the bottle of Maker's Mark in a glass in his hand.

Maid service had left what he hadn't finished, but also replaced it with a new bottle.

He'd be sure to give them a big tip because he knew, by the time this was done, he'd be obliged they kept on top of his bourbon.

He'd left the Bohannans and driven across town.

This meant he'd just returned from the Better Times Motel after getting Brad's written account of the man who questioned him about the killing.

He'd also given Brad a pep talk and shared the powers of meditation, melatonin, valerian, warm baths, aromatherapy, Zzzquil, no electronics or television an hour before sleeping and psychotherapy.

Barring all that, he shared, if he had the time, he'd be happy to sit down in the Double D with the guy, buy him a meal and have a chat so he could have someone he could talk to who understood where he was coming from.

Brad had seemed relieved by the simple fact someone gave a shit.

Rus didn't know if that'd help him sleep, but at least it was something.

He sat in front of the fire with his bourbon, reading Brad's account, noting it didn't have much more than what Brad had told him and Moran.

Of note, Brad thought it was weird the guy didn't stand too close. He entered the lobby, but he stood a good three, four feet away from the desk Brad was behind.

That and the fact he didn't take off his sunglasses, even if it was night, were the two big things that struck Brad.

He also was knowledgeable about the crime and as confident as a cop.

All things that would fit CK.

Rus believed Bohannan's take on the situation.

There were some who would argue, but not many, that the man was the best there was, possibly ever, at what he did.

But also, it all made sense.

He could see why CK didn't take his sunglasses off for Brad.

He might be ready to say hello, but after four years in the shadows, Rus could understand he'd still hold something back.

He tossed the paper on the coffee table, and no other way to put it, began brooding as he sipped bourbon and stared into a fire.

It wasn't a question. It wasn't a decision to be made.

It was a given that now, not only did he have to find Brittanie's killer, he had to lay a trap for CK.

He just needed to figure out how the fuck to do that.

He also needed to report this to his superiors tomorrow.

Good news, he liked Misted Pines, because he was probably going to be there for a while.

On that thought, one of the reasons he liked Misted Pines so much vibrated on his phone.

He took the call.

"Hey, honey," he greeted Lucinda, at the same time, in the back of his head, he began wondering if he should tell her why he was there.

Which meant CK might be there.

It would upset her, and maybe scare her.

But if he wasn't wrong, they were starting something, and he didn't want to start it by keeping anything from her.

Not something this big.

"Hey," she replied. "You seemed okay I brought Madden tonight."

"More than okay. You got a great kid."

"I know. She likes you."

"I like her."

"Of course you do, she's perfect."

He chuckled.

She said, "You were good with Jace. He seemed better when you guys came back in."

"I hope so."

"It was incredibly attractive, you doing that."

He smiled. "It's good you think that."

"Right, now that I've buttered you up, Britt's funeral is set for Wednesday and Tuesday night, they're calling a town council meeting."

Fabulous.

"This happens, Lucinda," he told her. "People get freaked about murder. It's a natural response."

"You can call me Cin, you know."

That felt better than her telling him she found his being a decent human being attractive.

Even so.

"Baby," he said softly, "everyone else gets Cin. I like that it's me who gets Lucinda."

"Mm," she purred, and he felt that noise in his cock.

"The cunning queen," he murmured.

"Sorry?"

"You remind me of the queen that's a lot more interesting than the fairy princess."

And that bought him the gift of her bursting into laughter.

He was unsurprised it was as beautiful as the rest of her.

When she stopped, he said, "Now, before I take us into a zone that's too soon when I haven't even bought you dinner, tell me about some of the bones at the bottom of the lake."

"Ah, so he's heard the lore," she murmured.

"People have mentioned it."

"That's because it's fascinating," she declared. "I can start with the fact that the man my many-greats grandmother shot is down there. Sadly, her and all the girls dragging him to the lake after she shot him was witnessed by everyone in town. Alas, her shooting him was too. She apparently wasn't in the mood to put too much effort in covering up her crime."

That made Rus laugh.

"What do you want to hear next?" she asked. "The story of philandering Cornelius Ruck, who, shades of things to come, was killed, along with his mistress, by his wife. Or at least, that's what people think since she was seen rowing into the mist in the middle of the night, and he and his mistress were never seen again? Both of them still haunt it, as the story goes."

"This is entirely unsurprising."

"Then there's the lore of the Bohannans, and warning, you fit right in. Prosper Bohannan was the big muckety-muck who made his mark on this town, including running the competition for my granny's whore-house. But there's both an Obadiah Bohannan and Lazarus Bohannan in that mix. Spoilers, the big daddy was all about making his fortune any way he could, including illegally. But Obadiah and Lazarus were both lawmen. So, apparently that's more foreshadowing for Misted Pines."

Rus chuckled.

"But my favorite is Pearl Buckle."

The change in her tone made him get as serious as she sounded.

"What's the story of Pearl Buckle?" he asked, his tone changing to match hers.

"Pearl trundled into town with a baby at her breast, two horses in front of her, a covered wagon at her back, a mule attached to it, and a husband who didn't survive the journey. She staked her claim, pupped her tent, cleared her land, set her own foundation and built her one-room log cabin on top of it. It wasn't big, but it had a fireplace and a roof, and she did all of it with her son strapped to her back."

Jesus.

"She sounds like she was really something."

"Yes," she agreed. "But the story says she was even more, because not only did she do all that, the tale tells she was also very beautiful. Every man in town wanted her, and most of them tried to woo her. But she loved her husband. She grieved him fiercely. And she'd vowed to herself she'd raise his son right and be faithful to her dead husband until the day she died."

Rus wasn't feeling this new bent to the story.

"Since we're talking about bones at the bottom of the lake, I'm not sure I like where this is going," he noted.

"Oh, honey, this is Misted Pines. Pearl built her own house out of logs with the help of only two horses and a mule. At first, she was this feminine beauty, this marvel of female strength, this prize to be won. And then men started avoiding her, because there were those who would get drunk in one of the saloons in town and talk big. Talk about how they were going to win Pearl, and if they didn't, they'd just take her. They'd head out to Pearl's log cabin. And they'd never head back to town, or anywhere, ever again. I might have forgotten to mention, Pearl had a shotgun, and she wasn't afraid to use it."

"I'm liking this story again now."

He heard the smile in her voice when she said, "The story goes, even though Pearl was a good Christian woman, regardless of her proclivities with a shotgun, Granny and her were the best of friends."

Rus was smiling too when he replied, "I don't find that hard to believe."

Lucinda finished the story with, "Pearl built her house close to the lake. I have a feeling she added a few things to it in her time."

As any good Christian woman whose virtue was threatened should do.

"Reckon so."

They talked longer. Lucinda telling him stories, Rus listening, sipping bourbon, gazing at a fire.

When he let her go, he took the final finger he had in his glass and walked out onto the balcony for the first time.

The chill of the night was now deep, the lake covered in fog so thick you couldn't see it, the mist creeping up the mountain and clinging to the pines like shrouds.

Pearl Buckle made it in those woods. As did Lucinda's granny.

And after what she'd lost, Lana was still standing, buying coffees and frosting anyone who looked at her, hiding the loving and considerate woman she was inside.

Prosper and Obadiah and Lazarus and Cornelius might have made their marks on the town, but these woods were there for the women.

Rus tossed back the last of his drink, then returned into the room, checked the locks on the door, turned off the fire, undressed, brushed his teeth, got under the duvet and arranged his pillows behind his head.

He then took his cock in hand, closed his eyes and called up Lucinda's sultry voice telling him stories.

It wasn't her voice that made him come, it was other thoughts about her.

But they were good thoughts.

So when he came, he did it hard.

TWENTY-TWO

On My Way

T he next morning, after his workout and shower, Rus was dressed and sitting at the table, finishing breakfast, his laptop opened in front of him.

He'd called in to headquarters and his superiors knew of Bohannan's take on things, the mystery man asking questions of a witness, and they, too, felt Rus should take Bohannan's read on the situation seriously.

With the real CK possibly in the mix, they wanted to send more men.

Rus pushed back on that.

He had a friend he could call who the FBI would be okay being brought on as a consultant, and he and his colleagues would blend in.

That way, CK wouldn't feel like Misted Pines suddenly was filled with G-men, get spooked and take off.

So he asked for approval, was told to wait for the sign off, and then he texted Moran to arrange a meet up that included Bohannan so they could go over this new situation and make a plan.

He then got back into the case.

During Rus's busy Saturday and not-as-busy Sunday, McGill's people had been filling in blanks.

They had Brittanie's bank records, and McGill had been over them. He summarized what he found, which was nothing, but Rus looked over the statements anyway.

And McGill was right.

It was nothing.

She had a small nest egg, lots of expenditures, and as they knew, Brittanie wasn't one to sit on her cash.

There wasn't anything big going out, nothing big going in, or anything weird at all. Bills. Credit card payments. Debit card purchases at the grocery store. Shit like that.

McGill told them her laptop had finally made it to a tech's desk, he'd cracked the password in about five minutes, and McGill had someone going through it. McGill would send a report and a bulk file with all her email that Rus could look through himself by that afternoon.

They were still waiting for data to be provided from her cell.

Ezra Corbin hadn't pinged anything, something Rus found surprising. The way he ran was a panicked escape. He had twenty thousand dollars, so he didn't have to use a credit card for some time, but he also had a BOLO out on him and his car.

Evading the FBI and all known law enforcement in this state and all the others was not a skill Rus thought he'd have.

Moran's deputies had been out, combing places they knew someone like Ezra might hide, and that had produced zilch, or Rus would have heard about it.

It was too bad Jesse and Jace were out of the picture. They seemed to know what stones to turn in this area.

But even though Jesse might work it and be able to hold his shit, Rus had a feeling they were as successful as they were because they shared a mind. Rus was not a twin so he didn't know how that worked, but he sensed for them it was their hidden superpower.

So, before he headed into town, he needed to get back with Thea and—

His phone vibrated with a call.

He picked it up, looked at the screen, and it was Moran.

"Lazarus," he answered.

"Rus, need you at the station right away."

Rus was already rising from his chair.

"Ezra?"

"No. But I need you here. And fast."

Rus didn't ask any further questions.

He said, "On my way."

And two minutes later, he was.

TWENTY-THREE

Fetish

He was not met by Polly this time when he walked into the station.

Wade Dickerson waylaid him.

"Sheriff's in with her," he said.

Her?

"So's Polly," Dickerson went on. "I'll take you back. But quick brief, she came in and she said she heard it going around town we were looking for Corbin. She said she had a story to tell. I don't know what that is, but Harry wasn't in with her long before he came back out, told me to tell you what I just told you when you got here, and to bring you back right away."

Rus lifted his chin to him, then Dickerson continued following orders and guided Rus to Moran's office.

The deputy knocked twice and waited until they heard Moran call out for them to come in.

"Special Agent Lazarus is here," Dickerson announced. There was a grandiosity to it Rus wasn't thrilled about, but he saw there was a reason for it when he walked in.

She was curved into herself sitting between Polly and Moran at Moran's small round conference table.

She wasn't this way because something had happened. Or at least not recently.

That posture was habit.

Making herself small. Not earning anyone's attention.

She wore an oversized hoodie, no makeup, hair a mousy-brown and pulled back in a ponytail.

She glanced up at him as he walked in and Dickerson closed the door behind him, but she didn't make eye contact and immediately aimed her gaze back to the table in front of her.

He did not like this.

"Rus, glad you're here," Moran said, friendly, familiar, we're-all-buds here, but his voice was careful, modulated and quiet. "I want to introduce you to Shannon. She's come forward to share something about Ezra Corbin."

"Hi, Shannon," Rus said, slowly pulling out the only remaining chair, and with equally slow movements, folding his body into it.

Shannon didn't return his greeting.

Rus exchanged a look with Polly. She was hiding being pissed under a thick layer of compassion that was genuine, but she was still ticked.

He wasn't sure what to do with that.

"Shannon gave us a little of her story, but we asked her to wait to tell us all of it," Moran explained. "We told her we needed you here to listen in too, and we didn't want her to have to share it twice."

Fucking shit.

Not good.

"Right, okay, now I'm here," Rus said slowly. "Shannon, before we start, do you need anything?"

She had an Aromacabana takeaway cup in front of her, he knew, because he'd noted someone there tended to get creative with markers, so all of the cups he'd seen had pictures drawn on them.

Shannon's was no exception.

However, she wasn't touching it.

"No, I'm good," she mumbled to the table.

"Do we need to hurry?" he asked. "Do you have to get back to work?"

"No. Worked this weekend. Today's my day off," she answered.

"All right," Rus said.

He then said nothing else.

She didn't either.

They gave her time.

Eventually, Moran prompted, "Start whenever you're ready."

She pulled in a visible breath, slumped back in her chair, curled even deeper into herself, put her hand on the table and drew a mindless pattern with the tip of a finger, her nail having once been painted a deep blue, but now it was chipped and the polish was nearly all gone.

"Okay, so, like, years ago, I was raped."

Taking her in, years ago would mean, his guess, she was fourteen, fifteen, maybe younger, maybe a bit older, since she couldn't be much more than eighteen right now.

Yes, this was not good.

Rus felt his skin get tight.

"Like, more than once. Like, a lot. Like, by the same guy, the guy I had a crush on in high school, and, um…all his buds."

Rus clenched his teeth, sliding his eyes to Polly, whose face was bright pink, then to Moran, who's lips were thin.

Rus got a lock on it.

"Okay," he said gently.

She rolled her head on her neck. It was an exaggerated movement, but still real, releasing tension, preparing.

They were disappearing for her, she was placing herself not in that room, but in a world all to herself. She had to so she could tell what she was going to tell.

"So, you know, that's what I knew, of, like…*sex*. Because the first time they did it was my first time. And then they kept doing it. So, eventually, they got tired of me, and it was over. But then I got a boyfriend who was real, I mean, not like them, and we couldn't, like, he didn't, you know, we tried things, and it didn't…*work*."

Rus said nothing.

Polly and Moran did the same.

"I mean, unless, you know, he...you know, I told him what I might like, and it weirded him out."

Rus wasn't sure he was following.

Or, more aptly, he was, he just wished he wasn't.

"So, he dumped me," she continued. "And one of my friends hooked me up with a new guy. She said he was perfect for me. We would click. And I liked him loads. But it was the same thing."

A breath and a moment as she remembered losing a guy she liked.

And, "Then he goes off and tells her what it was because they're friends. And she has a big mouth, so she told another one of our friends. Then that friend comes to me and says she's heard, like, there were people who would, you know...like, *do* things for you. And I should...maybe...just try it out to see if that's what the deal is with me. She's pretty cool, and has it together, and she was really mad all the earlier stuff happened. But when she told me what I could do, I got kinda excited."

She paused, stared at her finger drawing, then began again.

"I told her I was. I mean, the excited part. And she said that just proved the whole thing and I had to try it. So I'd know. So I could figure it out from there. She helped me raise the money, 'cause it costs a lot, and we got online, and we did the whole thing. I think, you know, it took so long for it to happen, I thought they just took our money, and it was all bullshit."

Another pause.

More drawing.

The next, she was whispering.

"And then, it happened."

This pause lasted so long, Rus had to say, "What happened, Shannon?"

Keeping her head lowered, she lifted only her eyes to him, and said, "I paid for them to rape me."

Rus's stomach turned over, and he immediately felt sick.

Stranger danger.

She looked back at her finger, which never stopped moving.

"It wasn't what I paid for," she said. "I had a safe word, but he taped my mouth so I couldn't say it, which I would have, but I couldn't. And I didn't pay for that tape, no way, because I wasn't sure I was going to like it, and I wanted to be able to tell him to stop. So...so..."

She went silent and it was Polly who said, "Take your time, Shannon."

Shannon moved in her chair, side to side, like it was a cushion she could get deeper into.

Then she said, "And I didn't want two of them there. And not a woman. No offense to lesbians, but I'm not gay."

Two of them.

Fucking hell, *two of them.*

"Are you reporting a crime, Shannon?" Rus asked, and he was pissed with himself because he wasn't able to take the strain out of his voice.

Again with the looking under her brow at him.

"No. I paid for it. I just, you know, heard you were looking for a guy named Ezra, and she didn't touch me. He did. But she called the shots. She told him what to do. And he touched me. And it was worse than what those boys did. Rougher. Mean. I paid to be raped because I would, they would...they'd rub me and put their mouths on me and make me, you know."

"We know," Rus said quietly.

"So I paid to be raped because my friend thought maybe that was how I'd like it now, and she was right. When he showed, I got excited. But then she pushed him to hurt me, and he was into it, so he hurt me. She pushed him more, and I could hear her doing things to him if he didn't do it fast enough or hard enough or whatever. I heard, you know, like a fly swatter. And he'd jump. And moan or shit. And he took me like...*back there*, and those boys *never* did that, and like, regular too, and she kept pushing him to do it harder and smack me around. And..."

She dropped her head further, stopped drawing with her finger, put her hand in her lap, and finished it.

"And then it was done. I was fucked up when they left. Bleeding and shit. So no, you know, I'll never pay someone to do that to me again. But I did pay. I consented. I just thought you should know, she called him Ezra."

Rus stopped himself from getting up and throwing his chair across the room, but only barely.

He then kicked Moran's boot under the table when he saw his face reflecting that same need.

When he had control, he asked Shannon, "Did you see her?"

Shannon shook her head. "No. It was dark. I was instructed to keep my window unlocked so they could get in, if that's what they decided to do when they came for me. They came in while I was sleeping. He was on me before I knew they were in my place. It was dark. I heard her, never saw her."

"Okay, can you give us the website where you found them?"

A mini-shrug and, "Sure."

"It was important you came to talk to us," he assured her. "I know that was hard, but it's been very helpful."

She lifted her chin to look right at him and asked outright, "With that girl, in the motel, they went too far, didn't they?"

"We don't know," Rus told her. "But maybe."

"He got off on it," she bit out. "Like *big time*. It was *sick*."

Yes, he got off on it.

Because the thing that was missing with Thea was the thing she'd never think to try with him or refer him out to someone else to do.

What he needed was to be told to hurt someone else.

That was his kink.

That was what he was missing.

He wasn't big on the pain, but he was big on inflicting it, and bigger on being ordered to do it.

That was what they did in the motel room.

And either Ezra, or the woman he was with, had a serial killer fetish, or a snuff fetish, and they used CK's MO to cover it up.

Because that was what Brittanie got in the motel room.
And that was why Ezra ran.
Because their play didn't take.
Ezra knew they knew it wasn't CK.
And he'd been found out.

TWENTY-FOUR

Keycard

That evening, Rus was back on the balcony with his bourbon.

McGill had the stranger danger website address, which also catered to a variety of other unusual or intense fetishes, and the FBI would get names, particularly of the dominatrix that accompanied Ezra on their assignment.

Rus had called Thea in, interviewed her again, but just as he suspected, although she knew these options were out there, she didn't know much about them, and she definitely didn't know any Domme who was into that kind of shit.

And although she wasn't a person to vilify what any individual might need sexually, she was infuriated to know anyone's hard limits were ignored.

She agreed with Rus, even if he didn't share names or details, but with what he had given her, Thea declared it was not a service rendered consensually.

It was rape.

However, even upon explaining this, Shannon refused to press charges or name the boys who started this nightmare for her in the first place, which was unfortunately what many women in her situation decided to do.

She wouldn't even name names so Moran would know who he had in his town capable of that shit.

She might look eighteen, but they found out she was twenty-three.

Polly took her away to talk to her about victim's assistance and finding other support she needed.

In the meantime, in the mix of all the comms coming in from people who had hints and tips and information about the motel murder and Ezra Corbin (and Moran hadn't asked for any of this, but Moran told him the phone never stopped ringing), the sheriff's office got a viable call.

Therefore, Rus spent the early afternoon with his gun in his hand, his other gun in its shoulder holster, moving through the woods on a rental cabin they'd gotten word had activity it shouldn't have.

They thought they had Ezra.

Rus thought there was an outside chance maybe they had CK.

They found no one, except evidence likely high schoolers had picked that place to hang and party.

They contacted the rental company, who contacted the owners, and big win for the day: the party place would be shut down.

The last thing they got was, Brittanie's ex-boyfriend came in.

He had an alibi. He was gone for the weekend, camping with his new girlfriend, and he was with her last Wednesday night when Brittanie was killed.

He also was broken up Brittanie was dead. They didn't last long, but the break wasn't bad, so he was destroyed to come home and learn she was gone.

However, this was one more strikeout of a name, which further highlighted Ezra's.

But with Ezra in the wind, until their warrants came through to compel the people behind the website to give names and details of who they sent out on Shannon's job, they had dick.

So he'd spent the afternoon antsy and wanting to be out there, knocking on doors and scouring woods, even in the remotest chance of finding Ezra Corbin, dragging him in, and ripping into him in an interrogation room, just as he knew Moran felt the same.

But instead, both of them holed up in Moran's office with Bohannan, talking about how to flush out CK.

They came up with the stellar idea to wait until the next night to see if he, or someone who seemed to be wearing a disguise, or someone who didn't but looked like one of the disguises he'd worn before, showed up at the town council meeting.

Moran would handle getting Brad there so he could make the ID.

From there, well, obviously, they'd take him down and bring him in for questioning.

Rus did not hold a lot of hope for this, since all the men agreed CK knew that Rus knew he was in MP, and he wouldn't make it that easy, or easy at all.

But it was all they had, and all the bandwidth left in their heads for now, especially Rus and Moran, who'd listened to what Shannon shared, and it shook them at the same time pissed them off, because she then tied their hands.

There was nothing they could do for her except hope whatever Polly said got through, and she found some help.

Since crime was still happening in Misted Pines, the Seattle division sent a couple of agents to assist in the door-knocking/woods-scouring part of the investigation with the local deputies.

And Rus was left with hoping the go-ahead would come that he could call his buddy Eric, and he, or some of his team, could come up and add trained eyes and ears in the hunt for Ezra or the lookout for CK.

However, he commandeered Karen, one of Moran's deputies, gave her the picture of the crystal found on Brittanie, and told her he didn't care how many New Age shops she had to visit in her jurisdiction, out of it, into Idaho, down to Oregon, or up to fucking Alaska, he wanted to know where that crystal was bought, and he wanted it linked to Ezra or the Domme.

It was probably a wild-goose chase, everything was bought online these days. But the deputy was all in because she wanted to do something for Brittanie, and she practically tore out of the station.

He'd ended up at the Double D for dinner with Moran, and the waitress with the nametag of Heidi gave them a wide berth after they stared at the patty melts she served like they wanted to incinerate them.

Incidentally, the Double D was one hundred percent stuck in the fifties.

Needless to say, he was in no mood when he got back to the hotel, but he wasn't stupid enough to run it off in the dark on a lonely trail in the woods with a serial killer on the loose, no matter how much the guy might like him.

So he changed into his gear and ran five miles on the treadmill in the hotel gym before he realized how hard he'd been running.

He went back upstairs, showered and put on the lounge pants he kept in his go-bag at his daughter's insistence, but never had time to wear. He just liked the idea of her thinking he did. He threw on a thermal.

And he went, barefoot with hair wet, out to the balcony with his bourbon.

He was not feeling the cold, because he was deep in a very satisfying revenge fantasy of what he'd do to a pack of faceless boys who gang raped a young girl who committed the unforgiveable crime of liking one of them, when his phone in his front pocket buzzed against his thigh.

He pulled it out and saw a text from Lucinda.

He put his glass on the railing and checked it.

You'll forgive me, Thea called. I know people. As such, I've obtained a keycard to your room. I'm coming in in three, two...

He turned around and saw her walking in.

Christ, she was something.

Ivory this time.

Ivory overcoat with tall collar.

Ivory dress that fit like a glove.

Though the high heeled boots were a shiny taupe.

She walked across the room like she owned it and came out on the balcony.

Rus was glad it was dark because he was growing hard.

"Hey," he greeted.

"Tough day?" she asked.

"Less tough than some, tougher than others."

"Stop it," she whispered.

Yeah.

He liked her.

She got it.

And she was there.

He took a shot and held out an arm.

For once that day, he got a win.

She walked into him, rested her cheek on his shoulder, and wrapped her arms around him.

He wrapped both his around her.

As expected, she felt good. Add to that, she smelled good.

And she was warm.

"You shouldn't be outside in the cold with wet hair and bare feet," she admonished.

"It was all good. I was in the middle of a revenge fantasy."

She tipped her head back. "Do those guard against colds and flus?"

He smiled and shook his head.

"Can I take you inside?"

He kept smiling and nodded his head.

She smiled back, twisted, got his drink, took his hand, and walked him in.

She closed the door behind them.

She gave him his glass before he went to the fireplace to turn it on.

She shrugged off her purse and coat, threw the purse on the table, her coat over a chair, and they met on the couch.

"Want a drink?" he asked. "Apparently, you're buying."

Her lips quirked. "I'll get it in a second."

"I'll get it. I gotta get some socks. My feet are freezing."

Her eyeballs rolled up.

This meant Rus was grinning as he pulled himself back out of the couch, sauntered to his room, tugged on some heavy socks, went back, got her order of a glass of wine from a full bottle that was in the mini-fridge, and then he came back to her.

"Thea shouldn't be talking to you," he shared.

"She was worried about you. She said you weren't in a good way. She didn't tell me why. She just told me she doesn't know the whole thing, but it's bad and maybe you might need some company."

"What about the club?"

"Kleo is my second."

"Kleo?"

She looked surprised. "You've met her. You met her before you met me."

"Ah," he said. "Security Sue."

That was when he got what he'd wanted from her since he first met her.

Or at least part of it.

She busted out laughing.

Finally, he could see it as well as hear it, and it was just like it sounded over the phone.

Amazing.

She took a sip of her wine when she was done laughing and said, "I won't tell her you call her that."

"She scares me," he teased.

"Good," she replied. "That's her job. She also stands in for me when I'm not there. It runs well on its own, regardless. But I have a nanny because I have a daughter. I still don't tend to stay deep into the night because I like to be home with her, not to mention, Hillary gets off at midnight."

The explanation of why she disappeared the night he spent in her club.

"You have a nanny?"

"Nighttime nanny. I do all the mom things, to and from school, after school, etc. But when I have to go to work, Hillary is there."

"When did Brittanie watch her?"

"Nights when she was off and...other times."

Goddamn.

She just kept getting better.

"Times you made up so you had a reason to pay her because she needed money, and Madden would have time with her," he deduced.

She hid that eyeroll behind a sip of her wine.

Yeah.

"Something to know about Brittanie," he said gently. "She had a nicely decorated apartment and maybe a designer bag or two. But she also had three family members who had their hands out often, and she might have hated her mom, but she looked after her dad and brother. This being something you already know about Brittanie, she was loyal and loving to those she cared about."

Lucinda buried her reaction in another sip of wine, but he saw the bright hit her eyes before she did it.

This was only part of the reason why Rus reached out slowly, and when she didn't pull away, he wrapped his fingers around her neck and stroked the soft skin there with his thumb when he said, "As for you coming to my rescue, this is part of the job. I hear shitty things. I deal with shitty people. And I deal with the people who the shitty ones hurt. I'm okay."

"Are you more okay with me being here?"

"Yes," he said, no hesitation.

"Then we're done with that topic."

"Bossy," he muttered.

"Not always," she said into her wineglass.

Yep.

That stirred his dick too.

So she heard he had a crap day and drove all the way through her forest to get to him.

This, what was going on with them, was something.

And since it was, right now, it couldn't be about his dick.

It had to be about her, them, and where they needed to go.

Transparency.

"I have something to tell you."

"Hmm?" she asked, raising her eyebrows, making it casual, but those amber eyes were focused penetratingly on him.

"I need to explain why I was called to Misted Pines."

She rested her wineglass to her leg and shifted so she was more fully facing him.

But he noticed she did this with care so she didn't lose his hand at her neck.

Nice.

"It's going to be upsetting," he warned.

"I figured that," she said softly.

"And maybe frightening."

Her eyes widened.

"I'm lead on the hunt for the Crystal Killer," he announced.

Her response was both anticlimactic and easing.

This being, her brows drew down in confusion, and she asked, "Sorry?"

"The Crystal Killer, he's a serial killer."

"Oh," she said offhandedly. "I don't really keep up with those kinds of things."

Thank Christ.

"Wait, is Ezra this Crystal Killer?" she asked.

He shook his head. "No, but extenuating circumstances kept me here."

"All right."

"Make me a promise?" he requested.

"Maybe," she hedged.

"Don't look it up until this is all over."

"Oh shit," she whispered.

He moved closer to her. "I have something else to share."

She nodded.

"He's not Ezra. But he might be here, in Misted Pines."

She nodded again.

"And that would be, he's here…for me."

It was only then her eyes got huge.

TWENTY-FIVE

Be Good

H is phone was rattling on the nightstand.

Rus opened his eyes, and for a second, he didn't know what was happening.

Then he smelled Lucinda's perfume.

He put his chin in his throat and saw her form through the dark, draped down his side, arm across his stomach, head on his chest, in his bed.

She was still wearing her dress, but she'd taken off her boots.

Last night, when she'd started to settle in, get comfortable, watching her unzip and tug them off had been one of the most erotic things he'd ever witnessed.

He couldn't say he'd given her the same. He was in his lounge pants and thermal.

They were on top of the duvet, but the plaid blanket was over them.

And she'd finished the bottle of wine, he'd finished the bourbon, she'd shared she didn't know how bad it was going to be when she came to him last night, so Madden was spending the night with her brother, who Madden adored and who was going to spoil her ridiculously, and then he was taking her to school that morning.

Rus had shared that was the most meaningful thing a woman had done for him in a decade.

Then they'd talked deep into the night, moving it from couch to bed because it was more comfortable. They'd started cuddling, and Rus had the sneaking suspicion he was the one who fell asleep first.

But she'd stayed.

And now she was draped on him, he had his arm around her, he was on his back, and she felt great.

Best morning he'd had in years.

By far.

He reached to his phone, mostly to silence it, but took the call because that was what he always had to do.

"Lazarus," he said quietly.

Lucinda stirred.

His body went tight, and his morning erection vanished when Jennifer snapped in his ear, "You're on assignment?"

"Hey, just a sec," he said, still talking quietly, now trying to extricate himself from Lucinda without waking her.

This failed.

Her head came up.

"Why are you talking like that?" Jenn demanded.

At this demand, Rus stilled.

Completely.

Because, first, she didn't say hello.

Second, it was still dark, so it had to be early, even for her, where it was four hours later.

Third, it was no longer her business if he was on assignment. She made too much money to get alimony from him. He left her in the house they'd bought together. They'd saved for the kids' college, a fund she managed at her decree.

So in all things that mattered, they were covered.

Outside incidental Acre and Sabrina things, there was no reason for them to speak anymore, and definitely no reason for her to be up in his shit first thing in the morning.

He looked into Lucinda's shadowed face.

"I'm talking like this because I have someone with me, but don't worry about it, she's awake now."

He heard Jenn gasp.

"I can—" Lucinda whispered, making a move, but he answered that by tightening his arm around her.

"Are you on assignment?" Jenn asked.

"Yes."

"Are you working right now?"

"I was sleeping."

It was high-pitched when she asked, "With someone else?"

He looked to the clock. "Jenn, it's five thirty here. Why are you calling?"

Lucinda tensed against him at the name.

Yeah, they'd talked a lot last night. With stories that were accompanied with showing her numerous pictures of his kids, his brothers and sisters-in-law, nieces and nephews, she now knew a good deal more about Jenn.

"Why do you have someone with you on assignment?" Jenn returned.

"Are the kids okay?"

"Are you…are you…*fucking someone*?"

He pulled himself up in bed, and this time, Lucinda came with him, doing this herself, keeping a hand on his chest.

While he was on the phone with his ex, she was claiming him.

Very nice.

But sadly, with Jenn in his ear, not nice enough.

"Are. The kids. Okay?" he pushed.

"Yes, they're okay. But you told Sabrina you're on assignment and you know how she worries," she snapped.

"This has been her life since she could cogitate. I know she worries. It comes with the territory of having an FBI agent for a dad."

"I've told you I don't like you telling her when you're out doing that kind of thing."

"And I've told you that's between me and my grown-ass daughter. And she disagrees with you. She wants to know. 'That kind of thing' is my job, Jenn, and my girl is proud of what her father does."

"It upsets her."

"Since she's an adult now, it's her call."

Lucinda leaned into him to reach across to turn on the light, and when it lit up the space, he squinted against it.

"She's not grown, she's only eighteen. It's your job to protect her from these things."

"Jesus Christ, you're calling just to get on my ass. Is your husband away on business or something? Not there to ride his?"

He could see in the room now, and what he could see was Lucinda smiling.

His cunning queen was enjoying this.

Yeah.

He'd told her all about Jenn.

"Leave Royce out of it."

"Royce is your husband. I'm not. How about leaving *me* out of it?"

"What's gotten into you?" she clipped.

"Some sense," he retorted. "Now, if there's nothing pressing with the kids, I'm ending this. Later."

He then hung up on her.

Lucinda went at it immediately.

"Does that happen often?"

"You know, she was such a part of my life, it didn't filter in that she never really stopped being part of it. So yes, it does," he replied. "And hello, gorgeous, good morning."

She smiled, white teeth and all.

His phone buzzed in his hand.

He looked down at it.

Jennifer.

"Take it," Lucinda urged.

He shook his head. "No. She can stew. Want coffee?"

"Rus, honey," she purred, a light in her eyes that might make his morning erection recover even after an episode with his ex-wife. "*Take it.*"

Feeling his lips twitch, he took it.

"Jenn, this isn't cool," he said, but it sounded like he was smiling.

"Am I amusing you?"

It was close to a shout.

He took in Lucinda, her cloud of dark hair framing her face and falling down her chest. Her makeup seeming fresh, as if she'd just put it on.

There she was, in his bed, after keeping him company all night because he'd had a shit day...hell, a shit few days. Driving from work and making arrangements for her kid so she could be there.

And he hadn't even kissed her.

She didn't freak out at serial killers but threw a mild fit to demand to pay for the funeral of a girl who wasn't blood.

He reached out, ran the backs of his fingers down her soft cheek, then he turned, threw his legs over the side of the bed and knifed out.

"Right, it's important you listen," he said into the phone as he walked to stand at the window. "I'm not yours to jerk around anymore, Jennifer."

Another gasp.

"We divorced. We're done. You made that plain by fucking another man in our bed. I didn't want you after you took some other guy's cock, and you didn't fight it."

"You didn't fight it either," she fired back.

"Is that what I was supposed to do?" he asked. "Beg you to come back to me when it was you fucking somebody who was not me?"

"We had a marriage, Rus, we had children."

"Yeah, we did, so why did you fuck another guy?"

"Well, my husband wasn't home to fuck so..."

"So? So you fucked another guy? So you, *you*, Jenn, put an end to our marriage by betraying it, and somehow it was on me to save it for you and our kids?"

There was silence from her end.

Yeah.

Fuck yeah.

"Do you hear yourself?" he pressed his advantage. "Do you know how fucked up that is? Christ, I loved you, Jenn. But that died instantly when you looked over his shoulder at me standing in the door to my own damned bedroom watching my wife get fucked. We're divorced three years, I woke up with a woman next to me, you knew it, and threw a fit. What if I did to you what you did to me?"

"Rus, maybe—"

"Answer me."

"What's gotten into you?"

"I told you. Some sense. I felt so much guilt for not being everything you needed me to be, it escaped me that you weren't what I needed either. You were demanding. You were unappeasable. And in the end, unforgivably cruel. I didn't make you happy, and you didn't make me happy, and we're over. So why the fuck do you keep calling me?"

"I'm trying to protect our daughter."

"No, you're trying to lead me around by my dick. Take this in, Jenn, when you took his, you lost hold on mine, and you can't have it back. Yeah?"

"You can stop being crude now, Rus."

"You can stop calling me, Jennifer. The kids. That's all we talk about. Are you listening?"

"Fuck you, Zachariah."

Christ, she knew he hated that name.

"Right," he bit off then ended the call.

He turned to Lucinda who was staring at him not with fear, or revulsion, but like she was proud of him.

So yeah, there was something happening between them.

Trial by fucking fire.

"A twenty-three-year-old girl came in yesterday and explained how she'd been gang raped by a guy she had a crush on when she was fifteen, and he invited his friends to the party. They didn't do it once but came back repeatedly. She's so fucked up by it, she might be in a position where the only way she can get pleasure from sex is to be raped. To test this theory, she set up a stranger danger scenario to get raped again. But it didn't go down how she expected. She wasn't raped. She was *raped*. She paid someone to rape her."

"Rus," she said quietly, her eyes melting, her beautiful face full of sympathy.

"That's my job. That's my life. That's the shit I have to deal with. And that's not the worst of it, Lucinda."

"I know that."

"Okay. You're smart. You're getting this. You know I mean to freak you. It sucks I gotta jump ahead when I haven't even kissed you, but you're into me. I'm way into you. And you need to know what you're getting into with me."

"We can remedy part of that now, honey, if you kissed me," she invited.

And damn, sitting on her hip and propped up on her hand in his bed, she was inviting.

"No way, baby," he whispered. "It's not about morning breath. I've wanted to fuck you since I met you. Now you, in my bed, so damned beautiful, it wouldn't stop at a kiss, and I got shit I gotta do."

"Okay," she murmured, the invitation still in her eyes.

He used her words of last night.

"Stop it." And added, "Be good."

She bit her lip.

Jesus.

She let him off the hook. "I cared about Brittanie a lot. You have to find who hurt her. I know what you do, Rus."

"Okay," he muttered.

"And I know this won't help, but that was an outrageously serious turn on, listening to you make mincemeat of your ex."

"It helps, but it doesn't help. And that isn't being good."

"She deserved it."

"You're way into me too."

"Yes," she said simply. "I am."

Well then.

Fuck it.

He went to her, pulled her to him, twisted to his back on the bed, and held her on top of him as he kissed her.

He didn't experience morning breath.

She tasted musky and forbidden and fucking delicious.

And she might be queen of her domain, but she submitted totally when kissed.

Fuck.

He rolled her to her back and broke away to stare down at her.

"Wow," she whispered.

"Yeah," he whispered back.

"You were right, that wasn't a good thing to do."

"I know."

"I'll be good from now on, I promise."

He kind of hoped she wasn't.

Still, he said, "Obliged."

"Rus?"

"Right here?"

"You're a remarkable man, and even though the why breaks my heart, I'm really glad I met you."

Goddammit.

He was right.

He was glad she couldn't keep her promise for even ten seconds.

He kissed her again.

He got hard doing it.

But...fuck it.

She earned it.

TWENTY-SIX

Seeley Booth

They made out for a while, and Lucinda's body felt even better under him than it had on top of him, but eventually, he needed to end it.

Lucinda ordered room service while Rus showered, shaved and dressed.

Now they were both at the table, Rus with his laptop open at the side of his plate, and he was watching it boot up as he spooned steel-cut oats into his mouth.

Lucinda, keeping that fine ass of hers in perfect shape, was eating a waffle.

"Now, Special Agent Lazarus."

He looked to her to see she'd lost interest in her waffle for now.

She had her elbows on the table, fingers linked, chin resting on them, her gaze on him, and seeing her like that, knowing how she tasted, he also knew it would take superhuman control he did not have to wait until this was all over to be with her in all the ways he could.

Seriously.

The woman did not know how to be good.

"It's not romantic," she began. "But it would seem apropos for us. So how do you feel about our first date being at the town council meeting tonight? If you're able, we can go to The Lodge after for dinner. That being The Lodge, the fancy restaurant with a chef not as good as Angelina, not the restaurant here at Pinetop. They have a delicious thick-cut pork chop. As I'm sure I don't have to tell you, it's not as good as Angelina's brown sugar-glazed one, but it'll be a change of scenery for you."

With the thought he'd just had, he wanted to say yes.

With what their plans were for the town council meeting that night, he wasn't sure.

Bohannan had said CK would not hurt him or anyone he cared about.

But Rus didn't want to take the chance he was being watched, and walk into the council meeting with Lucinda, and Bohannan being wrong.

Instead, having it be that CK felt he owned Rus, his time and his attention, and anyone else taking it would be in danger.

Therefore, regrettably, he had to respond, "I have to have my wits about me at the council meeting tonight, and since this guy I'm hunting may be close, I'm concerned about his reaction to anything…and anyone. This means I don't want you on his radar. I can come up to your club to have dinner with you there, if I'm not busy after the meeting."

He reached out and stroked her jaw.

And then he finished, "But even though it's important you know I'm all in to move this forward, honey, I think we need to be low-key."

Her gaze had turned soft when he touched her.

When he was done speaking, it turned shrewd.

"Is this about the killer or the town?"

This was an excellent question, and in case she was worrying about any aspect of it, Rus took his hand from her in order to get into it so she wouldn't be concerned.

"This is the thing," he started. "Cop shows are great. But they aren't real. People watch them and think they know what policework means. The truth of the matter, it's a slog. It's talking to a lot of people who don't know anything or don't want you to know what they know, so you gotta figure out how to get it out of them. And half the time, you fail. It's witnesses who misremember or have ulterior motives who send you in the wrong direction. It's others who are scared to talk, or don't trust cops, so they don't say anything."

Chin still on her hands, eyes riveted to him with fascination, Lucinda nodded.

Rus kept going.

"It's also a lot of waiting. You don't find evidence that needs processed and boom, techs have nothing better to do and they're on it right away. In the TV shows, it's sent off and in the next scene, detectives are in a lab that looks like it's on the Starship Enterprise and not in some inner-city police precinct. And they're talking with a technician wearing a lab coat who has a lot of time to do their hair, and suddenly, they've got all the proof they need to get their man."

Her lips curved up.

Rus's did too.

And he continued.

"That's not how it is. There's a backlog. There's always a backlog. Sometimes it's days, sometimes it's months. I mean that. Most DNA, for example, takes months to run, and I don't mean one or two. I mean it could be six or eight, or even longer. Every crime is important. You can't skip the line."

"That makes sense," she said, lifting her chin from her hands and reaching for her coffee cup.

She did this, but she didn't take her attention from him.

Rus was realizing as he was talking, and with how she was responding, it felt good for someone to show they were interested in what he was saying, especially about his work.

Jennifer had never asked and didn't want to know. His kids were too young to tell and would be probably until Rus left this earth.

Though, it felt more than good Lucinda made it so obvious she felt this way.

But this wasn't the only reason he kept talking.

"Yeah," he replied. "It took until Saturday for a tech to have the five minutes needed to get into Brittanie's laptop, and it's a surprise we didn't have to wait longer. Not to mention, cops don't spend all their hours working one case. That's happening now for me, but that's extremely rare. At my office, I have more than one open file. I'm not just tracking CK. All cops have several open cases they're working. They'll also have superiors telling them what to do, when to do it, and how many resources they can expend. There are only so many hours in a day and only so many tax dollars allocated. Every victim or family wants justice, and they're pushing for it, not having any idea how fucking hard it is to do this job."

Lucinda nodded again.

He took a sip of his own coffee.

When he put down his cup, he told her, "I'm used to people thinking I'm John McClane or Seeley Booth. Seriously. This might be my first town council meeting, but it's not the first time I've experienced pressure to provide answers to people who are flipped out. They don't get it. Even if I explained it, they wouldn't get it. They want answers and they want to know they're safe, and they're depending on me to take care of both."

"That's a lot of stress," she remarked, still following him word for word, but there was concern in her expression now.

He shook his head.

"Not really. It's the job. You learn what to care about. I care about finding the people who did this to Brittanie and building a solid case so they'll be punished for it. I care about you and Madden and Keyleigh, and even her dad and brother having answers and closure. I also care about this town not living under a cloud, but that's low on my priority list. I don't give it time or headspace. I also don't answer to anyone but my superiors. If people don't like I'm spending time with you, fuck 'em. I answered to Pastor Richard for sixteen years, and that wasn't my choice. I choose who has authority over me and a say in how I spend my time, and I do this in a way that, if I'm done with it, I'm free to quit and move on. What I know right now is, that entity isn't the townspeople of Misted Pines."

"So, in short, you're going to be fine at the meeting."

He felt his lips twitch. "In short, yeah."

"If you can come to the club after, I'll wait to eat, and we can have dinner together."

"I'm ordering that brown sugar-glazed thing."

She smiled.

He leaned slightly her way, hand lifted, crooking a forefinger at her.

He saw her eyes flash before she leaned a lot farther his way and offered her mouth.

He took it, just a quick stroke of his tongue because he wanted another taste, but he didn't have time for more.

"You seem to be okay with the fact there might be a serial killer in Misted Pines," he noted.

"I'm not," she returned. "But I have tight security on my club. Also on my house, which is close to the club. And I'm a realist. I'll be alert to the danger. I'll have a face-to-face with Kleo to tell her what's going on, making sure she keeps it confidential, but she heightens things as they need to be. And I'll look out for myself and my daughter. There's nothing else I can do, but if there is, I'll do it."

"It's sexy-as-fuck how rational you are."

He was teasing.

He was also relieved because she was being rational.

"Of course it is," she replied, cool as always.

That was sexy as fuck too.

That said, a woman had been murdered, and a serial killer was in town.

He and Lucinda were feeling their way. At this point, it was nowhere near his place to make demands.

It was attractive she was rational.

But if this was going to go anywhere, she'd have to understand he was protective.

"How close is your house to the club?" he asked.

"Walking distance, honey," she said, her voice soft, indicating she understood very well he was protective. "So…very close. We'll be fine."

Right.

Then, walking distance from a building that had lots of lights, cameras and great number of people coming and going until the early hours of the morning.

He could live with that.

He shot her a smile and was looking back to his laptop when she spoke again, so he returned his attention to her.

"Just so you know, you're a lot better looking than David Boreanaz. I mean, on a normal scale, he's a nine or ten. But you're on a different scale, one where he's only about a five."

Rus burst out laughing at that, and this time, he leaned all the way to get to her mouth.

When he was done kissing her, he'd started to return to his laptop when she waylaid him again.

He knew by the expression on her face what she had to say next was of a significantly different bent, so he braced.

"I'm enjoying getting to know you," she stated. "I'm excited to know more. I admire what you do. It's incredibly interesting." She wrapped her fingers around his wrist. "But I want to make sure you know you don't have to explain yourself to me."

"I go overboard in the debriefing?" he asked self-deprecatingly.

She squeezed his wrist and said firmly, "Not at all."

She seemed to struggle for a second.

And then she carried on.

"This isn't my call to make, Rus. And at this juncture in our relationship, I don't have near the information I need to make it. But my preliminary read on a situation with a man I very much enjoy being with and very much enjoy getting to know, I also very much enjoy kissing,"—she gave him a small smile—"is that he's been shoved into a corner and forced to defend his choices, pretty much all his life. This includes with his ex-wife. I'm just saying, that isn't me. I want to know you. What I don't want is you feeling you have to twist yourself in knots to convince me of anything. If I don't get you, I'm not the person for you." She gave him a much bigger smile. "Fortunately, I feel like I get you."

She leaned in close before she finished.

"What I'm saying is, you can be you with me. It's you I'm attracted to and have been since you walked into my office. And everything I've learned from that moment on only makes me want more."

Rus felt that sear through his chest, it was strong, it was lasting.

And it was a burn he hoped never healed.

He'd also never made out with a woman over oatmeal and a waffle, in a suite with a view, but he did it then.

It was terrific.

When they came up for air, she had her cat's-got-her-cream look, which almost meant they were going to have to make out more, preferably in the bedroom.

But he had to focus.

So he rubbed his thumb along her lip as a way to end it gently at the same time tell her how meaningful it was what she said, just in case she didn't get it from the making out.

After that, he turned to his laptop, this time made it all the way, so he opened his email.

He saw one from McGill with the subject heading: 61 FR 2659, BI/7690 / 09-16-22 - EMAIL.

Brittanie's case file.

He pulled it up and McGill had typed, OF INTEREST, LINE ITEM 3.

Rus opened the attached file, typed in the shared password and waited until the big file opened.

The top was a table of contents with hyperlinks.

He was not thinking happy thoughts when he clicked on line item three, which was titled, INCOMING JASN.BOHANNNAN@GMAIL.COM.

First, both names were spelled wrong.

Second, anyone could get a Gmail account in about ten seconds.

Third, he knew what he was going to see, he wouldn't like it, and if Jason ever found out, it would gut him.

He clicked on the hyperlink and was taken to a screenshot of an email from that address to Brittanie's.

It said,

B-

No texts. You and me. Back together. Better Times Motel. We'll talk. Work it out. Meet me there. Tomorrow night. Don't text me. Just be there.

Check into room seven.

Reconciliation.

Love you,

-Jace

She was into him. She wanted to live with him, marry him.

She'd think this was romantic. She'd think this was getting away from the Bohannan Compound and being about nothing but her and Jace.

She'd go there. No thoughts. No doubts.

Happy.

Excited.

Reconciliation.

Love you.

Motherfuckers.

He wondered if they'd ever exchanged emails so she'd know what his address was. People texted. You lived close to each other, there was no reason to email.

It wouldn't matter. Rus got emails all the time from people in his life, and he only ever cursorily noted the address to see who it was from.

A glimpse of *Jasn Bohannnan*, excited he was reaching out after a breakup she didn't want, and she'd assume.

And she'd go to the motel for Jason. From what everyone said, he might be the only one she'd go to that motel for.

Which meant…

He surged out of his chair.

Lucinda was startled at his sudden movement and was looking up at him.

"Gotta go," he said.

Her eyes dropped to his laptop, but they came back to him when he bent to press a kiss to her lips.

"You're good to—?" he began.

"Go," she urged.

He didn't delay.

He strode to the bedroom. He strapped on his guns and shrugged on his blazer.

Back to her, he slapped the laptop shut, nabbed it and gave her one last kiss before he prowled out the door.

He texted Moran in the elevator.

Then he got his key fob from the valet and jogged to his vehicle himself.

TWENTY-SEVEN

Tracks

———

M oran was at the motel before he was.

Rus parked next to his cruiser and angled out of his SUV with his laptop under his arm.

"Got the key?" he asked.

Moran, who'd walked to Rus, held out a key with one of those large, old-fashioned, diamond-shaped, plastic, motel keychains.

Rus took it but moved to the hood of his SUV, opened his laptop on it and hit a button so it would wake. He typed in his password.

The email came up.

He stabbed a finger at it to indicate to Moran he needed to read it.

Then he jogged to room seven.

He yanked off the crime scene tape.

He opened the door, walked in and used his elbow to flip on the overhead light.

Brittanie gone. Plastic gone. The bed was rumpled, but otherwise, the room looked ready to rent.

To Rus, it still felt like death.

He walked straight through to the bathroom.

Above the toilet, a window. Opaque glass.

It was closed.

It was a sash.

It was also plenty big enough for a man to fit through.

And a woman.

In fact, you could stand, take a piss, and look at that cloudy glass right in front of you, and you didn't have to be as tall as Rus.

Which meant you could get in without a ladder, the bottom ledge maybe three inches above the back of the toilet.

I was instructed to keep my window unlocked so they could get in...

I park at the back and walk all the way around on the outside so I don't have to go by that crime scene tape.

The Seattle team didn't fuck around, there was fingerprint powder all around the frame of the window and all over the toilet.

He pivoted and nearly ran into Moran.

"Jace is gonna fucking lose his mind," Moran gritted.

He had Rus's laptop under his arm.

"Yep. That's why he can't know."

Moran's head jerked in surprise.

Rus pushed through the sheriff and walked back outside, beyond his SUV, and stood in the middle of the parking lot.

Making slow circles, he took everything in.

The motel was L-shaped. Lobby in front, fourteen rooms, swimming pool with high chain link fence surrounding it. The pool was to the side but closer to the front of the property, better to be seen by cars passing by.

The lobby and nine rooms down the long side, five rooms down the foot of the L. Open breezeway at the angle where there were vending machines and ice.

Rooms big enough for two parking spots in front of both.

Sign out front by the street, about twenty feet from the front edge of the fence to the pool.

There was another chain link fence that closed off the motel property from the open-nature, grass-scrub-and-boulder-filled lot beyond the pool to the side. The fence ran the length of the property and ended before the steep incline of the mountain that was the backdrop of the motel.

One entrance from the street to the property. It was wide.

No true reception area for a car. No overhang. You parked in one of the spots outside the lobby to check in.

But the concrete that covered all the property the hotel sat on, save a narrow rectangle of grass around the decking of the pool, ran across the front of the building too.

This was how Brad drove around back to park his vehicle without having to pass Brittanie's door.

Moran had joined him, and Moran silently followed when Rus jogged to the front of the motel and stopped.

The desk clerk on duty was watching them through the panorama windows.

Rus ignored her.

The lobby was all windows, but the ones to the side of the building, which would be the back of the units, were covered with display units that had pamphlets for local attractions and businesses. Also obscuring the view, from what he could see, there was a bulletin board covered likely with advertisements and event announcements.

You couldn't see out those windows.

In the dark, you might not think there was anything to see from what was on that other side.

All that shit there would also muffle noise coming from that direction.

There was no additional street entrance on that side and nothing but nature that led to the sheer wall of another very steep mountain about twenty yards out. And by nature, he meant it was more tall grass, scrub, brush, and big boulders. Impossible to drive through, even if you had an ATV. A tank couldn't make it through that mess.

Rus walked slowly to stand looking down the side of the motel, which was the back of the units.

There was a vehicle-wide lane to the rear, but you'd have to drive in the street entrance and around the front of the motel to get to it. There was more chain link fencing lining the concrete down that side, closing it off from that vacant lot.

If a car came in, and it crossed the front by the lobby, especially at night, the desk clerk wouldn't miss it.

He loped down the side of the motel, Moran with him, nothing there but the windows over the toilets to the rooms.

He stopped at what he knew was room seven, not only because he was counting, but also because there was a ledge from the roof protecting the building from the elements, and the black fingerprint powder was still visible around the outside of that window.

They'd be thorough. He knew it because he'd read the reports.

But...good.

He started jogging again, Moran with him.

They hit the back of the motel and stopped.

At the angle to the L, there was a door, now open, and he could hear the laundry machines going.

So, laundry, linens, supplies.

No other doors. But more bathroom windows. All the units had front entry only.

There was also parking back there. There were two cars parked. The maid and clerk.

Unless they were told to park back there, it seemed everyone was avoiding Brittanie's room.

And this was probably where they did any unloading of supplies.

But you could drive around either the front or the side of the motel to get to it, easier access was around the front.

He turned his back to the motel and looked left and right.

The chain link fence went to the end of the concrete on either side.

No back fence.

Also no back road.

You entered the property from the street, and it was closed in at both sides.

And regardless of those pamphlets, you'd see a car enter, whether it went to the main parking lot, or around the side.

But there was no access to the property in the back. There was another very steep hill close to the edge and that was it.

Fuck.

He'd thought he had something.

He was sure they'd come in through the window. Though, unless they left fingerprints, he couldn't prove it.

He also couldn't offer an explanation as to how they got on the property at all, because there were no witnesses who saw them there and it was impossible to enter the property in a vehicle without the desk clerk seeing, including being on break or away from the lobby, but noting the car parked in the lot.

Considering Brittanie checked in at around five thirty, depending on how long they were there, they might have had to evade the attention of three clerks—the evening clerk, the night clerk and/or the morning clerk. Not to mention other customers, all two of them, who had been contacted and interviewed and they hadn't seen or heard a thing.

Though, none of those clerks or customers would have reason to see someone parked at the back by the vacant lots, nor would they see someone rounding the rear of the property and going down the side to the bathroom window.

And unless they got sloppy and his team lifted prints around the window, they'd left no trace.

You just couldn't drive a car back there.

It wasn't impossible that two people walked to the motel carrying a massive amount of plastic tarp, sex toys and a hammer.

But it was improbable someone did it without anyone seeing them.

They'd have to park somewhere close and walk the road, which was highly traversed. And how they'd navigate rounding the fence at the front without being seen by the clerk would be a miracle.

Unless you wanted to take your chances stumbling in the dark next to a mountain, or through one of two vacant lots strewn with boulders, and climb the fences at the sides.

But if Rus had a mess of plastic tarp, sex toys and a hammer, heading to a motel where he was going to torture and murder some-one, he wouldn't want to sprain his ankle stumbling through the dark or break his neck falling off a six-foot chain-link fence.

And chain link fences were noisy. If you climbed them, they clanked and banged. Maybe not enough to be heard by people in the motel, but these weren't two cat burglars.

Nevertheless, they'd managed to evade being seen or heard by street traffic, employees and customers.

And with the town as interested in the murder as Misted Pines, a passerby seeing them would have reported it.

Even if they did come up from the back along the mountain, they'd probably need flashlights, and those would be seen too.

Bottom line, though, none of the reports shared evidence of vegetation, gravel, mud or dirt in or outside the room. And unless they took their shoes off outside the door and were careful to clean away any residue when they vacated, if they hoofed it there, they'd track at least some of that in.

He couldn't see them dragging a vacuum or cleaning supplies with them either.

Maybe the lab would turn something up.

But until now, Rus would have sworn they got there in a vehicle.

Rus had halted, but Moran kept walking.

Rus watched as the man stopped beyond the concrete in the dirt. He stared at the ground, looked up the mountain, and then stared at the ground again.

He was as pissed as Rus that they hadn't found the perp's ingress and egress.

It wasn't strictly necessary to know.

But when you were investigating a crime, everything you could learn was necessary to know.

More importantly, if you could gather convincing evidence to tell the story of how they did it, you could help the jury members raise their hands for a guilty verdict, or better, convince the perpetrators to plead it out.

He watched as Moran squatted, still staring at the ground.

The sheriff lifted his head and looked off into the distance.

He then turned to Rus in a way Rus went to where he was.

He saw it before he got close, something easily missed, unless you knew the only way it could be was right there.

This was why his team, who thought to print the outside of a bathroom window, and according to their report also inspected this area and saw no road, no easy access, and no immediate tracks, missed them.

It was a definitely a miss, they should have looked closer.

But it still wasn't easy to see.

He saw it where the concrete ended, and a narrow area of gravel and mud began before the mountain started to ascend.

It was barely enough room to fit a vehicle.

But if they wanted it bad enough, went slow enough, it'd not only work, you could go without your lights because the motel lights would guide your way. Your car was dark, no one would see you from the street.

Or the motel.

Rus felt his heart start to pound.

"It was raining that night and had been raining off and on for a few days," Moran said. "Including the day we found her and the day after."

Yeah, it was.

That was why it was muddy enough, a vehicle left deep depressions that wouldn't go away, even if there was more rain.

Because those motherfuckers were still right there.

You could barely see them. There were no tread marks anymore. Some of them had been completely washed away. They looked like grooves in the mud.

And they were.

Grooves made by car tires.

Rus turned his gaze where Moran had, and he saw, less than a quarter a mile away, another business.

It looked closed, but there was activity because it was under construction.

They started walking that way.

"Place used to be an Italian restaurant. They closed about a year ago. Now, believe someone's opening an outdoor gear store there, sales and rentals," Moran said.

"Mm-hmm."

Rus's eyes didn't leave the tracks. They were broken, there were full yards where they'd been lost to the elements, but then they returned.

They led all the way to the back of the store.

The broken concrete around that property was lousy with dirt washed in from the rain, gravel, blown in pieces of litter and construction debris.

But there was a lot of dirt washed in from the rain.

And through it, car tire tracks, not construction vehicles, *car* tire tracks turned onto that back area that wasn't actually a back lane, but it had served as one, and then those tracks returned to drive through that business.

"They came previously, unlocked the window, and rolled in from back here," Moran deduced.

"Mm-hmm," Rus agreed.

Rus stared at some men coming from inside the building and tossing some demolition materials in a dumpster.

Then, at the same time, he and Moran both turned and raced back to the motel, phones to their ears.

TWENTY-EIGHT

Two-Point-Seven Stars

R us sat in one of the chairs in front of Moran's desk with his phone resting on it. Moran was behind the desk. Both of them were listening to McGill talking through the speaker.

"They gave it up, no warrant. They're pissed as shit. This is a big deal to them, beyond the fact it's a big fucking deal," McGill was saying. "I'm sending you some pictures of her they have on file. Her name is Carrie Molnar. She lives in Tacoma. She's a dominatrix with several subspecialties including stranger scenarios, public play, the kind where you do sex shit in alleys or wherever with a possibility you'll get caught, and consensual rape. Usually it's male rape, but to do that, she always works with a partner, she'll do what they do to a female, and they confirmed she was assigned Shannon."

Carrie Molnar.

It sounded innocuous, like Ted Bundy or Ray Andrews.

Until it wasn't.

McGill continued to lay it out.

"She's been registered as a contract worker with them for sixteen months. She has a two-point-seven-star rating out of five, so they weren't real hot on her to start off. They want their people to strive for at least a four-point-five, anyone below a four is flagged. She's been flagged awhile, and that while would be for around sixteen months. They've been considering losing her. Reading subtext into all this, she gives them the heebie-jeebies."

As she would.

From what Rus knew about the BDSM+ world, it was about openness and communication. It was about making promises and keeping them.

Paramount: Trust.

You might not click with the woman you hired to work you, but you didn't give a three star and below to someone you didn't click with.

You gave that to someone you didn't like.

McGill's voice kept coming at them.

"She also got a complaint eight months ago that was so bad, they gave her a warning, one more and she was out. As far as they knew, until now, she was toeing the line. Subtext to that, it's clear they wished they hadn't blown a golden opportunity. They were both surprised and not surprised when the FBI came calling."

"What was the complaint?" Rus asked, but he knew.

There was a knock on the doorframe to the open door behind him, but even if Moran looked that way, Rus ignored it as McGill continued speaking.

"Not observing hard limits," McGill told them. "We sent agents to her place last night, but the folks from the website informed us she had a new client booked in. He requested her specifically, which they were already shocked about, because she doesn't get a lot of referrals, and as of this morning, she hasn't checked in as they require their contractors to do. They told me this isn't unusual. Customers pay by the scene, not by the hour. We got guys out there sitting on her place and they'll grab her when she comes home. I'll let you know the minute we have her."

"Moran and I'll be on the road when you do."

"Right."

"Ben, I want the fingerprints around the back window processed first," Rus told McGill.

"I already added that to the request," McGill replied.

"Great. Thanks. Keep us in the loop. Later," Rus ended it.

He hit the screen to close the call and saw Dickerson rounding Moran's desk with a laptop.

Moran jerked his head to Rus, but Rus was already out of his seat and moving around the desk.

"Once they sent it in, didn't take long to find it," Dickerson said, hitting a button on the laptop, and the black-and-white video on the screen played.

The date on the feed was the night of Brittanie's murder, eight thirty-nine.

The feed was from the opening-soon outdoor gear store who really didn't want anything stolen while they were setting up shop, so they had cameras. And they were all over offering up feeds to the local sheriff to help in a murder investigation.

On the feed was a BMW driving through the lot. The video was small, and grainy, but you could easily make out two people in the front seats of the car.

You couldn't make out faces, and definitely not license plates, not from what he could see. Someone could enhance it, though they probably didn't have those programs at Fret County Sheriff's Office.

But they didn't need it enhanced for now.

Ezra Corbin owned a BMW.

His chest felt tight.

Fucking hell.

They had the who and they had the how.

He didn't give a fuck about the why, just as long as they could say who and how.

And they could.

Dickerson's finger moved over the mousepad, that feed minimized, and he hit go on the next feed.

Same car exiting the lot, this time it was the next morning at four twenty-three.

Seven hours.

They tortured her for seven hours.

Rus kept himself perfectly still.

Dickerson spoke. "You know we already talked to all the desk clerks about him. No one checked Corbin in ever, to their knowledge. We got this feed, we called the motel."

"Anyone specifically ask for room seven?" Moran asked.

Dickerson shook his head. "But the clerk on duty said a dark-haired, Caucasian woman came in for what she thought was a matinee the day before. She didn't have anyone with her. The clerk on duty that day is the one there now. She didn't notice anyone joining her. That doesn't mean someone didn't, but in the comings and goings during the day, they couldn't say for sure if someone did. She didn't check out in person, just left her key in the room and was gone by the next morning. The clerk said she saw her leave mid-afternoon, but thought she went for food or something, or was just done with her tryst. She didn't remember seeing her come back. She'd never seen her before. But she was put into room seven."

"And Jason's supposed email came in that afternoon, telling her which room to ask for," Rus said. "And Better Times Motel doesn't have very many amenities, but they do have Wi-Fi."

Dickerson nodded.

"Log that," Moran said, dipping his chin to the video. "I'm going to get you a picture of the woman we're looking at. I want you going right out to the clerk who checked her in, and I want an ID."

Dickerson nodded again, grabbed the laptop and left.

Rus's phone was vibrating on the desk, so he went back to it.

He had a text.

We're coming up. We have a brief. No contact in case you're being watched. But we got your back.

It was from his friend, Eric Turner, who used to be an agent. He'd left the Bureau a few years ago and went to work for a security outfit in LA. They were good at what they did, and this wasn't the first time Rus, or the FBI, contracted with them.

He looked to Moran as he sat back in his seat. "That crew I was telling you about?"

"Yeah?"

"They're in."

"Thinking of CK here, in my town…" Moran shook his head and didn't finish except to say a heartfelt, "Good. "

"I wanna brief Bohannan," Rus told him. "And I want more of a plan than what we got for tonight's meeting. We weren't in shape yesterday to put our minds to it. I got some—"

"Rus?"

He turned to see Polly in Moran's doorway.

"Hey, Polly," he greeted. "What's up?"

"Uh, Porter Sexton is here to talk to you."

"Who?"

"Porter Sexton, Cin's brother."

They didn't have the same last name?

He knew Bonner wasn't Jaeger's surname. Not only did Lucinda and he never marry, his last name was Rhett, as was Madden's.

It seemed he did a lot of talking with Lucinda. It was time to do some listening.

Rus stood, shot a glance to Moran, whose mouth was quirking, and he moved out.

Rus wasn't feeling this, considering one of the things he had learned last night was that Lucinda was not only the mother of a nine-year-old, she was thirty-six, had been with Jaeger for ten years, living with him for nine before he left for Oregon two years ago.

In other words, she was way out of the realm where a big brother paid a visit to her new suitor to lay the ground rules.

With reserve, Rus approached the man who was standing out in the lobby.

"Porter," he greeted, not offering his hand.

"Agent Lazarus," Porter replied, and he did offer to shake.

Rus still was a new suitor, so as not to appear rude, he took him up on it.

And Porter didn't beat around the bush.

"Listen, Cin doesn't let anything get to her, which is great, when women aren't being murdered in motels. This only a year after a dead girl was found floating in our lake and a little girl was kidnapped from a slumber party and brutally killed. Cin can be chill, but I'm tripped out. This is uncool, me coming to you, but she keeps shutting me down, and not only me, but Mom and Dad want her and Mad off that mountain and staying with one of us. If she's not into that, she can check into Pinetop and be close to you."

He lifted a big, calloused hand in a *don't take offense* gesture before Rus could say anything, and he kept going.

"People are talking, I'm not listening, exactly. She's my sister. When she wants me to know what's going on in her love life, she'll tell me. But there's murder shit happening, and I suspect you're trained to take care of yourself and other people. So, if you two are…whatever you're doing, me being here is not about pressure, it's about safety. They don't have to stay in your room, but I want her and my niece close to somebody who can offer some protection, something she doesn't have on Bonner Mountain."

Bonner Mountain?

He didn't have time to get into that.

He said, "She told me she had tight security."

"Of course she would. And yeah. There's a security system on the old house. And the club is wired up better than the Pentagon. But that doesn't stretch to the old house."

"The old house?"

"She had Granny's Victorian renovated. She lives there. Go out the back door to the club, down the incline about a hundred and fifty yards, around the face of the mountain, closer to the river, that's where she lives. And no, you can't see it from the club. And yeah, that means it's more in the middle of fucking nowhere than the club is."

Rus's voice was tight when he said, "I'll talk to her."

Porter was visibly relieved.

"And, 'whatever' is happening between us, so thanks for coming to me," Rus went on.

"Obviously, not a problem. And if you need anything to help her make the right decision, tell her she either does that, or I'm pitching a fucking tent in her front yard."

If she didn't make the right decision, Rus would go to an open outdoor gear store and rent something to pitch right next to him.

It was at that belated moment Rus endured the big brother giving him the full once-over before Porter offered his hand again.

Rus took it.

They squeezed and let go.

"See you at the council meeting tonight. Advice, brother, wear a flak jacket."

And with that, Porter left him alone in the lobby.

He looked to his watch then pulled out his phone.

Depending on if they flew commercial, or boarded their super security jet plane, which was how they'd probably do it since they'd need weaponry, it would take between five and seven hours for Eric's team to gear up, roll out and arrive in Misted Pines.

Even so, he broke a rule and texted, *Bon Amie, club and theater on Bonner Mountain, house down the slope and around by the river. I want eyes on it until I can have a few words with one of its inhabitants and get her ass closer to me.*

It wasn't cool to ask a contractor the government would be paying to cover someone you had a personal connection with solely because you had a personal connection with them.

But Rus didn't give that first fuck.

As Porter said, murder shit was happening.

Unless you knew the person or it was covered in emojis, you couldn't read humor in a text.

But Rus knew Eric.

So he knew he was killing himself laughing even though the return was two words.

On it.

TWENTY-NINE

Mashup

R us knew one thing.

Misted Pines Town Council would be in serious trouble if they didn't have the lady who was a taller, more attractive version of Liz Cheney sitting in the main seat.

He wasn't sure three of the four other members were even awake.

Though one was on his phone constantly, and Rus didn't have to follow him on Twitter to know everything that was happening was now in the Twittersphere. How that was more important than listening to his constituents and their concerns, Rus had no clue. But that seemed a general issue with elected officials across the board.

When he'd gotten himself loose of the cult, Rus had caught up on some TV, and one of the things the kids at school talked about most, which was one of the first things he made sure to watch, was *Northern Exposure*.

And Sabrina was devoted to *The Gilmore Girls*. So devoted, he couldn't escape it even though he wanted to.

So, standing next to Moran, holding up a wall in the standing-room-only space, Rus felt caught in a mashup of a town meeting of Cicely, Alaska and Stars Hallow, with most of the residents freaked way the fuck out, and half of them being characters so bizarre, only a writer for a fictional TV show could make them up.

Needless to say, Brad was there, but they'd had no thumbs up.

And Rus had looked at every face in that room more than once, and no one matching Brad's description, or no one obviously in disguise, or even not obviously, was in that room.

As suspected, CK didn't show.

Nevertheless, the room was filled with colorful characters.

Case in point, the man currently at the lectern who looked like Mad Jack from *Grizzly Adams*, including wearing a fringed, Native hide smock.

And he clearly didn't read newsfeeds because he was on a tear, *not* about a woman's murder.

"So I wanna know what you're gonna do about it. 'Cause last time I stood here, you told me to post more signs, and I did. Before that, you told me to build up my fence, and I did that too, and I'm gonna say, that didn't cost me nothin', it cost me a whole lotta somethin'. And they still keep coming. And I know this, next option open to me that I'm takin' is fillin' them full of buckshot."

Explanation: he wasn't a fan of tourists hiking across his land.

"Siddown!" someone yelled. "We wanna know what's happening with Brittanie!"

"Ain't no Brittanie walkin' cross my land, that's all I know. It's a bunch of weekend-wannabe GI Joes!" Mad Jack shot back in the direction where the yell came from.

"Owen," the Liz Cheney look-alike said with admirable patience (there was a nameplate sitting in front of her that shared she was Megan Nichols, President). "You can't shoot at tourists."

"Can and will," he fired back. "It's *my* land. You see a fence, you don't climb over it, for heaven's sake!"

Megan looked like she agreed.

Rus definitely agreed.

"How's this?" Megan asked. "I will personally call every hotel, motel, B&B, inn and rental property company in this town and suggest to them, strongly, that they be sure to advise all their patrons, when in pursuit of their relaxing time in Misted Pines, to

stay off private property. In the meantime, we'll discuss a referendum to reassess trespassing fines and jail sentences. It might not
stop it. But I know if I would get fined, say, five thousand dollars,
and I'd also sit in a cell at our sheriff's office for the weekend I was
hoping to relax and enjoy the out of doors, and then the next week,
and I'd leave Misted Pines with a criminal record, I would probably
keep to the public hiking trails."

Owen worked the chew in his mouth considering this option,
then he said, "I'd be votin' for that referendum."

"Your time is up!" someone shouted from the line.

"Hold your horses!" Owen shouted back. "Darn!" He leaned
into the microphone so close, when he said, "I'm done," people
cringed at the feedback, including Rus.

He circled off and the next lady came up.

She gave the rigmarole the three before Owen gave, about how
uncomfortable she and everyone in the town was about the lack of
information the sheriff's office was releasing about the murder of
Brittanie Iverson and the hunt for Ezra Corbin.

Rus didn't listen to her.

After he shook his head in understanding and looked away from
Porter Sexton, who was sitting next to his mother and giving him an
I told you expression, Rus's attention focused on Ellen Macklemore.

She was again wearing a lot of denim, silver and turquoise, and
she was in line next up to speak.

He looked back to the front when Megan spoke sharply.

"Okay, Mandy," Megan interrupted the speaker, then she
scanned the whole congregation, before she demanded, "Anyone in
line waiting to complain about the Brittanie Iverson case, step to the
back. We'll hear you at the end, but I'll warn you, we won't be
listening. As I said the last three times someone complained about
this, and I won't say it again, *active investigations are confidential.*"

She zeroed in on Mandy.

"Now you tell me, Mandy, if someone you loved was hurt, do
you want Harry Moran out front of the sheriff's office, gabbing to
media, or with his boots up on his desk, talking to citizens, or do you
want him out doing policework?"

"Policework, of cour—"

"And do you want the media to know every little thing about what's happening so the bad guys know what the good guys know so they can make sure to cover all their tracks?" Megan demanded.

Mandy was getting red in the face. "That's not what I mean, Megan, and you know it."

"What do you mean?" Megan asked sharply. "That *you* should know because you're interested and you're not a bad guy? Or *you* should know because you're scared and knowing they're working hard at finding who hurt Brittanie will make you feel better? Well, rest assured, Mandy, they're working hard. But even though you knew that already, you don't feel better, because something awful happened. And no one ever feels good when something awful happens."

Megan looked through the congregation again and kept lecturing.

"Not one person in this room is entitled to know the intricacies of how Harry is handling this case. That's for starters. But it would actually hurt Brittanie even more if he parceled out all the information. He is not Leland Dern. He's Harry Moran. He does his job well. And if you don't like it, don't vote for him in four years. For now, you have to trust him, because you voted him in. As for me, I want them to find who murdered Brittanie, so I'm going to let him and his men do their gosh darned jobs."

She glared at the line.

"Anyone got anything else to say?" she asked, each word sounding like a threat.

The vast majority of the line, heads hanging, melted away from the aisle.

"She's a ball buster," Rus said under his breath. "I like it."

"Our last president was one hundred and seventy years old, so the whole council was dicked up with corruption and complacency. In real life, she's a very nice woman. Up there, she has to bust balls, because she has her work cut out for her."

Even though Rus knew he liked her, he felt sorry for her.

"And," Moran continued, "you see what she has to work with."

That was the truth.

"Right, Ellen, what's on your mind?" she asked as Mandy slunk away and Ellen took the microphone.

Ellen looked back and forth across the five-person council seated across the continuous arc of a desk at the front of the room.

Then she announced loudly and elaborately, "*Tyler Cook!*"

Startling Rus with her urgency, suddenly, a woman in the crowd stood up and shouted, "Ellen!"

"*Michael Mitchell!*" Ellen said.

Another woman stood up.

Both of them were pale and clearly rattled.

Just from the look of them, Rus came away from the wall.

"Don't, Ellen!" one of them yelled.

Ellen ignored her.

"*Dylan Rogers!*"

Rus looked questioningly to Moran.

His face was set in granite.

What the fuck?

"Ellen, stop it!"

Another woman had stood up, actually, three more of them.

"*Austin Brooks!*"

"Why's my boy's name in your mouth?" a man yelled.

Ellen turned his way but kept leaned into the microphone, "Because eight years ago, he and his friends gang raped a high school girl repeatedly."

A groundswell of shock rippled physically and audibly through the crowd.

"*Holy fuck,*" Rus bit off, already on the move.

Moran was too, shouting to Megan, "Shut it down!"

"The fuck he did!" the man yelled.

"Ellen, if you—" Megan started.

Ellen turned back to the microphone, "Her name is Shann—"

She got no more out.

Rus had her by the arm and he was pulling her toward a door he hoped led to the council's private chambers, but wherever it led was out of that room.

The noise of a microphone being unplugged cut through the space.

"What the fuck's she saying about my son!" the man yelled, and his voice seemed close to Rus's back.

"Take your hand off me," Ellen snarled, struggling in his hold.

He did not take his hand off her.

He manhandled her to the door and through it.

He'd looked at every face out there.

And Shannon's wasn't one of them.

"How dare you put your hands—"

He whirled her in front of him, let her go, but got nose to nose, and growled, "Shannon ask you to come here and do that?"

"They don't deserve—"

"Answer me."

"They're walking free—"

"*Answer me!*" he thundered.

The door behind him opened, he heard pandemonium, looked over his shoulder, and watched Megan slide in, closing the door firmly behind her.

"What on earth is going on?" she demanded.

Rus returned to Ellen but took a step away.

"Talk," he ordered.

She crossed her arms on her chest and set her jaw. "I don't have to say a word."

"Yes you fucking do and you fucking know it," Rus gritted.

"Special Agent!" Megan snapped.

"Did she ask you to come here and do that?" Rus challenged.

Ellen remained silent.

"Did she ask you to come here?" Rus yelled.

The door opened.

Rus twisted, Megan whirled, but she didn't try to stop the women from filing into the wide hall they were now populating.

All who had stood out there came in, a few more…and Lana.

He didn't have to ask.

The coven.

"*What were you thinking?*" one of them shrieked at Ellen.

"Wendy," Lana said coolly.

"She came to us," Ellen stated.

"Shannon did?" Rus asked.

"No, she did not," Wendy declared, answering Rus's question, but her eyes were on Ellen. "Her friend did. She wanted us to do something." She slashed an arm toward the door, nearly hitting two other women. "But not that. *Not that.*"

"They should be named and shamed," Ellen decreed.

"You don't get to make that decision," Wendy retorted.

"Too many women are silent!" Ellen shot back.

"Well, congratulations, because now, you've managed to silence their concerned friends too," Lana drawled.

Finally, what she did seemed to begin to sink in, and Ellen started to appear chagrinned.

"That was reprehensible," Lana stated. "And you better hope those boys, or their friends, or their parents do not take retribution against that young woman, Ellen. Because I vow to you right now, if they do, it's *you* who'll regret it."

And with that, Lana turned and strutted out the door.

"You've got a week. I don't see a for sale sign in your front yard, there's gonna be a problem," Wendy, the now obvious ringleader, announced. "In the meantime, I think it's safe to say, you're out."

"*So* out," another woman agreed.

"That was disgusting," a third one said.

"I'm so ashamed of you, I could spit," a fourth put in.

"Ellen," a fifth one said with great sadness. "How could you?"

All but that fifth one shot lethal glares at Ellen, but she was with them when they filed out.

Leaving Rus, Ellen and Megan.

"Let me get this straight," Megan said with bone-chilling calm. "The friend of a survivor of an assault came to your group, and you decided to make public an assault she did not wish to be made public?"

"Megan—" Ellen started.

"First," Megan cut her off. "You women are skating on thin ice. If any of them will talk to you again, you tell them that. This stunt didn't help. And second, shame on you, Ellen Macklemore. *Shame on you.*"

And with that, Megan walked out.

Rus turned to Ellen.

She was visibly shaken, and he knew that because she was visibly shaking.

"She told me her story herself," he said low. "Because it's hers and hers alone to tell. I think you know you fucked up, but I don't give a shit. You victimized a victim. With that shit out there, you raped her too, Ms. Macklemore."

Her face drained of color.

"Shame is too good for you," he concluded.

He left her looking wrecked, as she should, and went to help Moran deal with her fallout.

THIRTY

Golf Cart

They hadn't had an official date, but they had an official table.

Rus sauntered through the club, feeling eyes move to him, but his were on Lucinda seated at the table where he'd eaten dinner with her a few nights before.

She was in a dress, the only way he could describe it was the smooth color of buttermilk. It had a low circle of a neckline showing cleavage, and long, full sleeves gathered at cuffs at her wrists.

She watched him coming too, and she stood when he got close, stepping away from the table.

That was when he saw the matching tie belt, the full skirt that hit her below the knee, and although the material was clingy, the whole thing was designed to bring attention to the sexy-as-fuck bronze, high-heeled pumps on her feet.

When he arrived, she wrapped her fingers around his blazer at his biceps, noting, "You've had quite the night."

He was unsurprised the news beat him up her mountain.

"Word gets around," he replied.

Her head was tilted back, and since he'd already made the decision this was happening, and she was giving the invitation, he dropped his face down and touched his mouth to hers.

He could swear he heard the room quiet, then he felt the low buzz that went through as he lifted his head.

And now that was going to head down the mountain.

They moved away from each other, and he stood as she sat and didn't take his own seat until she was settled under the table.

Her gaze rested on something beyond him, and he knew it was a hovering server when she asked, "Bourbon, whisky, vodka tonic or a beer?"

It was nice to know she paid such close attention.

"I don't know," he replied. "Am I staying at yours or are you and Madden moving to Pinetop?"

Her mouth got tight.

He turned, and yes, a server was hovering.

"You got Macallan?" he asked.

"Yes, sir."

"Neat."

She strode to the bar.

"Porter's been at you," Lucinda stated when he looked back to her.

She was peeved.

"Do you live in an out-of-the-way Victorian house by the river?"

"It isn't out of the way."

He turned to the windows. "Can I see it from here?"

"Okay, it isn't *far* away."

He leveled his eyes on her.

"I have a sophisticated alarm."

"I bet the security at Pinetop is more sophisticated."

"Rus," she said warningly.

"For between twenty-four and forty-eight hours, the Crystal Killer rapes his victims, vaginally and anally, as they're tied to plastic tarping on a bed, their mouths duct taped. When he's done, he bludgeons them in the back of the head with a hammer until they're dead. He leaves a crystal in their palms and a note for me. And he's probably in town. I just kissed you. Everyone in this room watched.

And the news of what happened at the council meeting beat me up the mountain. Now, am I moving up here? Or are you moving to Pinetop?"

Her eyes were wide, and her face was pale. "Did Ezra…?"

She didn't finish.

He answered anyway.

"Yes. They used his MO, probably thinking it would send us in the wrong direction. And straight up, if they hadn't gotten a single detail wrong, they would have. That's why I'm here. It's also why CK is now here. So?" he pushed.

"I…need to think."

She was flustered.

He hated that.

He hated that he'd just told her exactly how Brittanie died too.

But if it got her and Madden staying somewhere else, somewhere safe, he was okay with it.

"Pinetop would be better," he said gently.

"Because Porter or Mom would be in danger too?"

Yes.

Or maybe.

He didn't answer with either.

He said, "It's more populated. He's careful. He'd stay well away from Pinetop. Especially since he knows I know he's here. And I know what he looks like now."

His whisky was served as she said, "Okay. I…it's closer to Madden's school too. It'd be nice to have a break from taking her up and down the mountain five days a week."

He looked pointedly at her phone, which was lying face down on the table.

"Now?" she asked.

"You don't want the suites all booked up, do you?"

"You're as annoying as Porter," she complained.

He nabbed his whisky and took a sip, totally okay with the fact she thought that.

Mostly because she said it while reaching for her phone.

RUS STOOD ON HER BALCONY.

He saw a swirl of buttermilk in his peripheral vision, turned and looked in through the windows.

The Presidential Suite at the Pinetop took up the whole corner of his floor.

It had two bedrooms, two bathrooms, a powder room, a much more elaborate bar than his, two seating areas—a smaller, more intimate one for talking, a larger, more comfortable one for watching TV—a pool table, a dining table that sat six, two fireplaces, and a wraparound balcony that had three different doors to get to it.

He wasn't sure, but he sensed it was bigger than the condo where he lived in Virginia.

Harking not too far back, the brown sugar-glazed pork chop at Bon Amie was inspired, they both had it, along with an appetizer of crab-stuffed mushrooms.

But they didn't linger over it, and she'd ordered it before he got there, so the mushrooms were put in front of him by the time he took his second sip of whisky.

After their dinner, where conversation, when it was had, was stilted, it was all kinds of hilarious that, to get to her house, on a paved road that hugged the mountain, she drove a golf cart wearing an uber feminine dress and bronze stilettos.

She was being prickly while acquiescing to something that meant something to Rus, so he didn't give her shit about the golf cart.

Her house, he could see even in the dark, was something.

Nestled on the slope very close to the river, it looked what it was.

A bastion to a bygone age.

It had a decent-sized garden, was painted—you guessed it—cream with some coordinating accents, had three brick chimneys jutting into the purple sky and a ton of fretwork.

Walking in, though, was like stepping from another world into a set decorated as a clean-lined, modern home. There was nothing Victorian or antique, homely or rustic, old-fashioned or traditional.

It was open plan. The kitchen was massive and state of the art. The furniture comfortable, but stylish.

All pure Lucinda, including the shock to the system from outside to in.

He loved it.

She went up the stairs.

He shot the shit with Hillary, her nighttime nanny, who he'd peg at Brittanie's age or a bit older, and a woman Porter might be interested in, because she had fresh-faced, hike-three-miles-and-picnic mountain woman written all over her.

It was unsurprising it took Lucinda forever to pack.

It was also unsurprising his job, once he got the six suitcases loaded in her car, was to go up and carry a dead-asleep Madden to Lucinda's white Jaguar SUV.

Madden woke up along the way, barely, but she was back out after he got her buckled in.

And Rus realized he forgot how precious it felt, carrying a nine-year-old girl in his arms.

Lucinda drove him to his vehicle, and he followed them down the mountain.

The bellman dealt with their luggage.

Lucinda dealt with checking in.

Rus dealt with carrying Madden to bed.

But he left her with her mom, snapped open her Maker's Mark and headed out to the balcony.

He walked in rather than her coming out in that dress.

She was at the bar, opening a bottle of wine.

"She good?" he asked.

"A little confused, but my baby is always up for an adventure."

Excellent.

"I'm sorry this is affecting you and Madden," he said as he stopped opposite her outside the bar.

"I'm sure when I cease being annoyed our first somewhat-official date was disturbed by the looming threat of a serial killer, I'll be thrilled the man I've started to see is the kind of man who hunts serial killers," she replied while pouring wine.

She stopped doing that and rested her gaze on him.

"I'm not there yet."

He fought a smile.

She put the bottle down, picked up her glass, took a sip, and leaning into a hand on the counter of the bar, she brought them full circle to the start of their evening.

The town council meeting.

"How bad was it?"

"Chaos," he told her. "Accusations flying. A couple of fists flying. The boys named, they're men now, don't have the greatest reputations in town from what I could tell. Once the initial news sunk in, this didn't seem much of a shock, but it sent a shockwave through the meeting. Only one set of parents was there. Two other sets showed at the sheriff's office before I left, shouting slander, wanting him to arrest Ellen Macklemore and demanding to know the name of the accuser." He took a drink of his bourbon. Then said, "It's not something I can wade into, so once we got things calmed down and people on their way at the council chambers, and Moran was facing it at his office, I felt shit, but I had to leave Harry to it."

That wasn't exactly true.

He had a few things to say to the parents before he left, but he didn't need to relay that now.

Fortunately, an FBI agent held sway pretty much anywhere, so after he gave his lecture, some of them calmed down because they listened to reason, and others did it because they were scared of him.

Either way, they'd stopped shouting and making demands so Moran could talk to them.

"This won't go well for the coven," she noted.

"They were, no other way to put it, enraged at what Ellen did."

"Even so."

She was right.

"Is there something I can do for this young woman?"

Of course she'd ask that.

"I don't know. She might need a hideout. She's definitely going to need advocates. Moran sent a deputy out to check on her. I'll keep on top of it and ask Polly. Okay?"

"Okay," she agreed and changed the subject "You raced out this morning, is everything all right with that?"

"We're making headway. It isn't looking good for Ezra."

Her lips thinned.

"It means it'll be over soon, sweetheart," he placated.

She took another sip, looking him right in the eye, then asked, "And then?"

He knew what she was asking, and it wasn't about his plans to catch CK after they took down Ezra Corbin and Carrie Molnar.

"And then, I'm going to go back to my office. I'm going to ask for reassignment to the Seattle division. But before I go, I'm going to see if Moran has any money in his budget for a dedicated detective. He doesn't have one now, and the way things are going in Fret County, he needs one. He's a good cop, and he runs a clean shop, but I don't want to brag, they'd get something unexpected with me. If he finds money in his budget, I won't ask for reassignment. I'll just quit."

"Are you being serious?" she breathed.

And there.

Fuck.

He wished he could take a picture.

The happy, excited look on her face.

Yeah, he was so fucking quitting.

He got that look honestly, he gave her honesty in return.

"It's beautiful out here and you're beautiful and your daughter is beautiful, and I'm tired of seeing beautiful girls with their heads caved in lying on plastic. I decided it before I met you, but I can't say that getting to know you better isn't high on the priority list of things I'll do once I move here. And just so there's no mistake, it's at the top of the list. Still, bottom line, I need something else in my life, and I like it out here. It feels right. It feels like I fit. And I haven't fit anywhere since I was two."

She stood, leaning into a hand, her other hand holding a glass with some pink wine in it out to the side.

She was wearing a gorgeous dress, looking gorgeous, holding his eyes, and she said, "I really, really, really, really, *really* wish I could make out with you right now."

It was the most girlie thing she'd done.

And of course, his body responded as did his mouth, which he used to say, "Then get over here. We'll go lightly in case Madden wakes up."

She walked around the bar right into his arms.

She kept hold on her glass out to the side, her other hand resting on his chest, her head tipped back.

"I take Madden to the airport to go see her father on Friday afternoon. Can I ask for a sleepover Friday night?" she requested.

His answer was a growl. "Absolutely."

She smiled.

And Rus kissed her.

THIRTY-ONE

Cunning Queen

L ucinda had given him a keycard.

Even so, late the next morning, Rus still knocked before he used it, stuck his head in and called, "It's Rus!"

Madden came around the corner.

His heart shrank when he saw her in a cute black dress with tiny white polka dots and black velvet hearts on black netting that over-laid a shell. It had a pleated skirt, short sleeves and a satin bow tied at the throat.

"Hey, Mr. Lazarus," she greeted.

"Hey, doll," he returned, coming in. "How you doing?"

She scrunched her mouth to one side.

Yeah.

Indira came around the corner, also in black. Hers was a shiny material that looked like a buttoned-up coat and had sleeves that ended below her elbows.

She looked him head to toe in his suit and tie and gave him a small smile.

"Rus, come in. Do you want coffee?"

He shook his head.

Madden took off, calling, "Mom! Mr. Lazarus is here!"

He moved to Indira who held out both hands.

He took them, squeezed, let her go and asked quietly, "How're your girls doing?"

"Cin, fine. Or at least, she hides it well. Madden, not as fine," she answered.

He nodded.

It was the day they were saying goodbye to Brittanie.

Indira walked him in, stopping them at the pool table at the corner. "I hear you're making progress."

"Yes."

"Good." She looked up at him. "Thank you for getting her to move down here."

"It's temporary. Then they'll be safe to go home."

"I know." She gazed off into the suite where the primary bedroom was, undoubtedly also to where Lucinda was still getting ready and to where Madden had disappeared, and said, "When Alice Pulaski was missing, I didn't sleep for a solid three days. Although she was better at putting her makeup on to hide it, I don't think Cin did either. Jaeger took time off, came up and slept on their couch for two weeks. By then we knew Alice was gone, and we were wishing she was back to missing. Even now, sometimes I hold on to a hug so long, Maddy squirms and thinks I'm weird." Again, she looked up at him. "With this going on, I'm glad they're close to you."

He didn't know what to say, so he simply nodded.

"Thank you for taking us to the funeral," she said.

"My honor," he replied.

She reached out and took his hand.

Rus thought that was sweet, his fingers closed around hers, and he squeezed.

The thing was, when he was done squeezing, she didn't let go.

THEY WERE SAYING goodbye to a beautiful young woman who died too soon.

And he was going to kill the middle-aged skank who was sitting in the front row.

The burlesque was dark, and the club was closed, and neither would open until the next night.

Lucinda wanted Brittanie's friends to have time to say goodbye, think of her and grieve.

The tables had been moved, and chairs that were covered in a light pink material were lined up to face an expansive array of huge bouquets made of cream, light pink and dark pink roses. These nestled around two poster-size pictures of a happy, alive Brittanie on easels, as well as a table filled with other photos and mementos of her.

There was a reading stand to the side where a female pastor was handling the ceremony.

The seating was theater style, curved, and Lucinda had Gary, Dakota, Keyleigh, her boyfriend Declan, as well as Melanie seated front and center.

She and Indira, with Madden sandwiched in between, sat at the front, but off on one of the wings.

In the congregation, among the other mourners (and the house was packed), Cade sat with Jason and Jesse, and sandwiching stone-faced Jace, who Rus didn't see take his eyes off the display at the front once, were Celeste and Delphine.

The pastor had clearly done her homework and had lovely things to say about Brittanie.

After a thankfully short prayer, she opened it up to the crowd and several friends walked to the front to share.

Keyleigh was the last, turning to a portrait on an easel, talking directly to Brittanie but telling them all Declan had asked her to marry him that weekend, and she'd actually sent an entire, excited text to Brittanie before she realized she'd never receive it.

She got this out before she dissolved into sobs and Declan had to go fetch her.

It was also when Rus got choked up.

Gary wept silently through it all, and since his dad was showing emotion, Dakota did the same.

But Melanie spent the entire service shooting filthy looks Lucinda's way.

On one hand, he got it.

The streamlined, black turtleneck dress Lucinda wore, with her healthy hair hanging straight around the sides of her face, the silver pumps on her feet, the thick silver bangle at her wrist and large, interesting silver ring on right middle finger, she was the height of funereal elegance.

And Melanie, wearing a too-short dress that looked like a black-and-white print of a patchwork quilt, and she had not taken the time to deal with the roots in her hair, was not.

On the other hand, her daughter's ashes were sheltered among the roses in an ornate urn not ten feet from her, she'd been murdered at twenty-five, so how the woman could be anything but destroyed, Rus couldn't fathom.

He was worried she'd get up and say something, ruining all the effort it was clear Lucinda put into the service, before the pastor closed the proceedings, asking everyone to stay and share a light luncheon buffet that would soon be served.

At first though, no one moved, because suddenly, static played over the sound system, like someone was changing the channel.

Rus knew what was coming, so he clenched his teeth so he wouldn't lose it.

When the guitar hit, Gary's quiet weeping became audible. Not loud sobs, but he could be heard, and Dakota wrapped his arm around his old man's shoulders and tugged him close.

It took Jace until the lyrics started to drop his head, and when he did, Celeste curled into him, burrowing her face into his neck.

Jesse visibly swallowed and both his hands were clenched into fists. It didn't take long before Bohannan's hand covered one of them and remained there.

And, "Wish You Were Here" by Pink Floyd played.

Rus was glad she did it.

It was wholly devastating.

But at least Lucinda got to say what she needed to say to Brittanie.

It was beautiful, how everyone stayed seated until the very last moment of the song, the wind whistling, taking Brittanie away.

And then it was done.

She'd never be there again.

But those who were kept going.

As folks got up to mingle, and Melanie made a beeline to Lucinda, Rus, who'd been standing off to the side with Moran and Porter, strode forward.

"Take Madden," he murmured to Indira as Melanie arrived at Lucinda.

He felt her startled look, but she bundled Madden away just as Melanie demanded, "I want her ashes."

Rus put his hand to the small of Lucinda's back, opening his mouth to say something, but he should have known better.

"You can't have them," Lucinda replied sedately.

"She's my daughter, I want her ashes," Melanie spat.

"I'm aware she's your daughter. And next weekend, Gary, Dakota, Keyleigh, Declan, Madden and I are going to put her in the river. She loved the river and that's where Gary and Dakota want her to be. It's going to be a private ceremony. Of course, if you'd like to be there, you're welcome."

"You don't get to pick where she goes," Melanie retorted.

"I didn't," Lucinda replied.

"I'm taking her with me," Melanie declared.

"Then how 'bout you give Cin the twenty K she dropped on this shindig?"

Gary was there, and even if his face was haggard and still wet with tears, his words were snide.

Melanie turned on Gary. "I'm not sure what this has to do with you."

Gary's bloodshot eyes bugged out and his face turned purple.

Rus pressed in at Lucinda's back, because he knew Gary was going to blow, and he wanted her out of there.

And then, Gary didn't blow.

"You're a miserable individual, Melanie Iverson," he said in a defeated voice. "And you can't have her. She hung out with little Maddy by the river, and they played in it when Maddy was a little thing and that's where Maddy wants her. So that's where she's gonna go."

Rus got choked up again.

Melanie started to say something.

But Gary kept talking.

"I knew you'd pull shit, so I asked. And as her dad, I got rights. And as the person who claimed her and paid for all this, Lucinda has rights too. You got nothin'. You wanna fight it, punch at the sky all you want, woman. By the time you rake together enough cash to take us to court or whatever, my beautiful Brittanie will be free and breezy."

Melanie looked fit to be tied.

Not reading the situation, that being that Gary had sorted it, Dakota butted in and asked, "Where's my dog?"

At this point, Rus guided Lucinda away while looking toward Moran, who had Dakota's dog on his four acres south of town. He'd been rechristened Smokey. And Moran's two chocolate labs had adopted him as one of their own.

Fortunately, Melanie didn't know that.

And Dakota would never find out.

HE SAW her outside on the deck alone.

So he left Keyleigh, Declan, Gary and Indira with Lucinda in Lucinda's kitchen, since they'd moved the final mourners down to the more intimate space of her house once everyone else had left.

Rus walked out to the deck.

To Madden.

He stopped next to where she was leaning against the railing, her ankle twisting, staring at the river.

"You wanna be alone?" he asked.

"Not really," she answered.

"You hanging in there?" he asked.

"I guess," she answered.

Regrettably, that was all he had.

"Mom says you have a daughter," she remarked.

"Yep. Twice as old as you and at the University of Florida. Her name is Sabrina. I have a son too, he's older. He's called Acre."

"I'm gonna have a daughter."

"They're the best."

"Britt loved Jason Bohannan and said they were gonna make baby girls, and she said I could be their big sister."

Shit.

Rus pulled his thoughts together and then gave it to her straight.

"Well, sweetheart, as horrible as it is, and as much as it hurts, there was a lot that Brittanie wanted to do that she won't get to do. But she leaves us with things that make her stay special, even when she's not with us. All the memories you have with her in them. But also, she taught us to live it up while we're here, because sometimes, we just don't know what's going to happen."

"Yeah," she whispered. "Live it up."

He looked down at her shining dark head. "It's not fun to know all that."

She didn't look at him but kept her eyes to the river when she spoke.

"No. It's funny, though. You said that. You said it just like her. One of the things Britt always said was, 'Live it up.' We'd make popcorn and she'd melt butter for it, and she'd melt a whole lot, look at me and say, 'We gotta live it up, baby.' Or she'd do my hair before we'd go to the grocery store, and it'd be all fancy, and she'd say, 'Who cares, we're living it up, you and me.' So I guess that's right."

"I know it is, honey."

Finally, she tipped her head back to look at him. "Do you think she lived it up enough before she went, Mr. Lazarus?"

No, he didn't.

"I think a woman who knows to melt all the butter they want for popcorn knew how to live life, Maddy."

"I hope so."

He ran his hand over her hair then turned and leaned into his forearms on the railing.

He knew that conversation went okay when Madden returned her attention to the river too, but she did it leaning down his side.

The water rushed over the rocks like it had before either of them made it to the earth, and as it would after they were both gone.

Together, they stayed close and watched it race away.

And they did this for a long time.

HE WAS WALKING BACK to his SUV after hitting the grocery store when his phone vibrated against his pectoral.

He pulled it out of his inside suit jacket pocket, looked at it, and saw he had a text from Moran.

He opened it up and read, *Carrie Molnar hasn't checked in and hasn't come home. She's in the wind.*

Goddamn.

Shit.

"MOMMA! I don't wanna be an immunologist when I grow up! I want to be a fashion designer!"

They were in the big seating area of Lucinda's suite.

When Rus had hit the store, he'd got what they needed, and he'd microwaved several bags of popcorn, then melted extra butter to pour on.

They'd gone through a slew of napkins.

After Madden said that, he turned his head to look at Lucinda.

She didn't look thrilled with this announcement.

But he should have known.

They were all on the couch, Madden's head on his thigh, her feet in her mother's lap.

They were watching *Cruella*.

And he was learning Disney had already figured it out.

The really interesting story was what went into making the cunning queen.

THIRTY-TWO

Man-to-Man

R us sat with his laptop at the conference table in Moran's office.

Moran had been called away for something.

Rus was going through email, writing reports, and texting Lucinda.

He'd started it off with, *Madden okay this morning?*

Her return text didn't take long. *Yes. She's not her normal self.*

Then came her next, *But I think she's shored up by making a new friend.*

Being that new friend, he liked that.

How are you? he asked.

Glad the service is over. I'll be happier when Ezra is caught, she replied.

He agreed.

He decided to take them out of that topic and texted, *So, I'm gonna need an explanation of this Bonner and Sexton thing.*

She replied, *Hillary will be with Madden at the suite tonight while I work. I can come to your room when I get back, and we can have a drink before we turn in. I'll share it all then.*

You're on, he agreed. Then added, *I'll also want to hear all about Bonner Mountain.*

To that he got a gif of Julie Andrews twirling on a mountaintop. He smiled.

It was then, like the man was monitoring his texts, he got one from Eric Turner.

Notice you're on her and her girl. You still need cover for her house and club?

How many of your team are up here?

Just two.

For that crew, two was more like six.

Still.

Keep it on your radar, but when Lucinda is at the club, and Madden is at the hotel, they should be covered.

Yeah, saw her security. Trying to get a bead on the lead of her detail. She carries herself special forces, but we ran her, no military training. Her employment history has all been private details.

Military was Rus's bead on Kleo too. Even though only a few women had passed special forces training courses, so it would be impossible for her to have that tag, he would have said she at least had military training. He was surprised she didn't.

We'll keep on them when we can, Eric finished it.

Or not quite.

He then sent, *You're cute with the girl, and her mom has a great wardrobe.*

Rus sent him an okay sign emoji.

He then sent a middle finger emoji.

After that, he went back to his report, but wasn't working on it long before his phone rang.

McGill.

He took the call.

"Hey, Ben."

"Yo, Rus. Right, got some more for you. Ran the prints, what we got from his house versus what we got from the outside and inside of the window places Ezra there."

Fucking fantastic.

"Forensics team also took some samples from around the frame. Someone recently used WD-40 so it wouldn't squeak," McGill carried on. "We called motel management, they haven't treated those windows, as in, never."

Carrie Molnar had a few things she needed to do when she set up for a murder, and she did them.

And the story was coming together.

The story of what happened to Brittanie.

The story, if these two assholes didn't cop a plea, the prosecutor would tell a jury that would convict them for what they did to take away the friend who was the first Keyleigh wanted to share her good news with, the daughter a dad could have pulled his shit together (maybe) and shown some love, the only big sister a child had ever known.

"What about Molnar's prints?" Rus asked.

"No go," McGill said. "Maybe Ezra helped her through the window. Maybe she was smart enough to put gloves on early. Maybe he got access, neutralized the victim, and let her in the front door."

A lot of maybes.

But at this point, they didn't matter.

"For you," Rus started. "One of Moran's deputies went on the hunt, and at a New Age shop in Seattle, she located an owner who recalls selling the crystal placed on Brittanie to Carrie Molnar. The ID is solid because she said Molnar struck her attention. She wasn't the type to shop there, even just to have a look around. And she didn't seem to give a shit what she bought. She went to the crystals, picked one, and then took it to the cash register. She paid for it in cash but bitched about how much it cost."

"I bet when we can get into her laptop, she'll have serial killer searches and receipts for online purchases of plastic tarp."

They hadn't found Molnar, but they'd gotten a warrant and searched her house.

They didn't turn up a bloody hammer (same with their search of Ezra and Sherri's house), but they got her prints and her computer.

"So the clerk who checked her in the day before at the motel in ID'd her. She bought the crystal. We can place Ezra at the motel. If they can enhance that video, we have both of them there that night, or at least they'd need to explain why they were driving through the lot of a business that wasn't open but was in the vicinity. It's enough to indict. Now we just have to find these two fuckers."

"Yeah, that's what we gotta do. We're on it here."

"We got no stones left to turn here, but we're still on it too."

"CK?" McGill asked.

"Bohannan is coming in. We're going to see if we can come up with a plan to flush him out."

"You know that just gave me a shiver, Rus."

He knew it did.

He knew why.

There was only one plan available.

Somehow use Rus as bait to get him to expose himself.

"We got this opportunity, Ben. I'm not squandering it."

"Yeah," Ben agreed, but he didn't sound happy about it.

They disconnected, and Rus was at his report for five minutes before Moran walked in with Bohannan.

He exchanged chin lifts with Bohannan, but mostly, his attention was reserved for Moran.

"What's going on?"

Moran all but collapsed in a chair at the conference table.

Bohannan took his with far more control.

But he had his attention on Moran too.

"Good news, Lana has taken Shannon under her wing," Moran shared. "She isn't a lioness, ready to tear you limb from limb if you get close to her cub. She's an ice queen perfectly willing to pierce your heart with the icicles she can shoot from her eyes. I don't know how she got Shannon to move in with her and Dean, but she did. I sense part of this is to protect and look after her, and part of it might be her jumping at a chance to replace Malorie. I don't give much of a fuck which it is. I'm just relieved Shannon is covered."

"That's good," Rus said hesitantly, also relieved, but this didn't explain Moran's mood.

"Bad news, Tyler Cook, Michael Mitchell, Dylan Rogers and Austin Brooks are all pieces of shit. I've known that for years. Most of the town has too. Built. Good-looking. Athletes. Popular at school. Acted like they owned this town then, and that hasn't changed much since they graduated. Straight up, when Shannon told her story, they were the first ones that came to mind. We've had trouble with them. Nothing as serious as Shannon. Underage drinking, and with that driving. Intimidating behavior. They're banned from Aromacobana because they acted like such shits in there. And Double D got close to doing that too."

"All right," Rus said when he stopped talking.

"Now they're getting shit from folks in town," Moran went on. "Dylan's been fired, and he's pissed, says his boss has no reason. He's been to Ellen's house, banging on the door and shouting. Twice, she called us, and we had to cite him to get him to leave her alone. Dean says he caught him on the way to his door. Dean's a serious guy. He walked out with a baseball bat in hand, Dylan had second thoughts."

Rus had not yet met Dean, but he already liked him.

"Tyler's always made my skin crawl," Moran shared. "No empathy in that guy. He's the leader and probably the one who Shannon had a crush on. Only light shining on this is that he went away to school and didn't come back. I don't know where he is, and I haven't seen him around for years."

Rus nodded.

Moran kept going.

"Michael is dumb as a rock and would follow them off a cliff. Austin, he probably was a good kid, until he got messed up with them. He's trying to distance himself from all this now. But you rape a fifteen-year-old, that clings to you no matter how good you were before you gave into peer pressure like that."

"Gotta ask, Harry, outside members of your team having to go and give citations, not sure why this is a problem," Bohannan noted. "They're reaping what they sowed."

"I just don't want them to sow any more. That's my concern," Moran replied.

Both Rus and Bohannan nodded in understanding.

A man felt entitled to do what he wanted, it took a serious knockdown for him to learn differently, and unfortunately, this wasn't the kind of knockdown it took. This was the kind of thing that brought to the surface how much he felt the world owed him for just being born.

"But that isn't what we're here for," Moran said. "We're here to discuss CK. Let's get into that."

They started, with Bohannan sharing some ideas, but Rus's phone rang while he was talking.

He was in an active investigation and had given his number to a lot of people, so he gave the men a *one minute* and took a call from a number he didn't know.

"Lazarus."

"Zachariah, I need your help."

He tensed at his given name being used, and he tensed more because he recognized that voice.

He couldn't be sure, but…

"It's Ezra Corbin, and I didn't do it."

He took his phone from his ear, hit speaker, twirled his hand in the air, then jabbed a finger at Moran, and put the phone on the table.

"You didn't kill Brittanie?" he asked as Moran got his phone out to start recording.

"No. I mean…no, I didn't. That is…no."

"Ezra, we need you to come in," Rus said. "We need to talk about this."

"I'm not coming in unless I have a deal. I didn't kill her."

Rus glanced at Moran and said, "Okay, let's get that on the record. Let's get your story down."

"Not without a deal. You talk to Harry. You get me a deal."

"Were you there?"

"Not without a deal, Zachariah."

This man-to-man shit he thought he had stuck in Rus's craw.

He ignored it and said, "You know how it goes. You're a businessman. Harry can't give you something if he has nothing to go on."

"I can tell you who did it."

"We know who did it. Carrie Molnar."

His voice was a squeak when he said, "You have her?"

Yep.

She was there. She either did it, or she was involved. He was involved too. She could confirm that.

And Ezra was terrified of what she'd say.

"What can you tell us about that night, Ezra? Something to go on," Rus pushed.

"Not until I'm promised a deal. In writing."

"How are we going to get something in writing to you? We don't know where you are. I have to tell you, and this is no lie, you need to talk to us. You need to give us your story. You need us to hear your side."

"*Just get me a deal!*" he shouted.

And then the line went dead.

"*Fuck,*" Rus bit.

"Ezra Corbin disconnected," Moran said for the recording before he turned it off.

They all looked at each other.

"He's not far," Rus said.

"No, he isn't," Bohannan agreed.

"Shit," Moran said.

Then they all got up from the table and exited the room.

Because they had more stones to turn.

THIRTY-THREE

Vixen

It was after ten that night when there was a knock on Rus's door.

He checked the peephole, saw Lucinda with another knot in her hair, wearing something the color of porcelain, a camelhair coat over it, and he opened the door.

"Hey," he greeted.

Then he was going backward while kissing her because she threw herself at him.

He heard the door snick shut as his thighs hit the arm of the couch, and she leaned all her weight into him.

He went down.

She came down on top of him.

He flipped their positions and lifted his head.

His voice was gruff when he noted, "That's a lot to avoid telling me how you own a mountain. Understand, though, that is not me registering a complaint."

She smiled slyly at him, and seeing it, he was done talking for a while.

He had her body under his. He had her smell. He had her mouth. And he had her hands all over him.

He managed to tug off her coat.

She managed to get her hand down his jeans at his ass.

He pulled her skirt up and went for hers, but she caught his hand and took it in a different direction.

He broke the kiss.

"Baby," he murmured questioningly.

"Please, Rus."

She needed it. He heard it, he saw it, and when she guided his hand into her panties at the front, his hard cock beaded, because he felt it.

It didn't take long, he kissed her between watching her while touching her, listening to her excitement escalate, then with a soft rasp, her face flushed, her eyelids drifted closed, and she came for him.

Rus cupped her for a few moments before he slid his hand out and wrapped his arm around her. He shifted them so he had his back to the couch, her held close to his front, and what he expected would happen next...happened.

The orgasm knocked loose her hold on keeping it all together and being strong for everyone.

She shoved her face in his throat and started silently weeping.

He held her and stroked her and stayed silent, giving her the time she needed.

She didn't need much.

He listened as she got it together but didn't take her face out of his throat.

"Okay, I just used you and it wasn't cool."

"If I didn't want a part in that, I would have let you know. So put it out of your mind."

She pulled her face out of his skin and looked up at him, eyes still teary, a little smear of mascara, but otherwise her usual gorgeous.

"It's been romantic. The tall, dark, handsome agent from the FBI rides into town in the pursuit of justice. He meets the local vixen with the heart of gold...that's me."

He smiled gently at her. "I followed that."

Her return smile was much smaller than his.

"They connect," she continued. "And their attraction grows during his dogged attempts to get his man. Along the way, he gives her daughter a strong man to lean on in a sad time, and her parents and brother peace of mind. I think when it happened, it was supposed to be rose petals and candlelight and soft touches and simultaneous orgasms. Not...*that*."

"Alternative story," he returned. "The FBI guys shows in pursuit of justice and meets the beautiful, interesting, classy businesswoman with a heart of gold. He still carries bruises from a long-term relationship that she helps him realize wasn't healthy for much longer than he thought. She also helps him understand he's carrying a weight of blame it wasn't his to carry, and I can guarantee you, unloading that was a serious fucking relief. But this class-act woman was so together, she was giving him a complex. So, when she attacks him one night in his hotel room, he's fucking thrilled he has something to offer. Even if it's an orgasm and holding her while she lets go, it's an honor he gladly accepts, because he figures she doesn't do that very often."

"I'm not sure your version will make it into a romance novel," she critiqued.

"Don't give a shit, since I'm living it, and damned if I'm not trying to find two motherfuckers who killed a sweet, loving woman, and still, I'm happier than I've been in maybe two decades."

Her face scrunched like she was going to cry again, so she hid it back in his throat.

She got it together without crying that time, but said into his skin, "She'd come over just because. Because she loved Maddy, and she loved me. She'd grab my grocery list and take Madden to town. She'd get my dry cleaning. She'd bring me an Aromacobana in my office just because she swung by there on the way to work. She and Keyleigh would have Madden over for slumber parties, especially around the time Jaeger and I were ending things, and he was getting ready to move. Also, when Gram died. We were functional and we were loving, and we loved her, and she never had that, but it wasn't the only reason she came around. It was because that was Brittanie.

Madden was closer to her than me, but she was nearly a daily part of our lives, and I miss her."

"I got that, baby," he murmured, stroking her back.

"I worry sometimes I keep such a tight rein on everything because I have so much responsibility, I'm teaching Madden the wrong things. I don't know, maybe it's not good to control your emotions the way I do."

"Sweetheart, you have no choice, life is going to kick you in the teeth. You'll never see it coming. Jenn for some reason wants me to make Sabrina a little girl until...I don't know when. But there's danger out there in the dark. Men are going to break her heart. Bosses are gonna suck. I don't want a daughter who'll fall apart at a slight breeze when the hurricane gales are what's coming next. She's gonna be her, girlie and womanly and feminine and soft, all her life. That's who she is. But I don't want that softness to be weakness. I just want it to be soft."

Again angling her head back to look at him, she waited.

He gave it to her.

"I think Jenn is weak. I think she expected the world to be as she wanted it, and when it wasn't, and she couldn't deal, that soft became hard."

"Yes," she agreed.

He shook his head and pulled them up to sitting. "Enough about me. I don't own a mountain."

She chuckled quietly.

"I'll get you wine, you get comfortable," he offered.

"Can I use your bathroom?"

He nodded.

She took off.

He rinsed her from his fingers in the sink at the bar and poured her wine.

When she returned, she had the knot out of her hair so it had tumbled down in waves around her face and shoulders, and the mascara smears were gone.

They met at the couch.

"It's not that exciting," she said to start.

"I don't have a mountain named after my family. Let me be the judge of that."

Her eyes glittered and she cozied into him in front of the fire, head on his shoulder, wineglass in hand.

"Well, you know my family has been here for a while. And many-greats Granny didn't put up with a lot of shit."

"Yes, I know that."

"She was also a savvy businesswoman. As money came in, she decided to differentiate herself from the other saloons and whorehouses in town, built the Bonner bordello where the club is now. We've rebuilt it since, but back then, it was clean. You could get a delicious meal there. The beds were soft. The girls were dressed nice, and they were pretty."

"Sounds familiar," he quipped.

She gave him an elbow, took a sip of wine and went on.

"Because the bordello was there, and then the house was built there, it became known locally as Bonner Mountain."

"That's pretty cool."

"It's also why whoever takes over the club goes by the name of Bonner. That's just a tradition, not an edict. Legally, I'm Lucinda Margaret Bonner Sexton. But I drop Sexton for pretty much everything but my taxes, bills and driver's license."

"And why Madden is Madden Emery Bonner Rhett."

Her head moved on his shoulder with her nod. "Though I have a cousin. She's younger than me. You may have met her. Esmae. She manages the downstairs club."

"Yeah, I think I talked to her."

"She'll probably take over from me. As much as Madden wants to be something new every other week when she grows up, fashion designer and CEO are not where she lands for the most part. She's good at languages, but she's a STEM kid. She wants to go to a big geek camp next summer. I honestly think she'll be a doctor, but she's good at tech, so she could be an engineer."

"Right. So…CEO?"

He asked because he was surprised at her title.

"Of Bonner Enterprises."

"The club?"

She lifted her head, and when she caught his eyes, he saw she had a funny look on her face.

"No. My many-greats Granny was a savvy businessperson," she repeated.

"Okay," he said slowly to indicate he wasn't getting it.

"Rus." Her voice was quiet, cautious, maybe even unnerved. "My family's company owns about a quarter of the buildings on main street. We rent them to the businesses who occupy them. We have a stake in a half a dozen other concerns as well. And I'm in the presidential suite not because I have a successful restaurant, bar and club, and I can afford it. I couldn't if that was all the income we had. I'm here because Bonner Enterprises owns this hotel."

"You're shitting me," he whispered.

"No. I thought someone told you."

She seemed mildly tweaked.

But Rus couldn't process that, because he was busy resting his head on the back of the couch and busting a gut laughing.

"No wonder you have such great fucking shoes," he pushed out, still laughing.

She'd got up high on her knee in the couch, hand on his chest, and was looking down at him, lips quirking, when she remarked, "This doesn't seem to turn you off."

"Why would it turn me off? If we work, you might buy me a Jaguar for Christmas."

That was when she started laughing.

"Though, I'm fonder of Porsches," he was sure to add.

"Shut up," she replied.

He lifted his head to kiss her and then, still amused, but being serious, "It doesn't turn me off at all, baby."

"Good."

He kissed her again, then asked, "How long do I have you?"

"Hillary works from five to midnight, so awhile." She tipped her head to the side and her eyes started heating. "I have a favor to return and the time to do it right."

That was seriously tempting.

However.

"We'll wait until tomorrow when we have all night," he murmured. "Though, you might be wiped from driving to Seattle and back to get Madden to the airport."

Her brows drew together, cleared, and she mumbled, "I should have been sharing more."

"I should have asked more questions," he corrected.

"Stalemate," she blew it off, then informed him. "My father is a pilot. He flew for the Air Force. He then flew for Alaska Airlines for about ten years. He was sick of the commute runs to Seattle from Misted Pines, so he bought a couple of planes and opened a commuter airline outside MP and also does some wilderness drops. He has two pilots. Porter is one of them. Jaeger used to be one of them. Dad or Porter fly Madden to Jaeger every other weekend. Jaeger flies her back. That's how I met Jaeger. When he started working for Dad."

"Right, of course. I don't know why that wasn't the first thing to spring to mind," he teased.

"I'm never going to hear the end of this, am I?"

"Female wilderness mogul in tight skirts and high heels driving her personal golf cart from her exclusive club and burlesque show to her Victorian mansion built on a mountainside?" he asked. "No fucking way. You're who Beth Dutton wishes she could be."

Big score, because this time, it was Lucinda who burst out laughing.

Lamentably, his phone rang while she was doing it.

He looked at it, and he felt his heart kick up a gear when he saw it was Moran.

Her laughter died and he knew she saw it too.

"Gotta take this."

"I know."

He took it. "Hey, Harry."

"Rus, remember that rental we checked out a few days ago?"

"Yes."

"Could you make your way up there without someone leading?"

"No."

"Right, go to the station. As soon as you can. I'll have a deputy guide you up here."

"What's happening?"

Moran blew out a huge breath.

Then he said, "We have another body."

THIRTY-FOUR

Rhodonite

They had the floodlights on her, the forensic techs in their suits crawling all over the place, but Rus stood at the foot of the bed and just stared.

He was certain it was the Crystal Killer, even if it was not his MO.

There was plastic.

She was tied to the bed.

She'd been violated. It had been prolonged and sadistic.

But she was on her back, spread out.

Her head was not caved in.

Instead, there was a knife in her heart and he'd left it there.

Her eyes were open, not closed, and they stared at the ceiling. Her face was a mess, not only blood splotches, but she'd been beaten. There was swelling, splitting, bruising. The last could be seen on her body, particularly around her ribs and neck.

There were two messages in stone for Rus. They were left on the tarp between her spread legs.

One was a pile of crushed milky grayish-pink powder, the other was a triangle of Rhodonite. Rus knew the crushed substance was Rhodonite as well, even though it was obliterated. It'd have to be tested, but he'd wager his condo and car on the fact it came up as that stone.

Since he had this shit down, he knew the stone was about love and friendship. Stability. Emotional balance. In healing, it helped to assuage negativity.

Crushed, it would mean the opposite of those.

The crushed was for her.

The triangle of stone was for Rus.

There was another message left for Rus.

It was carved five times in her flesh: on her forehead, across her chest, along her stomach and down each thigh.

He's next.

The victim was Carrie Molnar.

THEY SAT at Moran's conference table, Rus and Moran.

"He's been investigating it along with us," Moran said to the table.

They were both sitting there, motionless, staring at the tabletop in front of them.

"Yes," Rus agreed.

"He's following us…or you," Moran went on.

"Yes," Rus agreed.

At the same time, they looked to each other.

And at the same time, they said one of the worst things either of them could say out loud.

"He's a cop."

THIRTY-FIVE

Or, Alternatively...Alive

"**I** can't believe I didn't fucking see it," Rus gritted.

It was the next day.

The media were losing their goddamned minds, so Moran, Dickerson, McGill and Bohannan were in Rus's room at Pinetop, mostly so Moran and Dickerson could escape the commotion and have some quiet to meet and think.

Moran had made a statement early that morning, standing just outside the doors to the sheriff's office.

It had been short and carefully crafted by Moran, Megan Nichols, Rus, Bohannan, McGill and an FBI communications officer.

He'd said, "Last evening, the body of a woman was discovered in a rental cabin. The victim was a suspect in the Brittanie Iverson murder. We're still gathering evidence, and the investigation is in its infancy. The victim's family have not been reached, and we won't identify her publicly until that's taken place. When there are details the public needs to know about this case, we'll share them through statements to the press and our department's social media. Until that time, we have work to do."

Questions were shouted, including if this was a revenge killing and if the people of Fret County, especially the women, should worry.

Moran had turned to go into the building, but he turned back and answered, "We have no reason to believe the citizens in this county are under any threat. I would say to them now what I'd say to them two weeks ago and two months from now. Be smart. Be safe. Be aware of your surroundings. But don't panic. I cannot stress enough, there's no reason to panic."

With that, the presser ended as he turned and walked into the building.

He'd gone out alone, no cadre of officers or men in suits or hangers-on to share the limelight or make this seem like a bigger deal, even if it was.

Moran was a man who didn't need to be propped up by a posse, and it came off that way, at least in Rus's opinion.

It was agreed by all, the less said, the stronger it was communicated, the better.

If they wanted to fill in the blanks, they could print their retractions or deal with their canceled subscriptions later.

Rus had already talked to his Section Chief.

He'd also made certain they passed on what they knew to Turner and his crew.

And last, he hadn't slept at all, not only because of the state CK left Carrie Molnar in, but also because he'd sat in on the interview of the couple who'd rented the cabin.

They'd had a long day's drive up from Nevada to enjoy a long weekend in the Washington State wilderness. They'd hit town, the grocery store, then found their rental, only to discover Carrie Molnar's dead body in the bed in which they'd intended to sleep away the daily grind of stress. At least for a while.

They were traumatized.

"It's a blind spot," Rus declared.

"There are a lot of things narcissists and control freaks do, Rus," Bohannan said. "They're all not cops."

"It's a viable theory," Rus returned.

"I agree with you," Bohannan replied. "With this new development, if this person didn't have advanced investigative skills, I'd be surprised. I'm not convinced he's a cop, but I agree that's the working theory we need to go with."

"What else would he be?"

"PI. Military police."

"A cop," Rus stated flatly.

Bohannan sighed.

Then he said, "You didn't miss anything, Rus. With all you had before, I'd say cop was a leap. For one, cops don't move around that much. Not unless he has a problem on the job. And this guy won't have a problem on the job. He'll close cases. He'll be on the softball team. He's not gonna dick up at work and have a messy record following him around. He's going to be proud of his work and do it well. He's going to be liked, at least by colleagues. They may feel close to him, but when he's found out, the thing about him they can't put their finger on that makes the hair stand up on their necks will make them not surprised he is who he is."

Like usual with Bohannan, this made sense.

One thing Rus had learned, you never really knew anybody.

Sometimes, not even yourself.

"If that's the case," Bohannan kept at it, "how does he have the opportunity to scope out victims and locations that far apart with the time he takes to murder them? Is he doing it on vacation? With his very specific MO, that's a stretch."

Rus couldn't argue the point either.

"Two," Bohannan continued, "my bead on a cop, especially a malignant narcissist, especially if he kept getting away with it, would be that he'd do it more often. He'd get cocky. He'd start taking risks. You get someone in an authority position with a growing god complex, a real one, not just an asshole who thinks his shit doesn't stink, a cop, judge, doctor, it doesn't take long for them to start doing crazy shit because they think they're invincible. You make that person a serial killer, you'd be finding dead women all over the place."

Rus couldn't argue that either.

"With what you had, I would not leap to cop," Bohannan finished.

"Well, now the working theory is, we have a cop, or someone who did a like job, and to answer your question as to how he gets around, he's retired. Brad said he was older than me. He had gray in his hair. He has a gut, but he's built. All the profilers said he'd be vain. He'd take care of himself. If he does, he could look younger than he is."

Bohannan nodded his agreement.

But he said, "He's following you. He knows how to do it so you don't spot a tail. He knows how to blend. Maybe that's work, say he was undercover at some point. Mostly, it's his illness. You can't scope out victims if you don't learn how to blend. He's connecting dots because who you're talking to and what you're doing is feeding him leads. Don't get it in your head he's superhuman. He's doing what he'd be furious if you did. He's stepping into your space."

"Is this going to be an issue?" McGill asked a great question.

"I worry," Bohannan admitted, and Rus's gut clenched. "I think he'd be all about professional courtesy. Especially if he's a brother, as much as that word is hard for me to say, it's true in this context. Molnar was double trouble. She was a gift to Rus, having horned in on their relationship, and Rus was forced to investigate her. Someone our guy doesn't think is worth Rus's time. Complicating this, he killed her. He may have gotten her story before he did, but him doing that took away Rus's ability to learn why she did what she did. Cops know that's important. We wanna know the whys and hows. I think he's going to have concerns Rus is not going to think she's a gift, but not in the same ways we, as normal, functioning adults, would have those concerns."

Fantastic.

This was not good news.

"He's also pissed she impersonated his work," Bohannan kept at it. "If you asked me which of those was bigger for him, considering the state of her, the rage he left behind, I'd say the latter. I think he's on a tear, and he's looking for Ezra, but he's conflicted. He's doing Rus's job. And that doesn't fit in their relationship."

"Okay, now, is *that* going to be a problem?" Rus asked. "Remember, he could have random bombs set up anywhere."

Bohannan leveled his gaze on Rus.

"It's tough to make this statement in case I'm wrong, and that's one of the reasons why I haven't made it yet."

That was an interesting opening.

And not very promising.

Bohannan got into it.

"But I don't think the bombs are a thing with this guy. It doesn't fit. I've been going over it since I got the file, trying to make it fit. It just doesn't. He can't be everything. A master of disguises. A master of the con to lure these girls to a hotel room. An expert in crystals. Finding the perfect victim and taking her to the perfect place and getting away with the perfect murder in seven different states, leaving no trace, which means pretty intense scouting trips. All of this without being seen or noticed by anybody. Then add being an expert in remote-detonated bomb making too?"

Bohannan shook his head.

And kept going.

"It's easy to buy a hammer. It's a lot harder to buy shit to make bombs without the FBI knowing you're doing it. So he'd have to be a master at that as well. Now we also know he can spend an entire week in a town where LEOs are a heavy presence, investigating a murder and looking directly for this guy at the same time, and he's been seen by only one person, because he wanted to be seen."

Rus wasn't feeling awesome about this, because if that wasn't CK, then they had a bomb go off that they didn't fully investigate.

"And he has to feed himself," Bohannan said. "He has to make a living. He probably has a wife. Kids. Those things take your time and attention. Your presence. We can't fall into a trap of thinking this guy is omnipotent. He thinks he is, but he's not. I don't know how to explain the vague threats in his notes to you and what happened in Alabama with that timing and that follow-up call. I can see those dots connected, it's a mad coincidence if it isn't him. I still don't think that was the correct call. I'll just say, right now, even if that was him, he's not thinking about it. He's placed himself in this position. He's here not because you forced him to be, but because he's made the decision to be here. And things are getting out of his control."

Bohannan paused, probably so Rus could brace, so he did.

Then Bohannan finished it.

"This might be a boon. He's going to get more erratic. Erratic will mean he'll fuck up. But it's also a concern. Because he's going to get more erratic, and he's proved with what he did to Molnar, that could mean anything."

Shit.

Not great, but they couldn't get mired in it.

They had to keep moving.

"Talk to us about Corbin and Molnar," Rus demanded.

Bohannan again delivered.

"Corbin is a piece of shit who couldn't brush his own teeth if he didn't have someone handing him the toothpaste. That's why he married a woman who could make the money. That's why he's a submissive. His hatred for himself and his weakness is why he gets sexual release by being told what to do, and that's hurting someone else. He doesn't even have the strength to take the pain and punishment himself."

Rus nodded he got that because it all fit.

Bohannan carried on.

"But he was her sub. It's rare, especially with violent murders where there's no emotional component to it, say attacking your abuser, for a woman to kill in that way. She's off, I don't know how she was off, but it was her. Ezra didn't lie. He probably had no idea they were going there to kill Brittanie. Rape, yes. Non-consensual rape, all the better in his fucked-up head. But he didn't wield the hammer. He's the kind of man to be told to shut up and go along with it, and he will. He's also the kind of man, if you assure him you have it covered and it's all gonna be okay, he'll believe you, because women from his mother to his wife to Molnar have made it okay for him since he came out crying."

"And now?" Moran asked.

"Now, we need to find Ezra, because CK made it clear he's

next," Bohannan answered. "And Rus has to be visible, out there, working it, frustrated, pushing CK, who feels affinity with Rus and will commiserate with these emotions, to act. And we need eyes, so if he's following, we can catch him. I want Jace and Jess working with that crew from LA."

"I'll arrange it," Rus said, pulling out his phone.

"Rus?" Bohannan called.

Rus looked to him.

"This ends here."

"I know."

"No, I mean, he's done. He might not know it consciously, he still knows it. It's just the scenario playing out as to how he goes down. In a blaze of glory or simply walking into Moran's shop."

"Are you serious?" McGill was incredulous.

But Bohannan didn't take his gaze from Rus.

"His work has been desecrated. His relationship with you has been jeopardized, to him, to the point it can't be resurrected. It will never be the same. I don't know how he's going to do it. I don't know if he knows yet this is his trajectory. But the Crystal Killer isn't leaving Misted Pines a free man…or, alternatively…alive."

THIRTY-SIX

Time to Think

Purposefully, standing outside his SUV before he got in it to go up to Owen Larson's property, because the man in the town council meeting complained about "wannabe GI Joes," and it was a shot in the dark, but they'd received his permission to have a look around, Rus made a call.

He set the call to record and hit go on a number that he'd touched a half a dozen times in the day and a half since he'd received from it, and unsurprisingly in those times, Ezra Corbin hadn't picked up.

Surprisingly, with some of the twenty thousand dollars of his wife's money, he'd managed to get his hands on a privacy phone that had no GPS receiver, so they couldn't track him.

But now, he picked up.

"She's dead?"

His voice was the definition of panic.

And he was keeping on top of local news.

"We need you to come in, Ezra," he said.

"Is she dead?"

"Yes, and we have reason to believe you're in danger."

"Oh my God, this is *so fucked up!*"

"If you're in a place where it's difficult to get into town, or you fear the travel, if you tell me where you are, I'll make arrangements for someone to come get you."

"It was just a fucking *scene*," he bit off.

Rus was losing it, and the reason why wasn't because he'd had zero sleep.

"You killed a woman, Ezra," he clipped. "She had friends. People who loved her. She was kind."

"She was an Iverson, for fuck's sake."

Rus went solid.

"And I had no idea Carrie was going to take it that far. Listen, Zachariah—"

"Do not call me that. I didn't give you permission to call me that. I'm Special Agent Lazarus," he growled.

"We're both just men."

"No, I'm a man. You're a criminal wanted for the rape and murder of a twenty-five-year-old woman."

"It was just a scene," Ezra snapped.

"Did Brittanie consent to being raped and murdered?"

"*I didn't know she was going to kill her!*" he screeched.

Rus was done.

"We have the fake email sent from Jason Bohannan. We know Carrie Molnar checked into room number seven, unlocked and lubricated the back window. We have a statement from the witness who Molnar bought the crystal from. We have your fingerprints inside and outside that back window. We have you and Molnar on security camera footage from the business next to the motel. You have no alibi. We have Molnar's computer and will soon have evidence she researched the Crystal Killer and purchased plastic tarp. We have a hair left behind, in other words DNA, and we have a sample of your DNA to compare it to. We know you lured Brittanie Iverson to that motel room. You left her body there, so we know you overwhelmed her, you sedated her, you raped her, and we know you at least stood there and watched while Carrie Molnar caved her head in. Now, someone out there is getting revenge for this, and you're next. You can take your chances, and they found

Carrie, Ezra, so I wouldn't say those chances were good. Or you turn yourself in and face what you did."

A long silence and then, "Okay, okay, what's the difference in time served between rape and murder?"

Rus took the phone from his ear, pressed it to his chest and looked to the sky.

It was gray, lots of clouds.

It was going to rain.

He put the phone back to his ear.

"You're an accomplice, Ezra. You're worrying about the wrong fucking thing. We're talking you live, you do your time, you maybe get out while still breathing, or you're dead when someone hunts you down. And let me just say, they weren't nice to Carrie. Carrie had a *good fucking idea* how Brittanie felt when you two did what you did to her. But she was not sedated, and she was beaten, badly. If it takes a while to find you, this guy has time to stew and think of all sorts of things he's going to do to you. *Come. In. To. The. Station.* When you do, I'm gonna book you and I'm gonna go balls to the wall to make sure you don't breathe free for as long as I can manage it. But you'll be alive, not tied to a bed, bleeding from the ass, mouth raped, carved up, and left with a knife in your heart."

"I need time to think."

Jesus.

This fucking guy.

"You don't have time to think."

"*Give me time to think!*"

And then Ezra decided he was going to take time to think.

Because he hung up.

So yeah, he didn't have to act.

If CK was watching him, he'd see Rus very fucking frustrated.

On that thought, Rus got in his vehicle to drive into the mountains to tramp through the woods.

THIRTY-SEVEN

There
___

R us was goddamned fucking pissed when he knocked on
Lucinda's door that evening, used his keycard, and let
himself in.

No GI Joes. No leads to Ezra or CK. He couldn't go into the
station without reporters rushing him and asking questions. They'd
also shouted questions from where they were cordoned off when he
entered the hotel fifteen minutes before, wet from being out in the
rain, exhausted…

And angry.

"It's Rus," he called into the suite.

The lights were out in the small living room area, but he turned
the corner and saw the fire going in the TV space, candles lit all
around, including on the dining room table where there were
flowers and a bunch of plates with silver room service covers on
them.

Lucinda was coming out from behind the bar with what looked
like a bourbon in her hand.

She was wearing one of those feminine lounge outfits in a shim-
mery satin pearl color—camisole, drawstring pants, and a long robe
that floated out behind her.

Her feet were bare.

Her toes were painted red.

He'd seen it before when she'd taken off her boots the other night. It still was so wildly erotic, he nearly got a hard-on at witnessing the racy color on her toes that she hid in her shoes, like it was a secret she kept and exposed only to him.

She handed him his drink.

"Is it too soon to ask you to marry me?" he queried.

She smiled, got up on her toes, kissed the underside of his jaw, and even with how great that felt, he adjusted his head for a better fit, so she kissed his mouth.

That felt better.

"On a scale of one to ten, how bad was your day?" she asked gently.

"Seven thousand."

"I have food."

"I see."

"Did you bring your sleepover bag?"

Having had no sleep the night before, then the day he'd had, and their first time?

He wasn't going to do that to her.

He cupped her jaw and whispered a disappointed, "Baby."

"Rus, I don't mind. I still want you sleeping over."

He could absolutely do that.

"I'll need my charge cord."

"You have the same phone as mine, I have more than one."

His answer girl. Get it done. No nonsense.

He wasn't sure he ever wanted to get married again, his earlier comment was a joke.

But he could see himself committing to Lucinda Margaret Bonner Sexton for the rest of his life.

One hundred percent.

"Did Madden get off okay?"

"Gone after school. Dad's already back."

"Good."

"It's late. Come eat. Then you can get some sleep. I worry about tomorrow for you, and I want you covered."

He worried about tomorrow for him too.

So he took a sip, found it was whisky, and from his discerning taste buds on the subject, whatever whisky it was, it was a damn good one, even better than a Macallan 18.

And then he let her lead him to the table.

THEY WERE in bed watching mindless TV.

Lucinda had lost the robe, and the pants, and was cuddled up to him under the covers in nothing but her silky camisole and matching panties, which was a sight to see, and feel, and it was stirring, but also intimate and comforting.

And he was wearing his shorts, he had a full stomach, along with three glasses of whisky and two of wine, and he was fatigued as fuck.

But even with all of this, Rus couldn't drift off.

With how still she was, her head on his shoulder, he thought she had, though, and was about to turn off the TV—that and the fire under it the only things that lit the room—when her hand smoothed down to his abs.

"Cin," he murmured.

"Mm-mm," she denied, and her lips hit his skin.

He pushed up a bit.

But he didn't stop her, part because he was a man, part because this was Lucinda and he'd wanted it since he clapped eyes on her.

Though it was mostly because she wanted it.

She worked her way down.

He was straining the front of his shorts by the time she pushed the covers off him.

She pulled his boxer briefs down, tucking them under his balls, and that felt good.

Then she took him deep.

Christ.

Yeah.

Now, that felt *great*.

Watching her work his cock was almost more of a turn on than how good she was at doing it.

When his movements and noises meant she knew he was almost there, she released him, hit a hip, but then pulled off her panties.

"Baby, I don't have a condom."

Her reply was to swing a leg over.

Guess she was covered with birth control and trusted that he wouldn't let her continue if he carried something to harm her.

Which was the case.

She latched onto his cock with her hand, positioned him, and he came up off the pillows when she buried him in her wet heat.

Oh yeah.

Better.

Better than he imagined.

Better than he'd fantasized about when his mind was filled with thoughts of her when he jacked off.

The best.

"*Fuck*," he groaned, going under her camisole and pulling it up.

She lifted her arms, he got it free and tossed it away.

This woman.

Christ, he'd waited forty-five years to find this remarkable woman and be right here.

He slid his arms around her.

She moved.

He alternately sucked her tits and watched her.

She moved faster.

He trailed his hands down and dug his fingers in the flesh of her ass.

She moved faster.

"I can't—" he grunted.

"Go," she invited.

Rus wasn't sure she knew what she was inviting, but he went anyway.

He whipped her to her back, hooked a hand behind her knee, yanked it up to his side, and drove into her.

As he thrust, she gasped and panted and used her nails.

Fuck.

This needed to happen.

Soon.

He dropped down and kissed her.

She came, moaning in his mouth.

He came, groaning into hers.

He collapsed on her then rolled them so she was on top.

He felt her breaths against the hairs on his chest, her hand moving there too, his hand exploring the smooth skin of her naked back and ass.

She eventually slid away, went to the bathroom, he got rid of his shorts, and she came back, naked, switching off the fireplace and sliding into bed.

He hit the remote to blank the TV.

She cuddled into him.

"At least we had firelight," he joked.

He felt her smile against his skin.

Then she kissed him there.

"It was perfect," she whispered.

She was right.

It was.

"Thank you, baby," he whispered in return.

"Think you missed it, but it was my pleasure," she replied.

He smiled into the dark.

Within seconds, he was losing it.

And right before sleep claimed him, he could have sworn he heard her say, "There."

THIRTY-EIGHT

Daddy

R us was in his SUV, two counties to the west of Fret, about to raid a kids' summer campsite that had been closed for the winter, but it was reported someone was squatting up there.

Since everyone wanted in on the takedown of Ezra Corbin or the Crystal Killer, against his advice, they were working with a huge team that included the local sheriff, some of his deputies, Moran, some of his deputies, and a cadre of FBI agents.

Over-fucking-kill.

As the men geared up for what would either be a shitshow, or more likely, pissing in the wind and a waste of all their time, Rus took some of his own to make a call.

"I haven't made a decision," Ezra said by way of answer.

Last night, Lucinda had fucked him, before he'd finished it by fucking her. But it was all him doing the fucking that morning. He'd also had good whisky and a full night's sleep. And when he returned to his room after they shared breakfast in her suite, he saw she'd had his clothes taken away and laundered. So he further had fresh running gear, pressed shirts, the whole thing.

There.

Yeah.

He wasn't even her man, and she took care of him how he needed it.

Or maybe he was her man. He'd been in high school the last time that happened to him. He wasn't sure when that shit became official.

Though for him, he could peg it at her pressing the whisky in his hand the night before, then kissing his jaw.

Or when he'd told her to do it, and she'd got off on it, when he fucked her that morning, and she got an orgasm from her new daddy.

Needless to say, he was in a lot better mood.

"I know you're scared. I get that," he told Ezra.

"I honestly didn't know she was going to do that to Brittanie. It was sickening."

"Where's the hammer, Ezra?"

"Dunno," he mumbled. "It was in the bag with her stuff. She took it with her when we parted ways and she took off."

"Who sedated Brittanie? You? Or Carrie?"

"I don't know why she did that," Ezra said. "I mean, that's when I knew things were going to get weird. It was supposed to be about…about…"

He didn't finish.

But Rus knew.

Apparently, Ezra found it a lot less fun to rape a sedated woman.

Jesus, this guy was a piece of shit.

"How'd Brittanie get the carpet burns?" Rus asked.

Ezra was silent.

Then he said, "Okay, yeah, it was me. I moved her around. I did what Carrie told me to do. And she kept messing with the tarp. She had some big thing about that tarp. Like, keeping it super clean. And when I moved her, I kinda…dropped her."

Total fucking piece of shit.

"Why was that? Her thing with the tarp?" Rus asked. "Did she have some fetish around serial killers?"

"I didn't even know what all that was about. I mean, at the time, it was just like…a new dimension. She told me when I was freaking out after we left that I didn't have to worry. You'd be chasing your tails looking for a different killer. I'd heard of this crystal guy. It's on the news. But I don't keep up with that kind of thing. Though, I remembered it after she told me we'd be cool."

So she told him it was about throwing them off the scent.

Rus didn't buy it. Not completely. She'd planned intricately to murder someone. There was something else there.

But now, since Molnar was dead, he'd never know.

"You're not the only man with a kink," Rus said to try to lull him into doing *something*.

"No," Ezra sulked.

"Let us help you."

"Like a deal?" he asked hopefully.

"Ezra." He sighed. "You need to get what's going on here. This is serious. It's very serious. There aren't going to be any deals. The killer is dead. If you'd come in, talked about what Carrie did, you would have had leverage. Now, all you got is our desire for you not to get dead. And you share that same desire, I'm assuming. So work with me here."

"I don't think I'll make it in prison," he whispered.

He'd be perfect for prison. Fit right in being somebody's bitch.

Rus didn't tell him that.

He was done with this conversation.

"I sense you need more time. I just hope for you, you don't take too much of it."

He disconnected that call and jumped out of his SUV.

Dickerson was there, staring at his phone.

"Something up?" he asked.

The deputy looked to Rus.

"My girlfriend. She's a real estate agent. She says Sherri Corbin put her house on the market and put an offer on a place in that neighborhood where the coven lives. She was accepted."

Rus didn't blame her.

"We doing this?" one of the local deputies called, giving whoever was in the campsite not too far away, but at least they had cover of a thick copse of trees, audible indication someone was coming.

It didn't matter, nothing would come of it.

But they were doing it because the sheriff in the next county ran a boondocks half-ass operation.

Rus reached in his SUV, pulled out the vest with FBI in white on front and back, and he put it on. Then he shrugged on the blue windbreaker with FBI in big yellow letters on the back, and little ones on the chest.

He clicked the safety off his gun.

And they rolled out.

IT WAS LATE, he was in the elevator going up to his room.

Lucinda was at work. She told him she'd be back at the hotel around ten or eleven, and he told her he wanted her in his bed that night.

She was going to sort her sleepover bag and head his way.

He'd had dinner with Moran and Dickerson at the Double D.

Dickerson had gone home to his girlfriend.

Moran had gone home to his dogs.

Rus had at least two hours until Lucinda came, and until that time, he was going to do absolutely nothing.

His phone rang, and it was Jennifer.

It was late for her, so even if he wouldn't have taken the call if it was at a decent hour for her, since it was after midnight her time, concerned something was up with one of the kids, he took the call.

"Hey, everything okay?" he asked as the elevator doors opened.

He kept sharp as he walked down the wide hall.

No one there with him.

"I just…do you have a second to talk?"

Goddammit.

"Jenn, is everything okay?" he asked, touching the keycard to the pad on the door of his room.

"No, it isn't."

His blood pressure spiked. "One of the kids?"

He entered the room, flipped a switch, focused on her but did it still trying to stay alert.

He didn't sense anyone there, but with one hand on his phone, one hand on his gun at his hip, he did a walkthrough.

He did this while she talked.

"No. The kids are fine. It's me."

"It's you what?"

"Well, you and me, really."

He stopped and closed his eyes.

"Jenn—"

"I think I made a mistake."

That was said quickly.

The room clear, he walked back to the door, flipped the latch, then shrugged off his windbreaker as he headed to the couch.

"This is going to sound harsh," he said. "I don't mean it that way, I'm just going to be brutally honest so we can get past this because, frankly, I don't want to be here with you."

"Rus—"

He didn't let her get in there.

"First, you're married. If you've used up your man like you used me up, that's not on me. I don't want any part of it. Second, we're divorced. I do not want you anymore. You betrayed our marriage and my trust. But truth, we stopped being happy a long time ago. We're never going to get that back. Though, I need you to understand I have no interest in trying. Third, again, we're divorced. I'm not yours anymore. So in case you've been fixating on the fact you phoned when I was with someone else, there's nothing between us to make your jealousy rational. But so you know, I'm with someone else. It's serious. And I'm not going to have you insinuate yourself into something that works for me. So I have to say, I don't want to get to the point where I'm not picking up calls from my kids' mom in case something happened with them. But if you don't back off, I'm going to stop taking your calls, Jenn."

"You're right, Rus, that was harsh," she replied, sounding hurt.

"Did it get through?"

"I think I'm still in love with you," she said nervously.

"That's not my problem," he replied firmly. "I know that's harsh too, Jenn, but you fucked another guy knowing I'm a man who would not countenance my wife fucking another guy. It's your mistake, but I'm not the one who's going to live with it. I've moved on. Honestly? If you love me? Let me go."

"That was harsh too."

Now he was on the couch, the fire lit, his still-wet boot up on the edge of the coffee table.

But he said nothing.

"Are you still on assignment?" she asked.

"We're not now going to have a conversation. And no, I'm not close for you to come over. But honestly, I'm tired and I'm done talking to you."

"Rus—"

"Take care of yourself, I mean that. But if I get this again, I'll hang up before we get anywhere near this far. And if you call after that, you won't get me. Bye."

With that, he hung up.

Then he reached for the remote, flicked on the TV, hauled his ass out of the couch and got himself a beer.

LUCINDA CAME out of the bathroom from cleaning up after sex wearing a beige satin bra and what looked like a matching loose pair of short shorts.

She just kept getting better.

He knew she intended to sleep in this awesome getup.

He also knew the next morning he was going to fuck her in it.

Though, those sexy shorts would have to go, obviously, but maybe he'd just drag them down to her thighs and do her on her knees.

"It'll catch on fire if you keep staring at it like that," she interrupted Rus making mental plans as she put a knee in the bed.

He reached and dragged her the rest of the way, mostly so she'd end up on top of him.

"Madden comes home tomorrow," he noted.

She smiled huge. "Yes."

"She doing good at her dad's?"

"He's concerned about what's going on here, but she's doing okay."

Rus wasn't surprised about this. He'd be concerned too.

"He the kind of guy who'll go carefully since she lost someone?"

Her face got soft, she trailed a finger down his hairline, and she nodded.

"Ready to sleep?" he asked.

"Yes."

As a demand, or she could consider it an invitation, Rus touched his mouth with a finger.

Whatever way she took it was the right one.

She kissed him.

They turned out the lights, snuggled under the covers, only Rus making the pillows the perfect fit, because he was acting as hers.

He was not a man who had trouble getting to sleep, he was a man who had trouble staying asleep.

Night two, he was out in a way he wasn't going to wake up.

Until his phone rang.

THIRTY-NINE

Terrific

"It's funny."

"It isn't funny, Jess."

"Wrong," Jace stated. "It's seriously fucking funny."

Rus was sitting at Moran's conference table, his legs stretched out in front of him, crossed at his ankles, his fingers linked behind his neck, and he was grinning at his chest.

Because it was totally fucked up.

But it was still funny.

"Okay, so we hauled in Ellen and Wendy and Dean and Lana, and none of them jumped Michael Mitchell, rang his bell, forced benzodiazepines down his throat, stripped him, trussed him, ball-gagged him and shoved a dildo up his ass, leaving him in front of the high school," Moran said. "Now, my guess, we have about a thousand other citizens with a myriad of reasons why they might be moved to do this to Michael. What are my chances it's a citizen taking justice in their own hands, and not the Crystal Killer frustrated with not finding Ezra, acting erratically?"

"Your chances are zero," Bohannan answered. "He didn't like doing that. He's not gay. That's why it was quick, clean, efficient, and he didn't take it to climax. But somehow, we missed him, or he's

293

listening, and he heard about it. Ellen's performance at the town council meeting. Rus's reaction to it. And with Ezra holed up wherever he's holed up with no one able to find him, he's fidgety, wants to do something, and decided to clean up some local messes as presents for Rus."

"Do I need to take Austin and Dylan into protective custody?" Moran asked.

"I wouldn't," Jess said.

"Jess," Bohannan warned.

Jess and Jace exchanged identical smirks.

Bohannan was much like Rus, sitting in his chair at the table. Jace was in a chair in front of Moran's desk, Moran was behind it, and Jess was leaning against a wall.

And in that "much like Rus" scenario, Bohannan's tone might have held warning, but he was amused.

The amusement left the room when Moran asked irately, "How is this guy walking around my fucking town? We've been everywhere asking about him, he's fucking watching Rus, and no one has seen him?"

"He's very good at disguising himself," Rus reminded him. "Not a single witness at any of his scenes had the same descriptions for the guy. He was shorter. He was taller. He was blond. He was bald. Heavyset. He had a lisp."

"Could it be more than one guy?"

Rus shook his head but looked at Bohannan.

Bohannan shook his head too.

"So we got another victim, at least this one's not dead, and otherwise nothing," Moran groused.

"First, he might have come prepared for Molnar, but he didn't come prepared for Michael," Rus remarked. "You have a sex shop just out of town, we need to go talk to them and see if they have internal cameras. He bought Michael's gear here. He might have taken the trip to Seattle so we couldn't track him local, but that's five hours in a car alone, much less finding somewhere to go and make his purchase. He's got his ear to the ground and shit's happening fast. My guess, he's not wasting time driving."

"I'll send Dickerson out," Moran decided.

Good.

"Next, Ezra is keeping tabs on news in town," Rus said. "I know your deputies hit his friends for interviews, I want you and me to go back personally and lean on them in case he's got someone he's conned into thinking he's still a decent guy. Someone who might be hiding him. Or bringing him supplies wherever he is. And when he does, keeping him in the loop about what's happening."

"Why isn't he a million miles from here?" Moran asked.

"Twenty K won't get you far, and he's probably watched a least one cop show. He knows credit cards aren't safe. He knows what a BOLO is. And he still thinks he can swing a deal," Rus replied.

"Remember," Bohannan put in. "He's had people taking care of him all of his life. He's just waiting for whoever is going to do that next to slide in."

Moran huffed out an aggravated breath.

So Rus hated to do it, but he had to when he said, "We got people to talk to, brother."

Moran pushed out of his seat.

Rus did the same.

"LISTEN, I don't know why you guys keep coming to me. He'd come to our Super Bowl parties because my wife is friends with Sherri. If we were one short, we'd ask him to complete a foursome for golf. But I really didn't ever like the guy," Justin Ingram told them.

Rus's phone vibrated in his pocket.

"Honestly, if I heard from him, the first thing I'd do is call you," Ingram went on.

"We're trying to be thorough," Moran said as Rus pulled out his phone.

"No offense, I can tell you're not twiddling your thumbs," Ingram returned. "But wish you could be more thorough in some other way and find this asshole. I heard what happened to that Mitchell kid. Don't know him, but I also heard what was said he did.

Just desserts, but this town is fucking crazy. Dead girls in the lake. Dead girls in the motel. Wives texting videos to everyone in town of their cheating husbands doing kinky shit. Naked guys on the lawn of the high school with sex toys shoved up their ass. What the fuck?"

It might be the case getting to him, but Rus was having trouble not laughing.

He looked to his phone and saw he had a text from Lucinda.

He opened it.

I know you're busy, but I need to ask if you can find time to swing by the hotel. Jaeger wants to speak to you, and he won't be put off. I don't want him to find you and there be an issue. I'm sorry, but do you mind?

His thumbs moved over the screen. *I'll be there in thirty.*

"I completely understand," Moran responded to Ingram.

Ingram looked sorry for Moran as he replied, "I bet you do."

"We'll leave you to your Sunday," Moran ended it.

"Thanks, and good luck. I hope this ends soon for you and all of us," Ingram bid.

Rus dipped his chin to the guy, and they moved away from his front door.

"I need to get to the hotel. Jaeger's there and he wants to talk to me."

"Coulda called that," Moran muttered. "Should have warned you."

This was new territory for Rus, so he asked, "You got any advice?"

Moran stopped at the cruiser and turned to Rus.

"My take?"

Rus nodded.

"Jaeger didn't want to lose Cin. He let something stupid get in the way of what was important. So he lost Cin. He lost time with his daughter. And he was too damn proud to admit it and move back. He's living with that fuckup. I thought they'd reconcile when he came back when Alice was taken. But Cin's too smart for that. She doesn't need a lifetime of juggling a man's insecurities. This situation is going to tweak him, and he's gonna wanna know you have it in hand. But he's not a dick. He's a good guy."

Moran took a breath.

And then they hit Bro Time.

"I like you. I like working with you. Never worked with a partner as simpatico as it's been working with you. I respected you right off the bat. Just so you know, Jaeger's my friend. We're not tight anymore only because he left. And I told him not to leave. But he didn't listen. We're still friends, we keep in touch. Because of this, I know he's going to be protective of what's not his anymore, it's yours. And because I'm getting to know you, I know it might get under your skin. Last, because I like you both, you need to go in knowing he'll always be Madden's dad, and you can't fuck this up."

Terrific.

"Lucinda says he's got another partner," Rus remarked.

"I know he does," Moran returned. "But I think we both know, there's only one Cin."

Yeah, they both knew that.

And Jaeger did too.

He thanked Moran for his advice with a clap on the arm, rounded the cruiser and got in.

He received another text from Lucinda as they pulled out.

Just so you know, Dad's here too.

Fantastic.

FORTY

I Passed?

R us knocked, used his keycard and walked in.
He rounded the corner and was pleased, on the way
there, he'd girded for what he knew he'd see, because he saw it.

First, the dad looked like James Brolin. He'd be vital, virile, and
riding the high of skimming clouds until the day he died.

And he still chopped his own wood, absolutely.

Then there was Jaeger Rhett.

Thick black beard. Overlong black hair. Maybe two inches
shorter than Rus, but with the build of a middleweight fighter.
Heavily tattooed. Hazel eyes.

His first look at Rus, he wanted to rip his head off.

Yeah, he was still in it for Lucinda.

Madden saved it by running to him, crying, "Mr. Lazarus!"

She threw her arms around his hips.

He ran his hand along her hair, looked down at her and
murmured, "Hey, honey. Good visit with your dad?"

She looked up at him. "I know how to make hot fudge sauce
now, so when we go home, I'll make some for you."

He wasn't sure her dad teaching her something and then her

giving it to Rus was good for this situation, but it was how they were going to have to roll.

"Sounds awesome. Can't wait," he replied.

It was then he realized Indira was there too.

"We're going to Rus's room to watch TV," she announced, holding a hand to Madden.

Madden turned to her grandmother.

"Why?" she asked.

"Because your mom, dad, granddad and Rus have something to talk about," Indira explained.

Madden wasn't stupid and proved it.

She knew her dad was in the same room with the man her mom liked. So, with both suspicion and that vibe kids get when they didn't want to be left out of the loop, she asked, "What do they have to talk about where I have to be in Mr. Lazarus's room watching TV?"

Indira went from sweet grandma to stern grandma in a blink, and for the first time, Rus saw the retired CEO make an appearance.

"If you were permitted to know that, you'd be in here while they spoke."

As noted, Madden was not stupid. She was also a good kid and she'd pushed it as far as she was allowed, so she didn't push it further.

She took her grandma's hand but looked up at Rus as they moved to the door.

"Can we watch another movie tonight?"

"That'd be great. When I go back out, I'll pick up more popcorn."

He dug his keycard out of his wallet and handed it to Indira.

Madden shot him a smile, looked over her shoulder at her family, then disappeared out the door.

"Rus," Lucinda called. "This is my dad, Darragh Sexton."

Rus approached James Brolin with hand raised. "Sir. Zachariah Lazarus. Everyone calls me Rus."

The man's attention was sharp on him as they shook, his grip was stronger than it needed to be, but not in a competitive way, he just had a strong grip, and he said, "Rus."

"And this is Jaeger, Madden's dad," Lucinda continued when he and Darragh broke off.

He turned to Jaeger, hand raised.

"Jaeger."

Now that grip was strong to make a point.

Rus wasn't immune, and he gave as good as he got.

"Rus," Jaeger grunted.

They broke.

"Jaeger feels that he should take Madden back with him to Portland," Lucinda announced, Rus's skin immediately started itching and his eyes went back to Jaeger as Lucinda continued, "I'm trying to allay his fears."

Shit.

His attention returned to Lucinda.

He could tell by looking at her she liked putting him in this position even less than he liked being in it, which meant either Jaeger pushed it so she didn't have any choice, or Jaeger and Darragh double-teamed her, again, making her feel she had no choice.

Though, Indira might have made the decision for her, leaning on his authority to end the debate, but in doing so, throwing him under the bus.

However it went down, there was nothing he could do.

"I'm sorry, baby," he said gently to her.

The *baby* was in-your-face and claiming.

What could he say? He had a dick. It had to happen.

Her lips quirked.

Yeah.

She liked his dick.

But when he turned to Jaeger and Darragh, it was all about being a dad.

"There's nothing I can say to allay your fears," he admitted. "Even if there was something, I'm a father. I get it, and nothing anyone could say when shit is going down like this would allay my fears. I can tell you the people we're looking for have no interest in children. I can tell you I've communicated the danger to Lucinda, and she's taken steps, including staying here, where there are always people around, they have security and I'm down the hall. However, the people I'm seeking are not healthy or functional, so I can't predict their behavior. And in this conversation with you, I wouldn't try. If I were you, I'd be worried. And nothing, even knowing everyone involved is doing everything they can to stay safe, would stop me from being that."

Jaeger and Darragh looked at each other.

They turned back to Rus when he kept speaking.

"That said, life goes on, and as I understand it, the situation is this. Lucinda doesn't want Madden taken out of her routine, but Jaeger, you do. It's Lucinda's turn to have custody. I don't deal in family matters when it pertains to the law, but it's my understanding, if you two disagree on this strongly enough, you need to get a judge involved."

On that, Jaeger turned to Lucinda. "How about this? I check into the hotel, and you got more coverage?"

Fabulous.

The ex on the scene.

Rus's phone vibrated again.

"I can't stop you, Jaeger," she replied. "So, if that's what you feel you need to do, do it."

"You take her to school, I'll pick her up," Jaeger started bargaining.

"That works, but she has plans tonight with Rus and I."

Jaeger's beard jumped at his jaw.

He didn't like that.

Rus beat back laughing again. He'd been in your face and claiming already, laughing would take it over the top.

"Fine," Jaeger bit out.

"Is there anything else you need from me?" Rus asked.

"Thanks for the honesty, Rus," Darragh said.

Knowing Rus had things to do, Lucinda's father reapproached with his hand up, firmly putting an end to this. This meant it might have been a double team, and Rus figured it was, but he'd gotten what he needed from Rus, hopefully in more ways than one.

Rus took his hand, shook it, offered his to Jaeger, who did the same.

"Thanks for coming around," Jaeger said.

He was in it for Cin, but he loved his daughter. He saw what was happening with Rus and Lucinda.

And Rus was relieved he wasn't going to be a dick about it.

He jerked up his chin to the man.

"I'll walk you out," Lucinda offered.

She took his hand when she made it to him, which was good, since he was going to take hers.

She walked him to the elevator.

"I'm sorry I had to take your time with that," she said. "You have much more important things to do. But to them, other things are more important."

He totally got that.

"This is part of my job," Rus assured. "I've never been sleeping with one of the locals when I'm trying to keep others who have concerns calm. Other than that, I've been here before."

She shot him her sly smile, but it faded before she replied, "It was escalating to an argument. Dad was worried too. I sensed he was going to side with Jaeger. I don't like arguing in front of Madden. I thought you might be the easiest way to end it, and I'm afraid I used my new guy's position of authority to do that."

They stopped at the elevator, Rus tagged the button and replied, "I think we've established I'm there for you when you need me. There's payback to be had for candlelight dinners and blowjobs, and I'm here for it."

She laughed softly.

"I had to be honest," he told her.

"Of course you did. But if you'd given them a song and dance about how you had everything handled, not only wouldn't they believe you, they'd not think very highly of you."

He grinned. "So I passed?"

She leaned into him. "You passed."

He kissed her.

The elevator doors opened.

He kissed her again quickly, let her go and walked in.

He winked at her as the doors closed.

She was still smiling.

He pulled out his phone to check the text that came in, and saw it was Moran.

Know you're doing something important, but soon's you can, get back to the station.

That had already been his plan, so he'd asked the valet to keep his car close.

He drove to the station, did some greetings to deputies as he walked through, and hit Moran's office.

Dickerson was in there with him.

Moran didn't even say hello before he flipped his laptop to facing Rus and shoved it closer to the top edge.

Rus felt something he didn't like crawl up his spine.

There was a black and white still on the screen.

He stopped in front of the desk and saw it was an angle from behind a register of what had to be a sex shop, considering on the counter was a ball gag, the boxed dildo medical staff extracted from Michael Mitchell's ass, and a few other things.

"Hit play," Moran said, his voice strange.

Rus didn't even look at him.

He hit play.

The man on the other side of the counter had a baseball cap on.

Washington Nationals.

Rus's team.

His face was obscured.

Then it wasn't when he reached up, took off the cap, set it on the counter, then looked, dead at the camera, lifting his hand...

And he gave Rus a salute.

FORTY-ONE

Ride It Out and Keep Sharp

L ucinda came in his mouth, but he didn't give her a break.

He sucked hard on her clit, earning a mewing cry and her nails digging into his scalp before he got up to his knees.

He flipped her to her belly and ordered roughly, "Up."

She slid her knees in.

He positioned his cock and drilled her.

Her taste on his tongue, her ass in his hands, her cunt soaking wet, he wasn't going to last long.

She went for him again anyway before he buried himself deep and shot deeper.

He slid out, put pressure on her hip, she dropped to the side, turned to her back, and he rested on top of her, weight on a forearm.

He kissed her neck, then under her ear, then looked down at her, her hair all over his pillow, her eyes liquid gold.

"Knew you'd taste good," he muttered.

"Knew you'd give great head," she muttered back.

He grinned at her. "We have that in common." She started to smile but he kissed her before she finished, lifted his head and added, "Better than room service."

"I hope so."

"Appreciate you fitting me in your busy schedule after you dropped off Madden at school."

She'd come back to him.

He was glad he'd slept in.

She was moving her hands on his back. "I'll always make time for you, Rus."

He believed her, and Christ, he liked that.

He kissed her again.

Then he rolled, pulling her on top.

"You doing okay?" she asked.

"I'm great," he responded.

Her face grew wicked with pride, but she shook her head. "I mean with the case."

No.

He was not good with the case.

He sighed, pulled them up the bed, kept her close as he shoved pillows behind him to make it more comfortable, and returned his attention to her.

"It is what it is. Am I thrown? Yes. But I don't have time to descend into that shit. If I lose focus or patience with the process, I can fuck shit up. I just have to ride it out and keep sharp."

"Have you talked to Harry yet?"

She wanted him to move to town.

Since he wanted to move to town, he found that excellent.

"No, thought it best to close a case before I asked him for a job."

She chuckled.

He kissed her again, but had to say, "Baby, it's late. This has been all kinds of fun, but I need to hit it."

"Okay. Me too."

"You showering here?"

"Are you offering to keep me company while I do?"

"Absolutely."

"Then I'm showering here."

That meant Rus had far more energy to throw his legs over the side of the bed and drag her out with him.

HE AND MORAN were at the Joy of Joy sex shop outside of town, visit number two in twenty-four hours, when the call came in.

It first came to Moran's phone.

As he was talking, Rus's phone went too.

Since it was Lucinda calling, and she was calling the same time Moran got a call, Rus felt something close around his throat.

He forced it open enough to answer, "Hey, sweetheart."

Her voice was sheer terror when she said, "Ezra took Madden from recess."

He locked eyes with Moran.

And he kept his phone to his ear as the two of them sprinted out of the shop.

FORTY-TWO

The Hammer

There would be a time, hopefully a joyous one, where he'd find out what Harry Moran liked most in the world, and whatever it cost, he'd buy it for him.

This was because Moran stepped back, and while Polly ministered to a terrified Lucinda and Indira, he personally took on the different kind of terror that was happening with Jaeger, Darragh and Porter.

But Rus stayed visible to them in one of the conference rooms in the back of the bullpen at the sheriff's office.

Jason, Jesse and Cade Bohannan were there.

Dickerson was there, as was Sean Stoll, another deputy, and Karen Wilkins, the deputy that tracked the crystal.

McGill was en route.

Turner knew what was happening.

And Rus had called in Kleo.

Having them gathered, he made the call and put it on speaker.

Ezra picked up.

"That was not a good move," Rus growled.

Bohannan lifted a hand and flicked his finger at Rus.

Cool it.

He pulled a breath into his nose.

"You told me I needed something to bargain with," Ezra said.

God fucking dammit.

"You just made the really bad situation you're in worse," Rus warned. "Is Madden safe?"

Ezra didn't answer his question.

He said, "I want you. Just you. I also want five hundred thousand in cash. No tricks. None of those marked bills or whatever. The Bonners have it, you could have it in an hour. No sweat. Just you bringing it. Come in a car with a tank full of gas and the money, just you, and you can have the girl."

"Is Madden safe?"

"She's safe."

"I want to hear her voice. Put her on. Now."

There was silence then, "Mr. Lazarus?"

Her voice was trembling.

God fucking dammit.

He was going to fucking *kill this guy*.

"See? She's safe," Ezra said. "She's fine. She has a candy bar."

A candy bar?

Going.

To fucking.

Kill this guy.

"Exactly what are you gonna do to dig this hole deeper, Ezra? Carrie isn't here to call the shots."

"I lied, *Special Agent Lazarus*," Ezra sneered. "I have the hammer."

Rus's blood ran cold.

"I also have a gun."

Rus nearly dropped his head, but he didn't, because he knew Lucinda was watching.

"*Just you*," Ezra demanded. "Get the cash, call me back."

The line went dead.

In that instant, he picked his team personally.

If they weren't still deputized, Moran could do it on their way out.

And add one.

If questions were asked, he'd finesse it later, but he wanted people with a personal stake.

And he wanted Moran to head shit up if things went south.

His picks?

Jace.

Jess.

And Kleo.

FORTY-THREE

The Cave

Rus was focused.

So, unlike Jace and Jess, who stared at Kleo with surprise and respect at the no-nonsense, practiced way she strapped up, checked her weapon, gave them a nod and rolled out, Rus was too busy trying to talk himself out of killing a man with his bare hands to appreciate her obvious skills.

The twins bumped fists and rolled out too, in different directions.

Rus checked his watch and tracked the second hand as it dialed around the face five times in order to give his team what they needed to take the long way around quietly and without being seen so they could get into position.

He did this thinking of Lucinda's face when she'd run to him and thrown herself in his arms after they'd left the conference room.

She wasn't holding in her emotion now.

It choked the entire space.

It tore at Rus's flesh.

And he'd looked in her terrified eyes and made a promise he hoped like fuck he'd be keeping.

"I'll bring her back to you, baby."

Now, it was go time to do that.

Their five minutes were up, and Rus began to move in, a heavy backpack that looked like he carried the money on his back.

Unlike the others, he was going to take the direct route to the cave.

Turner and his bud were out there somewhere, he didn't know where. He just knew they wouldn't screw the pooch, so he didn't care, as long as they were there.

Backup.

Moran and Stoll and two FBI agents were at the base of this mountain forming a roadblock should something go wrong and Ezra had his vehicle stashed, or got one of theirs and tried to get away. Wilkins, Dickerson, McGill and another deputy were at the top of the road, cutting off his exit that way.

Before he and Moran had made it to the station from the sex shop, Bohannan had called a man named Paddy Tremayne. He did this because Tremayne knew every inch of the woods around Misted Pines, and the entirety of Fret County.

So when Ezra gave Rus his instructions and he'd given up his surprising location, even though no one else knew of it, Paddy knew exactly what Ezra was talking about, and standing over a map, he gave them everything they needed.

Ezra's instructions?

To bring the money.

Ezra would then take Rus and Madden with him as insurance as he started his getaway.

Once he felt safe, he'd let Madden go. Once he was wherever he intended to go to make his final escape (Rus's guess, even though Canada was not even an hour away, they were driving to Mexico), he'd release Rus.

If this went wrong in any way, Madden would get the hammer.

Rus knew why he threatened that and not the gun.

Because he wasn't a killer, but he did like to inflict pain, and he knew Rus would be just as worried that he'd harm Madden in some way that couldn't be tended as he was that Ezra would kill her.

They'd heard no tell of him having guns, but since, for fucked-up reasons, any piece of shit could get a gun in this country, Rus didn't disbelieve he had one. Ezra was a piece of shit. He also had twenty thousand and a day to figure things out. They had a ten-day waiting period in Washington state, but a private sale would take five minutes.

Rus agreed with Ezra's plan.

That was the deal.

But that wasn't what was going to happen.

Rus was certain he could take him out before any of this shit would go down. The key was Kleo getting Madden free with Jace and Jess covering her while Rus set about doing that.

Rus liked to think he had a cool head.

But he couldn't wait to get his hands on this fucking guy.

He took his time and he kept alert because he was very well aware there was a wildcard out there who could fuck this up in a way that could make him break his promise to Lucinda.

A promise he'd also made to Madden.

And Indira. Porter. Darragh. Keyleigh.

And everyone else who loved her.

So he hoped like fuck, if he was there, that CK liked him enough not to fuck this up.

With each step, his breath grew shallower. Even though the intel from Tremayne said he had a good half mile to hike in from the road, and he had to keep sharp and stick to the route, because the cave was small, well-hidden and Ezra thought he had half a million dollars in his backpack he could just take if he shot Rus, he moved sideways in a half crouch, making himself less of a target.

He was maybe halfway there when he heard the crashing in the trees.

His heart spiked, he crouched and lifted his gun in that direction.

The sky was gray, the wood was dense, he didn't have a ton of light, and he'd been praying the rain would keep at bay until this was done.

But he saw her.

Racing through the woods, right his way.

His focus went beyond her.

Nothing. No visual. No sound.

No one chasing her.

He didn't question this.

He stood, holstered his gun, then crouched again, catching Madden on the fly.

Without a word, he pivoted, holding her in his arms, hers locked around his neck, and he sprinted back to the vehicles.

At the side of his SUV, he put her down in front of him, did a quick check of his margins, saw no one there, then he went back to her.

He ran his hands over her head, neck, shoulders, cupping her jaw and forcing her to look up at him while taking in the rest of her.

"You okay?" he asked.

She nodded, full body shaking.

Shock might be setting in.

He let her go, beeped the locks, reached in the back, grabbed a blanket and pulled it around her.

He picked her up, put her on the seat and made a decision he hated to make, but not knowing what the fuck was going on with her getting loose, and with the pieces that could be in play on the gameboard, he had to get her as safe as he could as fast as he could while figuring it the fuck out.

"Get on the floor, sweetheart. Stay down. Don't look up for anybody, except me, or if someone comes and they say, 'Cruella.' That means they're with me and they're coming to get you and take you to your mom. Yes?"

She nodded.

"Somebody's going to be here soon. Five minutes, tops. Okay?"

She kept nodding.

"What are they going to say?"

"Cruella," she whispered.

He kissed her hard on the forehead and watched as she tucked herself on the floor.

"Stay bound up tight in that blanket, honey. Keep yourself warm."

She nodded again.

He shut the door, locked the car, and was shrugging off the backpack, making a decision of who to call in to take her home—one of the twins, Kleo or Turner—when he spun, yanking his gun out of the holster and aiming it.

The guy came out of the trees, hands up, fingers splayed, but still holding a weapon in one.

Very tall. Handsome.

Kai Mason. Turner's boss.

Rus re-holstered his weapon and beeped the locks before he tossed the key fob to Mason.

He again yanked open the door. "Mr. Mason is here already to take care of you. He's gonna take you right to your mom. Okay?"

"Yeah." Her eyes were huge in her face, and she was still nodding mechanically. "Yeah, Mr. Lazarus."

"Rus, baby. Call me Rus. Quick hug?" he asked.

Struggling slightly with the blanket, she came at him, but he helped, pulling her to him.

He held her tight.

"You're okay now, right? We got you."

"O-okay," she whispered in his ear.

He set her on the seat, made sure the blanket was again tight around her and belted her in.

Mason was already in the driver's seat.

"Let's get you home, darlin'," Mason said.

Rus winked at Madden, shut the door, and locked eyes with Mason before he started a three-point turn.

Rus sent a quick text to Moran so he'd let them through.

They were on their way down the mountain when Rus took off, racing through the trees.

He slowed as he closed in on it, again with slinking movements, legs bent, arms up, gun aimed at the mouth of the cave.

He took cover behind a tree and shouted, "We got her, Ezra. She's on her way home. So let's not make this bloody."

Kleo heard him, he knew because she crept into the open from the terrain over the cave, her gun pointed down to the mouth of it.

He sensed Jace and Jess taking positions to either side of him.

"Ezra, it's over! Come out, hands linked behind your head!" Rus shouted.

He saw movement in the cave.

He focused on easing his finger on the trigger so he didn't do something stupid.

A tall man came out, hands linked behind his head.

He walked into the small clearing in front of the cave, and without being asked, he dropped to his knees.

Rus's heart was hammering in his chest.

Carefully, he moved forward.

Jace moved in from his left.

Jess from his right.

Kleo covered them from above.

Rus stopped five feet in front of him.

His head was tipped back, his eyes on Rus.

And he said, "Hello, Zachariah."

Rus holstered his gun.

And he replied, "Hello, Pastor Richard."

FORTY-FOUR

Pure
———

R us was pissed as shit.
He was wet because it was raining.

And he'd just come from the cave.

Good news, Richard let Madden loose and told her which way to run to get to the road before he got to work on Ezra.

Bad news, he didn't have a lot of time, so he made light work of dispatching Ezra after it took little effort to neutralize him.

He'd slit his throat.

And while Ezra was bleeding out from that, to add his personal flair so no one could make the mistake and not connect his handiwork, Richard had stabbed him through the heart and left the knife there.

In other words, Ezra Corbin was very dead.

More bad news, since Ezra was dead, Rus couldn't punch that fucker in the face.

But more good news, it had been reported to Rus that Madden didn't see Richard putting Ezra down, just witnessed the takedown, and she thought he was there to save her.

It was going to suck, trying to figure out how to explain that wasn't the case.

The last was more good news.

Ezra had been in that cave for a while. From how it appeared and the state of his person, he'd been there likely since he first took off. He might have changed clothes, but he hadn't had a shower for days, and, probably scared to come out of it, he'd used that cave to relieve himself and he didn't know enough about outdoorsmanship to bury it. A week's worth of a man's urine and feces in that small six-by-twelve niche did not make the place smell good.

How he knew of the cave, Rus would never know. Paddy Tremayne knew of it, but Moran, the Bohannans, nor a single deputy had been there. It wasn't on a trail. It wasn't large.

But it was the perfect hiding place.

And the prissy little boy-man who never grew up spent his final days on this earth in that cold, musty, fetid space with only a camp light, a sleeping bag, a portable radio and a small generator he used to charge his electronics. He'd been eating chips, cookies, candy bars and sandwiches, along with some pop and bottles of water, the only things he'd thought to buy before he went into hiding. And what probably drove him to make his move was because he was running out of food.

The man hadn't even brought a book with him.

It had to have been a lonely, terrifying week up there out in the elements knowing life as he knew it was over and having only that to dwell on.

Rus knowing all of that and seeing Ezra lying in a pool of his own blood, wearing a sweat-stained Lacoste shirt and filthy dockers, it wasn't the justice he deserved.

But at least Rus had that to hold on to.

He prowled to the interview rooms at the station and knew he had an audience observing when he opened the door to room one and let himself in.

Richard was in there alone, cuffed to the table, legs shackled.

Rus ignored the surge of feeling, both historical and current, that coursed through him and sat down across from Richard.

He didn't bother with pleasantries.

"Did you get her to talk while you were torturing her?"

"Haven't cracked her laptop yet?" Richard asked back. "Or was she smart and wiped her search history?"

Rus didn't answer.

Something that would bump your shit straight to a tech?

A kidnapping.

Carrie Molnar had been smart.

She'd wiped her search history.

There were traces they could follow, but it'd take more effort, something they could do at their leisure since the case was very closed.

Though, in a folder titled Work Receipts in her inbox, the invoice for the plastic tarp and other items was found.

"You...*we* were fortunate she picked me first," Richard continued. "She found her helper in that cretin in the cave. She had a plan. A whole list of acts she wished to follow. She wasn't getting what she needed out of that repugnant lifestyle she lived. But she kept trying. Searching. When she found Ezra Corbin, she knew it was time. He was the missing link. So it began. If she'd never found him,"—he shrugged—"it wouldn't have happened. She told me that. In the end, she was wishing she'd never met him."

Undoubtedly.

Undoubtedly Ezra died with much the same thought.

"Too much access to true crime these days," Richard went on, shaking his head in a *I know exactly what's wrong with this world* way. "Documentaries. Reddit. Podcasts. People are fascinated by it. I understand. It's fascinating. But you can learn anything. You know the whole story. It's like a how to. Fortunately, most of the human race is stupid. So they might know the how, but not how not to get caught."

In other words, Richard Sandusky was smart because he never got caught.

He gave himself away.

"Save me some time here," Rus requested. "Is that how you figured out how to do the things you do?"

"Zachariah." He tsked. "You know better than that."

He did.

"You were a cop."

He beamed. "Yes, in another life."

"That's how Dad met you. You recruited him. You knew about his accident."

He looked like a proud father. "Yes. He wouldn't meet me until later. I'd just started collecting then. People at their lowest. It was too easy. But I was at the scene of his accident. I knew his story. He was a perfect candidate."

God, he hated this guy.

"It might be easy, but too easy, though, yeah?" Rus asked. "You needed a challenge. You needed more."

"Is it ever enough?"

"For me, there are limits."

"There aren't many like you."

"Is that why you picked me?"

Now he was delighted Rus had figured it out. So thrilled, Rus could taste it.

His stomach twisted.

"You were special," Richard said.

"How's that?"

"Obadiah wanted out because he was greedy. It was all about money for that boy. Greed isn't good."

"You were greedy."

He shook his head. "No, I wasn't. I was smart. I found a way, with very little effort, to enjoy my life, do the things I wanted to do, learn the things I needed to learn to do my work, and get someone else to pay for it. It came fast. You were young. You don't even remember me being a police officer. The celebration we all had when I made detective. The one we had a few years later when I was able to retire."

Correction: When he'd fleeced enough money off his followers to retire.

Rus wasn't going to get into that.

"Okay, but that doesn't explain why me."

"Jedidiah followed the leader. Not Obadiah. *You.* You're a leader."

"Again, we're talking about my brothers, not me."

"You're pure, Zachariah."

Rus said nothing, but that shitty taste was back in his mouth.

Richard kept talking.

"Impossible to sully. Free thinking. Free of pride. Free of lust. Envy. Gluttony. Sloth. Greed. Wrath. You were honest. You listened. You cared. You didn't want the system to control you, but you were perfectly comfortable working within the strictures of the system. Unless, I would find out, those strictures were too strict. I had plans for you in my work with my congregation. At first, I was disappointed you left. It took some time, I despaired, but eventually the path became clear."

He sat back in his chair, but he was already warm to his subject, and he kept living in it.

"You were fascinating to me. You loved your mom. You didn't agree with your father, but you loved him too. Loyal to those people who took you from us. Loyal to that girl who won your heart. Right off the bat, got a job so you were loyal to our country. But you couldn't be led. It was impossible to lead you. It's an anomaly. You were strong, your own person even when you were a teenager. You couldn't be knocked off the path to righteousness because you were just all around...*good*."

"If you admired me so fucking much, why'd you put me through this?"

He looked confused. "Put you through this? We were partners."

Oh fuck.

"This was the path. This was when I knew I could finally do the work I was meant to do. I took care of them," Richard said. "But I couldn't finish it. And I knew the only one whose hands I could trust them in was yours. You are *me*, Zachariah."

Fucking hell, Bohannan had this asshole pegged.

Still.

"That makes no sense, Richard, because to take care of them, I needed to find you."

His cuffs clanked when he spread his hands, palms up, fingers curled, like the grace of God would shine from them, and he said, "Here I am."

"You came to me. I didn't find you."

"It was always going to be the way, Zachariah. I knew it from the beginning. There'd be a sign. It was when true evil darkened your life that it would have to be. True evil darkened your life." He tapped the table once with his forefinger like he'd do to a pulpit before making a point to his congregation. "You go to your god. But your savior comes to you."

Jesus Christ.

And that was literally.

He thought he was Rus's Jesus.

Enough of this mindfuck.

"How'd you find Carrie Molnar before me? And please, tell me you didn't go after Shannon."

"Of course not," he scoffed. "Though, when she left the sheriff's office, I sensed with the way you tore in there, she was important. So I followed her." He gave a father's disappointed shake of his head. "She relies too much on her friends. She went right to them. They then went right to that coffeehouse and had a conversation anyone could hear. I contacted the website they mentioned and asked personally for someone in this area, a female with male partner, to assist me. They suggested her and sent the photos I requested. I knew the minute I saw her picture she was the one I needed. It's all in the eyes, Zachariah. All in the eyes."

Looking in his crazy-as-fuck eyes, Rus knew this was true.

"I booked it," Richard went on. "I did this all at the coffeehouse. On my phone. It took maybe half an hour."

There were so many things creepy about his story, Rus closed the lid on it to unpack later and kept to theme.

Though, he'd be a damned sight more careful about public conversations, and he was already careful.

"How'd you know he'd take Madden?"

That was how he'd gotten to the cave first. He'd been watching the school, and he didn't intervene when Ezra grabbed Madden at recess.

No, the fuck didn't neutralize him there so it could all be over, and Madden didn't have to live with it. He let him take her and followed Ezra to the cave.

"It was all he could do. The only play he had to make. He was so weak, the only shot he had was going after a child. And the only child who would get your undivided attention, and he thought, though I knew it wouldn't be true, make you do what he wanted you to do, was that little girl."

They should have called that.

Though, Rus wouldn't have expected Ezra to have the balls to make that play.

Still.

"If you could take him down so easily, why didn't you let her loose earlier?" he asked Richard.

"You needed to be on your way to rescue her, Zachariah. I couldn't have that little girl wandering in the woods while he lay dead in a cave. She could get lost. You hadn't found him in days. I don't blame you. He was not a man I'd peg who could live in that squalor. But he'd grown complacent because you hadn't found him. I was just outside, listening to the whole thing as he made his arrangements. I knew when you'd be on your way. When the time would be right. In the end, he only had her for four hours."

"You could have let us know where she was. He was. You could have intervened."

"No, I couldn't."

Not true.

He could.

But he wouldn't.

Because it was all about the drama with this fucking guy.

"Are there things you did I don't know about?" he asked.

"You mean, when I was cutting my teeth, as it were?"

Cutting his teeth.

Fucking hell.

"Yeah," Rus forced out.

"Of course you know I had disciples, and although they didn't seem to enjoy it, in order to reach for their salvation, the women were very accommodating. And to seek their own deliverance, the men had no hesitation offering their wives. Then again, women always find ways to endure, just as men always find ways to use them to get what they need."

Oh fuck.

"My mother?" Rus clipped.

"No," he murmured. "Your father had his limits. I knew that. I didn't even ask. Many of the other men didn't feel the same, though. We were a special group within the larger whole. A secret society."

It was thin, but at least there was that.

"It did get to the point where the women were wondering why things were how they were between us," Richard shared. "How they didn't seem to be able to touch the light, and why their men allowed it to happen. It was a period I found very frustrating, because, obviously, back then, I couldn't bring it to fruition. I couldn't complete their redemption and send them home. Not really."

"So you started doing that, the bringing it to fruition gig, when I got in the FBI, thinking I'd catch the case so I could clean up after you."

A dead, flat, sinister light hit his eyes and he said low, "You weren't cleaning up after me, Zachariah. They weren't *messes*. They were *saved*. You were part of the process. You took care of them, didn't you?"

"Yeah," he grunted. "I took care of them."

It was eerie as fuck how that evil light flickered out like it hadn't been there, before, straight back to his we're-all-friends-here conversational style, he shared, "If the FBI hadn't given me to you, I would have requested you. I think they would have obliged. Though I knew you'd advance very quickly, so my chances were good. You are, as we both know, *you*."

Fuck him and his compliments.

"You're sitting there, looking me in the eye, telling me you started killing women because of me. How am I supposed to live with that?"

"Zachariah." It was a parental snap. No, it was a reverend

scolding a wayward deacon. "You don't have responsibility for me. Don't you dare take responsibility for me."

It wasn't an admonishment to make Rus feel better.

It was an admonishment not to claim dominion over his actions.

Those were his.

And he was proud of them.

"You know you're never going to get out," he said.

The man smiled.

He actually smiled.

"I'm excited for things to come," he shared. "So many minds to mold. A captive audience. It's going to be very satisfying."

Christ.

He'd let the criminal psychologists and profilers work at figuring him out.

He wanted to see Lucinda and Madden and figure out what was next for…no big deal, just the rest of his life.

Rus stood. "I think we're done."

"Wait," Richard called as he started toward the door.

He looked down at a man who took very good care himself. Tall. Nice-looking. Strong build.

And criminally insane.

If he didn't know him, he'd think he was maybe ten years older than Rus.

But Richard Sandusky was seventy years old.

His dad had been taken in by a guy that was three years younger than him.

And Richard Sandusky had been five years older than Acre when he already had the beginnings of his cult.

What was wrong in a society that people were so lost, so desperate to find meaning, that if they looked, they could discover in a single pine tree, and they were so reckless with these needs, they grabbed hold of anyone who told them they had the answers?

Rus's father was going to be wrecked by this.

And like all of it, that was on Pastor Richard too.

"What crystal did Molnar give you?" he asked. "She had no idea, and I'm dying to know."

Rus wished that was true.

"A Pyrite," he told him.

He wrinkled his nose. "Flashy."

Yeah, that was what was wrong with Carrie Molnar's whole thing.

But...

It was over.

Brittanie had justice.

Rus had answers to give her friends and family.

And he had the same for all the other victims' families.

He didn't have to dwell on it anymore.

He could leave the Bureau with this case closed and get on with his life.

Clean break.

New start.

Yeah.

On that thought, Rus turned his back on the man.

And he walked away.

FORTY-FIVE

Scotch

Lucinda and Madden were passed out on the couch, Madden tucked so tightly to Lucinda, she was covering her, and you could barely see anything but a hint of Maddy.

Jaeger was in an armchair across from them, staring at them, possibly counting his blessings, possibly rethinking his decisions and learning some lessons.

Darragh was asleep in the other armchair.

Indira was cleaning up after making cookies in the kitchen.

Rus was out on the deck with Porter, his eyes aimed inside.

He looked to Lucinda's brother.

"I got something I have to do," he told him.

"I figure you do," Porter replied.

"If she wakes up, tell her if she needs me, call, and I'll come."

"Man, just come back when you're done. Save her the call."

Rus looked him in the eye and then nodded.

He turned to take the steps that would lead him through the garden, up and around, to where he'd parked his SUV.

But Porter stopped him.

"Lazarus."

He turned back.

It was guttural when he said, "Thanks."

Rus jerked up his chin.

He jogged up the steps and to his SUV.

He angled in, did a tight turn in the vehicle-clogged space, and drove up and around the club, then headed down the mountain.

It started to rain before he hit the main road that would lead him to Misted Pines.

It was dark and it was foggy, it was also late, and Rus didn't rush.

There wasn't a lot of traffic, barely anyone out.

Maybe folks were sticking close to home and taking the time to cherish what they had before they forgot to do that on a daily basis. Maybe the rain and haze kept them inside.

For Rus, it didn't matter which way it swung.

It was just nice that the drive was easy.

He pulled into a parking spot outside the sheriff's office.

He went in and it was a skeleton crew. Quiet. Strange. Foreign. It'd been bustling every time Rus had walked in from the first, and it had been mayhem that day.

Now, he got some chin lifts and that was it.

Everyone was spent.

Even though it was well after business hours, it came as no surprise that Polly walked out of her office when she spied him through her window.

He stopped for her.

She knew what she was about, and simply wrapped her fingers around his wrist and squeezed, all she needed to say that Rus needed to know was in her eyes.

When she let him go, he caught her hand and squeezed back.

He headed the rest of the way to Moran's office.

He didn't knock.

It was dark, but Moran was there, as Rus knew he'd be.

He was sitting at his desk, his chair turned so he could look over the pictures on his credenza out the window to the rain falling on the street.

So he could look out to his town.

Rus sat in the chair opposite him. The same one he'd sat in twelve days ago when he first showed in MP.

Moran knew he was there, swiveled and reached to the bottom drawer at the side of his desk.

He took out another glass and grabbed the bottle of Jameson sitting on his desk.

He splashed some in the glass.

He then reached a long arm out to Rus. Rus stretched his to Moran and took it.

Moran sat back in his chair.

Rus did the same.

They both sipped.

They did this in silence for a while.

And then Rus invited, "Tell me about her."

No hesitation, Harry said, "She was daisies and sunshine and mine for a time."

Rus settled in, lifted his boot, rested his ankle on his knee.

And he listened.

FORTY-SIX

Aftermath

T his was what shook out after Richard Sandusky surrendered himself, Carrie Molnar and Ezra Corbin were killed, and the town of Misted Pines was left to face the fallout.

THE MURDER OF BRITTANIE:

The DNA from the pubic hair was a match for Ezra. They didn't need it, but they had it.

Further, for profiling purposes, considering a female assailant of this kind was out of the ordinary, agents made inquiries in an effort to develop a perpetrator summary. Through these inquiries, former sex partners of Carrie Molnar were interviewed by the Seattle division of the FBI.

They shared she was regularly too rough, ignored safe words and hard limits, and for a good number of them, she frightened them.

They expressed surprise she took it as far as murder, but she was known in the scene as very bad at what she did, which was likely why she needed to find her submissives by being assigned to them through a national website, mostly for scenes that would play out anonymously.

For obvious reasons, they talked to the FBI but did not talk to the press.

The website Molnar was contracted to, due to serious holes in their vetting procedures that led to the inevitable lawsuits filed against them, was forced to shut down.

A CITIZEN CAME FORWARD to the Fret County Sheriff's Office, gaunt, pale and heavy with guilt.

An associate of Ezra.

A lifetime Piner.

He'd been interviewed once by Deputies Wilkins and Stoll, and once by Moran and Rus.

He recalled telling Ezra about that cave, where he and his brother used to hang out as kids during the summer. He shared he "never in a million years" thought Ezra, who he described as, "not really an outdoors kind of guy, unless there was a bag of clubs involved," would find the cave, much less go there to hide, or he would have reported it. He himself hadn't been there in twenty years.

But that was how Ezra knew it was there.

Ezra did have a gun. He did because, according to an email from Molnar to Ezra, Molnar ordered him to purchase it prior to what they did to Brittanie.

At her orders, he'd brought it with him during her murder.

The suspicion for this was that she wanted it handy as a threat to Brittanie, and if things got out of control. Or if, in the end, Molnar didn't have the stomach to commit the crime as she came there to do.

Unfortunately for Brittanie, Molnar proved capable of carrying out her plan.

Ezra did not purchase the gun legally. There was no record of it. They still had no idea who he bought it from. And this was likely because his wife, who paid the bills, would have wondered why he bought it.

He had it with him at the cave.

Also at the cave, he had the hammer and the gear used on Brittanie. They still had her body fluids, blood and hair on them. In another email from Molnar after the event, she had ordered Ezra to clean them and hide them and have them at the ready for their next scene.

It was suspected she did this so, if things didn't go as she hoped, she would not be caught holding the evidence.

Why he didn't clean them was likely for the same reason. Maybe he had an inkling his shit would soon be in a sling, and he thought he could use them as bargaining chips.

Why he didn't actually use them was anyone's guess.

But then again, the man was not right.

Why Molnar had deleted her search history but didn't delete a variety of incriminating emails was also anyone's guess.

Fortunately for the profilers, unfortunately for anyone who had to watch it, she also had quite a bit of video of her work, much of which it was clear she did not have consent to take. Though the video she had of Ezra appeared consensual, and it was filmed in ways it could easily be used for future coercion and blackmail. This consent did not include the video of them raping a man in a way he clearly did not want, nor did he want it filmed.

After Brittanie, for unknown reasons, Molnar didn't delete any of that either.

But then again, Molnar was far more off than Ezra.

Or maybe Pastor Richard was right.

Maybe they were just stupid.

THERE WERE NOW no doubts Carrie Molnar planned and carried out, and Ezra was an accessory to the murder of Brittanie Iverson.

For the Fret County Sheriff's Office and the Federal Bureau of Investigations, the case was closed.

. . .

MELANIE IVERSON finally managed to make money off her daughter by selling a sensational story of Brittanie's life to a gossip magazine.

It was mostly lies.

Gary Iverson, with the backing of the attorney on retainer to Bonner Enterprises, sued Melanie and the magazine.

They settled out of court.

The magazine was forced to print an apology and a retraction and write a very large check.

Melanie was forced to sell her house, which wasn't worth much, and the land around it, which was.

Gary bought himself his own cabin in the woods and made his son go to the home improvement store and apologize to the manager.

At this point, Gary had enough money he didn't have to work for a good while, but he was offered and took a job at the store.

Dakota worked for Lucinda as a busboy and lived with his dad.

Melanie left town and no one knew where she went.

No one cared either.

FOR SEVERAL MONTHS after it was over, once a week, Brad and Gentry from the Better Times Motel met at the Double D with Harry Moran and Karen Wilkins.

They didn't talk about the murder.

They just talked.

Several months after they stopped meeting regularly, Gentry moved in with Brad.

Several months after that, they were married.

Around that time, they managed to get a loan and bought the Better Times Motel.

The first thing they did was replace the chain link with an attractive fence down either side, which went from the road to the mountain at the rear of the property.

The next thing they did was gut the rooms and tear down the sign.

They had help from townsfolk, free services and even some materials were offered.

And six months later, they reopened the newly christened Blue Mountain Motel.

They had Wi-Fi, and great cable with premium subscriptions, and set cute chairs outside the rooms to sit in and watch the cars go by or stare at the stars overhead.

They'd built a deck and bar by the pool and got their liquor license.

They'd taken out the pamphlet stands and had a giftshop in the lobby with local wares for sale.

With Gentry's flair, the rooms were trendy and comfortable, and even though Gentry and Brad were up to their necks in debt, that didn't last for long, because the place became a mecca for Millennials and Generation Z to have affordable Instagrammable adventures, and it was booked every season.

In the midst of renovations, a local artist known for his work on the Aromacobana building showed out of the blue and started painting a mural on the side of the building.

The mural was a river rushing through pine trees.

And if you looked close enough, in the spray of the water, you could see the name *Brittanie* streaming over the rocks into infinity.

THE WOMEN:

It would take some time before Shannon visibly reentered life in Misted Pines.

She did this getting a job at Aromacabana, which helped her pay for her online classes.

She was studying to be a teacher.

The transformation was slow, but it happened, and the hoodies, mousy hair and chipped nail polish gradually disappeared, and the woman Shannon was meant to be before that journey was interrupted emerged.

Rus would run into her later, and at first, he didn't recognize her.

Part of that was because she was smiling.

RUS WOULD ALSO OFTEN RUN into Lana and Dean, who was an extremely good-looking man and younger than her. He was all about affability and warmth, and he openly doted on Lana and her two boys from her previous marriage.

To Rus's way of thinking, they were the perfect couple.

Lucinda agreed, and on occasion, the four of them would have dinner together at Rus and Lucinda's table at the club.

THEA'S CLIENTELE kept growing so much, she was able to quit her job at the Joy of Joy and do it full time.

This didn't last long because it stopped being fun and started to become a grind.

She then limited her clients to the ones she liked working with and got a job working for Kimmy at the holiday shop on Main Street.

ELLEN MACKLEMORE SOLD her house and moved out of town, her whereabouts also unknown.

Sherri Corbin reclaimed her maiden name, Nagle, and moved into a home in that neighborhood.

The exact number of members of that crew was eighteen by the time of Corbin's death, with Sherri being number nineteen.

By the time things settled down, there were only two families in that subdivision of twenty-five homes who weren't members of the group, and their houses were for sale, both in escrow, because they'd accepted offers of women moving in from out of town.

They didn't cause any trouble.

The sheriff's police kept an eye on them anyway.

THE MEN:

Michael Mitchell, Dylan Rogers and Austin Brooks all eventually moved away.

It was rumored that Michael was having grave issues dealing with his assault.

It was also rumored that Austin had tried to take his own life, twice.

Dylan Rogers left to accept a job in Las Vegas, but it was rumored he was fired from it shortly after. Even so, he didn't return to Misted Pines.

Tyler Cook's folks still lived in MP, but if they ever wanted to see their son, they went to Spokane to visit him.

THE CRYSTAL KILLER:

The media was frothing at the mouth after the FBI Seattle Division Chief held a press conference where he made the announcement that the Crystal Killer had turned himself in to an FBI agent after murdering Ezra Corbin and Carrie Molnar because they copied his crimes.

The fact this happened in the sleepy town in rural Washington state that had another high-profile case alongside a salacious scandal just a year before sent them into a frenzy.

The townsfolk of MP were experienced hands with this and weren't fond of the reputation they were getting.

Outside of Melanie Iverson selling her daughter's faked story, the only one who would talk to them was Kimmy Milford. And she didn't have a lot she wanted to say about Richard Sandusky, Ezra Corbin, Carrie Molnar or Ray Andrews.

But she had some ideas about what happened to Jimmy Hoffa, and she claimed to have evidence that aliens visited the area on a frequent basis.

THE MISTED PINES monthly town council meetings were sheer bedlam for two months.

And then Megan Nichols felt they should have it out of their system, and she cracked the gavel with an iron hand.

But by that time, the press had lost interest and the town had gone back to the sleepy oasis it pretended to be.

IT WAS DISCOVERED that Richard Sandusky had no knowledge of bomb-making and had never been to the state of Maine.

The investigation into the bomb that exploded in Alabama was therefore reopened. It took some time, but evidence led to a retired veteran who was having trouble with his neighbor who had a dog he didn't clean up after when that dog used his lawn to see to business.

This vet also was suffering from PTSD.

He decided to do something about the situation, and he accomplished that, living some time with his lawn free of droppings.

It would take him going to prison to get the therapy the government should have given him for serving his country.

As for the call that came in from a vacant house in Maine, that remained a mystery.

RICHARD SANDUSKY'S victims came out of the woodwork. Members of the cult he still headed were either confused, lost or enraged. Wives left husbands. Additional charges of assault, rape, unlawful imprisonment, and a dozen other offenses were lodged against Sandusky.

His wife, Elaine, was sued by several ex-members.

She had a great deal of money, very powerful attorneys, and they lost.

Many members didn't leave the church, and for reasons unfathomable, the notoriety of the case brought in more.

Elaine Sandusky took over her husband's pulpit, with the support of two elders—their sons.

This was until evidence came to light that she, and they, were aware of Sandusky's "work" with his victims, including the killings, and the entire family had a hand in assisting him in conducting his crimes.

The sons' involvement, particularly, explained why a sixty-something man could lure women a fraction of his age to hotels, no matter how fit and attractive he was.

Elaine, an ex-hairdresser, was a dab hand with makeup, hairstyling and wigs.

They were all indicted as accessories.

The sons copped pleas.

Elaine, righteously indignant for herself and her husband, maintaining their work was holy, sat before a judge and jury. Regardless of her assertions, she was deemed fit to stand trial and was later convicted and sentenced to life, eligible for parole in twenty-five years, which, if she made it, would mean she would be out at age ninety-three.

An ex-elder stepped into the breach.

The church's tax-exempt status was stripped through all of these activities, and they were currently in a battle with the IRS to have it reinstated.

They felt positive they would win.

RICHARD SANDUSKY PLED guilty to multiple charges of abduction, false imprisonment, sexual assault and homicide.

He was sentenced to life without the possibility of parole.

As an ex-cop, he didn't find it as easy to cultivate a following in the penitentiary as he thought it would be. And his beliefs that the human race were all stupid didn't hold up well in a place filled with hardened criminals who established their own hierarchy.

His hubris was so overwhelming, he had no idea he entered a situation where he did not have a captive audience of potential disciples, but instead, there was no way out.

He was not the apex predator.

He was prey, a trophy to be won and proudly held in infamy.

Until eleven months into his sentence, when he lost his life during a brutal beating in the cafeteria during chowtime that had no witnesses, he wrote letters to Rus every week and sent them to the FBI office in Virginia.

Rus never received those letters.

Not only because he no longer worked for the Federal Bureau of Investigations.

Epilogue

QUIET AND WILDFLOWERS

Rus and Karen leaned against Karen's cruiser, which was parked behind the Nissan Pathfinder.

They watched the two women walking warily toward them through a field of wildflowers.

"Your take," Rus said. "How's this gonna go down?"

"If it was just you, they'd try to cute their way out of it by flirting, thinking they're young and pretty, and you got a dick, so you'll let them do whatever they want."

"Mm-hmm," Rus agreed.

"They don't like me being here."

"Mm-hmm," Rus repeated.

The women climbed the ranch rail fence about ten yards from a sign that said PRIVATE PROPERTY NO TRESPASSING and made their hesitant way to Rus and Karen, eyeing the situation, not only the two law enforcement officers, but their Pathfinder blocked in by two cruisers.

Rus was wearing jeans and a blue button down under a brown quilted vest that had FRET COUNTY SHERIFF stitched in yellow on the left breast, DETECTIVE in smaller lettering under that.

"Is something the matter?" the blonde asked.

"I'm Zachariah Lazarus, detective with Fret County Sheriff," he introduced unnecessarily since his vest already told them that. He tipped his head to Karen. "This is Deputy Karen Wilkins."

"Okay," the brunette said hesitantly.

Rus pulled out his phone, which was already called up to what he needed on his screen.

He hit play and turned it their way.

"Do you recall this incident?" he asked.

Owen Larson had learned that recording these situations was a lot less messy, legally, than filling people with buckshot.

Therefore, Owen could be heard cussing them out for trespassing on his land.

"We—" the blonde began.

Rus turned his phone around, shut down the video, shoved it in his pocket, all while interrupting her.

"That incident happened yesterday. Mr. Larson made it clear when he caught you on his land that he was not happy about it, and he did not want you here. He might not have been nice when he did that, but he doesn't have to be. You vacated the premises at that time. Now, you're back. Where are you staying?"

"I don't think we have to answer that," the brunette guessed.

Rus nodded.

"Correct. You don't. Though, I'll point out right now,"—and he did just that, he pointed—"not only is that a fence, which indicates this is someone's property, there are also signs posted there,"—he moved his hand—"there,"—he moved his hand again—"and there. Not to mention about every fifty yards all along the boundary of Mr. Larson's property. These signs are clearly visible and share the fact the owner of this property does not welcome visitors. He informed you of this personally. You returned today, when he wasn't around, and jumped his fence."

With a quick glance at Karen, the blonde got a little closer to Rus and smiled.

It was a pretty smile, and she knew it.

But she was a fairy princess (she knew that too).

And that was not Rus's thing.

"Listen, we're kind of a big deal." She pretended humility under a flirtatious look. "We're vloggers. We travel and vlog about it. We have a big following. Over a million followers on TikTok alone. This wildflower field is gorgeous. Our followers are going to love the footage we have from here."

Rus sighed.

Then he stated, "I'm uncertain why you're not understanding me. Yes, that field is pretty, but it's private property. You can see it from this road, and video it from this road, a road that's public property."

"It's totally better in the field. You wanna see our footage?" she offered.

"No," he answered. "I'm afraid I don't have time since I need to arrest you for trespassing. We have a fine of five thousand dollars, this will need to be paid by each of you, and a mandatory jail stay of one week. So now, I have to take you in."

They both went deathly pale.

"Are you kidding?" the brunette breathed.

"No," Rus repeated. "This is why I asked where you're staying. Since we have such steep penalties for trespass here in Fret County, hotels, rental management and campsites tend to be real communicative about that to their clientele."

He could tell by their expressions they'd been warned.

It was annoying, but since that happened a lot, he didn't get into it.

He also didn't share that, if they didn't act like assholes, Harry had a habit of letting people go early.

As in, within a day.

Though, Harry wasn't as lenient about the fines.

"Now, Mr. Larson was okay to let it slide once. But you came back. He called it in and communicated he wishes to press charges." Rus shrugged. "I got no choice. Please turn around and put your hands on the car."

"You can't…you can't do that!" the blonde cried.

"I can, and if it makes you feel better, you're not the first, and I suspect you won't be the last," Rus told her.

"This is crazy!" She was getting louder.

"Ladies, if you could do as Lieutenant Lazarus asked," Karen requested, reaching for her cuffs.

The blonde was frozen.

The brunette took a step back. "This is just…it's *nuts*. We *walked* in a *field*!"

"You walked in someone else's field," Rus corrected.

"It's just a fucking field," she snapped.

"It's still someone else's field. Listen," he started to explain. "You clearly don't agree, but to Mr. Larson, you jumping that fence is like you helping yourself to his living room and fridge. He's a private person. He moved out here for peace and solitude. That's why he lives here. That's why he spent a good amount of money to buy a good stretch of land that's surrounded by nothing but other good stretches of land. And he has the law on his side. Which means, as much as you think you do, you don't have the right to interrupt his solitude just because you want to. We have a lot of beautiful places in Fret County. Right now, there are wildflowers everywhere. Many of them you can get video of without jumping a fence. You made a choice. Unfortunately for you, it was the wrong one."

Rus was trying to educate them.

Karen was done.

"What he's saying is," she boiled it down, "you fucked around and found out. Now, hands to the vehicle."

The women looked at each other and fortunately, for once in their pretty-girl lives, they made the right decision.

Rus stood as Karen relieved them of their backpacks, patted them down, Mirandized them, cuffed them and informed them to pay their fines, the county accepted all major credit cards, PayPal, Zelle and Venmo.

When Rus had their packs stowed, and they were in the back of Karen's cruiser, the brunette threatened, "We're gonna vlog this and everyone is going to know about this insanity in Fret County. All the shit that goes down here, we should have known. This place is *crazy*. No one should come here."

"I'd be obliged if you would," Rus replied. "You have that many followers, it'd help a lot."

He shut the door on her.

He moved to his cruiser.

He made sure Karen was all good and rolling out.

Then he followed her into town.

AN HOUR AND A HALF LATER, guiding him by the hand, Madden led him to the front of her class.

"Okay!" she called out. "This is my kinda stepdad, Lieutenant Zachariah Lazarus. He's a detective with the sheriff. But before that, *he was in the FBI!*"

Rus buried a smile as she paused to preen from the excitement coming from the class.

She mostly gave up the goods with that, but tried to rally by finishing, "So he's gonna talk to you about being *in the FBI!*"

She gave his hand a squeeze, beamed up at him, let him go and went to sit at her desk.

He waited until she was there, scanned her class, who were all staring at him expectantly, and he started it with, "Hey there."

From just those two words, there was a ripple of anticipation through the crowd.

No pressure.

On that thought, he launched in on a very condensed, G-rated version of working with the FBI.

"AND SO, I was like, 'Jeremy, if you save the world from a serial killer, you get to quit and kick back with a cushy detective's job.' And Jeremy was all, 'If I was an FBI agent, I would *never* quit.' And I was all, 'How do you know? You'll never be an FBI agent.' And he was all, 'Yes I will!' And I was all, 'No you won't. I should know what it takes. Even though Rus isn't in the FBI anymore, all his FBI friends come to the house when he cooks steaks on the grill.' And he was all, 'You think you're so cool because you were kidnapped.' And I was all, 'Well, *obviously*. I mean, they're making a TV show about me!'"

They were.

Well, not about Madden, specifically, but what happened to her would be in it.

Lucinda was openly annoyed, which meant deep down inside, she was infuriated.

Rus was a lot more obviously infuriated.

Nevertheless, it was bound to happen. Not even a week had passed after Richard Sandusky surrendered himself, and Hollywood and a variety of producers of documentaries, podcasts and the like had been in touch.

Rus shut them down. Lucinda shut them down. Surprisingly, Gary and Dakota Iverson shut them down.

Melanie was in negotiations, but when Gary landed the big lawsuit on her, and it was clear she knew little about her daughter and couldn't contribute anything substantial, not to mention, she might lead them to a massive libel payout, they backed off.

None of that stopped them.

So now they'd been informed there was a docuseries being made.

More true crime fed to the world.

And the beat goes on.

After his talk with her class, which ended the day, Rus was bringing Madden home from school.

This was his job on days when Jaeger was flying, and today, when Rus was there anyway.

Yes, the man moved back. Too much shit going down in Misted Pines, his daughter kidnapped, that was inevitable too.

His girlfriend, a lifetime resident of Portland, as were all of her family, had decided not to come with him and was heartbroken he'd left.

History repeating.

It worked though, because Jaeger was a solid individual who loved his daughter, and Rus respected him. Jaeger gave that back.

There were times, however, that Rus couldn't wade into, when Lucinda and Jaeger butted heads.

They did this about how she was raising a confident girl to be a confident woman who didn't feel anything was out of reach, and Jaeger was raising a beloved girl who he thought one day would be as awesome as she was now, no matter what she did (though, while she was doing it, she'd be trained to make some man really happy).

It could be said the hot fudge she learned to make wasn't just an activity father and daughter did together.

It wasn't overt, it was just the way of the world, which was why Jaeger didn't quite get it.

Lucinda might lose patience along the way, but for the long haul, she was in it to win it.

Madden changed the subject.

"So, do you think Sabrina will like me?"

"Of course she will, honey. She already does. You FaceTime her all the time. Why would you ask that?"

"Because she's going to be here...*for real*...for hamburgers in, like, *two hours*."

Sabrina was coming up, meeting everyone in person for the first time, spending her spring break in Misted Pines. Darragh was right then heading to Seattle to pick her up and fly her back.

Sabrina was in fits of happiness at getting a ride in a personal jet, having not really cottoned on that a jet was not a prop plane.

Darragh had a small, personal jet he used for his clients who could pay for it, and his plane was nothing to sneeze at.

Still.

In a week, she'd overlap with Acre for the weekend when he came up to do the same.

Like everything with Lucinda, it all seemed to happen naturally.

Rus took two weeks of vacation after the Iverson case closed, all of it with Lucinda and Madden in Misted Pines.

He'd then worked two months' notice for the Bureau.

When he was done with that, he'd taken two months off to pack and get his condo on the market.

In this time, he also dealt with his family, who were reeling from the Sandusky arrest, particularly his father, who was now a shell of the man they all once knew. Rus hoped he'd snap out of it, but that hope wasn't high. And Lucas, whose fury had been renewed by all the things they learned about the man who shaped all their lives.

He'd left that mess in an uneasy détente, but that was how they'd been when they first reconciled, so the hope he had that would get better was higher.

He'd taken some time to end things with Ruth and Penny, doing so remotely.

And he'd spent time with the kids when they came home for the holidays, both of them excited he was moving, and more excited he found somebody who made him happy.

He had not been able to completely avoid Jenn during this time, but he discovered he had a new outlook on that, because her sullenness, sulks and snappishness had zero effect on him.

He frequently flew to Washington in this time period.

He moved to Misted Pines in early February, setting up temporarily in an apartment that was owned by Bonner Enterprises.

Lucinda was in his bed every morning after she dropped off Madden, and Rus was at their house nearly every night for dinner and TV and homework checking and babysitting, which was good, because Hillary transitioned out and into the chorus line to take Brittanie's place.

He would sometimes spend the night.

But in deference to Maddy, usually, after midnight, he was driving back to his apartment.

It was Lucinda who got fed up with it first.

She wanted to sleep beside him, wake up beside him, and Rus and Madden were so tight, she wanted him to be a fixture in her daughter's life.

Rus wanted the same things, so he didn't argue.

Madden and her mom had a convo Rus wasn't invited to, and

Madden was gleeful about the idea. He knew this because Lucinda told him, and because Madden expressed that same thing.

When this was shared, Jaeger was not gleeful, but he didn't cause a problem.

In mid-March, Rus moved in.

Now it was early April, and his kids were coming to have their first face-to-face time with Lucinda and Madden.

He was thrilled. He couldn't wait to have all the people he loved together.

"You have nothing to worry about. She already loves you," he assured Madden.

"'Kay."

"Let's go back to Jeremy," Rus suggested. "Were you okay with the whole—?"

"Rus," she began, like she was forty-five and he was ten.

He grinned at the windshield because she said his name like that a lot.

"Like I said *thousands* of times, I'm *okay*," she stated. "That guy smelled stinky, and his cave smelled worse, and the good guy turning into the bad guy was weird. But it was just like he grabbed me, then he took me in the woods. Then he gave me a Snickers and talked on the phone with you a lot. So I knew you'd be handling it. Then the good-bad guy came, you were right there in the woods and BOOM!" She clapped her hands. "Ice cream every night for two weeks and Dad moved home."

That was pretty much how she'd described it from the get-go.

They kept a close watch on her, because even though she remembered it like this, and the therapist Lucinda had found shared Madden had astounding recuperative emotional powers (not a surprise, she was a Bonner woman) and a very solid foundation of support, it was something they didn't want to creep up on her.

As for Rus, he saw her shaking, her wide eyes, the perfunctory nodding.

He felt her fear.

So yeah.

He kept a finger on the pulse.

They all did.

"Right, I'll let it go," he murmured.

"Like, *forever*?" she demanded.

"No, because I love you and want to make sure you're okay. But I won't ask again for two full weeks."

"I'm counting," she warned.

He chuckled.

They drove past the club and then they drove down the slope to the house.

He'd been right all those months ago, Lucinda had a beautiful garden around her house. It wasn't formal, it seemed to grow wild and carefree, but something he'd learned about her since everything went down, she gardened.

She said it was her meditation.

He was unsurprised her meditation created beauty.

And now that things had started blooming, they had fresh flowers in the house all the time.

He parked next to her Jaguar under the overhang that was hidden by the bulk of the house, and like always, he smiled to himself. Because he knew she wasn't home (being a wilderness mogul, she worked a lot), but she'd taken the golf cart to her office.

They went in, he and Madden worked together to sort her afternoon snack, and Indira showed so Rus could go back to the office for a few hours before coming home.

As he was driving by the club, he saw a beautiful woman wearing a creamy dress standing at the window in the room above the overhang.

He saluted her as he drove by.

She didn't move.

Though she was too far for him to see it, he knew she smiled.

RUS WOKE WITH A JERK.

"Honey?"

She was right there.

Always right there.

He touched her anyway.

Lucinda felt warm.

Good.

He tossed the covers off himself and got out of bed.

The house was dark.

It was quiet, save the constant sound of the river rushing over the rocks.

He moved down the stairs and opened the first door to the right.

He looked in.

Shit.

His blood pressure spiked.

No one was there.

The bed was still made.

He turned immediately to the door to his left.

He looked in.

There was a strange glow in the room that came from the dark screen with the word Samsung appearing and disappearing on it in different places.

And two girls, well, one was a woman, were cuddled in bed, asleep, the detritus of the kind of food frenzy that accompanied binge watching littering the duvet.

Sabrina had introduced Madden to *Gilmore Girls*.

Rus felt his breath coming easier.

He shut the door quietly behind him and walked through the rest of the house, going all the way down the stairs, checking locks on doors, even scanning the garden and the deck.

She was waiting at the top landing for him.

"Okay?" she asked softly as he joined her.

"Yeah," he replied, still slightly sweaty and wondering if he should take a quick shower.

Lucinda made the decision for him, taking his hand and closing the door behind her as she guided him to bed.

She sat him on the side then knelt on the floor in front of him and sucked him off.

She was insanely good at that.

It was a gift.

Lucinda then pushed and nudged him back between the sheets and joined him there.

"Sorry," he murmured.

She pressed closer. "It's okay, baby. Now, sleep."

It happened.

Too often.

These days, it was Madden racing through the trees, but she wasn't alone when she found him. She had someone chasing her and one side of her head was caved in from a hammer blow.

Sometimes it would switch up, and he'd walk in to see Brittanie again, round the bed, look at her face, and the face would not be Brittanie's. It'd be Sabrina's.

This situation would calm down.

And the longer he was arresting privileged girls who did what they wanted because they were privileged, having no idea Owen Larson might snap and send a shotgun shell through their spine or some predator hiding in the trees could wander into a wildflower field, and they'd never find their way out…

Yeah.

The longer he had of them making their way to Karen's cruiser, safe and alive, the calmer his nights would be.

He curled Lucinda closer into his body, and she held on tight.

He let out a long breath.

He was having these dreams now.

They wouldn't last.

And then something would happen, and they'd come back.

But he'd always have this.

His cunning queen with a heart of gold.

So it would suck.

But he'd be okay.

"OKAY, NO."

Rus looked to Kleo. "Why no?"

She turned to him. "Are you trying to set your daughter up?"

From his chair up on the deck, sitting next to Kleo, he scanned the crowd.

Cade and Delphine had thrown a big barbeque for Sabrina and Acre. And it was with zero surprise that, when they arrived, Rus saw Sabrina clock Jason and Jesse Bohannan.

Knowing both of them better, it was with less than zero surprise Jace then clocked Sabrina.

"Jesse's going to go for someone edgy, like Lucinda, or another take on that, you," he told her. "Jace needs a princess he can spoil."

"Oh my God." She sounded close to hurling. "You're setting your daughter up. She's your princess, and the king is picking who to hand her off to."

"It's not active." He didn't quite deny it. "I just showed Delphine a picture of her—"

"And conned the most meddling stepmother in MP into throwing a big barbeque so they'd meet."

Rus shrugged. "Now it's up to them."

His gaze went to the pier, where both of them were sitting next to each other with their feet in the water, the lake their view.

Sure, Madden was with them. And Celeste. And Keyleigh and Declan.

But it was a start.

Maybe.

"This is convenient," Kleo noted. "Since, if they click, she'll move up here to be with him, which means close to you."

"Mm," Rus hummed.

"You're diabolical," she muttered.

He turned to her. "Do you know anyone who might fit with Acre?"

She shook her head vehemently. "Don't drag me in. I'm not going to be a part of this."

And to emphasize that point, she got up and walked away.

Lucinda, who was standing at the deck railing, talking to Megan Nichols, was watching them.

He grinned at her.

She shook her head and gave him a small eyeroll, but he saw her lips quirking.

She had told him, later, it meant a great deal to her he'd added Kleo to his team when they went after Madden. With Rus and Kleo going to get her daughter, she was still terrified, but it gave her a measure of calm.

Rus had essentially adopted Kleo as his little sister.

Which meant, of course, he piled as much shit on her as he could shovel.

She pretended she didn't love it.

But she absolutely did.

Moran took Kleo's place.

"Heads up, brother"—he tipped the neck of his beer to the dock —"think there's a situation happening there."

Rus just sat in the sun, took a sip of his own beer.

And smiled.

LUCINDA WANDERED in wearing her preferred pajamas.

These were ivory satin, a bralette and what she described as tap pants.

She matched her bedroom, which matched her house. It was clean-lined, modern, intensely feminine and, as for that space, it was all done up in ivory, taupe, soft gray with accents of gold.

She'd told him she'd happily redecorate it for him, but since he felt surrounded by her there, and he'd never felt safer in his life than he did with her, he didn't want her to change a thing.

He was in bed reading, pillows shoved up against the gray upholstered headboard, his back and shoulders to them, his legs in pajama bottoms stretched out on the ivory covers.

She put a knee to the bed and then stretched out on her side close to him, elbow in the bed, head in hand, eyes to him.

"Happy?" she asked.

"I think the first part of what Kleo describes as my diabolical plan to matchmake Jason and Sabrina went well."

Her lips curled.

She knew of his plan.

She kept mute on the subject.

But he sensed she agreed.

Then she said, "I'm glad for that, honey, but I meant generally."

He was confused.

"Generally?"

She flung her arm out to indicate…what?

He didn't know but he took a stab anyway.

"I love this room, baby, I told you," he said low. "It's very you. And I'm very into you."

Her face got soft, but she replied, "You live in my house, Rus, with me and my daughter. Except for taking over the basement, which you've declared your intention to make your mancave, and then moved forward with that by starting demolition, it's us. It's not you."

"Is it you two? And not me?"

"No. It's all of us."

"Yes," he said. "I agree."

"I worry," she admitted.

His brows drew down.

He didn't like that.

"Have I given you a sense I have an issue with this?"

"Did you give Jennifer a sense that her demands on your time and attention, which were impossible to meet, especially with the career you chose, were dragging on you?"

Ah.

He put his book aside, took hold of her, pulled her up him then rolled them so he was looming over her.

"You aren't her," he said.

"No," she agreed.

"I don't care about décor. Your house is the shit. I love the kitchen. I love the garden. I love the river. I love the privacy. I love Madden. I love you. My kids have their own rooms where they can be here with us and know they'll have space. They won't need it long, but it's nice they know they have it. They both love it up here.

They both love me with you. They think you're cool as fuck, Acre's words. Sabrina said, 'She's *amazing*, Dad! I wanna be her when I grow up.'"

"I know, but—"

"I've never been happy, Cin," he whispered. "Not until I came to Misted Pines and met you. Not once. Not without questions or worries or weight. I don't care that my job is about investigating trespassers who property owners give me all the evidence I need for an arrest. Or high school pranks that are solved in a day. I come home to you and Maddy, and I'm great."

"Something ugly will come down the line," she warned. "It always does."

"It does and it will, but it's not relentless. It's not me working day to day in a sea of every possibility people can make of doing stupid, ugly, greedy, selfish shit that affects lives. I'll take months of quiet and wildflowers before the next big thing blows up in our faces."

He dropped closer to her.

"I'm happy. I promise. I wake up and go to bed happy. And part of that is, if something ever weighs on it, I know I can tell you and you'll listen to me."

"You're sure you don't want to get married?"

They'd had the discussion.

She didn't want it either, for different reasons, mostly having to do with the fact she thought it was an outmoded tradition that tended to levy heavy sociological and emotional burdens on women.

He couldn't disagree.

That wasn't why he didn't want to do it.

He didn't want to do it because he didn't need a piece of paper and a promise to the government to make him commit to the woman he loved…and her daughter.

When he started tearing down walls to build his mancave, that was when he committed.

And as far as he was concerned, the discussion was closed.

But in order to give her peace of mind, he'd reopen it.

"Yes," he answered. "Are you sure?"

She nodded.

Right.

Discussion closed again.

"Have fun at the barbeque today?"

She nodded again. "I think Madden has a crush on Acre."

"It's a different kind entirely, but Acre has a crush on Maddy. He won't grow out of his, but she'll grow out of hers."

"I don't know. She has good taste. Like her mom."

All right then.

Fuck it.

He kissed her.

They were in the attic room on the top floor, the better to give Lucinda a massive bathroom and closet.

And the walls were solid.

So Rus committed to something else.

Putting effort into giving his woman an orgasm.

Then, since everyone he loved was under one roof, and they were all like him—happy—Rus fell into a dead sleep.

And he didn't wake up.

Cin

THEY WERE DOWN by the river, her girl and her man.

Cin stood in the window, her arms crossed in front of her, and watched them.

Brittanie had long since been swept away, fattening up fishes and becoming one with the silt.

They had a date tonight, Rus and Maddy. There was a movie on in town that Maddy wanted to see. They were going to get popcorn and M&Ms and Reese's Pieces and have dinner after at the Double D.

Rus loved his second chance to be a girl dad, and he didn't hide it.

He was also so grateful for Cin, he let her feel it always. Sometimes in a glance over coffee before she left to take Maddy to school.

Sometimes not releasing her eyes when he was moving inside her in their bed.

She knew, here, with her and Madden, after a lifetime tethered to people who didn't let him be all he was, finally, he was free.

He'd been crouched, but she watched as he stood, so tall, those shoulders so broad, his body lean and muscled and strong, the sun glinting in his dark hair.

He was so fucking beautiful.

He was also a bona fide hero, the real kind who rode himself ragged in the pursuit of justice.

Last, he was her miracle, the man he was, the woman she was.

That he'd be hers.

That he'd return the favor, and love her as the woman she was, letting her be free.

There wasn't a Bonner woman in her line who'd encountered a man like Zachariah Lazarus.

Rus had told her what that man had to say, and Richard Sandusky got one thing right.

Rus was pure.

He was beauty.

On this thought, Cin walked out the back door, got in her golf cart and put it in gear.

She reversed out, her champagne gold, slingback pump pressing the pedal.

She adjusted it to drive, and in her head, she could hear Rus giving her shit about putting off in her golf cart to go rule her empire.

But she was putting off in her golf cart to go rule her empire, being the first in the Bonner line herself.

This being knowing a man she'd give it all up for was hanging with her daughter at the river.

Needless to say, these thoughts in her head, as she putted to work in her cart, Lucinda Bonner was smiling.

The End

Discussion/Reflection Questions

1)   Lucinda Bonner is confident in her family, in business, in motherhood and in life, coming from a long line of self-assured, independent women.

Were you surprised to be in her point of view at the end of the novel, where she marvels at the miracle of being a strong woman who finds a partner with alpha tendencies who not only accepts, but celebrates the woman she is? Something none of her ancestors were able to find?

Onward from that, were you surprised that Rus was happy to fit into Lucinda's and Madden's lives, content to build his mancave in the basement, but otherwise be absorbed as part of that family, rather than making his mark on it? Did it make him seem more manly that he was confident enough with himself and his masculinity that he would not only be able, but be completely comfortable doing this?

Last, this leads to them having a very open and balanced sexual relationship, where neither is entirely dominant nor submissive, but both are willing to get creative. Did you find that worked with their personalities?

2)   What did you think about Rus's trajectory in this book, from the first chapter, where he asserts his dedication to his job is what ended his marriage, to his final confrontation with his ex-wife, where he realizes he took on guilt that wasn't his? Also, he starts the book in an occupation that weighs on him incredibly, and in the end, gives little thought to the financial sacrifices, and instead, prioritizes personal peace? Did you admire how open to other viewpoints and introspection as well as being willing to take risks he was?

3)   There were many villains in this book: Pastor Richard, Carrie Molnar, and Ezra Corbin.

But Corbin, who lived his life being taken care of by women, considered Brittanie "expendable" to his needs and desires. On the surface, this was due to her family's reputation. However, it could be said all women were expendable to his needs and desires, and in many ways, he made his wife and mistress victims too.

What were your feelings around Ezra and the way he lived his life and handled the situation he maneuvered himself into? What were your feelings about his end? Do you think he got his just desserts, or do you wish Rus had been able to catch him so he could face justice?

4)   Pastor Richard, who is the epitome of malignant masculinity (and beyond), admires above anyone else, Rus, who is the exact opposite. Why do you think that is? Do you feel there's an underlying sense of envy Pastor Richard harbors, and as such, he punished Rus by drawing Rus into his crimes? Or do you feel

Bohannan's take on the situation is true, and Richard had twisted thoughts that they were partners.

5)   Rus worries about a world where people ignore important things, even important things that are extreme, in order to "belong." In Pastor Richard's cult, wives were being sexually assaulted, and husbands were condoning and championing it in order to obtain their own "salvations." A smaller illustration in this book is Austin Brooks going along with his friends by raping a young girl in order to belong to that group of boys.

Not all examples are that extreme, but it illustrates how vast sections of society can ignore bad behavior to remain a member of a group (continued fandom when professional sports players/coaches/owners do terrible things, continued elections of politicians who have been exposed for crimes or bad behavior, commercial churches growing and recruiting even if it's clear their leaders are profiting from their flocks, etc.).

Everyone can't be a leader, for society that would never work. And no one is perfect, we've all done things we regret. But blind devotion can cause irreparable damage.

What do you think we, as a society, are searching for that would make some of us overlook commonly accepted moral standards in order to belong?

6)   What do you think Lucinda's wardrobe says about her? Not only does she dress very sophisticated in a rural area, but her color palette is also carefully curated. What did that communicate to you? Which was your favorite outfit?

7)   What are your thoughts about the coven? Do you think they'll play a bigger part in Misted Pines and future novels?

8)   Do you watch true crime documentaries and/or listen to podcasts?

9)   Do you want Harry to find new love? Jaeger? How about a love story for Porter? Jason? Jesse? Kleo? Which would you want next?

Read **The 'Burg Series** for more
Kristen Ashley suspense.

For You
the story of Colt and Feb.

Try More Kristen Ashley Suspense

THE 'BURG SERIES

For You
The 'Burg Series Book One

Lieutenant Alexander Colton and February Owens were high school sweethearts. Everyone in their small town knew from the moment they met they were meant for each other. But something happened and Feb broke Colt's heart then she turned wild and tragedy struck. Colt meted out revenge against the man who brought Feb low, but even though Colt risked it all for her, Feb turned her back on him and left town.

Fifteen years later, Feb comes back to help run the family bar. But there's so much water under the bridge separating her and Colt everyone knows they'll never get back together.

Until someone starts hacking up people in Feb's life. Colt is still Colt and Feb is still Feb so the town watches as Colt goes all out to find the murderer while trying to keep Feb safe.

As the bodies pile up, The Feds move in and a twisting, turning story unravels exposing a very sick man who has claimed numerous victims along the way, Feb and Colt battle their enduring attraction and the beautiful but lost history that weaves them together.

For You

THE 'BURG SERIES BOOK ONE

Chapter One

Angie

Until that day, I'd made an art out of avoiding Alexander Colton.

All my work would be for nothing, all because of Angie.

Poor, sweet, stupid, dead Angie.

*****

Martin Fink and Christopher Renicki were the first two uniforms who responded to my call. I'd known Marty and Chris for ages. It was good they were partners. Chris was smart; Marty, not so much.

We were out in the alley, Chris doing crime scene stuff, Marty standing by me. A couple of squad cars with their lights silently flashing had pulled in on either side of the dumpster. Other uniforms had been dispatched to hold back the growing crowd and the crime scene tape was secured by the time Alec showed up.

He'd parked elsewhere and didn't come through the bar like I expected him to. He had keys to the bar, for one. For another, he knew the bar nearly as well as I did and not only because he spent a good deal of time sitting at the end of it, my brother standing inside the bar in front of him, both of them drinking beer and talking about shit I couldn't hear because I stayed well away.

Another surprise was he also didn't have his partner Sully with him.

I watched him as he walked up to Marty and me.

The detectives in town, not that there were many of them, wore ill-fitting, inexpensive suits or nice trousers and shirts with ties.

Not Alec.

Jeans, boots, wide leather belt, sports jacket that looked tailored for him (probably a present from Susie Shepherd) and a nice shirt.

Alec was a big guy even when he was a kid, just kept growing and growing. Dad used to say if he didn't stop his head would touch the clouds. Mom thought Alec and my brother Morrie were best friends because they were both the biggest kids in the class and it just grew from that. Morrie grew out as well as up, however. Alec just grew tall and broad but stayed lean. Alec was tight end to Morrie's offensive lineman during high school, and in all things life. Morrie did the grunt work and never got the glory. Alec knew how to block and was really good at it but every once in a while he got the chance to shine.

Alec's dark hair was too long but he'd always worn it too long, even as a kid. But he'd done it then because his mother was such a shit mother. She never remembered to get it cut. My mom finally ended up taking Alec to the barber when she took Morrie. Later he kept it long just because he was Alec. It curled around his ears and neck now and, as with everything Alec, it looked a little wild.

I stood there and watched silently as he made it to me and Marty, his eyes never leaving me. He didn't even look at Angie.

"Feb," he said on a short nod.

"Alec," I replied.

His eyes were a weird color; light brown with a hint of gold. His dad had the same eyes but his dad's eyes weren't exactly like Alec's. Alec's dad's eyes were mean.

Those eyes got hard as did his mouth when I called him Alec.

They always did. Everyone called him Colt. *Everyone.* Even my mom and dad started calling him Colt after what happened years ago.

Only his folks and I called him Alec anymore, not that he talked to his folks since his dad was in prison for the second time and his mom was never sober and he never spoke to her. Not that I talked much to him either.

He hated it when I called him Alec but I didn't call him Alec to be a bitch or anything, just that he was Alec to me, he always had been.

"Colt," Chris said, calling his attention and Alec looked his way.

That was when he caught sight of Angie.

I looked at her too and wished I hadn't. I'd already seen enough, too much, so much I'd never forget.

I'd gone to high school with Angie. We'd been friends once upon a time, good friends. You could say we still were, but not good ones.

No, we weren't anything anymore because now she was dead.

Alec's midsection came into my vision and cut off sight of Angie. I lifted my eyes to Alec's face, which was still hard but now he was directing his hard look at Marty.

"Why's she out here?" he asked, sounding pissed-off.

"What?" Marty asked back, sounding as usual, confused.

"Jesus, Marty," Alec muttered, still sounding pissed and his eyes cut to me. "Go inside, Feb."

I stared at him and didn't move a muscle.

"Feb, inside," he repeated.

I still stared at him.

He took a step toward me and said low, "February."

My body jerked and I nodded. Inside would be good. Inside would be fucking awesome.

I went inside, headed directly to Morrie and my office—Mom and Dad's old office, the office Morrie and Alec and I practically grew up in—and coffee. I could still taste the vomit in the back of my mouth. I hadn't actually puked but it had threatened.

I was pouring a cup when Morrie came in.

Alec was big but my brother was enormous. He was also demonstrative.

He walked right up to me, took the coffee cup from my hand, plunked it down, yanked the coffeepot out of my other hand, slid it under the filter and then engulfed me in a hug.

I should have started crying then, I suppose. But I didn't.

"You okay, Feb?" Morrie asked, and I nodded, my cheek sliding against his big, barrel chest.

I wondered briefly why he was there. It wasn't his turn to open, it was mine.

My guess, Alec had called him.

"Sis," he whispered at my nod and I closed my eyes. He didn't call me "sis" very often anymore. Hadn't since we were kids. I missed it.

Still, no tears came.

"You want coffee?" I asked.

Morrie pulled away and gave me a look.

He didn't like what he saw, I knew it but he still said, "Yeah."

I made him a cup and we were taking sips when Alec filled the doorframe.

In the light I caught sight of the scar under his left eye. It was a little, puckered crescent moon, about the size of your thumbnail. I thought that was weird, it being that small, considering at the time it was made it bled a whole helluva lot.

As it did anytime I saw it, it made flashbacks flood my brain. Flashbacks of Alec, sixteen years old and sitting silent on the toilet seat in my mom and dad's bathroom and me, fourteen, standing there wiping the blood off his face with one of Mom's wet wash-cloths. Morrie coming in, giving me ice, me wrapping it up and holding it to the gaping cut under Alec's swelling eye. My dad walking in, taking in Alec, his bloodied face, his knuckles torn, bleeding and swollen, the way he held his body like if he moved it would be torture, and saying, "Police are going to your place, Colt, you're going with me. Jackie and the kids to the hospital."

That was the first time my father called him Colt. He never addressed him as anything else since.

For You is available everywhere now.

About the Author

Kristen Ashley is the *New York Times* bestselling author of over eighty romance novels including the *Rock Chick, Colorado Mountain, Dream Man, Chaos, Unfinished Heroes, The 'Burg, Magdalene, Fantasyland, The Three, Ghost and Reincarnation, The Rising, Dream Team, Moonlight and Motor Oil, River Rain, Wild West MC, Misted Pines* and *Honey* series along with several standalone novels. She's a hybrid author, publishing titles both independently and traditionally, her books have been translated in fourteen languages and she's sold over five million books.

Kristen's novel, *Law Man*, won the *RT Book Reviews* Reviewer's Choice Award for best Romantic Suspense, her independently published title *Hold On* was nominated for *RT Book Reviews* best Independent Contemporary Romance and her traditionally published title *Breathe* was nominated for best Contemporary Romance. Kristen's titles *Motorcycle Man, The Will,* and *Ride Steady* (which won the Reader's Choice award from *Romance Reviews*) all made the final rounds for Goodreads Choice Awards in the Romance category.

Kristen, born in Gary and raised in Brownsburg, Indiana, is a fourth-generation graduate of Purdue University. Since, she's lived in Denver, the West Country of England, and she now resides in Phoenix. She worked as a charity executive for eighteen years prior to beginning her independent publishing career. She now writes full-time.

Although romance is her genre, the prevailing themes running through all of Kristen's novels are friendship, family and a strong sisterhood. To this end, and as a way to thank her readers for their support, Kristen has created the Rock Chick Nation, a series of programs that are designed to give back to her readers and promote a strong female community.

The mission of the Rock Chick Nation is to live your best life, be true to your true self, recognize your beauty, and take your sister's back whether they're at your side as friends and family or if they're thousands of miles away and you don't know who they are.

The programs of the RC Nation include Rock Chick Rendezvous, weekends Kristen organizes full of parties and get-togethers to bring the sisterhood together, Rock Chick Recharges, evenings Kristen arranges for women who have been nominated to receive a special night, and Rock Chick Rewards, an ongoing program that raises funds for nonprofit women's organizations Kristen's readers nominate. Kristen's Rock Chick Rewards have donated hundreds of thousands of dollars to charity and this number continues to rise.

You can read more about Kristen, her titles and the Rock Chick Nation at KristenAshley.net.

facebook.com/kristenashleybooks

twitter.com/KristenAshley68

instagram.com/kristenashleybooks

pinterest.com/KristenAshleyBooks

goodreads.com/kristenashleybooks

bookbub.com/authors/kristen-ashley

Also by Kristen Ashley

Rock Chick Series:

Rock Chick

Rock Chick Rescue

Rock Chick Redemption

Rock Chick Renegade

Rock Chick Revenge

Rock Chick Reckoning

Rock Chick Regret

Rock Chick Revolution

Rock Chick Reawakening

Rock Chick Reborn

The 'Burg Series:

For You

At Peace

Golden Trail

Games of the Heart

The Promise

Hold On

The Chaos Series:

Own the Wind

Fire Inside

Ride Steady

Walk Through Fire

A Christmas to Remember

Rough Ride

Wild Like the Wind

Free

Wild Fire

Wild Wind

The Colorado Mountain Series:

The Gamble

Sweet Dreams

Lady Luck

Breathe

Jagged

Kaleidoscope

Bounty

Dream Man Series:

Mystery Man

Wild Man

Law Man

Motorcycle Man

Quiet Man

Dream Team Series:

Dream Maker

Dream Chaser

Dream Bites Cookbook

Mathilda The Rise of the Dark Lord

Misted Pines Series

The Girl in the Mist

The Girl in the Woods

Moonlight and Motor Oil Series:

The Hookup

The Slow Burn

The Rising Series:

The Beginning of Everything

The Plan Commences

The Dawn of the End

The Rising

The River Rain Series:

After the Climb

After the Climb Special Edition

Chasing Serenity

Taking the Leap

Making the Match

The Three Series:

Until the Sun Falls from the Sky

With Everything I Am

Wild and Free

The Unfinished Hero Series:

Knight

Creed

Raid

Deacon

Sebring

Wild West MC Series:

Still Standing

Smoke and Steel

Other Titles by Kristen Ashley:

Heaven and Hell

Play It Safe

Three Wishes

Complicated

Loose Ends

Fast Lane

Perfect Together

Too Good To Be True

www.ingramcontent.com/pod-product-compliance
Lightning Source LLC
LaVergne TN
LVHW041355040325
804918LV00001B/68